Praise for Marion Zimmer Bradley's
Previous *Sword & Sorceress* Anthologies

"The late Bradley's skill in choosing quality short stories
is evident throughout this volume. Many characters and
problems are so engrossing that readers will not wish the
stories to end."   —*Voya*

"Together with nineteen other tales, this latest collection
featuring women who excel in their talents for magic and
war presents a varied and entertaining sampler of current
fantasy storytelling."   —*Library Journal*

"Solid writing and an engaging range of themes . . . a
series that is gaining in popularity."   —*Booklist*

"Typical example of this anthology series—good to great
stories emphasizing women/girls as strong females."
                                —*Science Fiction Chronicle*

"A rich array of the best in fantasy short stories."
                                            —*Rave Reviews*

"Female warriors, witches, enchantresses make up this
wonder-filled brew of horror and magic."   —*Kliatt*

"Each tale is extremely well written, holding the reader
in the grip of belief until the very end. A better collection
of fine writing would be hard to find."   —*Voya*

"A distinctive and quite varied collection of stories. . . .
we all should enjoy Marion Zimmer Bradley's latest collection of heroic fiction."   —*Science Fiction Age*

SWORD AND SORCERESS XXI

EDITED BY

Diana L. Paxson

DAW BOOKS, INC.
DONALD A. WOLLHEIM, FOUNDER
375 Hudson Street, New York, NY 10014

ELIZABETH R. WOLLHEIM
SHEILA E. GILBERT
PUBLISHERS
http://www.dawbooks.com

First Printing, November 2004
1 2 3 4 5 6 7 8 9 10

DAW TRADEMARK REGISTERED
U.S. PAT. OFF. AND FOREIGN COUNTRIES
—MARCA REGISTRADA
HECHO EN U.S.A.

PRINTED IN THE U.S.A.

ACKNOWLEDGMENTS

Introduction © 2004 by Diana L. Paxson
"Sword and Sorceress" © 2004 by Jennifer G. Tifft
"Dawn and Dusk" © 2004 by Dana Kramer-Rolls
"Spell of the Sparrow" © 2004 by Jim C. Hines
"The Woman's Place" © 2004 by Susan Urbanek Linville
"Kin" © 2004 by Naomi Kritzer
"Child's Play" © 2004 by Esther M. Friesner
"Ursa" © 2004 by Jenn Reese
"Red Caramae" © 2004 by Kit Wesler
"Parri's Blade" © 2004 by Cynthia McQuillin
"Necessity and The Mother" © 2004 by Lee Martindale
"Sun Thief" © 2004 by K.A. Laity
"Lostland" © 2004 by Rosemary Edghill
"Plowshares" © 2004 by Rebecca Maines
"Step By Step" © 2004 by Catherine Soto
"Favor of the Goddess" © 2004 by Lynn Morgan Rosser
"Rose in Winter" © 2004 by Marie M. Loughin
"Kazhe's Blade" © 2004 by Terry McGarry
"The Skin Trade" © 2004 by Heather Rose Jones
"Multiple Choice" © 2004 by Leslie Fish
"Oulu" © 2004 by Aimee Kratts
"A Kind of Redemption" © 2004 by John P. Buentello
"Journey's End" © 2004 by Dorothy J. Heydt
"Love Potion #8½" © 2004 by Marilyn A. Racette

CONTENTS

INTRODUCTION

by Diana L. Paxson

Two years ago I sat at a hotel coffee shop table with Betsy Wollheim of DAW and begged her to keep *Sword & Sorceress* alive. From its first volume, the anthology has been one of the few markets for fantasy short stories with a female perspective. In twenty volumes, Marion Zimmer Bradley created what amounted to a subgenre, and launched a generation of writers. It seemed to me that the field would be much poorer if the anthology were allowed to die. Fortunately, Betsy thought so too.

Fantasy writers apparently shared that feeling. When the possibility of another volume was announced, stories flooded in. By the time I was brought on board to edit it, the pile was almost overwhelming. I do apologize to those authors who had to wait while I was learning the ropes and catching up on the backlog to hear whether their stories were accepted. I've been on the other side of the desk many times myself, and I know how you feel.

To edit *Sword & Sorceress* has been an educational experience. I knew Marion well for almost thirty-five years, as her sister-in-law, fellow priestess, and student in the craft of writing, and over the years I absorbed a great many of her ideas about what makes a good story. To select stories for *Sword & Sorceress XXI,* I started with my memories of her criteria, and in the process of actually wrestling with the stories I began to discover what makes a good story for *me*. My choices may not always be the same ones that Marion would have made, but I hope that she would have enjoyed them as much as I hope you will.

Beyond the basics—length, competence with the lan-

1

guage, a sympathetic protagonist and believable setting—I realized that what I value most is a quality I can only call *focus,* a center around which the action revolves. I also found myself looking for the sense of weight and texture that makes even the most wildly imagined world seem real. Unfortunately, more stories met those criteria than I was able to include. In the end, choices depended on achieving a balance between swords and sorcery, humor and pathos and tragedy.

As Marion so often observed, as one begins to make choices from a group of submissions, themes emerge. This time, it was animals (alive and dead) and children, who as we all know are magic (what kind depends on the day, as any parent will tell you) that kept appearing. Instead of the stereotypical witch and the glamorous sorceress so well known to contemporary fantasy I found village healers and wisefolk. These days, readers of fantasy come in all ages as well as all genders, shapes, and sizes, and I was particularly happy to find this variety reflected in the stories.

In selecting the contents of this anthology, I have tried to apply the lessons Marion taught me about writing. I would like to thank Ann Sharp, the trustee for Marion's literary legacy, for dealing with the mechanics of gathering and processing the stories. Many of the writers you will see in these pages have been here before—some of them were given their start by Marion. Others are new. The one traditional element you will not see here is a story by Diana L. Paxson. So many excellent stories were submitted that I couldn't see buying one from myself unless I could be sure it would be better than the ones I already had on hand.

I won't delay your reading any longer—enjoy!

SWORD AND SORCERESS

by Jennifer G. Tifft

Marion was a good poet herself, but she had very high standards, and poetry was one of those things she refused to put in the anthology. However, her writers knew that if they showed her something that was good enough, she would break her own rules. I think this poem by Jennifer Tifft, a noted bard in the SCA as well as a famous costumer in fandom, so beautifully expresses the essence of this anthology that Marion herself would have succumbed to it. Jennifer would like to thank Lori, for many useful comments, and Prokofiev, for the *Third Piano Concerto*.

O maid sword-spirited
  Blade-bright, edge-eager!
Have a care you do not cut yourself
  In all your striving.
Adventures end—
  Swords are sheathed
  In scabbards
  Or in death.
Choose with open eyes,
  With heart and hand and mind
Lest your blade break in the forge,
  Lies rusting in the rain,
  Notched and nameless
    In an unmarked and unremembered grave.
Steel is not your only edge.

O lady magic-minded
  Fire-fierce, wonder-wielding!
Have a care you do not burn yourself
  In all your striving.

Adventures end—
   Fires go out
      Dimmed in ash
      Drowned in ice.
Choose with open eyes
   With hand and heart and spirit
Lest your light be but a glancing gleam,
   Or lie smothered in smoke
   Burnt and blackened
      In an unmarked and unremembered grave.
Wonder is not your only warmth.

O woman gift-given
Sword-maid:
   Scabbards come in many forms.
Sorceress:
   A lens of ice may spark a light.
Burnish your blades, hone your hands,
   Sharpen your skill,
   But stifle not your spirit.
Remember to have a home for your heart
   When adventures end.

DAWN AND DUSK

by Dana Kramer-Rolls

I first met Dana Kramer-Rolls sometime back in the mists of antiquity, at about the same time, in fact, that I met Marion. Then, she was working on a doctorate in biology. The Ph.D. she eventually earned is in folklore. Along the way she has ranged through a variety of interests, which give her writing richness and that gut-level sense of reality that can only come from someone who has "been there and done that." In this story, she blends the immediacy of experience with the flavor of a traditional tale.

These days she writes both fiction and nonfiction, edits papers for graduate students, and worships cats, especially her own. Her newest book is *The Way of the Cat* (Red Wheel/ Weiser). Her stories appeared in *Sword & Sorceress II, III,* and *V,* and *Marion Zimmer Bradley's Fantasy Magazine* (#14). She also wrote a *Star Trek* novel, *Home Is the Hunter.* She is a knight in the SCA (retired), an avid gardener, and a cook.

Dagne huddled in the little hut listening to the wolf howls getting closer and closer. She knew the stories about wolves, but nobody in her lifetime had ever been killed by one. On the other hand, her brother Thorgrim had brought back tales from the Rus, before he sailed again and never came home, about how wolves killed each other, just like men, and these wolves were circling closer and closer to the little house. And it was Midwinter night—when the Hunt was out.

The pitiful fire spluttered and hissed, threatening to die with every gust that blew through the many chinks in the abandoned house. The little kitten had finally settled down and was sleeping in her arms. Dagne tenderly put the kitten down on the tattered wool she kept for a bed and carefully placed another stick on the fire, crouching low to blow it into flames.

"Poor dear, you will probably die anyhow. But at least you won't die alone, and you won't die in a sack struggling for air."

The wind had brought first rain, sheets of rain driving torn branches every which way, and then snow, big sloppy plops of snow, which now had turned into a blinding powder of ice crystals.

"Dagsett, poor little Sunset! We won't see another day, neither dawn nor dusk," she cried out, "but I'm not sorry." Her outburst woke the kitten. "Hush, little one. You are safe." *If you live,* she thought.

The trouble had happened three days ago, just before Midwinter. Well, probably Dagne's troubles began some fifteen years before, when she was born, and born out of season, during the Blood Moon. Her birth had upset the annual ritual of the pig killing, and that meant her mother couldn't take her role as mistress, and Auntie Sigrid had to take her place. It was a bad year on the farm after that. The crops were meager, and the livestock didn't bear well.

Everybody noticed Dagne's eyes right away. Most babies have blue eyes. Later they might darken, but she was born as she would always be, with one green eye, one eye black as coal. Some thought she would be blind, but she could see. That was the problem. She could see everything, they said, as she stared at them from her little cradle-box.

All the kindred urged her father to put her out to die, but her mother had begged to let her be. There had been boys, many boys, big rough boys to take over the farmstead and to seek their fortunes, and to hunt and kill and fight, but there hadn't been a daughter. Her mother said she wanted a daughter to teach to weave and cook—and, perhaps, other things, too, but Alfgifu kept that wish to herself, even to her death. And so they let the odd girl live. And then, after her father accepted her and named her, and it was too late to put her out, her mother died. So father married Auntie Sigrid, who was already big with his twin boys, and everything got better again on the farm. For everybody but Dagne.

One or another of the servants had enough pity to nurse her, and after that she fell in with the other children on the farm, but she was always the outsider—the master's daughter in name only. They called her Twig, or Dwarf-girl, when they were being nice, but never New Day, Dagne. And that was before Sigrid had a beautiful blonde daughter, who grew into a pretty little thing they called Helga, all pink cheeked and blue eyed, obedient to her elders, and uppity with the boys who increasingly found reason to linger where the women worked.

Sigrid, whom Dagne refused to call Mother, dressed her own daughter in the finest linen and wool, and worked her own fingers to the bone embroidering Helga's apron and cloak. That was after Dagne had been buffeted once too often for failing to make the tiny even stitches which her stepmother required for her children's clothes.

So Dagne hid a lot in the barns and outbuildings, and went out into the forest, where she talked to the birds and the beasts. And they talked back, but she never told. At home, after that, they just called her Ugly One, and Dumb in the Head, and let her be, which was just fine with her.

She never cried, except when she saw her mother, all light and like fog drifting toward her, her ghostly arms outstretched for an embrace which she could no longer give. Then Dagne cried.

It was on her fifteenth birthday that it all started to go really wrong. She got her first blood just around the Blood Moon. Too early, some said, for this northern place where girls didn't become women sometimes until they were eighteen, but Dagne, they said, always had to be different. She heard them whispering about her, she looked at them with her one green eye and her one black eye, and they made signs with their hands, and spit.

When her stepmother caught the blood at the pig killing, Dagne hid at a distance with the rest of the household women as was traditional. The women could still hear the men making the usual rude jokes about the mistress being the pig, and the blood, and the sacrifice. Dagne felt a new gush of her first blood-time soaking past the rags, and down her leg, and she felt ashamed and frightened, and she ran away. She found fresh cloths for herself and ran into the woods. Nobody noticed.

That was when she found the empty house. She didn't know why she had never seen it before, but there it was, a broken shamble, but someplace no one else wanted, a place of her own.

When she came back to the farm that night, the pig-killing feast was going strong. Her stepmother was passing the mead cup, first to her husband, and then, in order, to the men who surrounded him, his own kin and men who could fight to protect the farm and who had a place of honor in the long house. But tonight, instead of the old retainers who should only have yielded their place for the first wife's sons, all away on ships seeking their fortune, Sigrid's twin sons sat next to their father for the first time. When Dagne came in, Sigrid turned and smiled at her, but the smile was as cold as the winter. When the mistress of the hall turned back to her duties, Dagne felt as if a door had finally slammed against her.

Stunned, she silently watched the feasting in the hall. The men were drunk and the women hot in a strange way, hot from blood and death. And Dagne now could feel the heat, the quivering, and it frightened her. She looked at the men, and they were looking at her. Her two half-brothers also looked at her, and Sven smiled, with his mouth, not his eyes, and leaned over to Eric and said something, and they laughed, but it was not a kind laugh. She tried to stare back defiantly, but they didn't look away. In the shadows of the great hall, who cared what color her eyes were. The word was out. She was a woman. She was meat. She was a pig, like the pigs on which they feasted, and which would be the meat for the winter season. Dagne lowered her glance and stared at the ground, her cheeks burning with shame.

When her father finally took his wife off to bed, Dagne knew that there would be another beautiful sister or big hulking brother by summer, and what little safety she had here was finally gone. In that new knowledge, Dagne felt a chill in her heart, and her bones all froze, and the pit of her stomach ached with fear. She moved warily like a cat out of the hall, until she was clear of the house, and she ran and ran and ran, into the black forest to her little house, where she rocked back and forth, and felt the strange heat in her loins, and shook until she finally slept, and dreamed. She dreamed of death, and the knives and the blood and the squealing pigs. And she dreamed of her mother, who again reached out for her, but this time touched her. And the touch was cold as death.

After that day, Dagne felt the fear, always. She became quieter than ever, looking down at the ground, not at the people around her, so they wouldn't see her eyes. But, as the weeks from the Blood Moon to Midwinter went by and her time came again, nobody seemed to notice anymore, almost as if someone or something had covered her in fog and they couldn't see her. It worked for everybody except for her half brothers, the twins Sven and Eric, Sigrid's firstborn by her father, born just after Mother had died. But at least they forgot Dagne was a woman and went back to punching her, and chasing her, and calling her names.

The twins were trouble. They always had been. There had been near blood feuds with neighboring garths, mostly about girls, even when they were as young as twelve, but sometimes about mutilated animals. But Father always bought them out of trouble, and the beatings were pretty much for show, and ignored by the boys, who could dish out more pain than that on each other on a normal day. And now they were being treated as men in the hall, and they strutted like two cocks around the yard, making trouble.

The kitten had been born out of season just as Dagne had been, the only one in her litter out of a queen from the tribe of farm cats that lived in the storehouse, or in the nearby meadow. She had fallen from a shed, and lay stunned when the boys rambled by. Dagne saw them huddled over something, poking it with a stick, and then throwing it back and forth. Her heart stopped when she heard the mewling.

"Stop that," she screamed, racing to them.

"Make us," Sven said, lifting the poor little gray limp thing out of reach.

"I will. I will. I'm a witch. I'll kill you."

"Take it then," the boy said, throwing it at her. And he made a sign with his hand and spat.

"Father was going to drown it anyhow," Eric piped in. "It is out of season. It is evil. Like you."

But Dagne didn't feel like a witch, and she was glad they hadn't called her bluff as she clutched the kitten to her, and ran for the barn. Anyhow, if the boys had intended to follow, the sudden crash of lightning and roll of thunder headed them off. There was more important work to do on the farm than torturing small animals and unwanted sisters.

In the barn, Dagne listened to the kitten's heartbeat, and felt her all over. She set her down, but the kitten cried out. She was favoring one leg. Dagne picked her up and felt the bones carefully. No breaks, but probably a sprain, or a tear inside. She gently massaged the leg, and tucked the now purring cat down her woolen gown, where it snuggled for warmth. She thought, *Let's see. It was born around my birthday, around the Blood Moon, so it is probably weaned, or nearly so.* And then she said aloud, "I won't let them drown you."

She spent the afternoon at her chores, still hiding the small cat in her bosom. But as the wind blew up, and the household gathered indoors, she slipped away to the storeroom and gathered a chunk of sausage, some cheese, a loaf of bread, and a skin of mead. There was water aplenty in the streams, but the strong drink would be handy in the cold. She had left a flint in the little house, some dry wood, and some old woolens and even a tattered skin. She would go and not come back. This was no longer her home.

When she was across the field and at the forest edge,

she turned and took a last long look at the garth. The winter days in the north were short and the long shadows hid her. The last of the farmhands and assorted relatives were making their way indoors, chasing in a stray hen or dog. They all looked like they were moving in mud to Dagne, so slowly, so coldly, as if they were all dead and merely wraiths.

It was raining in earnest when she finally plunged into the woods, the kitten cuddled between her breasts. The first two days were ones of great peace. It was cold and it was wet, but she and the gray kitten, a little queen cat whom she named Dagsett, shared the sausage and water, and were content. But by Midwinter night, the food was getting low, and the storm had turned ugly. It had been a warm winter until now. No longer. The icicles were jagged knives hanging from the eaves of the hut, and the snow piled up in drifts.

"I won't go back, Dagsett. I will find us food. I will stay here forever." Dagne pushed open the door against the wind, and plunged out in the dark to search for more wood, but she had picked the ground near the hut clean, and the blizzard drove her back in.

By now the kitten was moving fairly well, and had managed to dig out a half-frozen mouse from a rotting pile of old straw in a corner. Dagne smiled and said, "At least you are going to be all right, even if I die."

That thought comforted her, until the wolves started howling, nearer than she had ever heard them. By now the blizzard was tearing into the shuttered windows, and there was no going back to the farm.

THUD! Dagne jumped. She calmed herself, thinking that it had to be only the wind banging the door. Thud, thud, thud. Finally the door tore open, and the wind and snow screamed in, putting out the sad little fire. Where the light came from the girl did not know, but she could see, as if a full moon or the Northern Lights filled the sky. There were glistening crystals everywhere, brilliant, blue-white sparkles of light.

"Who's there?" she cried out, her voice almost frozen

in her throat. She tried again to call out louder, "Who's there?" but it was like in a dream when you couldn't scream, or speak, or run.

"I am," a woman's voice answered, "and this is my house."

A wizened old woman, bent with age—well, more a pair of shining, sharp eyes, peering out of a lump of woolens and furs on a pair of reindeer boots—came in. She had a sack on her back, which she tossed down, sending up a cloud of fresh powder snow.

"Well, girl, if you are going to take over my house, at least have the courtesy to help me."

Dagne was stunned, not only by the strange woman's appearance, but that she was being spoken to, not at, probably for the first time since her mother died, or at least the last time her brother Thorgrim went Viking, never to be heard from again.

"Well, cat got your tongue?" the woman snapped, stomping her feet. The kitten woke up with a tentative, "Meow."

"Well, there little one, let's see what *you* have to say," the old woman said, addressing the cat in a more friendly voice. Turning back to Dagne and pointing to the last smoky remains on the hearth, she snapped, "You call that a fire? Get some more wood."

"Yes, er, mistress . . . uh, *where?*"

"Outside, girl," she chided, but there was something in the way she said it that made Dagne not so afraid as she had been at home. Oh, she was afraid, but the fear was different. It was fear of something strange and wonderful and dangerous, but not mean and petty and cruel. She started out, but the woman shouted at her, making her jump.

"Not like that. Here," and she threw a wool shawl from the layers that she was peeling off.

"Thank you, mistress," Dagne said, as she hurriedly wrapped herself up and scuttled through the door.

"And close the door behind you," the old one shouted.

The light as not so bright anymore, as if the brightness had come from the old woman herself, but it was light enough for the girl to see a large pile of split wood peeking out from a drift of snow. She pulled out as much as she could carry, and piled on a few smaller bits for kindling, suddenly very aware that she didn't want to tumble down the neat pile, and not daring to wonder where it had come from.

She brought back the wood and laid a fire, the old woman watching her sharply. Dagne could feel her hands shake, and she could feel the old woman's eyes on her. She was blushing and she felt ashamed because she could not do something properly that she had known how to do since she was a small child. Then she took her flint and struck it again and again, but her hands were still shaking, and she couldn't get a spark. The old woman took her by the shoulder and eased her out of the way.

"No mind. Let me." And she snapped her fingers, and a spark flew out from them and landed on the wood, which immediately began to burn brightly, the tongues of flame like dancing tomten in their red hats from the stories. Dagne clapped her hands and laughed, instantly shocking herself into silence.

The kitten pulled herself out of the pile of shawls into which she had settled, stretched from one end to the other, and walked over to the fire pit, sat down and began to wash. The old woman reached out to stroke her.

"What's her name?"

"Dagsett."

"Sundown, when the ghosts come out. Good name." She ran her fingers through the kitten's fur. "Hurt, eh?" She looked up at Dagne, "Well, you did the right thing, child. Nothing broken. Rubbed the soreness out. She'll mend. She's almost mended already. What is your name?"

"Dagne."

"Ha, ha, ha. Sunrise and Sunset. Dawn and Dusk. Dagne and Dagsett. What a pair. What brings you here?"

Suddenly the whole story of her life gushed out of the girl, and she didn't stop until the tears choked her up, and then she was still, feeling emptied and unsure of having said so much. After all, who was this woman?

Dagne had heard about children who were eaten by creatures in the forest who could assume any shape. She looked up through her tears and said, firmly, "I don't care what you do to me. But promise me you won't hurt Dagsett. Promise."

"I promise I won't, littlebit, I won't ever."

The old woman went over to her sack and pulled out a ham, dried fish, a small pouch of dried berries, and a cauldron. But Dagne didn't have time to wonder, as the old woman sent her scurrying about tidying the little house and preparing their meal.

"Fold my shawls, and put them in the chest," and there appeared to be a chest where there had been none before. "Fill the cauldron, put it on the fire." And finally the old woman asked, "And what makes you think I would hurt you? You are marked. Your eyes mark you."

Dagne said in a squeaky voice, "What about my eyes?"

"You'll learn. Do you know what night this is?"

"Midwinter"

"And what happens?"

"The Hunt rides. I heard the wolves."

"And do you know who rides the Hunt?"

"Most say All Father, but the children and some of the women say Holda, oh, oh, my . . ."

The old woman grinned a grin so wide that the whole world was within it, "Yes, go on."

By now Dagne was stammering, "My brother Thorgrim said it was Thor, but he always liked Thor best. He told me that when he was little, he saw Thor riding in the sky, but when he told, they laughed at him, so he never told anybody again, except me."

"You miss him, don't you."

"Yes, and my mother."

"Oh, but you see your mother all the time, don't you?"

Dagne didn't answer right away. "But she isn't real."

"Not real!" the old woman shouted, disturbing the kitten from her bath, who gave Holda a very angry look and went back to her ablutions. "She is your ancestress, and was a great seer, until your father knocked all the

magic out of her. You are her daughter. You are Dagne Alfgifusdottir. She will not leave you. Don't forget that. But enough. Let's eat."

At Holda's direction, Dagne set out plates, and as she looked around the cottage she realized that it had changed. The walls were whole, and whitewashed, and the dishes were in a fine wooden cupboard, and there was a table and benches, and it was warm and lovely. And in the corner stood a fine carved bed piled high with fluffy feather beds. Tears washed down her face, but for the first time they weren't tears of sorrow.

"Now, you don't need to salt the food with tears. Just serve it," Holda said, not unkindly.

And they ate—first a creamy porridge and then ham and sausage and fish stew and dried winter berries soaked in honey, and they drank warm mead with spices. And the cat had her share of everything, except the mead, and she didn't like the berries.

"It is almost midnight. Now we must go to work. Come."

Dagne didn't know what she meant, but she did as she was bid, and she helped the woman to once again bury herself in shawls, handed her the sack, and opened the door for her. The storm had ended, and the air was still and the sky studded with stars, and the moon was out, as bright as a silver coin.

Dagsett rose and went out with them. "No, sweet, it is cold out," Dagne scolded, trying to hustle her kitten back inside. But before she could do so, Dagsett grew and grew until she was the size of the great northern snow tigers about which Thorgrim had told Dagne the last time he was home. Dagsett put out her raspy tongue, and licked Dagne's face. Holda lifted up the girl and placed her on the huge gray cat's back. "Hold on tight, now," she said.

Then Holda threw her sack on her back and whistled. A large broom flew up from the side of the house, and the old one leaped on, spry as a girl. And they rose into the air, Holda on her broom, her sack on her back, and Dagne on her cat.

"Look down and see all the world," Hold called out. And Dagne did, and she could see her farmstead, little lights from the smoke hole in the great hall, and all the neighboring farms.

But then she heard the wolves, and she nearly slipped off her mount in fear.

"That is the rest of the crowd," Holda crowed. "Heilsa! Heilsa!"

And through the night sky came a host, led by a fierce warrior who had one green eye and one black eye, who rode a mighty steed that galloped so fast that it seemed to have eight legs. The horse and rider were accompanied by two huge wolves. And then Dagne saw a great shaggy man in a chariot drawn by goats, and she cried out gleefully, "See, Thorgrim was right, too."

At one point a woman in all the greens of the forest with reddish hair flying, in a cart drawn by cats, wheeled through the air and spoke with Holda, pointing to Dagne, but she didn't hear what they said. As the woman raced past her, Dagsett hissed at the two haughty cats drawing the cart, but they ignored her, and Dagne could hear the throaty laugh of the wild woman in the cart as she rode her own way in the night sky.

Holda flew up close to Dagne. "Close one eye and look around. Close your left one."

Dagne did as she was bid, and looked at the flying horde with her green eye. All was as before, but somehow clearer.

"Now your other eye."

Dagne looked out with her black eye.

"What do you see?"

"Nothing, er, the same as the other."

"Look harder," the old woman shouted over the whoops of the horde, and the roar of the wind. Dagne did as she was ordered, looking afar as if straining to see something on a distant peak, and suddenly it all shifted. The Old Man on the horse was ablaze in light. They all were.

But there were also more beings. Wraiths, terrible dead things, streamed past her through the air, their breath colder than the winter night. They stared at her as they flew past, stared out of white dead eyes. And there were bright shining creatures, pale slender men and women glowing with an eldritch light, and singing, so beautiful as to take the breath away, but so foreign to nature as to be too dangerous to be near.

"Now look down," Holda commanded, and Dagne did as she was bid, and she could see creatures of stone, as if the hills themselves were slowly moving across the fields, and other things, dark and terrible, that darted in and out of the shadows of the trolls. The whole world was alive, and on the move.

Dagne felt herself get woozy and began to slip from Dagsett's back, until Holda's hand on her shoulder steadied her. "Now you know. With your one eye, you see the truth of the world. No one can lie to you. With your other, you see the world beyond. You can heal, you can kill. What do you wish to do about your evil brothers?" Holda asked slyly.

A day before she would have said, "I want them dead," but now she knew her words could make it so. "I don't know," Dagne panted, as her breath smoked in the icy air.

Holda grinned. "No matter. *He* wants them, although I don't know why. And that will be soon enough. And what shall we do about you?"

"I don't understand."

"You will. You will. Come, we have our own work this night."

And while the host soared through the night, putting terror in all humans and beasts, Holda dipped down on her broom again and again, riding close to the earth, throwing sweets, and shawls, and ribbons, and other useful things into the houses of all the folk. Only some got nothing, and others got what was needful—a bag of fodder for the livestock and a bag of meat for themselves.

As the night became day, and Dagne was almost asleep mounted on her cat, the host of the Hunt was beginning to fade away. But before they did, Holda guided Dagne back up to the higher realms where they still wheeled in the sky, taking Dagne closer to that terrible horde than she had really wanted to be. But then she could see that many of the riders were ordinary men, and a few women, and one among them.

"Thorgrim," she cried.

"Little Dagne, I never thought to see you again."

"Oh, Thorgrim, why did you leave me?"

"I didn't want to, littlebit. There was a raid, and I stood with my captain. And I died. Oh, littlebit, I did want to come home, and farm, and marry, and have many babies, and take care of you. But it was not to be."

She reached for him, but as it was with the shade of her mother, he was like fog and he faded away in the growing light of dawn.

"Home," Holda commanded.

And suddenly, Dagne was in the cottage, and it was dawn, or at least sunup, which was almost midday in the northern winter, and Dagsett was curled in her arms, and the cottage was as it had been before, shabby and bare. And Holda was gone. But through the chinks in the walls she could see that the sun sparkled on the new snow. And there was a warm fire, and a package of ham, and sausage, and a bowl of porridge, and Dagne was wrapped in the softest of dark wool shawls.

And Dagne wasn't afraid anymore. She wasn't afraid of anything.

She and her kitten ate a hearty breakfast. Then she gathered her self, her supplies, and her cat, and she marched back to the hold. Let those two get near her or her cat, the thought defiantly. She remembered that she had power, as she remembered the events of the night, although in the light of day they were like a dream. But the power was there, and she could wound them, those two bullies, far worse than the wound of any sword. Something had changed inside her. She was alive, very alive, a life that burned in her eyes like the tongues of flame from Holda's fire, from both her eyes, green and black. And as for her brothers, they were mean and nasty and weakminded and they had no power over her anymore.

But she didn't have to hurt them. Their own deeds had brought their own rewards. When she got back, there was smoke, and a bad smell, and a great commotion. One of the farm girls ran out to her shouting. "We thought you had died with the others."

"What others. What is going on?"

"Eric and Sven. They raped a neighbor's daughter, and tried to kill her, but she lived, and she told her father, and they came, with axes, and they burned . . ." The girl burst into tears. "They waited until almost daylight, when all were asleep. Your father is dead. Your stepmother and her daughter were taken away. The two boys are dead, and some of your father's men. We heard the screams, and ran and hid. They burned most of the mead hall, but the snow kept the fires from spreading before all was gone. It's terrible."

"Who is now master of the land?" Dagne asked calmly.

"It is being taken to judgment, but likely one of your mother's sons. She was kin to those wronged, so that will settle it. Maybe Thorgrim. He's eldest."

"Thorgrim is dead."

The girl looked wide-eyed at Dagne, "How do you know?"

"I know."

"Then Wulfstan, if they can find him, but he will have to pay for the girl's outrage."

*

It was so. Wulfstan was a fair man, and his wife a good woman, and their children raised with honor. And they welcomed Dagne into their home, but Dagne and her cat moved to the cottage and rebuilt it as she had seen it that Midwinter night. And she often sat by the fire, talking to her mother, and to Holda, and to her brother, and to her cat Dagsett, who lived as long as any human woman. And she learned all the ways of seeing and healing, and, over the years, she was often called upon by the folk from all the farms to throw the rune staves and chant the charms, to heal the sick, both folk and animals, to speak to the dead, and to see the wyrd. And when she and Dagsett died at a great age, quietly in each other's arms, they rose to fly with the night horde, Dagne sitting lightly on her cat companion. And Dagne and Dagsett ride the night sky with the Hunt to this day.

SPELL OF THE SPARROW

by Jim C. Hines

Jim C. Hines made one of his earliest sales to MZB with a story that appeared in the final issue of *Marion Zimmer Bradley's Fantasy Magazine*. He has since appeared in *Writers of the Future, Turn the Other Chick,* and many other magazines and anthologies.

Jim lives in Lansing, Michigan, where he fixes computers in order to support his writing addiction. This is his first fiction sale as a married man, and he would like to dedicate it to his wonderful wife Amy, and his equally wonderful daughter Skylar.

One of the things I particularly appreciated in this story was the protagonist's wish that her child will grow up to be something *respectable* but I feel I should warn Jim against such hopes for his daughter—I kept hoping my son Ian would rebel and become a stockbroker, but I'm afraid he too is becoming a writer!

Growing up, I had imagined my life would be full of danger, excitement, and fabulous riches. I wound up with two out of the three.

A family of two ex-thieves, a prepubescent wizard, and a dead cat stirred up a bit more excitement than I wanted these days. As for trouble, it seemed to find us as easily as a bloodhound, even at our small cottage in Larindale.

I was in the woods behind our cabin, trying yet again to dissuade my daughter from this wizarding business.

"I *like* magic," Mel protested. "And I'm good at it. Remember the spell I made up last week?"

"The spell that changed my daggers into caterpillars?" James and I were still pulling cocoons out of the laundry.

"No, the other one."

21

I crossed my arms and did my best to look parental. "The one that sent my undergarments on a mad dash for freedom?"

She covered her mouth, trying to hide a gap-toothed grin. "I got it right the next time. Don't your clothes smell nicer?"

"They do . . . those that aren't hightailing it for the border."

It was no use. After two years, I *knew* I couldn't win, but I kept trying. James and I thought that if we could teach her another skill, something *respectable.* . . .

"Try again. Hold the blade flat. The knife slides *between* the ribs."

We practiced a few more times before returning to the cabin. James arrived right after we did. He slipped through the door of our cabin carrying a string of trout at arm's length. The odor brought Snick scampering into the room, where he stood on his hind paws and waited for his share.

"Let him have a piece," I said, curious what would happen. Snick had died a few years back, and only Mel's magic kept his spirit around. We had first noticed Mel's magical gifts the day Snick's ghost tromped into the bedroom and poked an icy and insubstantial nose into my armpit.

Once I got over my initial bout of panic, I liked him better this way. He made my daughter happy, and I no longer worried about finding hairballs in my boots or disemboweled shrews on the chopping block.

James ignored us. He slapped the fish onto the table, grabbed a large knife, and whacked the heads off with four strong chops. Switching his grip, he began to clean his catch with a viciousness that made even Snick back away. Scales, tails, and fins flew in every direction.

'You realize they're already dead, right?" I took my knife back from Mel and used the blade to flick a bit of fin off my sleeve.

James' hair was a snarled brown mess. He had pinned up the sleeves of his shirt, and the lean muscles of his arms twitched as he worked. His trousers were tucked into mud-stained boots, and he smelled of river water.

Mel tugged my arm and pointed to the wall. "There's a woman coming."

James spun so fast his knife sprayed dots of fish juice onto the wall.

"Expecting anybody?" I asked, tightening my grip on the dagger.

"It's a tall woman," Mel announced, still staring through the wall. "She's got a bird on her shoulder, and she's dressed really funny."

The door opened.

Funny was an understatement. Our guest was dressed entirely in feathers. Stiff raven feathers made up the trousers, and her shirt was a shimmering blue, trimmed with yellow down. Her eyes were black and gleamed like lamp oil. Shoulder-length green hair hid her ears. She was barefoot, but her feet were so dirty I mistook the skin for leather—low-quality cowhide at best.

A mountain sparrow perched on her shoulder, looking rather dull by comparison. Black stripes came to a point over its eyes, giving it an angry expression. It chirped mindlessly as it studied the cabin.

"Who's this?" I asked.

Our guest leered. "James, my love. As I promised, I've come to take you home." She walked toward my husband, arms wide.

James' face was white. "Hello Basi."

I was between them before either could blink, and my knife-tip hovered a finger-width from Basi's chest. "Perhaps you should explain yourself. Quickly."

James caught my arm and pulled. We crashed onto the fish-cleaning table. It was a miracle I didn't stab one of us. I wound up with fish spines jabbing my leg and my husband beneath me in what, under other circumstances, could have been a very enjoyable position.

I was too stunned to enjoy myself. James had protected *her*.

"Thank you, darling," Basi said. To me, she said "I've

come to rescue him from this hovel. He will raise our children, cook and clean, and make an excellent mate."

I gaped at her. "James? Clean?"

I couldn't believe it when James stood up and quietly turned away. Could he possibly want this peacock?

'Mom, I think she's a Cloudling." Mel was staring at the sparrow on Basi's shoulder.

I didn't even know what a Cloudling was . . . probably something else Mel had learned from her books. Her magic books. James' actions began to make sense. "She put a spell on you."

"Of course." Basi smiled and helped my husband to his feet. "His feelings for me are as strong, if not stronger, than those he has for you."

Magic, was it? I smiled back at her. "Mel, do your mother a favor and remove the spell. Then turn Basi into something less bothersome. Another trout, maybe. We can wait for her to suffocate, then add her to the dinner pan."

"I can't."

Melanie could send my underwear on a mountaineering expedition, but she couldn't undo a little love spell?

"Cloudlings use bird-magic. I don't know how it works."

Basi scratched the sparrow's neck. "I'm afraid there is no antidote."

I scowled at my daughter. "Remember this the next time you ask why we hate magic."

She ignored me and tugged on Basi's feather shirt. "How can you and Dad have children? I thought Cloudling women didn't have—"

"Shut up, kid. It's complicated."

I raised an eyebrow. What sort of things was my daughter learning from those books?

"I can't undo the spell, but I *think* I can still turn her into a trout," Mel said thoughtfully. She didn't like being snapped at any more than I did. "We could let Snick play with her."

My scowl faded. "I think I'd like to see that."

"But your charming father would not," Basi said, slipping past Mel to sit at our table. In *my* chair. Next to *my* husband. If Mel hadn't grabbed my hand. . . .

"Men and women have killed themselves after the loss of a Cloudling lover. Suicidal devotion is a key part of the enchantment." She made a great show of considering the possibilities. Her forehead wrinkled and her green brows merged over her slender nose. "Even if the child succeeded, you would find that James' love remained. A human man and his poor, doomed fish lover. It has the makings of a song, don't you think?"

James wouldn't commit suicide. Not James, and not over this green-haired fop. He was too strong. I don't know what kind of humans Cloudlings were used to, but they had never met my husband. He was almost as stubborn as me. I grabbed my knife.

Rather, I slapped the empty sheath where my knife had been. James was still a very talented pickpocket. My confidence vanished, and my gut grew heavy. "James—"

"I'm sorry, Alycia."

I had to strain to hear his whispers.

"I love you, but whatever she did, it . . . worked. I love her, too." His gaze hardened as he turned to Basi. "Of course, as soon as my wife finds a way to break your spell, there won't be anywhere you can hide."

She winked at me. "Isn't he cute?"

I saw his hands tighten on the edge of the table. Even I couldn't get away with calling James cute. I waited for his retort, but his anger quickly faded, driven away by love and magic. James gave me a longing glance, then left the room.

Once he was gone, Basi smiled. "Sorry, dear. You lose."

*

For the next few days, Basi infested our home like a skunk beneath the floorboards. In the rafters, actually, since Basi preferred to sleep on the roof. Feathers and bird droppings showed up throughout the cabin, on floors, shelves, tables, and even on my favorite set of daggers. I tolerated the mess because the price of confrontation was too great.

Basi laughed at my attempts to talk James out of the spell. I guess she knew what the end result would be.

James wouldn't even let me touch him. "I do love you. But I love her too. I couldn't bear to lose either of you."

Instead, he did the only honest thing he could: he cut himself off from both of us. He slept alone, unwilling to betray one by sharing a bed with the other. The conflict was tearing him apart, and I didn't know how to stop it. The energy, the passion, the wit as dry as desert sands, all of the things that made James who he was were buried by Cloudling magic.

Logic wouldn't overcome magic. Nor could I threaten Basi—every time I tried, James came to her defense. I gathered that Cloudlings avoided physical combat. Instead, they enchanted others to fight for them. James would serve as protector and slave. Basi seemed determined to win him by simply outlasting me.

After three days, I decided to ask for help. James was more important than my pride. That night, I slipped out and waited at the edge of the woods, listening to a distant owl and watching the bats flap around in the moonlight.

The faint crunch of leaves marked the arrival of my coconspirator, who greeted me with a whispered, "Mom?"

"Did anyone see you?"

A small hood hid her face, but I imagined her eyes rolled with exasperation. "Of course not. I used magic."

I dread the day she becomes a teenager. "I need you to tell me everything you know about Cloudlings."

"Everything I know from my books? My *magic* books?"

My jaw tightened. "That's right."

"Does that mean you'll stop trying to make me give up magic?"

"Melanie Lapan. . . ."

"Yes?"

"If you don't help me, Basi might never go away. How would you like to have a third parent? She'll be like an obnoxious, overbearing aunt. With feathers."

She scowled. "My books didn't tell me much. Mostly gossip and rumors. Lots of stories about somebody whose friend's cousin was abducted by Cloudlings. The book said it's best to leave them alone.

"Their birds do all the magic. They tell the birds what kind of spell to cast, but nobody knows how the magic works. The birds fly off alone to do their spells, so nobody's ever seen them do it."

Her round face lit up. "Hey, what if I killed the *bird*?"

"If a wizard dies, does the spell go away?"

Her shoulders slumped. "I guess not. I'm sorry, I don't know anything else. I want to help, but—"

I knelt on the ground and gave her a tight hug. "We'll figure something out. A strutting peacock like Basi doesn't stand a chance against the most cunning thief in the country."

"But she already *got* Dad."

Sometimes Mel reminded me a bit too much of her father.

*

Mel and I spent the next two days waiting and spying on Basi. We took turns, though Mel did most of the watching. Her eyes were sharper, and I couldn't spend too much time around Basi without wanting to cram that sparrow down her throat.

I was in the backyard chopping firewood when Mel came racing through the weeds. Snick bounded along behind her like a rabbit. "The sparrow just flew off! She's heading east!"

She pointed to a fleck of black, almost invisible against the raising sun. I slammed the ax into the chopping block and followed her into the forest.

"I'm not sure this is going to work," she said.

"I am." I understood her doubts, though. Not even the best tracker could follow a bird through the air. Especially a magical bird.

Not unless that tracker had a magical cat. Snick had been licking the chops over that sparrow ever since Basi arrived. Being dead, Snick couldn't actually hurt anything. That rarely stopped him from trying. I pointed after the sparrow.

"Get 'im."

Snick sprinted through thorns, trees, and once through a very startled squirrel who didn't dodge quickly enough. We soon lost sight of him, but Mel knew where to go. She *always* knew where her cat was.

We had a harder time of it than Snick. Rather, I had a harder time. Being smaller, Mel had fewer branches to worry about. I think she used magic, too. I know I saw a cluster of wild raspberry lean out of her way. I only wish she had used enough magic to keep the raspberries from springing back and digging prickers into my trousers.

"Up there," she pointed.

I had to carry her over a wide stretch of mud to reach the pond she had indicated. At first I didn't see anything. We had come at least a mile, and we were high enough in the mountains that the only trees were evergreens. The cool breeze smelled strongly of pine. "Where are they?"

"In that tree."

I spotted Snick first. He had trapped the sparrow high in a narrow pine, where it stood on the edge of a nest. Its feathers were puffed so fat it looked like the ball for a children's game. Black beak open wide, it chirped defiantly at Snick.

Snick was unimpressed. His spectral tail lashed back and forth as he crept closer.

"Snick, get down here," Mel yelled.

One pointed ear flicked back, but otherwise the cat ignored her.

Nice to know I wasn't the only parent who couldn't control my kid. "It's okay. What can he do?"

Snick pounced. The sparrow screamed. I had never heard a bird scream before. It flapped so hard that feathers fell like snow, and I almost felt sorry for the thing as it tore through needle-thick branches to escape.

Snick pranced gracefully down the trunk until he reached the ground, where he proceeded to clean his hindquarters.

Mel hurried over to pet her cat. Don't ask me how

that worked. She rubbed where his fur should be, and Snick purred like he could feel it.

The one time I tried to pet Snick, it was like plunging my hand into a stream in midwinter.

"So how long before the sparrow does his magic?" Assuming we hadn't scared the thing so badly its heart had stopped.

"How should *I* know?"

The sparrow fluttered back a while later. It circled four times to make sure the tree was no longer haunted before settling into the center of the nest.

There, it began to hop back and forth, chirping merrily to itself as it rearranged bits of fluff and old grass.

"Housecleaning?" I asked.

She scrunched her forehead. "He's doing something, Mom."

"Up there?"

"Yeah."

I guessed the height at about thirty, maybe thirty-five feet. "I don't suppose you can—"

"I don't know any flying spells."

Heights didn't bother me. I could have scaled that tree with my eyes closed and my hands tied. Pine trees have so many branches it's almost impossible to fall, even if you tried.

Unfortunately, pine trees also have pine needles. And pine sap. And bark that flakes off and gets into everything. By the time I reached the nest, my hair was a tangled mess, my clothes bore dark streaks of sap, and the left side of my face was gritty with bits of bark and more sap.

I pulled myself up another few inches, wrapped one arm around a branch for balance, and peeked into the nest.

The sparrow puffed up gain. It was a spunky little thing. I couldn't bring myself to hurt it.

Fortunately, cats weren't hampered by such weaknesses. "Here, Snick."

Sparrow and cat vanished into the woods, leaving me to investigate the nest. It seemed like a typical nest to me: grass and pine needles and bits of green hair woven into a bowl the size of my fist. Three purple eggs, none wider than my little finger, sat on a cushion of white down.

"Nothing here but a few eggs," I yelled.

"It's a bird. The eggs must *be* the magic," Mel called back.

What had I expected? Sparrows wouldn't write long, spidery scrolls or lug around heavy, leather-bound tomes. They were birds. Birds laid eggs. That left only one question.

"What should I do with them?" We didn't know what the eggs did or how to use them. I had been hoping to find an antidote, despite Basi's claim that none existed. Could Mel use these eggs to figure out how Cloudling magic worked?

"Bring them down. Carefully." That wasn't my daughter's voice. My knife was in my hand and ready to throw before Basi finished speaking. My other hand held the branch, keeping me steady.

"If you hurt Mel—"

Basi laughed at me. "Gods above, I'm not going to harm James' daughter." She tried to pat Mel on the head, saw the look on her face, and thought better of it. "On the other hand, if you don't cooperate, maybe I'll slip one of those eggs into Mel's food. She could grow up to make a fine wife for my brother."

I wished James could have heard. If anything would break Basi's spell, it was a threat against our daughter.

Mel answered before I could find my voice. "Try it."

I couldn't let them fight. Mel couldn't kill Basi without endangering James. Basi might have been bluffing about that, but I couldn't take the chance. Nor did I trust Basi not to carry through on her threat. Mel couldn't protect herself every minute of every day. All Basi had to do was sneak in some night while Mel was sleeping and slip an enchanted egg into her mouth.

"Wait." I scooped up the three eggs and a bit of down, tucked them into a leather pouch, and clenched the drawstring in my teeth. I descended slowly, taking no chances with the eggs' safety.

Basi counted the eggs. From her shoulder, the sparrow chirped furiously at me. "Excellent. This should solve our problem nicely."

"How?"

"James' love for you is stronger than I expected. I should have given him a bigger dose." She gave me a small salute. "These should tip the balance. I've enjoyed our game, but James must come with me before first frost if our child is to be born early enough in the summer to survive." She slipped the eggs into a padded pocket on her shirt. "If it's a girl, perhaps we'll name her after you."

I shoved her against a tree before rationality caught up with me. My fingers crushed the blue feathers of her shirt. I could smell her breath, like spoiled fruit.

If I killed her, I could be killing James as well.

If I destroyed the eggs, Basi would simply get more from that sparrow.

If I antagonized her in any way, I put Mel at risk.

"What now, friend?" she asked.

I opened my hands, brushed her shirt to erase the marks of my hands, and let her go.

"See you back at the house." Basi whistled an old shepherd's song as she walked away.

"What do we do now?" Mel asked.

"We go home."

*

I insisted on cooking my own farewell dinner. Maybe it was the martyr in me. Maybe I just wanted to see the look on Basi's face when I shoved a roast quail under her pointed little nose. I would have used mountain sparrows, but they had too little meat to bother with, even if I had been able to catch one.

Nobody said a word. On any other day, I would have taken that as a tribute to my culinary skills. In addition to a half-dozen quail, all basted in imported Adenkar spices, we had golden biscuits with raspberry jam, wine from up north, and corn so fresh the farmer didn't even know it had been picked.

"This isn't going to work, Alycia." James jabbed a fork at his biscuit. "I don't want you to leave."

"So get rid of the Cloudling."

"Ever the fighter," Basi said around a mouthful of corn. "I admire your spirit, and I wish you luck in finding another man to warm your bed."

Somehow, I kept my temper in check. Did Basi know how close she had come to swallowing that ear of corn whole?

"Why are you giving up?" Mel demanded. This was the first she had spoken to me since we left the woods that morning. Her eyes shone, but she refused to let the tears fall.

"If I stay, we'll be miserable. You, me, your father. . . ." Maybe even Basi, though her comfort was the least of my priorities. "This is ripping your father apart. The only way to stop it is for one of us to leave."

"That's very noble of you," Basi said, helping herself to a biscuit.

James cocked his head. "Yes, it is," he said curiously. "Very noble."

No matter how strong a bond Basi's magic forged, she still didn't know my husband well enough to recognize the suspicion in his voice. Nor did she know me enough to understand that I ranked nobility right up with leprosy on my list of least favorite diseases. I spoke quickly to keep her attention on me. "Basi, promise that you'll treat him well. See that he's happy."

"How could he be otherwise?" She polished off the biscuit and gently patted the pocket that held the eggs. "He may pine over you for a brief time, but I assure you his grief will be short-lived."

I walked over to her chair. She shifted and raised her hands. Was she afraid that, having lost everything, I would risk one last assault? She needn't have worried. Like Cloudlings, I preferred the indirect approach.

I bent down to whisper, "Will you need both of those eggs, do you think?"

"Three eggs," she corrected, giving me a fond pat on the cheek.

I smiled. She smiled back, and a bit of genuine affection shone through the arrogance.

I lowered my voice even further. "Are you sure?"

Basi chuckled and checked her pocket. Those glassy eyes widened, and the way her mouth opened and shut made her resemble her sparrow. "Where is the third egg?"

I scratched my chin. "If I remember right, the last time I saw it was . . . ah yes. I think I may have accidentally dropped it into the batter when I was making your biscuit."

"But—" Conflicting emotions battled across her features. Horror and hatred propelled her out of the chair, but I wasn't worried. Cloudling magic had overcome even James' stubbornness. Basi had no chance.

Love triumphed. The expression on her face became one of adoration. "That's brilliant, my . . . love."

She moved toward me, one arm reaching toward my cheek as the other moved to a pocket on the side of her shirt and pulled out a dark brown egg.

I caught her wrist and bent her fingers back so that the egg dropped safely into my palm.

"The antidote?" I guessed. "The one that doesn't exist?"

She had to bite her lip to keep from speaking.

"You wouldn't lie to *me*, would you?" I blinked innocently. "Darling?"

Her lips trembled. "The egg . . . will counter the spell."

"Thank you." I leaned across the table and dropped the egg into James' hand.

For a second, I was afraid he wouldn't take it. If magic-induced love and loyalty made him refuse the antidote, then my entire plan had failed.

James smiled at me, the same brilliant, impish, loving smile I remembered from the night we got married in Adenkar. The same smile he often shared with me as we watched Mel play with the squirrels in front of the cabin.

He ate the egg whole, crunching the shell with relish and washing it down with the rest of his wine.

"That was the only egg I had," Basi said softly.

My attention was on my husband. "James?"

He grabbed my shirt and gave me a long, hard kiss. Then he turned to Basi.

Basi loved me. Trapped by her own spell, she probably felt such devotion that she would have died rather than leave me.

The look on James' face promised much worse than death.

Basi fled so fast she dislodged her sparrow. It fluttered around the chairs trying to find a way out.

With a lour *rowr,* Snick smacked a paw through the sparrow's head, scaring it in the general direction of the open door.

"Do you think she'll be back?" I asked. She was in love with me, after all. I wondered how long it would take her sparrow to create another antidote egg. I hadn't really thought that far ahead.

"I hope so."

The malice in James' voice enough that I almost wished Basi luck. To change the subject, I asked him a question I had been holding back for two weeks now.

"How could you let a woman who looked like *that* slip you a love potion?"

James hated being embarrassed. He flushed, but rather than answer my question, he tightened his grip on my arms and pulled me close. The other jabs I had planned were soon forgotten.

"*I'm* going to my room to read my *magic* books," Mel announced.

I broke away long enough to say, "That's nice."

"Nice?" James asked, his lips so close they tickled my chin. "I thought we didn't want her to study magic."

I didn't know how to explain my change of heart, so I kissed him. I planned to do a lot of that to make up for the past few weeks. Knowing James, he wouldn't mind one bit.

THE WOMAN'S PLACE

by Susan Urbanek Linville

Magic goes back a long way in human history. Just how far can be seen in this unusual story by Susan Urbanek Linville. Susan has a Ph.D. in biology and is presently working at Indiana University at the Center for the Integrative Study of Animal Behavior. She has been published in *Marion Zimmer Bradley's Fantasy Magazine, Writers of the Future Vol. 11, Sword & Sorceress XVIII, On Spec*, and *HMS Beagle*. She is presently finishing up an epic fantasy novel co-written with her husband, Stephen V. Ramey. She has a daughter Brittany who will be off to college in 2004. She would like to thank her paternal grandmother, Mary Martin Urbanek, whose oral stories about her life stay with Susan to this day.

Susan would like to dedicate this story to Eliette Brunel Deschamps, Jean-Marie Chauvet, and Christian Hillaire, speleologists who discovered Chauvet Cave and carefully preserved one of the most spectacular collections of cave paintings in the world. For a look at their discovery see the Cave of Chauvet-Pont-D'Arc: (http://www.culture.gouv.fr/culture/arcnat/chauvet/en/.

In underground darkness, lard-covered straw torches crackle and smoke, their acrid scent teasing the stomach with promises of meat. Light dances in the Mere's cavernous stone mouth: alabaster, salmon, and golden yellows, long white teeth that sparkle as if embedded with stars. Bones clap: leg bones, rib bones, toe bones, a constant clacking reminder that the bodies here are occupied. The dead must wait to return to the living world.

Draped in bear hide, the grand fem hobbles to the tongue, a sloping golden-white wall marked with auburn handprints. She stoops and ambles, rattling her tooth

35

necklace, growling, tricking the Mere into believing she is here to find a winter sleeping place. She sniffs a bowl of ochre on the floor, dips her palm into the paint and presses it into the wall, fingers and thumb held back.

The grand hom follows, snarling and growling beneath his lion skin, tricking the Mere into thinking he looks for bear to eat. He, too, leaves his palm-mark on the tongue. In unison, they turn to the hunters gathered beyond the mouth and motion them in. Five naked men strike bones together, two more hold torches. In summer these men were hard with muscle, but their shadows are thin now. Their bodies are painted in stripes and circles, red for blood, white for bone. Breath puffs from them in clouds. They shiver. The cavern, as always, is cold.

The grand hom rattles shells strung on dried tendon. The hunters pick up their tempo, clacking bones, stamping feet. The grand fem slips between jagged teeth that hang from the ceiling. The others follow.

The Mere's stomach extends in all directions as far as their torchlight. The grand fem walks through its center, careful not to disturb the bones of long dead bears. The cavern narrows. On one wall a great ochre hyena waits for prey, its spotted back arched. Below, a leopard watches.

"We are hyena," the grand hom calls out. He rattles his shells.

"Hyena," hunters chant.

"We are leopard."

"Leopard. Leopard." Bones clatter. Feet stomp. Torchlight ripples.

The grand hom growls. Or is it the leopard? The hunters' skin-paints darken and smear, red blood mixing with white bone. Breath clings to gray walls in glistening patches. Sweat and torch-smoke intertwine, the smell mimicking a lion's urine.

It is time.

The grand fem straightens and raises her arms. The grand hom hunches beneath his pelt, becoming small and unobtrusive. Hunters quiet, bone-clenching hands dropped to their sides.

The grand fem moves farther into the cavern, where orange and white formations form undulating curtains. The only sound is the echo of dripping water. Men follow quietly now, bare feet stepping gingerly across cold stone.

They reach the heart, where walls are burnt umber, cascading into rusts and alabaster. Torches flicker, exposing clear crystal teeth that hang from above and grow from below. Translucent white swirls through them like clouds. The hunters look neither right nor left. Only the grand fem watches their reflection in the pools to either side of their path.

The heart opens into the womb. Here, the Mere decides who will pass into the living world, and when. The grand fem stops before a wall streaked with white and gray, its center unfolding in draped concretions like a woman's opening. To the left, three black bulls run against shimmering light, across endless plains in the world of the dead. Horses and rhinoceroses give chase. To the right, reindeer and bison gather, nibbling long grasses. Charcoal pits smear the cavern's orange clay floor. Another tunnel leads into darkness.

The grand fem spreads her arms wide, bear skin dangling before the opening, blocking that mystical way from men's eyes. They are free to begin their hunting magic, chanting and dancing and throwing invisible spears, but the woman's place is forbidden.

The hunters find new energy. They cavort through the cavern, the grand hom overlooking like a smiling father. Now, the hunt will succeed and fill their bellies with sweet meat and marrow.

*

El waited in sunlight beneath a gray limestone outcropping, watching the river for signs of returning hunters. Her bones ached, a constant pain that woke with her every morning. Cold north winds rumbled through the gorge like stampeding horses. Junipers and box trees bowed. Snow skittered across rock, forming a drift beneath a barren honeysuckle. Her stomach growled.

She pulled the old bear skin tighter. The sun, now high in the sky's belly, *should* have brought green back to the land by now, new shoots and flowers to eat. But the air remained frigid, the winds fierce. The people's stores of roots, berries, and seeds were almost gone. If the hunters did not return soon, more of their clan would go to the world of the dead.

Two children had died already. A baby girl too young to be named: El's daughter Rouge's child, with her mother's auburn hair and gray-blue eyes. Rouge had carried the body three days before freeing it for burial.

Pom's death brought much sadness. He was a wiry boy, a trickster joke teller, his death sudden and unexpected from a breathing sickness that others recovered from. One never knew when the Mere would open her womb.

El noticed movement on the river's bank. Her heart lifted. She wanted to see Aul's graying-yellow hair above his black wolf hide, an animal carcass suspended from poles borne by younger men. But it was not her brother, or even hunters.

Ami and Noir trudged the river's bank, returning from their foraging. El released her breath, which steamed before her. Perhaps they had found new shoots. Or speared fish. It was to cold to catch fish the woman's way, wading with nets. Spearing was normally a man's right, but they were desperate now. If El spied a rabbit, she might spear it herself. An empty belly saw meat as meat whether it came from a man's spear or a woman's pointed stick.

Noir led Ami up the craggy path to the cave, bulging belly almost filled with child. El worried. Noir's first child came into the world with much difficulty and lived only a few days. Noir had nearly died also. So much blood, bright red, as slick as ice glaze. In a time when the Mere seemed to be reclaiming all the life she had set forth, how could they expect this *new* child to live?

Ami stepped around Noir and crouched like a wolf. Her flat face, once so soft, was pink and raw; her dark eyes watered. So young, El thought. Ami had come into blood only two seasons before. Several men showed interest, but she offered her affections to the new man, Chri, who came from a clan at the gorge's north end.

"We find no green shoots, grand fem." Ami unrolled a spotted horse skin. The cloak bore a sparse assortment of tangled white threads and yellow-brown lobes. Roots and lichen. Not nearly enough.

El tried to smile. Even her face hurt today. Her jaw felt as if it might break by merely speaking.

Ami stepped away. As grand fem, El had first pick. She crouched, clenching teeth against the agony that shot through her hip, and took only a few pieces of lichen. In time of plenty, she would take her true share. For now, she had Noir and the children to worry about.

Rouge approached from the shallow cave beneath the overhang, wearing her familiar gray wolf skin. She placed the back of her hand on her mother's cheek and stroked her graying brown hair. "I fear there is no greening this season."

"There is always greening." El clasped Rouge's hand and pulled herself up. Memories flooded her: the season of her first blood, the birth of her first baby, and the dead birth of her second, the summer all children died of the spotted disease. She remembered Rouge's birth and the birth of her son, Arbre. Sadly, she remembered, too, the day Arbre saw *others* fishing at the river and left their cave for a new life elsewhere.

She had no memory of snows that did not melt and give way to green.

"New life follows death," she said. "It is way of the Mere."

"I fear," Rouge said. "We are skin and bone. Maybe hunting magic not work, hunters not return."

Ami squatted, face bowed. Noir looked uncomfortable, holding her belly.

"Fear eats people like lions," El said. "Come, we grind seeds and make bread. Hunters return with meat. Do not worry."

A screen of woven plant fibers draped the cave opening to keep out winter winds and snow. It needed mending. When the greening came it would be taken down and burned, allowing warm air to circulate. Strands of rope would replace it, used to dry meats and summer fruits for storage in pits.

Soon, El reassured herself. The warm air will come. Her knee buckled as she stepped over a stone. Rouge caught her and supported her through the cave entrance.

Inside, five animal-hide tents paralleled the back wall, forming an arc around the fire. The smell was strong: sweat, urine, fire ash. Rouge helped El lower herself to a flat rock. She stretched her legs. The pain in her hip throbbed. The fire crackled and spat, warming boot soles worn almost through. Hope is like this fire, she thought. Tended, it warms body and spirit. Untended, it dies.

The Mere *will* bring green back to the world, she told herself.

Jee lounged opposite her, gray beard wound in knotted curls across his horsehair shirt. He looked old today. El's youngest sister, Oeuf, sat beside him with her most recent child, a toddler boy with yellow hair and pale eyes.

Ami wrapped roots in river moss and placed them amid hot coals. The eldest children entered the cave, three girls carrying bundles of sticks and twigs, a boy with a woven sack from their storage pit. Rouge joined them and poured seed from the sack onto a grinding stone.

So little, El thought. There would be barely enough bread to give everyone a taste. She looked to the four bone carvings of the Mere anchored in clay behind the tents. Faceless heads looked neither up nor down, did not judge nor stare, did not smile nor frown. Full breasts draped full bellies and generous hips. It was the way things should be, not the way they always were.

"Hunters return," children screamed. "Hunters return."

El crawled from the rabbit-skin and horsehide tent she shared with Jee, Oeuf, and her two younger children.

Pain arched from hip to knee, forcing a grunt through her lips. Ami and an older girl rushed to her side.

"I need no help." She nudged their hands away, hoping to banish that condescending look from their faces, and forced weight onto the sore leg. Pain twisted her sideways, off balance. Hands caught her and led her to the fire.

A slip, she thought. A good meal would fill her belly and chase this pain away. She hoped the hunters brought reindeer or bison. More likely horse, but even that tough meat would be welcomed.

Noir added sticks to the flame. Jee smiled for the first time since the snows fell. Children chattered and peered through the porous entrance screen, jangling strips of sunset that lined the back wall with violets and crimson. Smoke licked El's face.

Chri came through the screen, followed by other hunters. Where is Aul? El wondered. He had led their hunters through many seasons and should enter first.

Without a word of greeting, Chri leaned his spear against his tent and removed his reindeer cloak. El knew immediately from the downward turn of his brown mustache that they had not been successful. The others stood, heads hung.

"I want meat," a child whispered. Ami hushed him.

Coldness blew though El's stomach like wind through an empty cavern. Hope darted from her grasp. Her brother had not returned.

She remembered Aul's broken-tooth smile and light blue eyes that nurtured sparks of curiosity and warm wisdom. She remembered the day he watched her fish with a throw-net, smiling and nodding, the day he rescued her from strange hunters at stone arch, fearless, his fists like clubs. Tears welled. She remembered his glowing pride the day he brought back his first ibex. He'd slept with those horns for many seasons.

There would be no new memories.

She breathed deep, lifted her bearskin over her head, and looked through its round eyeholes. *You risk life to bring food,* she thought. *Come to fire and tell people.* She could not speak her part, her throat too twisted.

Jee pulled his lion cloak tight and crawled around the fire's edge to El, a purring growl in his throat. "Welcome hunters. You risk life to bring food to your people. Come to fire and tell story."

"Story is sad." Chri brushed curling hair from his face. A girl brought a deer skull filled with water. He sipped and passed it on.

Jee helped El to sit and knelt beside her. He took her hand into his and stroked her arm. It helped little. Her thoughts were a hot fog, a burning mist. She wanted to scream: *Why has the Mere taken my brother? Why is there no meat?*

She held her tongue. As grand fem, she must hear the hunters' story to make their hunt real in this world and the world of the dead. I do this for Aul, she thought. The way must remain open so that he can return as a child.

"From living to dead to living," she whispered.

"We travel three days," Chri said, pacing, using his spear as walking stick. His fingernails were black with dirt, his hand chapped-red. Other hunters joined him.

"We drink water. We eat bark and lichen. We see no fish. We see no tracks."

Chri pointed to the ceiling. "Aul see bison first on ridge. We climb." Hunters circled, grunting and panting, enacting the arduous climb.

"At top, plain stretch wide. We see four bison in distance. Darkness come. We sleep in tents." The hunters stooped and huddled, a mass of gray and brown furs, more bear than men.

Chri stood tall. "Morning come. Bison gone. We follow tracks in snow. It rain. We walk two days in mud. We dig roots, eat grubs.

"On third day, we see ibex. We circle to hide from wind." Crouched hunters waddled from fire to tents and back. One man snorted and extended fingers from his head like horns. The children's eyes widened with interest. El imagined with them.

The mud is thick and black and stinks of rot. They struggle onward, pushed by hope that their lean time is about to end. Muck sucks at their boots. They draw closer, raising their spears slowly so as not to spook the animal. The ibex snorts, breath steaming, its musk-scent goading their appetites. It sniffs through a black, wet nose. The ears pull back. The head turns toward them.

Hunters stop in mid-stride, barely breathing. Someone moves, a single slurping step. The ibex startles, jumping straight up, turning in midair. It bounds toward thick bush. The hunters pursue, frigid air biting their noses, throats, and lungs. The ibex stops. The brush is too thick for it to penetrate. It turns.

Aul raises his throwing spear. The ibex charges.

"There is a hole," Chri stated. "Aul not see." His voice lacked emotion but his eyes glittered. "He fall before he throw."

Clutching his stomach where the ibex horn penetrates. Writhing, face contorted, light-blue eyes seeking.

El's thoughts screamed: *Why take Aul when we need his skill most? He is our best hunter, our best leader.*

Chri lay still and silent.

My brother.

"Ibex run," Chri said. He directed sad eyes at El. She wondered when he had stood. "We bury Aul. It rain two days. We see ibex and bison in distance. Too far." He hung his head. "We return."

*

Snow fell in big wet flakes, blanketing the cave entrance. El's share of thin bread and two fish had not even quieted her hunger pangs. Oeuf sang to her boy. He had cried for two days. The dark circles beneath his eyes were a bad sign. El had seen them many times on sick and dying children.

She tossed a stick onto the fire and winced. Her pains meant little against so much suffering. Other women huddled within tents, saddened by the new snows. Even now, winter would not end. Hunters chipped stones, anxious and angry.

Chri's eyes flashed. "We need hunting magic." His mustache sagged with his frown. He scraped stone across the burnt end of his spear to sharpen it.

"The Mere is not fooled again so soon," El said. The Mere must be cajoled and convinced like a newborn offered a breast it does not realize it wants. Chri was a good hunter, but knew nothing of magic.

"It is five days since we return," Chri said. "Snow comes again. We need food." He shoved the half-formed spear back into the fire and removed a second. Black stone scraped white wood. "We hunt again. It is only hope."

"The Mere fills us when she is ready," El said. The Mere did not move in the people's time; they must move in hers.

"We cannot wait!" Chri shouted. "Do we leave world like wide-noses?"

It had been many seasons since wide-noses visited the gorge. El remembered meeting a group when she was young, just after Aul was born. They were quiet and traded furs for hand axes. Jee said they did not understand magic, but traveled the world of the dead without hope for return.

"We remain," El said. "Soon, warm winds bring green."

"Warm winds." Chri snorted. "I forget what they are." He stood and jammed his spear into the ground. "You help, grand fem."

"I do nothing,' El said. Her heart ached.

"Fem magic."

"Dangerous." Jee stood at the tent opening, hair flattened on one side from sleeping. "We wait, try hunting magic again soon."

Chri looked to the other hunters. "We hunt without magic. We kill reindeer. Ibex. We are lion."

"Lion," men repeated halfheartedly.

"Lion!" Chri smashed his spear against a rock. Splinters flew. "We are lion!"

Other men stood. "Lion," they said. El was not convinced.

Chri tied his hunting kit around his waist and lifted his hood. A reindeer face covered his curls, eyeholes staring upward. He lifted his remaining spear from the fire and pointed it at El.

"We return with meat," he snarled. "We not need magic."

El straightened her back as best she could.

"Hunting in anger not succeed." Aul had taught her that. She remembered fishing with him where water gurgled over flat rocks, she with her throw-net, he with his spear. Anger inhabited him that day. Another boy had bested him in a stone tossing game. That day Aul speared only one fish, while El trapped six.

He never hunted in anger again.

"Lion!" Chri screamed.

"Lion," the men chanted. They gathered weapons and followed Chri from the cave. Dread walked El's skin like a spider. For the first time, she feared there would be no green; they *would* vanish like the wide-noses.

*

Noir crouched on a bloodstained birthing hide before the bone carvings that depicted the Mere. She panted and groaned, belly clenched. This birth comes quickly, El thought. Often that was the case for a second child. Still, she wondered if it came *too* quickly, if the baby was dead or too small.

Rouge knelt behind Noir, supporting her back, combing fingers through her hair, speaking a gentle cadence: *it is good; the child is healthy and strong; you are strong; it is good; do not worry; do not worry; see how the Mere smiles?*

Noir cried out. The baby slid from her, small but not abnormal. Whiteness coated it, a powdery paint streaked with blood. El worked as quickly as she could with her stone-stiff fingers, turning the baby, clearing its nose and mouth, cutting the cord with the birthing blade. The tiny face puckered and reddened. The baby cried.

"It lives," Rouge whispered. Noir sagged in her arms.

"A boy." El wiped blood from the baby's face and head. Light yellow hair was just visible on his scalp. He seemed familiar.

"Aul?"

The baby quieted. Pale blue eyes stared directly at El. The corner of his mouth ticked upward.

El's heart raced. Tears filled her eyes. It was unusual for a spirit to return so quickly, but times were difficult. Great need brought many unusual things.

"The Mere does not forget us," she said to Rouge. She turned her gaze back upon the baby. "Welcome to our clan." She felt warmth in her stomach and chest. If only the cold winds would warm so!

She wrapped the baby in soft rabbit hide and held him close. Rouge rubbed Noir's abdomen and breasts, encouraging the afterbirth to expel. The baby fidgeted. El gave it her fingertip.

At last the tissue-mass splattered onto the birthing hide, exuding a smell that was too sour. El frowned. Afterbirth was normally dark red and smooth like fresh liver. This was green and wrinkled. Poisoned. Her hopes fell.

"Noir not eat this," Rouge said quietly. Her eyes demanded, then questioned, then went neutral. A new mother needed nourishment to produce milk for her child. In lean times, they depended on the afterbirth to feed her.

El gave the baby to Noir. "Hunters return soon with meat," she said. "Do not worry." She wished she could believe her words.

Noir held the baby to her empty breast. Women and older children foraged beyond the cave entrance. The snows were melting at last, but finding anything edible was still difficult.

Aul dies a second time, El thought. The pain of losing her brother again was greater than the pain in her joints.

She lifted the afterbirth by its cord and limped to the fire pit.

Jee sat at the fire, entertaining small children with sticks and bones.

"It is boy," El said. She threw the afterbirth onto the flame and listened to the spattering clamor of fire consuming flesh. It did not care that the meat was poisoned.

Jee frowned, watching her with full knowledge. He let out a sigh. "When does it end?" El had never seen him so weary, so absent of life and hope.

"No more," she said. "I use fem magic."

"No!" Jee looked up, a wrinkle gathering between his brows. "Hunters return soon."

Tears emerged from El's eyes. "Noir not live so long. Child not live."

"They must. Fem magic danger—"

"No time is left!"

"What of you?" Jee took her hand into his, skin as warm as springtime. She remembered lying with him, his arms cradling her, hands cupping her flesh. No other man had been so gentle.

"I go to the Mere," she said firmly. She could not watch her brother's new spirit die.

She wiped her tears.

*

El paused in the Mere's mouth and let her bear skin drop. She came as woman today not bear, not to trick, but to ask. The Mere's chill breath sighed down her spine. Water dripped like clacking bone. Oeuf and Ami crouched behind her, beneath bison and horse skins.

"I grand fem." El's words echoed. "The Mere not fear grand fem, who is old and weak, who no longer bleeds and stands only step from world of dead." She held the torch forward, but could no longer lift it above her head. Light bathed the Mere's tongue and teeth. Limping, she entered the stomach's darkness, her hip throbbing like a wound. The slick floor was marked by swirls of rust and crimson. Streams to either side gurgled.

Cave bear bones littered the area. Their sleeping pits

were still faintly visible, but they had long ago departed
the living world. El remembered accompanying grand
fem Ana when fire threatened to scorch the gorge. Ana
had stopped and spoken to these bears.

El repeated her words. "Great bears, I thank you for
guiding people back from the land of dead. Please guide
me. Keep me safe in body of the Mere."

El went deeper, passing leopard and hyena. She stopped
in the heart and worked her way to her knees and hands
to drink tangy water from a pool. Neither Ouef nor Ami
rushed to help her. She smiled. They had listened after all.
The Mere must not see through their disguises. Only grand
fem goes naked into the woman's place.

Her reflection stared back from the pool's surface: an
old woman with creased forehead, tired brown eyes and
downturned lips. When did I grow so old? she wondered.
It seemed only a short time since she awaited her first
child's birth, a mere eye-blink since Aul became man.
Where was the woman who once pranced, singing, at the
river's edge?

She struggled to her feet.

The heart opened onto the womb. Horses, bison, and
ibex lived in these walls. Lions stalked their prey. Blood
flowed. Men made their hunting magic here. Perhaps the
Mere was convinced by their pretenses, perhaps merely
amused by their childish play. Whichever the case, hunting magic worked in its limited way. Men usually returned with meat and skins.

Small magic involved no sacrifice beyond discomfort.
She wondered how many men actually believed their rit-
uals and how many danced to impress their friends or to
work warmth into their limbs.

Strong magic went deeper.

She gazed upon the Mere's birthing canal, the narrow
tunnel beyond the wall that resembled a woman's opening. The Mere nurtured and tolerated men in her womb,
but true power resided beyond this tunnel, where the
path between life and death took form. El's torch wavered, the flame pushing away from the opening, away
from her.

"It is time." Heart racing, she entered between wet, undulating walls, a dark placed filled with strange smells and sounds.

Feet shuffled behind her, more tentative with each step. She remembered her fear when she first followed grand fem Ana. Ana had not seemed afraid. That had helped. El tried not to show her fear.

They came to a black triangle painted on golden stone that seemed to float, unconnected to anything. Ami gasped, seeing for the first time this sacred place that was here when the people arrived in the gorge and would remain long after they were gone.

"This is woman's place," El said. "No man sees." She handed her torch to Oeuf and presented herself, arms and legs spread wide, ignoring the pain that roared like a lion from her hip and knee.

"I grand fem. I come in great need. I ask one gift. My people need meat. I must become." She must *become* hawk or lion, and take the hunters to prey. Just as grand fem Ana had become owl and soared above the gorge, leading the people to safety through the wildfires.

El's throat tightened. Ana had not been the same upon her return to woman flesh. Her thoughts flew beyond anyone's understanding and her eyes never settled. Girls had fed her and led her down pathways to water for the remainder of her life.

It not be this way for me, El thought. I not let it. Pain lanced her knee, nearly toppling her.

"I ask one gift," she repeated. "My people need meat. I must become."

Ami rattled shells. Oeuf emptied sticks and wood from her carry sling and started a small fire. El concentrated on the Mere. The triangle danced and floated, enlarged and dissolved.

Her arms grew tired. Her back and hip ached like a bad tooth, but one could not remove a bad back or a bad hip. The fire crackled and smoked, offering little heat. Shadows rippled alabaster walls.

"I ask one gift. My people need meat. I must become." Patient, she told herself. The Mere works in her own

time. It had taken a very long time for the Mere to
answer Ana's magic.

Time lost meaning. She might have stood there for a
thousand seasons or a heartbeat. Cold sliced her toes.
Her eyes unfocused, the Mere blending into shades of
gray and gold. Rattling shells became thundering herds;
smoke was musk. Lightening cackled and burned.

"I ask for . . . one gift. My people . . . need . . . meat."

Was that croaking her voice? Her throat was raw, her
mouth dry. How could she continue? A thought drifted
through her like fog: The Mere has abandoned us.

No. The Mere moves in her own time.

"I must . . . become."

Her vision cleared. A male ibex stood before her. She
saw the wetness of his eyes, his coarse tan hair, felt the
heat of his body and pounding heart.

A snuffling grunt pushed her lips apart. She smelled
acrid smoke with a vividness she had never known. Fear
entered her too. Why ibex? Eagle leads hunters to kill.
Or lion. Not ibex. Ibex prey, not guide.

Do not worry, her woman-self reminded. The Mere
provides what is required.

Pain vanished from her. She turned to the fire. Warmth
entered her fingers and flowed through her arms. Oeuf
extended an arm from her hide, offering a wooden bowl
half-filled with charcoal paint.

El crouched and took the bowl. The absence of pain
was nearly as intense as its presence.

She moved along the undulating cavern wall, repeat-
edly touching its cold surface until she felt a heartbeat,
until her own heartbeat grew loud in her ears. She
dipped two fingers into paint and spread blackness on
alabaster white.

A head.

*El stands in wet snow, frigid air stinging his black nose.
He sniffs and watches several ibex females graze.*

Long, curving horns.

*He scrapes snow with his horned head, digging for the
new growth his nose tells him lies within. He cannot concentrate. Something watches. He scans the plain.*

A back.

His hair prickles, sensing danger. A predator? He sees only yellow grass stems. Tough, tasteless grass. He sniffs again and snorts. Something *is near, but he can neither see nor smell it.*

Tapering legs.

He prances toward the females, inviting them to run. They scatter. He tries again. They kick and spin in nervous confusion but will not follow.

An ample haunch.

Muscle tenses, springing him high into the air, pushing him forward more quickly than wind. He runs alone, feeling invincible, the very force of life itself. Cold air fills his lungs and thunders in his ears.

Eyeless, blackened face.

Dark shapes crouch among boulders. He bounds to a stop, ready to bolt in any direction. Horns protrude from the shapes. Too straight. Too tall. The smell is not right. Energy surges. He jumps toward them, determined to intimidate and astound.

The horns leap too, flying with a sound like wind through tall grass. Pain jolts his hip and knee. Sharpness enters his chest. He staggers and drops to the snow. The pain is a familiar, searing agony. He tries to stand, but cannot. Panic.

No, a voice deep within El whispered. It is time. Do not fear this sleep.

The dark shapes surround him. A shorter horn descends.

*

In underground darkness, water drips from a ceiling. A fading torch crackles. Fur-shrouded women lift the grand fem's naked body, skin as pale as the cavern's walls except for the black paint smudging her chest. Gray hair sweeps the floor as they carry her from the woman's place.

The grand hom crouches beneath lion skins in the womb. He touches the grand fem's chill skin, growls and cries out. They bear the body through the heart's glistening waters, the stomach's darkness, not stopping until they exit the Mere's mouth. The day is bright and blue, warmer than the day before though snow still clings to shadowed places. Below, the river is swollen and flows fast through the gorge. Figures trudge beside it, a line of dark dots.

"Hunters return," children scream. "Hunters return."

The grand hom throws off his lion skin. He lays the back of his hand on the grand fem's cheek. Tears glitter his eyes. "Are two dead children not enough? Must you swallow us all?"

A woman in wolf's skin touches his hand. The man sobs and clutches it to his chest. "When does this end?" he mutters.

Blue-gray eyes look through the wolf's eyeholes, a steady gaze that will not yield. "The Mere works in her own time. Grand fem not fail us."

Voices rattle through the gorge, as loud as bones clattering or feet stomping. "We bring meat!"

KIN

by Naomi Kritzer

We'd all love to have magical powers, wouldn't we? But there may be a price, as Naomi Kritzer shows in this story. She lives in Minneapolis with her husband and two young daughters. She has a bachelor's degree in religion and worked as a technical writer for several years. (What does a degree in religion have to do with technical writing, you ask? She says she always claimed in job interviews that both were attempts to take the mysterious and inexplicable, distill it, and render it understandable to mere mortals.) Speaking of the mysterious and inexplicable, one of her favorite Web sites is the Urban Legends Reference Pages (http://www.snopes.com)—urban legends explored, debunked, and explained.

Naomi's first novel, *Fires of the Faithful,* sold on her older daughter's first birthday, came out in October 2002. "Kin" is set in the same world. Her next novel (set in a different fantasy world), *Freedom's Gate,* will be published in the summer of 2004. *Sword & Sorceress*—a *much* earlier volume, in 1988 or 1989—was the very first fantasy market she ever submitted a story to. She was a junior in high school at the time, and got a brief note back from Ms. Bradley saying that the story wasn't bad, but that typeface was still inelastic.

I'm glad she decided to try again.

When I was five years old, my father took me into town, to an inn, where a man in black robes waited for us. The man was old, and stern, and he frightened me, but my father gave me my doll, Emilia, and said that I needed to be calm and obedient to set a good example for my baby.

"Can you make a witchlight for me, Julia?" the man in black robes said.

Clutching Emilia with my left arm, I held out my right hand and easily willed a small glow into my palm. Witchlight was nothing. Everyone could make witchlight; I couldn't remember not being able to do it.

The man set a small log onto the hearth. "Can you make that burn?" he asked. I knelt down beside the log and touched it lightly to make it burst into bright flame.

"Oh, very good," the man said. "Very good indeed." I straightened up with an impatient frown. Most people could light fires. His praise was empty, and I knew it.

"Now," he said, and my ears caught a new note in his voice. "I have something else for you." Out of his pocket came a small gray pebble, which he tucked into my hand, where the witchlight had bloomed a moment before. "Can you make this burn?"

Still holding Emilia tightly with my arm, I turned the pebble over and over. Here, at last, was a new task—a new challenge. I set the pebble down on the hearth, so that it wouldn't burn me, and laid my whole hand over it flat, the way I had when I first began to start hearthfires. I took a deep breath and closed my eyes, and reached for the energy under my feet. The rock was different from wood—very different. But when I pulled my hand back, it glowed a deep orange-red.

"*Very* good," said the man in black robes, and from the look in his eyes when he glanced at my father, I knew his praise was not perfunctory. Nervous, I wrapped both arms around Emilia and retreated to my father. I heard the jingle of coins, and my father exclaimed his thanks as he pocketed what the man in robes handed him. Then the stranger crouched down to my level.

"In a few weeks," he said, "a young woman is going to come live with your family. She's going to bring gifts for you and your parents, and she's going to tutor you in magery. You're unusually good at it, for a five-year-old, but you're going to get even better. She'll teach you to work with others to create really *big* fires, to set fires from a long way away, even to make fires in the sky. When you're a grown-up, you'll get to come live in

Cuore with the other mages, isn't that exciting? But for now you're going to stay with your family, and this woman will come to teach you."

I nodded hesitantly.

"All I ask in exchange," the man said, "is your doll."

My doll? I wrapped my arms around Emilia as tightly as I could. "No!"

The man laughed, and my father laughed with him, and I realized that the request had not been serious. He straightened up and ruffled my hair. "Mages don't have babies," he said. "And you're a mage. You'll get used to the idea soon enough."

*

My tutor was named Anna. She was a few years older than my eldest sister, younger than my youngest aunt, and as promised, she came with gifts: a sack of apples, soft wool scarves, new needles, new boots for my father, even a tiny pouch of cinnamon. "I don't want to be a mage," I said to Anna at our first lesson. "They say mages can't have babies, and I want to have babies someday."

She laughed and took my hand. "Magery is better than babies," she said. "I'll show you; make a witchlight." When I summoned a light, she sent a surge of power through my body like liquid fire, leaving me gasping. It felt like flying; it felt like swimming in hot cider. "You'll be able to summon this power on your own soon," she said. "If you ever want babies, all you have to do is stop using magery, just as your mother does when she wants to conceive."

I nodded, relived to know that even as my pounding heart said *more, more, more* in my ears. Of course, it wasn't nearly so simple. My mother, an ordinary woman, could light her way with a candle instead of witchlight, and use flint and steel to start fires, and the only price was a bit of inconvenience. When I tried to stop using magery, a few weeks later, I was rewarded with racking nausea and pounding *need* until I gave in. The reward, though—the reward was magic, the soaring feeling that was there any time I cared to reach for it. The reward was *to be a mage*—one of the elite, one of the wielders of power, one of the privileged of Cuore.

It wasn't enough.

*

"What happened to Emilia?"

"I can't remember. I know I brought her with me to Cuore—just to annoy Anna, I think. And then I packed her in my bag when we went to war. I was thinking about her last night, and I don't know. I don't know where I lost her."

Silvia shifted, wrapping her soaking wet cloak tighter around her shoulders. It was raining, and the bottom of our rabbit-hole was a filthy, sodden mess. Silvia's hair hung lank and tangled around her face, and I knew I looked the same way. Ah, to be a mage, one of the privileged few. Silvia and I were the only mages who'd survived an ambush of our unit; a handful of Circle guardsmen had survived as well, and had dug a rabbit-hole for us and gone looking for reinforcements. Silvia had wanted to go along, but we'd been told rather forcefully that we'd just get in the way. I had known better than to try to argue.

"Maybe someone stole her to use the rags to line their hat," Silvia said. We'd both lost our hats somewhere before the ambush.

"She was a pretty small doll," I said.

"I never had a doll," Silvia said. "I used to have a pouch with a lock of my mother's hair in it, though."

"A lock of your mother's hair?" Mothers carried pouches with locks of their children's hair, so that they could pray for their children even when separated from them. But children did not usually reciprocate.

"Yeah, why not? Back when I was six, when my mother snipped a lock of my hair during the Birth of the World festival, I asked for a lock of hers. She thought it was cute. I carried that with me to Cuore, and then to war. I don't know what happened to it. The thong probably rotted out from being wet all the time."

"I think the rain's letting up," I said.

"Never," Silvia said. "I fully expect to drown in this pit."

But I was right; the rain slowed, then turned to a drizzle, then stopped altogether. I tried to wring some of the water out of my cloak, without much success. For some reason, now that the rain had stopped, I felt even colder.

"Listen," Silvia said. "What's that?"

I held my breath and strained my ears. "It sounds like a cat. No, I take it back. That can't be a cat. It sounds like—"

It sounded like a baby.

"I'm going to check."

"Gemino and Lucio told us to stay here."

"Yeah, well, I'm not going far."

"How do you know it's not the Vesuviani trying to lure us out?"

"Why would they bother? Do you think you could summon magefire worth a damn right now?" I hauled myself out of the rabbit-hole, getting even more covered in mud, and lay on the ground for a moment, trying to tell where the sound was coming from.

The rabbit-hole was on the outskirts of what had, a day or two ago, been a village. I looked around at what was left. *We made a really big fire, all right,* I thought as I picked my way over a pile of rubble that had probably once been a cottage. The war had begun over border raids from Vesuvia; in several cases, families of our farmers had been killed, their fields and houses put to the torch. Well, this was one village that certainly wasn't going to be put to anything as puny as a torch. The first time I'd seen the remains of a firefight, I'd been promptly and thoroughly sick, but the war had been going for almost two years now, raging east and west along the border with Vesuvia, and I'd been there for all of it; one more ruined village hardly made me blink.

Absurd to think anyone could survive, I thought, stepping over the remains of a stone wall, but I could still hear the high, lonely wail. I realized that the I was standing in what had been the blacksmith's shop; there was an anvil at my feet, and a fallen hammer close by. And there, behind the wall of what had been the blacksmith's furnace, sheltered in a niche made from stones and a fallen piece of metal, was a tiny, tiny, living baby.

"Lady's mercy," I said, and picked it up. The baby was as light as a kitten, fragile and delicate and terribly cold. It was a miracle it had even survived, first in the fire and then the cold and the rain. The baby was wrapped in a wool blanket, and the serendipitous shelter had stayed reasonably dry, but that didn't explain how it had escaped the fire. The baby quieted when it felt itself lifted in someone's arms, and started searching with its tiny mouth for a breast.

"I haven't got anything for you, little one," I murmured, and it let out its little birdlike cry again, flailing tiny fists in frustration. I couldn't take it back to the rabbit-hole like this; if there were any Vesuviani still around, the noise would bring them straight there. Finally, I sat down on the fallen anvil and offered the baby my breast, hoping that suckling would calm it down.

The baby seized on my breast with a ferocity that almost scared me; my eyes opened very wide, but it didn't precisely hurt. Before the war, back in Cuore, my bed had never been quite so consistently occupied as Silvia's, but I'd taken the occasional lover and most had touched my breasts. The baby's suckling felt nothing like a lover: the suckling was urgent, rhythmic, like a gasp for survival. Its suckling resembled love play no more than swimming to shore from a capsized boat resembled splashing in a hot bath.

At any rate, though the baby had to be hungry, for now it seemed content just to suckle. I pulled my cloak over both of us and went back to the rabbit-hole.

"It really *is* a baby?" Silvia said, disbelieving, when I showed her the tiny foot, blue with cold. "Girl or boy?"

I checked. "Girl."

"What are you going to do with her?"

I bent my face over the baby's downy hair. Even in the midst of muck and ashes, she had the same sweet baby smell I remembered from my youngest sister. "Well, I'm certainly not going to put her back where I found her."

"No, I suppose not."

"When Gemino and Lucio return and bring us back to the main encampment, I'll see if I can find something for her to eat."

"She'll need a wet nurse. You won't find one of those at the Circle camp." Silvia pushed her sodden hair out of her eyes. "Don't get too attached to her. She'll probably just die."

"I won't get attached," I said, tightening my arms around the tiny, warm bundle.

I sat up through the night, stroking the baby and letting her suckle. My breasts grew a little sore, as the hours wore on, but I feared she'd cry again if I made her stop, so I put up with it. Towards dawn, she fell asleep in my arms, her lips parted, her hands limp against me. *Lilla*, I whispered in her ear. "I'm going to call you Lilla."

Gemino and Lucio returned in late morning, with a detachment of mages, and horses and food and even dry clothes for us. I checked the food stores first, but there wasn't anything an infant could eat. "Milk," I said. "Is there milk back at the camp?"

"There's cheese," Lucio said.

"That's no good," I said, and started digging for a dry blanket, at least.

"Julia's had a baby," Silvia said. Dry clothes on, she was herself again: witty and sarcastic.

"A what?" Gemino dismounted.

"I found a baby," I said, irritably. "She survived the ambush somehow, even though I think everyone else in her village got killed. I'm taking her with us."

"And why not?" Silvia said challengingly to the other mages, when one raised an eyebrow. "We're allowed to have hobbies, aren't we?"

"There's a village not too far from where we're camped," Lucio said. "There may be farmers who haven't fled. You could try to buy some milk."

We had to ride slowly, because I didn't want to jostle Lilla. I was glad to be rid of the wet clothes, but Lilla still seemed happiest against my skin, and I tucked her under my robe and cloak. When we finally reached the encampment, toward the end of the day, Silvia tumbled off her horse and shouted that her body could be claimed by any man who found a way to arrange a hot bath for her. I stepped down carefully and went looking for milk for the baby. I had to wheedle money, first, from one of the unit commanders, and then I walked to a farm, reaching it finally in the fading light. They sold me milk, and gave me a clean rag when I explained that I had a little baby to feed. "Would you show me how, signora?" I asked, realizing that I had no idea how to feed a baby this way.

The farmwife sat me down and poured the milk into a bowl and warmed it. I pulled the reluctant baby away from my breast and let her suck milk off the rag a the farmwife showed me. "It's best to find a wet nurse for an orphan babe," she said. "The Lady intended goat's milk for baby goats, not baby girls."

I nodded. "That's not really possible right now," I said. "I wish it were."

Absorbed in my task, I heard the farmwife gasp suddenly. I looked up; she stared at my left breast, still bare. A single drop of milk trickled down, luminous as a pearl in moonlight.

"I heard you rescued a baby."

"Yes."

"Admirable of you." Martido, the High Commander of my Circle detachment, did not sound particularly admiring. "You do realize, of course, that this cannot excuse you from your duties. We are at war; you are a mage."

"I understand that." As one of the lesser mages, I was supposed to be as expendable as a pack-horse, capable of going anywhere, anytime, regardless of the danger. But with an infant at my side, I couldn't be sent anywhere that silence was necessary, and we both knew it.

"Then you'll understand that obviously this baby can't stay with you. I've started a letter to the High Circle, explaining the situation; someone back in Cuore will arrange for a wet nurse. You can send the child back to Cuore for the duration of the war."

A lump rose in my throat, looking down at her sweet, sleeping face, and I shook my head.

"Are you refusing me? This is not a request, this is an order. She isn't even your kin. Besides, you can't count on finding milk for her. If you want her to live, she needs a wet nurse."

"I have milk for her," I said.

Martido slumped back in his chair, frustration clear in his face. "That's what the rumor said. I didn't believe it then, and I don't believe it now."

I bared my breasts and squeezed out a drop of milk; since Lilla had just been nursing, it came out in a spray, like a jet from a tiny fountain. "Believe it," I said. The expression on Martido's face made me fall back a step, but I clutched Lilla to me and hardened my voice. "Why would the Lady send me milk if She wanted me to send away my daughter? Kin or not, She sent this baby to me, and She wants me to keep her." I licked my lips, trying to decide whether to try this next argument. "I think the Fedeli would agree with me."

At the name of that order—the fearsome priests and priestesses who enforced the law of the Lord and the Lady—Martido's lips tightened. As a mage, he didn't really need to fear the Fedeli—but that didn't mean he wanted to take them on directly. "The Fedeli aren't here," he said.

"Silvia has a friend back in Cuore," I said. "A Fedele priest." She didn't, but everyone knew that Silvia's selection of "friends" was both broad, and broad-minded. Martido's lips tightened even more.

"In that case, you can trust in the Lady to protect your child," he said. "It's often enough that silence is not important; you can take the baby into battle with you or find a temporary caretaker back at the camp when you go. You're dismissed."

I retreated, uncertain if I'd won a victory or been maneuvered into the worst of all possible corners.

Battles became frightening in a way that they had not been before. Before, I had feared for my own skin, hoping that if I died under enemy magefire, it would at least be quick; I knew that death was painful, but I figured I could endure a few seconds of anything. Now, though, I had Lilla with me, every time. Silvia, in one of her more sympathetic moments, helped me make a sling to carry her in, and as I clasped the hands of the other mages to summon power, I could feel Lilla's breath in the cold winter air. To imagine Lilla consumed by magefire was unendurable—but I didn't dare leave her back at camp. There was no one there I trusted to take care of her, not if Martido decided to arrange a tragic accident. If Lilla was going to die, it was better that she die next to me. She never seemed to be afraid, even when magefire lit the night sky like blazing dawn; the only thing that made her cry was when I gave her to someone else to hold, so I kept her with me.

On our way back to camp after one set of battles, Lilla started to sneeze, then cough. By nightfall, her face was flushed, her breathing labored. Though we would have only a few hours to rest, I couldn't sleep; I lay awake listening to Lilla's rasping breath. *The Lady wouldn't give me milk for her, only to take her away from me,* I told myself, trying to make myself believe it. Lilla napped fitfully, her cough sounding like a dog's bark. I remembered my own mother soothing my coughs with steaming teas, but I had nothing to offer Lilla. Despite the noise, Silvia slept like the dead. Toward dawn, Lilla's cough seemed to ease a little, and I was able to doze for a bit. I woke to find her tiny hand patting my cheek. I stared at her woozily in my own feeble witchlight, and saw her baby face light with a hesitant, luminous smile for me.

I had feared that if Martido heard that Lilla was ill, he'd send us out again as soon as possible. But the following day, he announced that our entire camp would be moving north. Silvia and I rolled our blankets and took down our tent. "You don't look pleased," I said to Silvia.

She looked surprised. "Surely you heard the rumors,"

she said. "No, I suppose not—you're the one person who wouldn't. There's a story going around that in the heart of where the fighting was, no one can do magery."

"How would you even know? What's left to burn?"

"Not even witchlight," Silvia said. "Some of the more sensitive mages swear it's harder to draw magefire down now, even at the edges of the fighting. I haven't noticed that, myself. But we're moving north, away from the where the battles have been held, and apparently the High Circle and the Emperor are sending messengers south to negotiate a truce."

"A truce." I straightened up, Lilla in one arm and blankets draped over the other. "That's good news, isn't it?"

"Oh yes," Silvia said. "That part's good news."

Our new camp was deep in friendly territory. The other mages celebrated the hoped-for truce with late-night feasts and dancing; some even made fireworks, colored witchlight in the sky, to entertain the people in the nearby villages. I wasn't in the mood to make fireworks and didn't want to take Lilla to the parties, so I mostly stayed in my tent, dozing with Lilla curled up against me.

After a few days I felt something I recognized as the craving for magery, blunted a bit by the fact that I still used everyday magic like witchlight. Despite my exhaustion, I decided that perhaps I was in the mood to make some fireworks after all. Tucking Lilla into her sling, I pulled my cloak around both of us and went in search of Silvia. Tent walls are thin, so I walked through the damp field listening for the sound of her voice.

"—with Julia," I heard Silvia say. "And Julia's babe."

"Oh yes." The tone of the young man's voice stopped me cold. "I've seen Julia out with her—*pet*."

"What a pity she couldn't have found herself a kitten instead," a young woman's voice said. "Kittens are cute. They're soft. They purr instead of crying, and they clean their own bottoms."

"You can't pretend you're a kitten's mother," the man's voice said. It wasn't Martido—I would have recognized Martido's voice—but his tone held contempt that

I'd never imagined any of my compatriots felt for me. Shaking, I turned away and went back to my tent. No magery was powerful enough to make me face the person who'd spoken about me that way. I curled up with Lilla and lay awake for a long time, my face against her hair. I did sleep, finally. When I woke up, I had a headache and my mouth tasted foul, as if I'd overindulged on wine the night before. But the craving for great magery, the desire to draw down magefire or create fireworks, had eased.

Silvia had also returned, and when she woke in early afternoon she looked at my face and asked, "What? What is it?"

"My—" My voice tightened, and I touched Lilla's hair "—pet."

"You heard that?" Silvia shook her head, raking her long hair back with her hands. It was almost clean, now that we were living at camp most of the time. "Don't let it bother you. Don't you know they're jealous?"

"Jealous?"

"Of course. You must have left last night or you'd have heard me tell them that, and you'd have heard their response."

"What did they say?"

"They denied it of course. 'Jealous? What would I want a squalling, prating, stinking babe for?' " Silvia nodded with evident satisfaction. "If I said you were jealous of my way with men, you wouldn't feel the need to deny it in *quite* those terms, now, would you? I don't think you'd say, 'Ugh! What would I want a trail of hulking, stinking, snoring men for?' You'd just laugh. And the lady I was talking with last night—trust me, Julia. She did *not* laugh."

Lilla laughed for the first time a day or two later. I had been lying on my side playing with her little toes, a game I remembered my mother playing with my baby sister: "This lamb plays in the meadow. This lamb stays with the fold. This lamb is warm and cozy; this lamb is out in the cold. And this little lamb is the sweetest lamb and we give her to baby to hold. Let's chase her back to the barn: chase chase chase chase chase!" On the last little lamb, I moved my fingertip to Lilla's palm, and then tickled her up her arm, under her chin, and back down to her foot. Lilla looked startled when I tickled her under her chin, and then giggled out loud and kicked with her feet. "You're laughing," I said. "Oh, my sweet Lilla, you're laughing!" I wished, suddenly, that my mother were somewhere nearby, so that she could hear Lilla's laugh, as well.

That night, I woke late to find Silvia shaking me. "What is it? What is it? Are they sending us out?"

"No, Julia. The truce is holding."

I sat up. The tent was lit by Silvia's bright witchlight. Lilla, sleeping in my bedroll, turned her face to look for my breast, but fell back asleep when she didn't find it.

"A woman came to the camp today. A woman with the same color hair as Lilla."

I stroked Lilla's red-brown fuzz and said nothing.

"She says that she heard there's a mage here with a baby, and she thinks that baby is her niece. She wants to take Lilla. If she's Lilla's kin, Martido will say it's her right."

My hand closed over Lilla's tiny one, and I swallowed hard. "If she's Lilla's aunt, where was she when the rest of the family was killed? Why did it take her this long to come looking?"

"She's a musician; she has a post in Pluma. She said she came as soon as she knew." Silvia bit her lip. "I thought you had a right to know. I heard they were going to wake you this morning and just take her. I figured at least—" Silvia reached out with one finger to stroke Lilla's downy head—"At least you have the right to keep a lock of her hair."

I had never cut a lock of Lilla's hair, even to keep in a pouch by my heart. There had never been the need; she was with me night and day anyway. Silvia had found a pair of scissors before she woke me, tiny silver shears for cutting thread. Lilla had very little hair, but I cut a little of her fuzz, slipping the hairs into the pouch that Silvia held out for me. Once they were safely inside, my hands began to shake so hard that Silvia had to slip the thong over my head for me.

"When are they coming?" I whispered.

"Morning, I expect," Silvia said.

If the woman was Lilla's kin, it was her right. I knew what the Fedeli would say, if any were here: that the Lady had given me milk to keep the baby alive for her kin to reclaim. I loved Lilla; that didn't matter. Lilla had taken me as her mother, after she lost her own; that didn't matter, either. I turned my head so that my tears wouldn't fall on Lilla's cheek and wake her up. The Law of the Lady was clear.

Lilla was still sleeping. Her lips puckered and she sucked briefly in her sleep, then smiled, dreaming of milk. A moment later she startled; her eyes flickered open and she flung out her hands. As soon as her hand found mine, though, she relaxed back into sleep.

"I don't care what the Lady says," I whispered. "You're my daughter. I'll give up anything else, but I won't let them take you."

Silvia had curled up in her bedroll and closed her eyes, but when she heard me moving around the tent, she sat up. "You're leaving with her, aren't you?"

"You probably think I'm crazy," I said, tying my blankets and robes in a roll with my belt. "Deserting the Circle, giving up power, giving up being a mage—all for a baby that isn't even my own kin."

Silvia touched her finger to the back of Lilla's hand. "No," she said. "She *is* your kin. I understand that." She looked up at me, her own eyes clear and her face calm. "You'd probably be best off fleeing to the south, into the parts of the country where magery doesn't work. They won't look for you there. If you think you can stand it, not using magery."

For Lilla, I could do anything. I nodded my head quickly.

Silvia fished a small velvet pouch out from the blankets of her bedroll. "Take this with you."

"What is it?" The pouch was heavy and lumpy, and made a clinking sound when I took it into my hand.

"Gifts from admirers." Silvia's voice was offhand. "If you sell it a piece at a time, you should be able to support yourself and Lilla for a while. At least in the style to which you've lately been accustomed." She gestured at the tent. "Wait a few minutes, then head east out of the camp. I'm friends with that guard, and I should be able to keep him distracted for you."

I clasped Silvia's hand. "Silvia—"

"It's going to be dawn in another hour," she said. "You'd better let me go if you want to do this. We don't have much time."

I slipped out of camp unchallenged in the deep darkness of the last part of night, Lilla sleeping in her sling against my heart. I listened for Silvia's voice as I passed the guard's post, but heard nothing.

I hesitated for one last moment, and then kissed Lilla's head and kept walking.

CHILD'S PLAY

by Esther M. Friesner

Nebula Award–winner Esther Friesner is the author of thirty novels and over one hundred short stories, in addition to being the editor of eight popular anthologies. Her works have been published in the United States, the United Kingdom, Japan, Germany, Russia, France, and Italy. She is also a published poet, a playwright, and once wrote an advice column, "Ask Auntie Esther." Her articles on fiction writing have appeared in *Writer's Market* and Writer's Digest Books.

Besides winning two Nebula Awards in succession for Best Short Story (1995 and 1996), she was a Nebula finalist three times and a Hugo finalist once. She received the Skylark Award from NESFA and the award for Most Promising New Fantasy Writer of 1986 from *Romantic Times*.

Esther is possessed of a devastating sense of humor, and she and Josepha Sherman should really *not* be allowed to sit at the same dinner table if you want to stop laughing long enough to finish your meal, but she can deal with serious stuff just as well. Marion's preference was always for short pieces. To get into *Sword & Sorceress* a longer story has to be really good. This one is. . . .

Mira heard her father and That Woman arguing in the middle of the night, long after good little girls were supposed to be in bed sound asleep. She frowned and buried her face against Isa's warm, nubbly side, thinking fierce, angry thoughts about the many sins of grownups, chief of which was their complete and total disregard for the rules of logic.

If they want me to be sound asleep, why do they fight with each other so loudly? *They were doing it when Papa sent me to bed before moonrise and they're still doing it*

*now! But I bet that if I got up and went out there to ask
them to be quiet, I'd get yelled at for being naughty and
not going to sleep.*

Mira sighed, and her breath stirred the loose threads
just under Isa's left forepaw. Moonlight streamed into
the child's sleeping chamber, casting shadows that whispered wonderful stories and dreadful secrets. Mira tightened her grasp on Isa. The stuffed animal was an odd
mismatch of real beasts—a bear's comfortable, cobby
body; a cat's bright, intelligent face and alert, pointed
ears; a dragon's shimmering wings but even at barely
six years old, Mira knew all about being a mismatch. The
other children in Tallyford town took pains to remind
her of it every chance they got.

It didn't help that Mira's father was the richest man
for miles around, a merchant whose storehouses were
always filled to bursting with the fine fabrics that were his
chief stock-in-trade. Children learned from their parents,
most often when their parents didn't even know they
were teaching them some very ugly lessons indeed. Envy
and sour-natured backbiting seeped through the walls of
the houses, snappish words and nasty innuendos slipped
from the lips of tradesmen who didn't have the same
success as Mira's father, of wives who only saw their
own worth in terms of how well their husbands' business
interests thrived. Their disgruntled mutterings became little trails of venom, a thousand poisonous rivulets that
trickled from parents' mouths into children's ears and
were at last spat full into Mira's face whenever she went
outside alone.

"Yah! Here comes Mira! She thinks she's just so
*wonnnn*derful!"

"Hunh. Little stuck-up princess. Her daddy buys her
everything she asks for."

" 'Course he does. That's the best way he knows to
make her go away and leave him alone so he doesn't
have to look at her."

"Who'd want to look at *her?*"

"Hey, Mira, if I give you this apple, will you go away?
Ooops! You should've caught it, Clumsy. It's your own

fault it hit you that hard. Only *babies* can't even catch an apple."

"Yeah, and only *spoiled* babies cry when they get hit."

"She's so spoiled, she stinks."

"Mira, Mira, satin and silk,

"Stinks as bad as sour milk!"

"Aww, is the baby princess crying? Is she gonna cry? Is she gonna run away and tell her mama on us? Nooooo. Because her mama's *dead!*"

"She's not *really* dead; she just ran away so she wouldn't have to look at ugly baby Mira and her ratty old doll anymore."

"*That's* not a doll. Dolls are pretty. That's a *monster*."

"Just like Mira. A stinky, stupid, ugly, crybaby *monster!*"

Alone in her bedroom except for Isa, Mira grabbed the pillow and jammed it over her head, trying to block out the echoes of the day. The children's taunting voices swooped and tittered through the darker corners of the moonwashed room like bats. Every day without fail That Woman forced Mira to leave the comfort of her room, the safety of her father's house, and go out into the street where her tormentors waited for her like a pack of hungering dogs. If Mira protested, That Woman brushed aside her pleas as if they were no more than bits of dandelion fluff.

"Don't be silly," she decreed with the confidence of someone whose definition of "silly" was: *Anything that contradicts the way I think things should be done.* "Children need fresh air. Besides, I don't want you underfoot here while I'm trying to set the house in order. Merciful gods, did your mother *never* dust? And the clutter! The piles of trash I've had to clear out of these rooms! What a disgrace! *Hardly* the way for a man of your father's social standing to live. What was she thinking? It's amazing you don't have rats in your beds."

In the end, Mira would go outside if only to escape That Woman's ranting on and on about what a terrible housewife her mama had been.

"But she *wasn't,* Isa," Mira whispered to her button-eyed companion. "Mama *was* a good house— house—"

The child paused. For the life of her, she couldn't think of her mother Gilli as a *house*wife. Gilli's joyful appetite for life and all its marvels was forever taking her far beyond the confines of her house. Under her hand, dust gathered unmolested on the bed slats, spiders found temporary refuge in the corners of the high shelves, and sometimes the breakfast dishes waited until well past sundown to be washed and put away, but the important chores always got done. Meanwhile she swept her darling Mira up onto her hip and carried the child down to the docks to watch the white-winged ships sail away to lands where the wind blew spicy-sweet, or else she bore her off into the woodland and showed her how to tickle trout from the brook, how to gather berries in a moss-lined basket, how to pick and choose roots and herbs and flowers to make tonics, elixirs, potions, and balms, the way that Teacher did now.

"She did house-stuff too," Mira concluded. "Maybe not how That Woman does it, but— but—" She sighed. How foolish to tell Isa things that the cuddlesome creature already knew! It had only been a year and a half since Mama closed her eyes for the last time.

"They said I was bad," Mira told Isa, remembering. "All the people who came to visit right after she died, they said I was bad for not crying. But I *did* cry! I *did!*" And the memory of those tears and the vision that had brought them made Mira's eyes sting anew.

She was weeping at the top of her lungs when her father came barging into the room. Sunden carried a little pinch-pot clay lamp in one beefy hand, holding the curved handle between thumb and forefinger with comical daintiness. He was that saddest of men, a sailor whose skill at driving a hard bargain had torn him from the lap of his beloved sea and marooned him behind a counting house desk. Lifting the lamp too high, so that his own head cast baffling shadows between the flame and what he was trying to see, he peered vaguely at the bumps and bunches of cloth cluttering Mira's bed, trying to catch sight of his daughter.

"Mira? Mira, child, what's wrong? Bad dreams?"

Mira sobbed and snuffled, wiping her eyes hard against Isa's side. Isa didn't mind. 'No, Papa," she said at last. "I— I wasn't even asleep yet," she confessed.

"Oh." Sunden set the little lamp down on the nightstand and settled himself cautiously on the edge of Mira's bed. It was huge, as befitted the only child of Tallyford's richest merchant, but sometimes he wondered whether Mira might not be happier to pass the night in a cozier nest. When Gilli'd been alive, sometimes they'd let the child sleep in the bed between them. Those nights, man and wife would stay awake for hours, content to gaze lovingly at the sweet miracle the gods had granted them, every breath they drew filled with the enchanted scent of a life so newly come into the world.

But Gilli was gone, and Porla insisted that children must sleep in their own beds at all times, even when thunderstorms or nightmares rode the skies. More, they must not have any light in the room but what the moon might give, and the door must be shut completely, to keep little ears from hearing things that were none of their business.

He sometimes wondered whether Porla thought doors were magical barricades, capable of sealing off all sound even when she got so enraged that she bellowed at him like a wounded stag. He knew for a fact that Mira heard more than Porla suspected, even with the child's bedroom door shut tight.

"Couldn't sleep, eh?" Sunden stroked his daughter's hair, softer and glossier than his finest silks. "Not much of a wonder. We were shouting mighty loud, weren't we?"

Mira didn't reply. Sometimes grownups asked you friendly questions when it was a trap. If you kept still and silent, no one could blame you for doing or saying the wrong thing.

The merchant took a deep breath and let it out slowly. From the moment of Mira's birth, he'd felt less like her father and more like her courtier, powerless to understand her but happy to serve her in any way she might allow. Gilli, now . . . Gilli'd had the knack for being able to share their daughter's thoughts, to partner the little one's strange, wild spirit. The happiest memories Sunden owned were of the times his two darlings opened the gate to their special world just wide enough to let him slip inside to share it with them for a while, a brief and golden while.

That all changed when Gilli died. It changed before, in a terrible, frightening way that even now he could hardly believe existed. It had happened just like this, with a cry from Mira's room in the middle of the night. It was easier to hear her smallest whimper then, for no inner door was shut in this house while Gilli lived. He'd leaped from his own bed and raced to his daughter's side to chase away the phantom terrors that sometimes were too big for Isa's powers to banish. He'd found Mira sobbing wildly, half-choked on grief, using Isa to stifle the worst of her sorrow.

When he asked her what was wrong, she struggled for breath, then fixed him with a dreadful stare and solemnly told him, "Mama's going to die."

Useless to offer the child words of comfort, useless to reassure her that it was all a dream, a bad dream, the kind of dreams that everyone has at one time or another. Mira just kept staring at him, her left eye blazing with reflected lamplight, her right eye holding the icy image of the crescent moon. She shook her head like a judge after pronouncing sentence, and went on to describe in detail— to the day, to the hour, to the smallest circumstance—how her adored mother would die.

Gilli'd come into the room then, her sweet face a crisscross of wrinkles from their bedding, her dark hair a tousled cloud. She took her daughter into the warm folds of her nightrobe and tried to soothe her while Sunden looked on helplessly, but the child refused to be comforted. Again and again she told them both how it would be. They'd laughed, trying to make her laugh, and told her all about what cheats dreams could be.

But Mira held fast to her mother, even to the point where she let Isa tumble from the bed, and refused to let go. Sunden sidled up and did his clumsy best to put his arms around the two of them at once, as if mortal strength and a desperately loving heart had the power to keep all darkness at bay. The three of them sat there like that until sunlight seeped in through the shutters and Mira, exhausted, slept at last.

He and Gilli had tucked her in and spoke no more of what was just a child's nightmare. How on earth could such a thing ever truly come to pass? How could a young woman, hale and in perfect health, be found dead on the kitchen floor while in the midst of preparing a feast for the Festival of Flowers?

Yet that was exactly how it happened. Even now, more than a year since that awful day, Sunden was haunted by the smell of freshly cut flowers, and of honey cakes left suddenly untended, burning to cinders in the oven. He had been the one to find his wife lying crumpled on the tiled floor among the carefully crafted images of dolphins, fish, sharks, and shells as if Gilli's delicate body were just another bit of sea wrack washed ashore by imaginary tides.

Since that dreadful day there had been other incidents, other times when Mira spoke of the future and her words came true. Sunden didn't think about it too much; it scared him, so he pushed it all aside in the old, childish hope that what you ignored would vanish and then you wouldn't have to worry about it any more.

He didn't *think* about it, but he did *do* something: He saw to it that Mira was accepted by the woman all Tallyford town called simply Teacher. If she owned a name like other people's, she never offered it. She lived alone, thoroughly respected and perhaps a little feared by the townsfolk for all the things she knew. Her small, trim house was a comfortable place, always fragrant with the scent of herbs and flowers. Sunden gave his precious child into this nameless woman's hands, and prayed to the god of all merchant seamen that he'd done enough.

"Mira," Sunden said, gazing down at his daughter. "Mira, I— There's something I need to tell you."

"She wants you to send me away," Mira said. "She thinks you're stupid to even think about lying to the king's messengers. They know how I can sometimes see things, things that are going to happen, and they'll give you lots and lots of gold if you let them take me with them. You don't have to give your consent—they've got the power to *take* me—but they were told not to *dare* do that, in case I get so scared that I never speak again. There was another girl-child born in the time of the king's grandfather who also had the power to see things moon-eyed, but they made the mistake of stealing her from her home and forcing her to go to the king's court. She never spoke another word."

Sunden stared at his daughter. Some of what she'd said might have been gleaned from overhearing Porla arguing with him, but all that talk of another child with Mira's power— This was the first he'd ever heard of it. To see things moon-eyed . . . That was her way of describing how the silver crescent glimmered in her right eye only when the door between dusks and dawns opened and let her look through. She didn't seem able to control it, didn't know whether it ever *could* be controlled. But if the other child-seer had lived in the king's grandfather's time, did all this mean that his darling could peer into the past as well?

Mira gave him a steady, solemn look. "I saw the story weeks ago, Papa, before the king's messengers even came to your door. I saw it in the sand picture Teacher made for me, saw the king himself telling them why they couldn't just pluck me like an apple from a branch and ride away. I didn't say anything about it until now because I didn't want you to worry and also because—because—" Suddenly she stopped talking and thrust her thumb into her mouth as if to dam up words she feared to say.

"What, my love?" Sunden asked softly. "Why else didn't you tell me? Surely you didn't dream I'd be cross with you?"

The thumb came out, the words tumbled after, *"Because I thought you'd want to send me away!"*

Sunden gasped, his heart gone cold. He hugged his child to him so forcefully that she squeaked like a startled mouseling.

"Child, precious child, how could you ever think that? How could you dream it?" Tears stung Sunden's eyes. His tongue tasted as bitter as if he'd bitten into a handful of uncured olives. He knew why such thoughts crossed Mira's mind.

"Mira . . . dear one . . ."

"Oh, it's all right, Papa," Mira said, squirming herself free of his too-desperate embrace and calmly setting Isa on her lap. "You don't have to explain about That Woman. You were lonesome after Mama died, and you needed someone to look after the house things. I knew she'd come."

"You . . . saw it? You saw that Porla would come here?"

Mira shook her head. "Just that you were used to having Mama to talk to about grownup things, and that you couldn't cook," she said. Meantime her thoughts added, *And that you thought it would be all right if you told yourself you were doing it all for me. But you weren't. You did it because you're too afraid to sleep alone. Poor Papa. You don't have Isa, like me, so you had to lie.*

"I used to be able to do a fair stew," Sunden said with a rueful chuckle. "Fish, mostly; fish stew and biscuits. That was in my sailing days. It's been a long time."

Mira gave him a sharp look. He was trying to distract her, or perhaps just himself, from talking about more important things. Mira was young, but wise enough to know that problems, like dragons, never disappeared simply because you pretended they weren't there.

"What are you going to do?" she asked him.

"Do?" he echoed.

"About me. About the king's messengers." She wanted to add, *About her,* meaning That Woman, but she held back.

Sunden sagged. "I don't know," he said. "I've told

them no already. I've done it a dozen times. They still come calling at my counting house, or the wharves, or even here, always with the same pleas and threats and wheedlings. A curse on every idle tongue in this miserable town that ever went wagging about your gift! How else could word of it have reached the king?"

"You told them no?" Mira repeated.

"For all the good it's done," her father muttered. "They won't accept anything but yes for a final answer. Seers aren't born every day. The realm that has one— But that's no matter to us, Mira. The messengers tried that tack on me, whining on about how you'd help keep our borders safe, our people fed and happy because of how you can tell what's going to happen. As if there aren't lands that know peace and plenty without the help of any magic at all, except a king wise enough to heed and give good counsel! A leader who looks beyond his own mirror's all any country needs to be happy, not a weathercock who'll dance to follow the latest gust of wind, nor a man who smiles in the face of war because he only sees his own glory, never mind if he climbs to reach it over the bones of other people's sons."

Sunden paused. He could feel Mira's eyes on him. He smiled sheepishly. "Sorry, lass; I forgot myself. Your mama was used to hearing me go on like that when I felt strongly about something. She was a patient woman, but no one's fool. Ah, how I miss her!"

"If you miss her, you should find her again," Mira said. "Not *her*, I know, but someone *like* her. You should, so you will."

"Well, that would be nice, love." The merchant chucked his daughter lightly under the chin. "But Porla looks after my needs well enough, and she's really not so bad as she sounds when she's angry. I expect I'm not the easiest man in the world to live with, as she often tells me." He stood up and tucked her snugly into bed before taking up the little oil lamp again. "It's nothing for you to be troubling yourself about," he said as he started for the door. "I'm a grown man. It's my lookout to stand watch over you, not the other way 'round. Now you just go to sleep and don't fret: I'll tell the king's men no as many times as need be, and the only thing that's like to stop me is if I wear my tongue clean off its moorings. But I doubt that'll happen. Sleep well."

"You should," Mira mumbled drowsily into Isa's pointed cloth ear. "So you will." And by the fading radiance of moonlight a silver crescent glittered in her eye.

*

If Sunden thought that the king's men would tire of forever being told that they could not have his daughter, he was wrong. These were men who knew to the penny just how much their skins were worth to their king, and the value of those skins varied according to how well they served him. They also knew that if they failed to bring the child-seer back with them, ready and willing to place her gift into the royal service, their skins were worth little more than the knife that would be used to peel those skins clean off their bodies.

They'd been given a goal and gold enough to reach it. That should be enough for them to do their job, as far as the king was concerned. He wasn't picky about how they chose to do it, as long as it was done. He'd give them more gold, if they had to have it, but as for how much time he'd allow them to accomplish their mission—

He wasn't a picky man, but he wasn't a patient one either.

That was why, little more than a week after Mira's midnight talk with her father, she returned home from her lessons with Teacher to find That Woman sitting on the old wooden bench outside the house, her apron covering her face, her whole body racked with sobs.

So it seemed. Yet when Mira came near enough to make a small "I'm here" noise in her throat, and That Woman dropped her apron and turned to look at the child, her eyes were as clear and dry as if she'd never shed a tear in all her life.

"There you are at last, the source of all our troubles!" she cried, pointing at Mira and raising her voice loud enough to force the attention of every neighbor with ears to hear. "It's all your fault, you and your mewling, whining, accursed selfishness! Oh, what's to become of us now?" She threw her apron back up to cover her face and howled loudly enough to outdo a whole troupe of professional mourners.

Mira felt herself go cold in every limb. Not even Isa's presence warmed her to the slightest degree. "I want Papa," she said, her voice unable to rise above a whisper. "I want my Papa."

The apron dropped again, revealing a demon's twisted face. "Want him all you like; you'll never see him again in this world, and you've no one but yourself to blame for it. They've taken him away."

Mira hugged Isa even more tightly than before, so tightly that one of the stuffed toy's belly seams parted. *"Who* did?" she asked That Woman. "Who took Papa?"

"Who?" That Woman gave Mira, a short, sharp slap. Passersby and nosy neighbors suddenly pretended that the two of them had turned invisible. "Who do you *think,* you stupid girl? The king's messengers! They got tired of my poor, foolish Sunden putting them off just because *you* haven't got the common sense the gods gave to a dormouse! All that time wasted, coaxing you, persuading you, acting as if *you* had any real say in the matter. When I was your age, children knew their proper place: We were obedient, biddable. We did as we were told, and if we didn't like what our parents served us, we swallowed it anyway and smacked our lips for more! *My* father never would have hesitated an instant if the king had asked for *me* to enter the royal service. He'd have said the word and I'd be gone before he'd finished speaking, and not a peep out of me if I valued my skin!"

"But *my* Papa loves me!" Mira protested, and as the words left her lips she realized she'd made a big mistake. She threw Isa up before her face to ward off the fresh slap she knew must come.

To her surprise, That Woman did not strike her a second time. Instead, she gave Mira a look that made the undealt slap seem like a blessing by comparison.

"So he does," she said softly. "So he must, to believe he has to get *your* consent to this. And because of that, because of his baseless love and your stubborn stupidity, he's been hauled away in your place to try explaining matters to the king. Do you think our lord will like being told that *his* royal desires aren't as important to Sunden as *your* pathetic whims? How do you think he'll reward *that* sort of loyalty, eh?" Her teeth, small and white, showed themselves in a wolfish smile. "Tell me, little seeress, what do you see awaiting your father in the king's own dungeon?"

Mira uttered a shriek so piercing and piteous that even those grownups who would sooner die than intercede for someone else's child took notice. But before they might say or do anything, Mira had taken to her heels and raced away. Cursing, Porla got up and went back inside the house, railing against herself for not having taken the precaution of getting the girl safely inside the house before playing all the cards in her hand.

"No matter," she muttered as she shut the door. "She'll be back; she must. The brat's got nowhere else to go."

"What's that you said, my dear?" Like a great bear newly awakened by the first breath of spring, Sunden came lumbering out of his study. His tongue was still thick from the dream-draught Porla had put in his wine, an oh-so-helpful gift from the king's messengers.

"Nothing, love, nothing," she replied brightly, hastening to slip a guiding arm around his waist and steer him back to the comfortable chair by the fireside.

"I guess I must have nodded off," he said sheepishly while she sat him down and poured him another cup of wine, deftly laced with a second dose of the pale blue liquid that brought sleep. There were enough doses of dream-draught in the vial that the king's men had given her to send Sunden slumbering at least a half a dozen times.

There was also enough left in the vial for one dose that would sink him deep into that final slumber from which no man ever woke. She hoped it would not come to that.

"Isn't Mira home from her lessons yet?" Sunden asked, taking the cup from her hands. "I think it's past her time. Maybe I should go outside and meet her."

"If you like," Porla said lightly. "But if you want my opinion, it would be better if you gave the girl a little room to grow up. You know the other children tease her about being a baby. Think how they'll taunt her if you're always mother-henning her!"

"If they do, I'll soon teach them better." Sunden scowled, half rising from his chair. Porla pushed him back down with surprising ease.

"You mustn't fight her battles. It won't help her at all. Come now, relax, drink. The hour's not so late as you imagine, and what child ever did come straight home after lessons?"

"I suppose you're right." Sunden sighed, and brought the cup to his lips.

"Of course I am."

I'd best keep a sharp lookout for the brat's return, Porla thought, watching contentedly as Sunden drank, then yawned and began slipping back into a drugged doze. *This is it, all or nothing. I must catch her before she can come into the house and find that her precious Papa's still here. If I scare her enough, it will be child's play to convince her that she must go with the king's men at once. After I've bundled her off, I'll simply convince Sunden that she changed her mind and went of her own free will.*

Porla left Sunden snoring in his chair and went to the front door to keep an eye out for Mira. She'd already taken the precaution of packing a few of the child's necessities in a wretched, small bundle by the door. If the girl were sufficiently upset about her father's fate, she'd never think to ask how Porla came to have that bundle ready.

And if the brat did manage to keep her accursed wits about her enough to ask, no matter: A good, hard slap across the mouth would soon cure her of stupid questions. Porla smiled and gave her apron a little shake. The gold coins that were her earnest money from the king's men jingled merrily, calling out for their brothers to join them as soon as Porla could manage to send that spoiled little chit packing.

It wouldn't be long now.

*

"Is that so?" said Teacher when Mira had poured out the entire story between gasps for breath and spates of tears. Isa's wings were soaked clear through. "How very . . . interesting. I've just been to the marketplace for greens and after that to the fishmonger's, down by the docks." She handed Mira a clean, sweet-smelling handkerchief with which to dry her eyes and wipe her streaming nose. "You'd think news so great as the arrest of Tallyford's foremost merchant would have reached *one* of those places."

Mira looked up sharply. Teacher was younger than her wisdom, a kind-faced woman scarcely older than Mira's own lost mother had been when she died, but she knew as much and more than those three times her age.

"You don't think he's been taken," the child said. "You think That Woman's telling lies."

"Now why would she want to do that?" Teacher asked quietly.

Mira didn't need to answer. "Good," she said fiercely. "I'm *glad* she lied. Papa will find out. He'll be angry, so angry that he'll throw her out of our house *forever*."

"Is that the only thing that might happen?" Teacher got up from her high-backed, hearthside bench and drifted over to her worktable. This was where she kept herbs and bones, pebbles and powders, paper and ink and enough pens to refeather a whole gaggle of geese. It was also where she kept the flasks of colored grit for the sand paintings she used when instructing Mira and her other pupils. It made them pay closer heed to her lessons when they saw how a single gust of wind could snatch the wisdom away.

Mira followed, taking Isa with her. By standing on tiptoes, she just managed to peep over the edge of the high worktable. She had hopes of seeing one of Teacher's more mysterious projects, something that might sparkle, or glow, or even go *boom!* Once she'd seen Teacher make a ring that sang out a warning when poison touched it, and another time she and the other pupils had watched wide-eyed while the young woman filled her house with butterflies who landed on the children's hair, whispering wonderful stories of all they'd seen in the lands beyond Tallyford town.

This time all Mira saw on the table top was a blue clay bowl, a pile of mushrooms, a handful of mixed greens, and glass vial filled with oil.

"Salad?" she exclaimed, feeling cheated.

Teacher smiled down at her. "You haven't answered my question. Why should I answer yours?"

"It didn't *sound* like a question," Mira said in her own defense. "Not a *real* one. And neither was mine."

"Those are often the most useful questions of all." Teacher filled the bowl with greens, topped them with mushrooms, and drizzled oil over all. "As you say, salad," she said. "But what sort? You remember our lessons about mushrooms, child?"

Mira nodded. Teacher had taken her pupils—only four other children in all Tallyford town who shared Mira's same bright, alert hunger for learning—into the forested uplands for three whole days. There she'd had them learn by heart the uses, for good or ill, of every growing thing they found. For Mira it was wonderfully like the lost times she'd spent rambling the wild lands with her mother. Teacher took special pains when it came to instructing her young charges about mushrooms and certain other plants, on account of the harm they could do.

Remembering those lessons, Mira gasped and clapped her hands to her mouth. *"Poison* mushrooms!" she cried. "And— and snakeweed greens?" She was too small to get a good look at what was in the blue clay bowl, but she could guess. "Or maybe . . . dreadwort? Oh! And the oil! The oil's been fused with poison too!"

Teacher laughed softly. *"In*fused, child, *in*fused." And after correcting Mira's word, she plunged a pair of ivory chopsticks into the bowl and gobbled down a huge mouthful, mushrooms and greens and all.

Mira shrieked, but Teacher only laughed again. "Sometimes a salad is only a salad. Sometimes, it's not. I want you to keep your mind open to every possibility. Now Mira, think before you answer my question, because I *will* have a sensible answer out of you: If you tell your father about Porla's lie, what might happen?"

"He *might* get angry and send her away forever," Mira repeated, somewhat less certainly this time. "But— but if he does that, I think— I think that she'll get angry too. She's *awful* when she's angry. One time an old peddler came to our door and he just wouldn't go away. I thought she was going to slam the door in his face, but instead she grabbed his tray and yanked it so hard she almost snapped the poor man's neck, too. Then she spilled all his wares into the street, stamped them into the muck, and then she beat the old man with his own tray until he ran off."

Teacher's mouth hardened. "And what did your father do when he heard about that?"

"Nothing," Mira said in a very small voice. "I was too scared to tell him. I was afraid of what she might do if she got mad at me." A look of realization touched the girl's face. "Or what she might do if she got mad at Papa!"

"Exactly." Teacher nodded briskly and finished eating her bowl of salad, sharing it bite for bite with Mira. "Easy to see what Porla's up to," she said. "It's no secret that the king's men will give a handsome reward to anyone who can *persuade* you to accompany them back to court."

"Papa said I don't have to go! He won't let them—" Mira paused, stunned, as understanding came. "What happens to me if Papa's . . . gone?" All at once the child's face assumed the grave mien of a grown woman. She had reached a decision, "I have to go," she said. "I have to find the king's men and tell them I'll go with them. It's the only way to protect my Papa."

Teacher stooped to cup Mira's face in her sweetly scented hands. "Child, why do you say that? There's no need for you to go. I'll deal with Porla and—"

"Porla's only one," Mira interrupted. "Even if we stop her from hurting Papa, someone else might try, to get the reward. The only way to protect him forever is to give the king's men what they came for." A tear trickled down her cheek. "Me."

"No." Teacher stood up, her face icy with anger. "I forbid it. You have power, Mira, the power of seeing past time's horizon, but you're still just a child. You were put into my care so that I could teach you how to master your power, and to master yourself as well. It's my duty to teach you discipline, limits, boundaries, that *No* means the same for the strong and the weak. Just because you hold a sword, you don't always need to draw blood. But the king's court—!" She shook her head. "The only limits there are the king's desires. What will you learn from that? That power is the be-all and end-all? That righteousness, justice, compassion are only words?"

All at once she dropped to her knees and clasped Mira's hands. "Once—" she began in a whisper. "Once upon a time there was a little girl who was gifted by the gods. She could make flowers blossom out of season, kindle fire with a fingertip, darken the skies with flights of birds or bats or butterflies. The king heard about this girl too, and he also sent men to bring her to him, men who carried gold. The girl's family was poor, desperately poor, peasants whose land seemed to yield scarcely a bushel of barley for every cartload of stones her father cleared away. The girl thought of all the good things they could have if she went with the king's men. Her parents agreed, but just as they were packing her things for the journey, the little girl's grandmother came in and stopped them, and made them understand that what they were planning was the worst possible thing they could ever do to their child."

"Why?" Mira asked. "Why was it so wrong, if the little girl *wanted* to go? They were poor; they *needed* the gold. What did the grandma say to them?" Silently she hoped for some magical words that might be used to good effect on That Woman.

But Teacher only shook her head and said, "Nothing.

My grandmother said nothing at all. She never did say a word in all my lifetime, nor my mother's either, as I was told. But she had her ways of letting others know her mind. When she planted one foot on the sack that we'd made ready for my journey and held her walking staff like an axman's blade, keeping all of us from laying hands on it, her message was clear. And all the while we could see the silver curve of a crescent moon—"

"—in her eye," Mira finished. "Was *she* the one, your grandmother?" The little girl beamed. "Oh, it felt so good when I first found out about her and knew that I wasn't the only one who'd ever seen things moon-eyed!"

Teacher nodded sadly. "Yes, that was my grandmother. She's the reason I recognized your talents as true when you were first brought to me."

"What did your parents do? They must have obeyed her . . . didn't they?"

"Oh, yes, they obeyed." A sigh from Teacher's heart brushed Mira's cheek. "Instead of sending me to the royal court, they took the few coins the king's men had already given them and bought me swift passage to a town where my father had old friends. I was told that I mustn't ever use my given name again, not for as long as anyone might recognize it, and that I must never try to send them any news, that when the time would be right, they'd contact me." Another sigh followed the first. "They never did. I grew up with a name that wasn't mine and a gift I had to hide forever. Even now I feel safer nameless, and I only give glimpses of my power to those like me, those I trust and love."

Mira didn't want to ask it, but couldn't help herself. "Didn't you ever get to see your family again? Couldn't they— couldn't they find a way to visit you, or—?"

Teacher looked away. "Years later I found an old paper in my guardian's keeping that spoke of the deaths of a poor peasant family, from the youngest child to the old grandmother who lived with them, all executed at the king's word."

Mira watched the tears slide down Teacher's face. She didn't know what to do but felt she must do *something*.

When no other remedy came to mind, she settled for pressing Isa into Teacher's arms and hugging them both. The three of them sat there in silence for a time, Teacher's fingers gently stroking Isa's soft, comforting body. When she next looked up at Mira, she was smiling.

"Gilli was a skilled seamstress," she said, examining the one spot where Isa's belly seam had parted and some of the creature's stuffing was peeking out. "But I'll wager she never expected you to be loved almost threadbare, eh, Isa?" All business, she hunted up her mending basket and went back to the bench beside the hearth where she proceeded to repair Mira's beloved toy. While she stitched, she spoke:

"Yes, Mira, she was a most creative person with a wonderful imagination. We were friends long before I knew you'd be my pupil. Whenever I had a problem, I'd take it to Gilli. Sometimes imagination finds doors where others only see walls." She finished the broken seam with a few reinforcing stitches. "We could use that talent now. If she were here—"

"If Mama were here, she'd say I had to go to the king," Mira said. "For Papa's sake."

"No, that's you talking, not your mother." Teacher bit off the thread cleanly and studied Isa's face. Truly Mira's favorite toy looked like nothing else on earth. There was a kind of bizarre fascination about the cat-dragon-bear thing. It looked impossible, but the way Gilli had crafted it you might almost imagine that the thing was laughing at you.

"You're afraid," Teacher went on. "That's understandable. You want to stay home, but you don't want your father to suffer the consequences. Going to the king is the easiest solution, not the best. You know, my grandmother wasn't speechless when she first came to the royal court. The sights she saw in the king's service, the unspeakable ways he demanded that she use her gift to serve him, the things that were done to her when she refused, *those* were what stole her tongue."

"But what else can I do?" Mira cried. "I can't run away—they'd hurt Papa!—and if I stay here and refuse

to go, That Woman will—will—" The child stamped her
foot in frustration. "Oh, I wish I could see things moon-
eyed whenever I wanted to! Then I'd know whether I
should even *try* to find a way out of this or if everything's
hopeless and I should just give the king what he wants
and be done!"

"Seeing your future, child, must never mean giving up
the mastery of your present life." Teacher spoke to Mira,
but her eyes were fixed on Isa. She regarded the stuffed
toy peculiarly. "Give the king what he wants, hm?"
Slowly she smiled. "Mira, dearest, your Papa's ware-
house isn't far from here. If I told you what I need, do
you think the foreman there would mind giving you some
scrap cloth of a *particular* kind?"

*

Sunden awoke to the piercing, peppery smell of highly
spiced hot soup. The pungent steam banished the last
cobwebby traces of Porla's potion from his brain. He sat
up straight in his chair and saw Mira, together with the
woman called only Teacher, kneeling by the hearthside
heating a small iron kettle just as if they were in the
kitchen rather than the parlor of his home. The soup
smelled delicious; his mouth watered.

"Ah, you're up! Good." Teacher glanced at him over
one shoulder and stood up from the fireside, a steaming
bowl in her hands. "Maybe this time you'll actually be
able to appreciate the taste of this," she said, bringing it
to him. "We had to spoon the first bowlful into your
mouth without you even knowing it. I'm afraid we spilled
half of it on your clothes."

Sunden looked down and was abruptly aware that he
had a large linen napkin tucked under his chin. The napkin was damp as was a goodly area of the fabric it had
tried so ineffectively to protect.

"Why did you do that?" he demanded. "It's lucky you
didn't scald me!"

"We did it to wake you up," Teacher explained calmly.
"Scalding would have done the job as well, but I'm glad
that didn't happen. You rich folk wrap so many layers
of cloth around your bodies that it's a wonder you feel

anything. You're *actually* lucky that you didn't *choke* when we were trying to feed you the first bowl, but I suppose that would have woken you up too."

"Did I *send* for you to wake me?' Sunden growled.

Teacher laughed. "No more than you sent for Porla to feed you dream-draughts. She really shouldn't have given you more than one dose; you were barely breathing when we came in. Mira was terribly worried."

"What—? Porla to—? Why would she—?" His scowl grew even darker. "Where is she? Where is Porla?"

Mira touched her father's arm. "She's gone, Papa; gone for good. Don't be mad." She plumped her stuffed toy down on her father's lap and added, "Isa doesn't want you to be mad. Isa never liked That Woman at all."

"Then why didn't Is— Why didn't you *say* something?"

"Maybe Isa didn't like the thought of eating nothing but fish stew," Teacher put in. "Or the idea of someone she loves very much being afraid to sleep alone."

"Oh." Sunden patted the stuffed toy thoughtfully. "I guess Isa didn't know that there's worse things than that." He looked up at Teacher. "So where is she? Porla? Don't worry, I'm not mad and I won't do anything stupid."

"Gone, as Mira says," Teacher told him. "Off and away with her pockets full of gold, the thanks-gift of the king's own messengers."

"The king's men!" Sunden started up from his chair, but a lingering dizziness from Porla's dream-draught made him sit back down. "What lies did she tell them, that she had any right at all to sell them my precious child? If they come here believing that she did, I'll   !"

"Oh, *Papa*." Mira spoke with the exasperation all children eventually express for the thick-headedness of grownups. "The king's men left *way* before she did. They rode out of Tallyford as soon as Teacher gave them what they wanted. They gave her a *lot* of gold for it, and she gave some of that to That Woman so she'd go away, and she's going to give the rest to the poor folk, and—"

While Mira prattled happily on, Sunden's mouth opened,

but no words came out. First he looked puzzled, then confused, then simply stunned. Giving Isa back into Mira's care, he stretched out his hands to Teacher. "Maybe all this will make sense after I've eaten another bowl of that soup," he said. "I don't understand; I thought the king's men weren't going to leave until they had my Mira."

"Almost right," said Teacher, carefully passing him the soup. "They weren't going to leave until they could bring their king a way to know the future. Once we gave them what they wanted, they were gone."

*

"Am I holding it right?" the king asked his messengers while all the court looked on.

"How could you do otherwise, Sire?" the senior of the two replied smoothly.

"Are you sure?" The king sounded peevish. "This would have been easier if that girl-child had had the seer's gift all along, as I was first informed."

"With respect, Majesty, I think you'll be happier that matters turned out this way. Children can be . . . difficult to manage and command. I for one am glad that the child turned out to have no powers after all. May the gods bless that good, loyal woman who came to us with the truth!"

"Aye," the younger king's man put in. "The true seer, a sorceress without equal, was the girl-child's mother. A pity Your Majesty heard nothing of her powers while she was yet alive. And yet, before she died she gave her daughter a wondrous gift: A device imbued with the magical ability to foretell the future. She meant it to protect her child, to warn the girl of impending perils. The girl was never parted from it. Her supposed predictions were merely the childish repetition of what she heard."

"But will it work for me?" the king whined.

"It must," the elder messenger replied. "The woman who came to us with the truth is your faithful, loving subject, but she was likewise the dead sorceress's dearest friend. She proved her loyalty to you by obtaining the device while the child slept. She told us all she knew about the proper way to operate it. Would she do that if she meant to give you something useless?"

"She did admit that the device can be capricious," the younger man· added. "It does not always answer questions the instant they're asked."

"But it does answer," the older man said hastily. "We have heard it speak with our own ears."

"Ears which you'll lose if *I* don't hear it speak," the king said grimly.

You will not harm these men, said a melodious voice that filled the whole throne room. *You will reward them well, instead.*

"It spoke!" The king gasped and stared at the device that his messengers had placed in his hands. The stuffed bear-cat-dragon, Isa's carefully crafted twin made by Teacher's own hands, stared back with button eyes. "O wondrous creature, speak again! Should I make peace or war against Lord Harrow's lands?"

And recognizing *war,* the spell that Teacher's loving sorcery had woven in the heart of a child's simple plaything plucked wisdom from the air and answered, *Peace.*

URSA

by Jenn Reese

Jenn Reese has published stories in *Sword & Sorceress XVII*, various other anthologies, and online at cool places like *Strange Horizons* (www.strangehorizons.com). She has been writing since 1995 and now lives in Los Angeles, where she practices martial arts, plays strategy games, and tries to suffer for her art. You can follow her adventures at www.memoryandreason.com. She is also very interested in women's self-defense and martial arts, and some readers might be interested in The Pacific Association of Women Martial Artists Web site (www.pawrna.org). In this story, however, the heroine is not only a fighter, but something more. . . .

The sharp cry of an infant shattered my sleep and brought me to my feet before I even realized I was awake. I sniffed the night air. Miles away to the west, in the mountains, a child was freezing to death.

I stumbled to the basin and splashed cold water on my face, smoothing the hair away from my eyes. I pulled the worn hides of my traveling leathers over my own worn flesh. I wanted nothing more than to crawl back under the blankets of my bed and sleep through the winter, like a respectable old woman. But the bear spirit had no patience for such weakness. She nudged me with her power until I managed to tug on my boots and kneel before the ancient chest at the foot of my bed.

The last few months had been peaceful, and the chest had remained closed. I'd hoped to find a successor before I ever had to open it again. But when a child cries, I must answer the call. It is my curse and my destiny both.

I knelt by the chest, opened the lid, and ran my hand over the cloak. The soft fur welcomed me, always warm.

I pulled it out of the chest and wrapped it around my shoulders. My body relaxed instantly. A little of my strength returned, and I would gain more and more each minute the great bear rested on my back. I pulled up the hood and the bear's head fit snugly and easily upon mine. My arms slid along the cloak's soft interior until I found the handgrips. I wrapped my fingers around the wooden rods and felt the comfortable curl of the bear's claws by my knuckles. The bear's senses had aroused me, but not her true power. I longed for that welcoming warmth and indomitable strength.

Out into the cold of winter I trudged. The child's cries rang clear in the ears of my mind. He was hungry and alone, but there was still time.

*

Only after the third set of knocking, did I sense the Mayor awaken. I knocked again, so he would not assume I was just wind and go back to sleep. As he approached the door I could smell the sleep still on him, mixed with a faint hint of ale. Other footsteps joined his just before he reached the door and opened it.

The Mayor's eyes widened, his breath caught. He stepped back for a moment and I saw the eyes of his fifteen-year-old son in the darkness behind him.

I couldn't blame them. No one liked to see me in the cloak, wearing the head, just as no one wanted the children to suffer or die. But some things cannot be avoided, especially in winter.

"Dead?" the Mayor asked.

"No, still alive." My breath was white around my face in the chill air. "I journey to the mountains, and I petition for aid. Someone to fight if necessary, and to tend to the child after the bear recedes."

"Yes, yes of course," said the Mayor. "Allow me ten minutes and I'll be fit to join you."

I nodded. The Mayor was not a young man, just as I am not a young woman, but he would ask none to do a job that he himself would not attempt. But without the cloak, the mountains would be more treacherous for him.

"No," a young voice said. The son. The boy stepped

around his father, into the silver light of the moon. He smelled healthy and awake, with no touch of the alcohol that lingered on his father. The bear within me grumbled low, but did not share her reasons.

"Matti, go back into the house," the Mayor said.

"I accept the boy's offer," I said, and the issue was settled. "Grab warmer things, boy, and some food. Find your sword, if you have one, but bring a knife if you don't."

The boy disappeared back into the house without a sound. The Mayor's shoulders slumped and he hung his head with a sigh. "He's still a child, Ursa. Young enough to deserve your protection. He knows nothing of the world or the night."

The bear spirit poured through me, filling me as if I were but an empty wineskin under a tidal wave. I was at once both light-headed and more grounded to the earth than I have ever been as a human woman. Intoxicated by her. I towered above the Mayor, angry but contained. I spoke, and my voice blurred into growls and rumbles and summoned images of dark fur.

"Do not presume," I growled. "Child or no, the boy will come." I sliced my arm downward, sparking my claws against the stone of the Mayor's house. The bear-skin around me flowed like a second skin.

The Mayor fled back into his house and did not return. The great bear slipped through me, her power trickling back into the earth until I called for her again. Or until she decided to come to me on her own. The Mayor's rebuke did not, to my human senses, deserve such a response. But the she-bear kept her secrets close, and I could only wonder at her fury.

The boy Matti came soon afterward and wisely did not question me. I smelled the dark metal of his sword as his side, untested but ready.

*

When we reached the mountain's edge, I led, first on two legs, then four, then two again. The snow and rocks were nothing to my hands and feet. The boy followed behind with the torch and stumbled often.

The baby whimpered in my mind, lonely and exhausted from screaming. I sensed little pain other than cold in his tiny cries. He tugged at me, pulled me up the mountain when even my bear-infused heart would beg for a break. Twice, the boy Matti thought he saw something in the darkness. We stopped and waited. Matti's breath made dim clouds. We saw nothing.

I watched the boy more closely now. To the bear, Matti smelled of his father and mother, and of himself. The bear did not tell me he was lying. No, for that I relied upon the wisdom of my countless human years.

I remembered the lad, had been present at his birth. Families in recent years chose blessings by the priest, but the Mayor—just a herder then—respected the older ways. The child had been bound to the earth, joined to the other animals in a simple blood ceremony. He'd broken legs, suffered through the red fever, but had lived healthy, grown strong and lean. Despite this knowledge, I knew nothing of the boy's mind. He was a stranger to me. I could only guess that the fear of what we might find at our journey's end made him invent shadows where there were none.

Dawn came, and we stopped to eat and drink. The boy said little as he built a small fire to heat the water. He shivered in his clothes.

"You carry another blanket, boy," I said, "put it around your shoulders as you work."

"I'm fine," the boy said.

In a tree nearby, a bird laughed at his pride. I glared at her, and she took flight.

"We'll find the babe." In my mind, the babe slept, free of tears. "There is still time."

Matti handed me a steaming mug of cider and returned to the other side of the fire to sit and drink his. "But animals could get it," he said, cupping the hot mug in his hands. "It's defenseless." The boy's face was too tight around the eyes and mouth as he spoke, his brow too heavy and dark.

"Yes, it is," I said slowly. "But there is a reason that

the child is out here and still alive. Someone made a mistake, and mistakes can always be remedied."

The boy stood abruptly, his drink spilling to the ground and melting small holes in the snow. "That's the stupidest thing I've ever heard," the boy said. "It's a lie, a complete lie."

I sipped my cider, drawing its warmth into my bones. "It's not a lie, boy. It's often unexpected, but there is a way to fix every situation and find happiness."

"Liar!" the boy said. "I've heard the stories. My papa knows them all. Both your children died, lost to the fever in the same winter. You'd have saved them both if you'd seen the priest, but you wouldn't!"

A dull ache resurfaced in my chest. No, the ache was always there, just hidden like bones under flesh.

"It's true, child. I lost my Sarra and my little Kiral both. I should have seen the priest."

"Don't you see?" the boy continued. He shook the mug in my direction. "You made a mistake, and they died, and now there's nothing you can do to fix it. You never got them back!" He sat down in the snow suddenly, heavily. "You can't go back and fix something."

The child's eyes rimmed with water, and not just from the snow. A child in pain. The bear spirit seeped into my soles and flooded through my legs and arms, offering her warmth as solace. "Do you have any idea how many children I've saved, boy? Do you have any clue?"

Slowly, the boy shook his head.

"Me neither," I said with a chuckle. "Think I lost track around three dozen. I'd guess it was well over a hundred now."

The boy clenched his jaw. "But that's no remedy. That's not fixing a mistake."

"In a way, it is. The old Ursa explained it to me this way," I put my mug down and looked deep into the boys' eyes. "Maybe my job is to help other people and their children, and my kids were keeping me from the job. I'd like to think I would have been a good mother, but I wouldn't give up all the lives I've saved since then, all the smiles I've seen and the tears of joy."

I stood and kicked snow onto the fire. "Only when you see the whole of your life laid out before you, will you be able to go through and say what was a mistake and what wasn't. Until then, you just have to do what you can to make right whatever is in your path."

"Yes, exactly," the boy said suddenly. "You do whatever you have to make things right." His face brightened, the hard lines forgotten, but I frowned. Only time makes room for wisdom. The boy's acquiescence came too easily.

We trudged forward into the day and up the mountain, slower than the night before. The boy grew even quieter than before, but also more agitated. His head never stopped darting from one direction to the other. The baby was crying again in my mind, hungry and cold from the urine freezing on its body. I walked faster, and the boy had no choice but to keep up with me.

We found the child at the same time as the wolves did.

Three of them circled a dark bundle in the snow. I had only a moment to see them for what they were— thin, hungry, desperate—before the bear spirit claimed me and erased my curiosity.

Power. Power so pure and intoxicating that it filled my body with thick energy and a need to roar. A deep rumbling started in my throat and tore from my lips like a roll of thunder. My hands gripped the wooden rods of my claws and they seemed to mold with my hands and knuckles, become extensions of me and my dark earth spirit.

The first wolf died whimpering, its spine broken against the tree where I flung it. The second leaped at my throat. I jumped backwards, away from the baby, and lashed out with my claws. The impact jarred my arm up through my shoulder, reminding even the bear spirit that her vessel had grown old.

The third animal smacked against my back. I fell on my hands and knees in the snow and slashed backward with my left. My claws connected with flesh and hot blood splashed the snow. I roared again.

The child, my cub, my Sarra, my Kiral. Protect, defend, kill.

Blood splattered again and another wolf lay dead at my feet. The last creature, its gray fur matted dark against its skin, loped towards the trees. I summoned my energy and leaped after it. I landed hard upon it and dug my dull human teeth into the back of its neck while my claws raked its soft underbelly. Soon only my heavy rasps filled the cold silence. Strangely, the Ursa stayed with me and did not ebb.

The child was still in danger.

I pulled myself off the dead wolf and turned back toward the clearing and the babe. Matti stood by the bundle, his sword drawn, his eyes frozen on the child. Slowly, still on all fours, I took a step towards them.

"She never said this would happen," Matti said. "She said it would feel good, that no one would get hurt . . ."

Another step.

". . . It did feel good. I didn't know, I didn't know she would die . . ."

And another. I could smell the child now, its quiet fear and its soiled cloth wrappings. And something else, something familiar.

"She's dead," Matti continued. "dead making the child. It's my fault, all my fault . . ."

In a quick rush, I recognized the smell. "Matti . . ."

"My child," the boy whispered.

He raised his sword above the bundle, and I'll never know if he would have struck; killed his own child in cold blood because abandoning it in the snow had not been enough, and because his child's mind blamed him for the mother's death. I'll never know because the great bear shook me and demanded action. We leaped and tackled the boy. His sword fell into the snow beside us, but he did not try to reclaim it. Instead, he stared up into my human eyes and dared me to finish the job.

I struck quickly.

Blood dripped in four long streaks along the boy's

cheek, bright red and warm. If he wanted to be punished for this crime, however ill-conceived, then I would punish.

We sat like that for some time, the boy's back in the snow and my great bulk pinning him to the earth. His breaths were shallow, his eyes unblinking. At some point, the baby's discomfort began to distract me, and I released Matti. I leaned back on my haunches and slipped my hands out of the claw handles to better tend the child. Its face was blue, but the boy Matti had apparently wrapped it tightly in many wool blankets before leaving it to die. That poor, confused boy. I began to peel the layers away but my old hands ached painfully from the effort, the joints stiffening with each movement.

Another, smaller pair of hands joined mine. The boy's face still bled, but slower. A few tears had crystallized on his eyelashes, but he paid them no heed. His lips pressed together as he worked, and I felt a new calmness, his own earth spirit, flow over him and through him as he held his son. His demon had been washed away in blood.

"There has never been a male Ursa," I said finally, as I sat back and watched him warm the child against his own skin. "But there will be. And sooner than you think."

The bear spirit touched all three of us then, an unlikely family, and bound us together with a bond older than thought, older than words, and older even than I.

RED CARAMAE
by Kit Wesler

Some stories leave us laughing, some with a tear, and some with an eldritch chill that is one of the oldest effects in fantasy. Kit Wesler is an archaeologist. Here he shows that sometimes there is more under the earth than bones.

Kit teaches at Murray State University in western Kentucky, specializing in late prehistoric and historical archaeology of eastern North America, west Africa, and the Caribbean, and the comparative study of complex societies. He is also the Director of the Wickliffe Mounds Research center.

His previous stories in the Red Queen cycle were published in *Marion Zimmer Bradley's Fantasy Magazine* #10 (Autumn 1990), reprinted in *The Best of Marion Zimmer Bradley's Fantasy Magazine,* volume 1; *Marion Zimmer Bradley's Fantasy Magazine* #16 (Spring–Summer 1992); and in *The Poetic Knight* (1993). He is also the author of *Excavations at Wickliffe Mounds,* published in 2001 by the University of Alabama Press, and numerous scholarly articles.

"Tasty!" said the ghoul on the wall, and leered.

She had thought it was a gargoyle. She half-drew her dirk, letting the lean blade glisten in the moonlight. The ghoul slipped off the far side of the stone wall and disappeared.

Caramae continued down the narrow, fissured steps, now wanly lit, now coal-dust dark as the flitting clouds crossed the silver moon. She reached the bottom, a flagstone pave as irregular as shattered ice. Before her stretched the cemetery of the wizard's school of Glaud, a landscape of chest-high vaults thrusting stony corners from shrouding tangles of ivy and bramble.

She thought she heard a scrape of claws behind her and turned, but saw nothing on the stair.

She faced forward again. Fifty paces ahead, a squat mausoleum loomed larger than the other crypts. She stepped cautiously through the rows of vaults, gathering the hem of her cotton shift to keep it from thorns.

She found a door, stout and blank. She felt for a handle. There was no lock, but an aversion spell nearly stole her courage before she was fully aware of it. She knew such spells, and already was stronger than this one. She broke it with a rap of her finger against the wood.

Caramae pushed the door inward, looked into utter darkness. A feeling of vast emptiness lay across the threshold. She had not intended to risk a light before entering the structure, but she called a small blue flame into the palm of her left hand, and reached it inside.

She saw that the mausoleum was merely a closet at the head of another long stone stair, and she began her descent.

She lost count of the steps. When finally she reached the bottom, she found only another door. There was no aversion spell here, only a sign, a rune, the one known as Harki's rune. It meant stop.

She pushed the door and strengthened the blue witch-fire in her hand.

The door opened into a cubical chamber, floored with slate. A stone pedestal stood in the center, perhaps ten paces from her. Each of the three walls was blank except for an inky rectangle in the center: other doorways, leading to—she did not know.

Caramae stepped into the cubical chamber, and caught glimmers of white in the corners of her eyes. She froze. She looked up carefully. For the first time, she nearly let fright turn her back.

On her right stood a tall skeleton, twice her height, the bones of a cave bear with claws raised ready to attack. On her left was the skeleton of a smilodon, a beast nearly as big, but crouched on all four legs. Even in her blue spark of a light their teeth shone like the scimitar moon in the midnight sky outside.

Caramae's senses were at a fever pitch, but she could find no breath of animation, no shiver of malevolence, no flicker of watchfulness in the bones. They were symbolic guardians, no more. Her heart beat less wildly, and she spared a moment to admire the artistry of whomever had wired the bones into such lifelike poses.

She walked over to the stone pedestal, no higher than her waist, and she looked down on another skeleton clad in tatters of shroud and robe, desiccated strings of flesh and sinew holding the bones together. A huge ring with a stone like a ruby encircled the third finger of the dead man's left hand, and the brittle shadow of a staff lay in the fingers of the right. Caramae could feel the echoes of power from both staff and gem, but they were not what she sought.

She heard claws scrape behind her again and whirled—but it was only the ghoul, ratlike face crinkled in a foul imitation of a smile, hairless wrinkled body obscenely like a man's, almost. She looked into its eyes and was surprised at the considering intelligence there.

"Eremion's litch," said the ghoul. "You need go no farther." The words were intelligible, but misshapen, like its snout.

"What do you want?"

"I know what you want," the ghoul countered. "And I know where it is."

"What do you know?" Caramae challenged scornfully.

"I know Eremion," it answered, unperturbed by her hostility. "Founder of the College of Wizards of Glaud. Eremion the long-lived. Taught the magic of discipline, because only by discipline could he control the evil that consumed his heart. Entombed here, at the head of the catacombs of the wizards, as a warning. Because eventually, the evil finished him after all."

"You're evil!" Caramae spat. "A foul beast. All your kind."

The ghoul shrugged. "We eat. All things eat. And sleep. And a few other things." It made no gesture, but somehow its nakedness was emphasized, and Caramae shuddered.

"How old are you, girl?" the ghoul suddenly demanded. "Fourteen?"

She did not answer, and the ghoul leered, as it had on the wall. "Fourteen and fancy. Caramae of the flame-red hair, Caramae the ice-eyed. Caramae of the alabaster bud-breasts, of the coral-pink—"

"What do you want?" Caramae demanded again. This time there was steel in her voice, and in her right hand.

"There's power in you. I can sense it. The wizards were fools to turn you away."

Her grievance got the better of her tongue. "They said I couldn't enter their school because I'm a girl! So what? I'll make them sorry!"

"Yes . . . the thing you want. Reach into Eremion's chest. You'll find it."

She looked at the remnants of fabric and gristle, and recoiled. To give herself time she said, "What is it?"

"You'll know. Or you won't deserve it."

"What do you want?" she asked for the third time.

"To be yours. To be your familiar. To eat at your table. To snuggle in your bed. To watch you become what you will become."

Caramae made a sound of rage and disgust, dropped her dirk on the stone bier, and thrust her hand into the long-dead rib cage. She felt desiccated tissue split, bones crumble, then—something frigid, and hard. It felt like a thick wire, coiled into a tight spiral. She grasped it and tore her fist out of the ribcage, spraying bone fragments.

She heard the ghoul hiss softly, but was too engrossed in her own conflicting feelings to care.

It sat in the palm of her hand, a coil of gold wire no thicker than embroidery yarn. Its end was blunt, slightly raised from the plane of the coil. No—did it have a slit, like a mouth? Did it have two eyes, red as rubies, slowly opening? Did it look at her with the purest glee in those eyes? Could it possibly—smile?

She tried to hurl it down, but it struck her wrist, directly into the vein. She screamed in agony, and flailed. The golden thing bit deeper, uncoiled, and slithered into her vein.

Caramae screamed again. She had never known such pain. She clawed with her left hand at her forearm, heedless that the blue flame might burn. She felt the thing in her vein wriggle toward her heart.

In her terror she turned toward the ghoul for help, but he was watching with a gleam of triumph in his eyes. She opened her mouth to curse it, but saw motion behind it, and the curse melted like fire on her tongue.

The guardians had awakened.

The great bear swung its skull from side to side, and lurched forward onto all four feet. The smilodon raised its sabre-toothed jaws in a silent roar.

Too late the ghoul realized its peril, and tried to dive away. The bear swung a skeletal paw and sent the ghoul flying in a spray of viscous blood. Even in her pain and horror, Caramae heard the crunch of bone at the impact.

The guardian beasts lurched towards her.

Then her vision failed in a final convulsion of agony as the thing inside her coiled around her heart.

After a timeless instant Caramae knew she would live, and felt a surge of power through her every artery, every vein, every nerve. She found herself supine atop the bier, having scattered the bones of Eremion in her convulsive leap. She rolled off the bier. The smilodon leaped. She blasted it with a surge of power that emanated from her heart through her outstretched fingertips and scorched the solid stone across the room.

The bear, a pace slower, she merely banished, watching the bones clatter to the ground in a heap.

She turned to the ghoul. It lay dying against the wall. It looked at her with pleading eyes.

The ghoul tried to speak. "You . . . owe . . ."

"I'll never have it in me to be a healer," she said. "But I promise you this: I will have armies. And your people will feed well."

"Please . . ." the broken ghoul whispered. Then it was dead.

Red Caramae left Glaud in the first burst of dawn, her heart cold as gold, but her feet light and her eyes aglow with power yet to be tamed.

PARRI'S BLADE

by Cynthia McQuillin

Cynthia McQuillin is one of the talented women I first met sitting around Marion's kitchen table. She is a prolific and versatile singer/songwriter with over two hundred songs published or recorded, and Marion enjoyed her music as well as her stories, many of which, especially those from her universe of the Stone Mages, have appeared in the *Sword & Sorceress* anthologies. She also makes beautiful, hand-crafted, one-of-a-kind bead necklaces, which are sold by various dealers—along with her CDs and tapes—at science fiction and fantasy conventions around the country.

Although Cindy has been absent from the convention circuit these last few years due to health problems, she has recently begun showing up at local cons and, as you can see from this story, taking an interest in the world of writing once again. She is currently working on several novels, including a vampire novel based on her song "Black Lace and Midnight" from the recently reissued *Moonshadows* CD and has completed a psychic fantasy called *Singer in the Shadow*.

As Hamli kept the ritual watch beside her brother Parri's body, she was startled by the sound of the Tako leaf mat as it slid across the doorpost of his once cheerful hut. She looked up to see his promised bride, Soela, slip quietly through, one hand hidden beneath her shawl. The ebony-haired woman appeared inhumanly calm, but her eyes were hard and hungry.

Hamli leaped to her feet, hand going instinctively to the blade she wore. "You're not supposed to be here," she said, alert and uneasy as she watched Soela pause warily just inside the doorway.

"No need to fear, Hamli." Soela glanced furtively

around the room, green eyes gleaming like those of the forest cat that had mauled Parri the day before. "I only wanted to see him once more."

The simpering, manipulative way in which Soela had clung to Parri always bothered Hamli, but for her brother's sake she spoke kindly. "To see him now, an empty shell rent by the claws of the beast, will give you no comfort. You must go."

"Don't be so high and mighty with me, little Hamli! In only a week, Parri and I would have been wed, and it would have been my right to stand vigil here." Soela suddenly bolted to Parri's side, deftly eluding Hamli's attempt to intercept her. With a little cry of longing as her eyes fell upon his body, which was draped in the funeral blanket of pounded bark, she stooped to pull the blanket from Parri's body.

"Stop!" Hamli pleaded, control crumbling at the sight of his once firm and supple flesh so hideously disfigured. "Please . . . don't!" Tears running hotly down her face, making her look like the child she still was, despite the status of adult she had been granted with the onset of her monthly courses. Unthinkingly she bent to retrieve the blanket and Soela struck her with the stone she had kept hidden beneath her brightly painted shawl.

*

Hamli woke with a start some time later, to be thoroughly and wretchedly ill. When she had emptied her stomach, she sat leaning against the leg of Parri's cot to reorient herself. The rush light had burned nearly to ashes, painting the walls with ominous shadows as it flickered.

"Soela!" Hamli's head throbbed as memories rushed in to fill the void left by shock. She must discover why Soela had desecrated Parri's pyre.

Rising in careful stages, Hamli went to the wicker table that held the rush pot, and sat feeding the flames till it burned brightly.

Cursing her own carelessness, she carefully probed the swelling on the side of her head. It was slight, about the size of a small nut, and the body-knowledge she had gained from her training with Ashamad, the Priest of the Forest Spirit, told her it would heal soon enough, though not as quickly as she might wish.

Everything looked the same as it had before she thought as she glanced around the room, except for the funeral blanket which lay on the floor where she had dropped it as she fell and her fire-hardened wooden blade that lay a few feet from the bed. Thankfully retrieving the blade, she turned to examine her brother's body.

It was important to make sure Parri had all of his possessions with him when he was burned, for the Children of the Forest believed that possessions could bind the spirit to the physical world. Unable to complete its journey toward completion until such objects were destroyed, it was doomed to wander aimlessly—unable to interact with the world, or with those it had left behind.

Gently she smoothed Parri's thick dark curls back from his smooth wide forehead. He looked so peaceful, almost as if he were only sleeping. Choking back a sob, she turned her attention to cataloging the personal belongings she had earlier placed on the bed beside him. This was her duty; she was the oldest now, and by all the traditions of her people, a woman. She must cling to that and forsake the weakness of childhood.

But panic replaced grief when she came to the end of her sorting to discover that Parri's blade was missing. *Soela must be mad to do this thing!* she thought, outrage at the sacrilege momentarily driving out the horror she felt for his death.

Hamli had chosen to walk the Path of the Forest Spirit, and though she was still a neophyte, she understood the spirit ways better than most. But her knowledge brought little comfort now, as she ticked off the magical uses Parri's blade could be put to.

Some of the dark shamans claimed to be able to raise the spirits of the dead, though Ashamad said they had no such power. Some created illusion to trick the unwary, but others . . . she trembled. In her youth Hamli had heard many dark tales of demon spirits eager to enter an untenanted body. Such incorporeal beings would willingly trade services for the privilege of flesh.

Surely Soela didn't believe she could keep Parri with her by taking his knife.

Hamli's head was beginning to pound and her body cried for rest, but her mind kept turning round and round. Fear for Parri's soul overrode her reason, urging her to go after Soela and take back the blade, but dawn was nearly upon her, and she could hear the sounds of the approaching funeral procession.

Quickly drawing the blanket back over her bother's body, she stepped outside to greet Ashamad and her family.

*

When the burning was done, Hamli slipped away as quickly as she could, stopping at her own neat little hut to gather her trail pack and cloak. Hearing a soft footfall behind her, she turned with a guilty start, to find Ashamad standing in the doorway.

"What troubles you, Hamli?" Though his gaze was mild, Hamli felt as though he was looking right into her heart. For a moment she couldn't speak or breathe.

"Why have you come?" Her voice was the merest whisper when she finally spoke.

"To help," he said, settling down on the bench near the fire pit and gesturing her to join him there.

She obediently sat down beside him and before she knew what she was doing, she had poured out the entirety of her failure to the solemnly attentive priest. Not daring to meet his gaze, she hung her head in shame. But instead of berating his hapless student, he simply asked what she was planning to do.

"I must find Soela and reclaim Parri's blade," she said.

He nodded thoughtfully, then said, "You have chosen the hardest path. But I will not say that it is the wrong one. But you know that you need not do this thing." His gaze riveted her. "You are still very young, Hamli, for all your skill and devotion, and there are others to take up the task."

"Mine is the failure, mine is the duty," she stubbornly replied, raising her chin a little higher.

"Since you have chosen, I will not interfere."

He rose and turned to go.

"Wait," she called as he lifted the mat that hung over the doorway. He turned to give her a questioning look and she softly said, "Please say nothing until I return."

"As you wish," he replied, then slipped through the doorway without a backward glance.

*

Once her preparations were complete, Hamli went to Soela's hut. Though she doubted the woman would be fool enough to stay in the village with a witness to stand against her, she might have left some clue as to where she was going. What Soela had done was the most serious of sacrileges. She would be expelled from the tribe and whipped naked onto the plains, to live or die as she was able.

As Hamli neared the clearing she smelled hot ash. At first she thought it was the reek from her brother's hut, then she realized that the wind blew from the wrong direction. Apparently Soela was still devout enough to destroy her possessions before she fled. That knowledge comforted Hamli somewhat.

There wasn't much left of the hut or its contents, but after carefully examining the area Hamli spotted a torn bit of the pounded bark fabric Soela customarily wore. It was caught on the branch of a small tree near the back of the clearing. The fabric was more fragile than the woven grass of Hamli's shift, and would have been stained had it been left out in the damp overnight. It wasn't like Soela to be careless about her clothing, so she must have torn it in her haste as she fled. With that as her only marker, Hamli struck off in the direction the fabric pointed to.

At first the going was easy. The loose assembly of huts that constituted the village was spread randomly throughout the edge of the forest and there were many well-kept trails. Soela's hut, as with most of the newer ones, was on the outskirts of the community, so the trails were less well traveled, making her fresh tracks easy to follow.

Hamli's tracking skills had been learned from Asha-mad, it was part of the initiation onto the Path of the Forest Spirit, and even he had admitted she had a keen sense for it. Even so, the lush rain-fed vegetation grew so quickly that breaks and tears were covered over almost as they happened, and the light grew dimmer, filtered through the thickly layered branches of truly ancient trees.

Hamli had never journeyed into the heart of the forest before and the liquid quality of the greenish light and the strangely muffled sounds were unsettling. Twice she heard the yowl of a forest cat, like the one that had killed Parri, and dropped to her knees, taking cover in the bushes, until she was sure it had passed. After turning her ankle when she stumbled into a mire-badger's lair trying to stay on Soela's track after it had grown too dark, she chose a small clearing and settled in for the night.

She made even less progress the next day for the track had grown harder and harder to follow and her swollen ankle had begun to throb. She fashioned herself a crutch from a fallen branch, but the going was slow and she was forced to pause frequently. By nightfall she had lost Soela's trail completely.

Too tired even to eat from her dwindling supply of trail rations, Hamli fell into a fitful sleep. Tossing and turning on the moss-padded branches she had pulled together to make a nest, she dreamed of Parri weeping, trapped in some non-place between the forest world and the spirit realm. She could see him wandering aimlessly through the giant trunks, a faint greenish glow outlining his body.

"Parri!" she cried, seeming to rise out of her body to follow. "Parri, come back. It's Hamli, your sister. Come back." But he just kept walking, moving farther and farther away, until finally she lost sight of him. Weeping with frustration, she woke to find herself on her feet walking away from the campsite. Luckily she had slept with her gear on her belt and her cloak wrapped around her.

Thoroughly lost in the dark, Hamli finally struck up a

small fire with a stone and some kindling from her pouch. Trembling as much from fear as from the chill, she huddled beside the fire's meager warmth, hugging her arms about her as suspiciously childish tears slipped down her cheeks. What was she going to do now? She could find food, and water was plentiful, but she had never been this far from the village alone.

Exhaustion finally loosened the grip of fear and Hamli knew she must sleep, but before lying down, she cut a strong supple vine from a nearby tree, and tied one end around her ankle and the other to a stout bush.

She woke the next morning with an unpleasant start, as something large and furry crawled across her body. Knowing better than to make any sudden moves, she opened her eyes just a slit and slowly raised her head. A rough tongue flicked out to lick her nose and she tensed, waiting for claws to follow. When they did not, she opened her eyes to find a half-grown forest cat lying partially on her chest. Forest cats weren't big, maybe six or seven hand-spans chest to haunch, but they were vicious when riled, and efficient hunters when hungry. This one still seemed rather cublike, more playful than fierce, but you could never tell with a cat.

One thing she knew for certain, any quick movement would bring its hunting instincts to the fore, and with half-inch dagger-sharp claws it could wound her badly even in play. Ever so slowly she turned over, easing the cat off her chest. It growled, but sat up, watching with interest as Hamli cautiously did likewise.

Oh, no, she inwardly groaned, as her ankle caught and she remembered the vine she had tied around it to keep herself from wandering. She cautiously tugged at it, testing the strength of the vine and the knot. But she had done too good a job; it wasn't going to give. As she released the tension on the vine, the movement attracted the cat's attention and he pounced on the bush, gnawing on the vine till it snapped. So much for that problem, but the solution had created another; now the cat wanted to play.

Batting softly at her sandal-clad foot, with his claws

sheathed, thankfully, the cat seemed harmless enough. But Hamli had no idea how long that would last and she was beginning to wonder where his mother was. The cub certainly didn't look big enough to be on his own. This close to the rainy season, most of the animals would already be snug in their burrows ready to sleep away the worst of the deluge. Perhaps this one had wandered away from the family lair.

Hamli's train of thought was broken suddenly by a bloodcurdling squall from the nearby brush. The mother-cat emerged into the tiny clearing with a low snarl, stopping to stare at Hamli. Heart pounding like a dance drum, the girl schooled her breathing to an even pace as she forced her muscles to relax. If the cat smelled fear or she tried to run, it would attack. But if she remained perfectly still it should leave her alone.

At least that was what Ashamad had said when they were learning the ways of the cat in Circle. It would be one of her initiations to track a cat to its lair and become one with the cat-spirit, but Hamli hadn't expected to have to face one this soon.

The cat was sleek, and her thick, golden pelt was dappled with dark spots. Her muscles rippled with deadly promise as she began to pace back and forth. Silent now, she seemed to study Hamli with eyes as deep and unfathomable as the forest itself. The light of intelligence shone in their depths, and oddly Hamli was reminded of the way Ashamad had considered her when she gave him her answer back at her hut. Suddenly the cat stopped pacing and came right up to Hamli, sniffing at her face. Unable to help herself, the girl flinched. When the cat's lips curled back in a silent snarl, Hamli forced herself to relax once again. *It's all right. She's only curious,* she told herself.

With an officious air, the mother-cat continued her inspection, whiskers twitching with interest. Then she turned to glare at the cub, who had dropped into a submissive posture and hadn't moved since she had entered the clearing. Stalking deliberately to it, she growled menacingly at her wayward child, then grabbing him by the scruff of the neck, sent him scrambling into the brush with a jerk of her powerful neck muscles. Then, with a single backward glance at Hamli, she followed.

Trembling so hard she couldn't stand, Hamli just sat there. She had never been so terrified in her life. When she could think again, Hamli rose, and taking the blade from her belt she drew a protective pattern on the ground around her, murmuring the words of warding as she worked. Then she sat down to compose her thoughts. She had never done the spirit-walk unguided, but lost and nearly out of food, she had no choice but to try. She would not return to Ashamad and admit that she had failed!

The ritual called for meditation to properly prepare the spirit for its journey. But she found it difficult to quiet her thoughts and relax into oneness with the forest and hills around her. This was crucial, for if her calling failed, or she was judged unworthy, she could well forfeit her soul, to be bound even as Parri was, or worse. But her thoughts kept returning to the scene in Parri's hut.

"I must stop this!" she told herself sternly, her voice sounding strange and muffled in the humid heat of approaching noon. Thinking back to her evenings in the forest with the other students, she could hear Ashamad's quiet voice, sonorous and assured, as he led them through the exercises.

Step by step she built that memory into reality, until it seemed that once again she sat, safe and calm, in the circle with her beloved teacher and all her friends around her.

"What do you seek, Hamli?" Ashamad asked, his expression softening with concern.

"Entry to the spirit ways. But I am barred by my own weakness."

"If you have locked the way, only you can open it."

"But I have forgotten the way." There was a note of weariness and despair in her voice.

"If that were so, you could not have found your way back to us, Hamli. Come, lead us in the invocation. You have not forgotten the way."

Obediently she began the chant and, as their voices joined with hers, Hamli knew exactly what was needed. She saw Ashamad nod in approval as the vision faded from her mind.

Murmuring the invocation of acceptance was like turning a key. Hamli felt her mind open like a flower as her focus turned inward. Raising her hands palm up as if to catch the pale beams of sunlight that streamed into the glade, she sang the five-tone Chant of Opening. Then with all the courage she could muster Hamli lifted her head to face what she had summoned.

"Who summons me?" The demand roared through her mind like a torrent of wind. Around her the world seemed to tremble and shimmer, but she held her ground, head high.

"It is I, Hamli, your daughter," she replied. "I have need of a favor." The ground beneath her thrummed with impatient inquiry. "The chosen of my brother Parri has stolen his knife, and I must destroy it before his soul can pass on. I seek the one called Soela, but cannot find her without help. Great Forest Spirit, I humbly beg you to allow me passage through your realm, vowing that I seek only to set the balance right once again." A sudden silence enveloped her, and it seemed almost as though the world held its breath for the space of a heartbeat as her soul was weighed and measured. Then the wind soughed through the trees, and its sound was the voice of the Forest Spirit whispering through her mind.

"So be it, daughter. You may trespass for this purpose." Then, as quickly as it had manifested itself, the presence was gone. Hamli's body sagged, drained of all nerve. She was almost giddy with exaltation. She could scarcely believe she'd succeeded, but she had to act quickly. Settling her body once more into a comfortable position, Hamli sent her thoughts questing inward, seeking the entryway the Forest Spirit had opened to her.

It hung suddenly before her eyes, an arch outlined in shimmering, ghostly white fire. Walking forward in spirit form, she stepped through as swiftly and fearlessly as she could. The sensation of crossing the spirit barrier was so much like breaking through a spider's web that she couldn't help but shudder. Sensing the sudden stir of movement all around her, Hamli kept her eyes turned straight ahead and began walking.

Then came the touching, like tiny insubstantial fingers tugging at her limbs and clothing, plucking at her hair, but she knew better than to let them distract her. She must walk straight to the forest and find the gatekeeper. Here in the outer dark were only elemental spirits, strange inhuman things without form or shape, despising those who walked the world in flesh. They were the stuff of nightmares, soul-eaters who fed on human misery and pain.

If they were able to claim Hamli's attention, distract her from her purpose, she would be lost. They would devour her soul to strengthen their own forces, or far worse, one of the great Dark Ones might bind her to its service. Then *she* would become one of the ravening, bodiless pack, while the Dark One entered into the real world using her body, there to work hideous evil upon those who loved and trusted her.

When the whispering began she thought she would go mad, for it seemed she had come so very far already and there was still no sign of the forest. "What if you chose the wrong direction?" a voice very much like Ashamad's seemed to say. "It does look different from the times before, doesn't it?" That was Parri's voice. "Come home, Hamli, we forgive you. Just turn around." The last was her mother.

Enough! she silently cried, but kept walking stubbornly onward, hands clenched at her side. The voices stilled as she came abruptly to the edge of a luminous forest that pulsated with unseen life. Before her on a dead tree branch sat an enormous owl, its feathers edged with silver light. Without hesitation she spoke to the Spirit-Bird.

"Sister Owl, I come seeking one who has enslaved my brother's spirit."

"You will need a guide on your journey, Daughter of the Forest," the guardian replied. "There is only one who may aid you, for it is he against whom this sacrilege has been committed. But first you must face the guardian of the way."

"Where is this guardian?"

"Within." As the owl spoke a great silvered surface hung suspended in the air before her, casting back her own distorted reflection. "Only you can judge yourself. Look into the mirror and see your soul, Daughter of the Forest!"

"No-o-o," Hamli whimpered, seeing all at once her own childish vanity, and the pride that had set her on this quest, kept her from seeking help when she knew she had failed. Was she really so petty and guilt-ridden? And see how she had floundered on the trail while Soela, pampered and useless as she was, eluded her. Twice Hamli had nearly been killed or injured, and for what? Her childish pride!

Faced with only that damning reflection she might have turned away to run screaming back across the Plain of Desolation, prey to all that haunted that desperate realm. But before she could move, she caught a glimpse of Parri's reflection standing behind her own. And her vision cleared. It was for Parri she had come, to free his spirit. Seeing him there, once more strong and alive, she suddenly longed to keep him with her.

The reflection wavered, as she remembered a still younger Parri and herself as a child. She sat playing with Parri's spinner while he wove a basket by the stream where the canes grew. After a moment she abandoned the toy to gather up some of the shorter pieces he'd discarded and began mimicking his craft. Parri smiled when he looked up and saw the lopsided thing she had made, hugging her and praising her effort.

It had been among the things laid on his pyre when she prepared it. But a thing was just a thing, just as a body was a thing. She would always have Parri's love, and for the sake of the love they shared, she would let him go. In the mirror he smiled, and she knew that in Parri's eyes she was worthy of the task she had undertaken. As she loved her brother, how could she judge herself less than worthy?

Slowly turning to look upon his shade, she feared to

see him as he had last appeared. But he was whole and unscarred, though very grave—which he had never been in life.

"Parri!" She reached to embrace him, joy and longing inextricably mixed with a deeper sense of sorrow and loss.

But he put her off, saying, "I am beyond your touch now. Why do you trouble me in my wandering?"

"I came to set you free," she said confused and chastened by his sudden coldness. But then, what warmth or joy were left to him? "I must find the blade you wore, since you are bound here until it is destroyed."

"Yes, I feel its pull even now." Without another word he began walking and Hamli followed, not knowing what else she could do.

They crossed great distances, moving tirelessly through the ethereal forest. But time was distorted so that it was only a little while before they came to the pitiful little cave where Soela huddled over a dimly flickering fire. In the shadowy light, tattered and filthy she had the appearance of some demon hag, a gleam very like madness dancing in her dark-ringed eyes. She rocked back and forth, crooning to Parri's blade, which she held lovingly to her.

"Oh, beloved," she whispered, pressing the handle to her cracked lips, "how can I live now that you are gone? No one will care for me, no one loves me as you do. If only I had the courage to follow you, I would plunge this blade into my own breast. But then you would still be bound while my flesh was devoured and my bones were broken and scattered by the wild beasts. But what if I were to throw the knife into the flames as I die?" She paused, caught in a fit of indecision.

"No, if the blade burned then you would go on without me, for there is no telling how long it would take for my bones to weather away. it might be years, and you would be gone." Her voice broke and she began to sob.

Shocked by what she saw and heard, Hamli scarcely recognized the woman, so much had she changed from the sly, self-centered creature she'd been before. Now she sat in squalor, murmuring endearments to the dead and tearing listlessly at the tangles of her once lustrous hair.

"She did this out of love for you!" Hamli was dumbfounded, watching helplessly as her brother's ghost hovered about Soela, vainly trying to comfort her. His longing to be with his tormented lover was palpable, and it wrenched at Hamli's heart. "She loves you so much she's willing to die to be with you," she whispered in a shaken voice.

"I will wait for her. I have sworn it." He looked at his sister then, eyes turned hollow with despair. "There is nothing you can do. Go back, Hamli, and leave us to our pain."

"NO!" With a start, she found that the force of his command had returned her to her body. But she stood now just within the entrance of the cave where Soela sat, oblivious to her presence.

"Soela," Hamli murmured, stepping further into the circle of light.

"So, you've come at last." Soela's voice was sullen and hoarse as she rose to turn defiant eyes on Hamli. "Well, here's the blade. Come take it, but you'll have to kill me first."

"No, Soela," Hamli said in a quiet voice, sitting down across the dwindling fire from the woman she had sought so persistently. "I haven't come to take Parri away from you."

"Parri?" Soela's eyes flickered anxiously around the chamber.

"Yes, Soela, he is here. It was Parri who led me to you." Envy and resentment mingled in the woman's expression, but she said nothing. "He still loves you, Soela. He has sworn to wait."

"What if he can't? If only I were sure. I could face living without him if I knew we'd be together again. But how can I know?" She looked like a desperate child.

Hamli moved cautiously nearer, sensing no threat in the woman, only despair. When she was close enough she reached for the knife, deftly withdrawing the blade from Soela's grasp. Sobbing like a heartbroken child, the woman collapsed into Hamli's arms. Touched as she would never have credited it possible, she drew Soela to her.

"Everything will be all right, Soela," she said. "I understand, truly I do. What you did you did for love of Parri. He is dead; you cannot bring him back. But if he will not go, then perhaps there is a way for you to speak to him." Yes that would be a kindness to both of them, Soela thought.

"Tell me," Soela demanded, her eyes brightening with hope.

"Ashamad has spoken of a dream-bridge which he uses to bespeak the ancestors of the world. Perhaps that would work for you and Parri. I will speak to Ashamad about it, but you would have to learn certain magics and apply yourself for once."

"I will do whatever you say," Soela pleaded, grasping Hamli's hands. "Just teach me the way! Ah, but where will I stay? The beautiful house that Parri made me is gone."

Hamli sighed, knowing the worst had passed and Soela was once more herself, though still badly shaken.

"I suppose you could stay with me, at least for awhile."

"What about Parri's knife?" Soela's eyes flickered suspiciously to the blade.

"*I'll* keep that," Hamli said firmly. "But I swear to you, by the Most Sacred of Oaths, that I won't destroy it while you live. And, if I should die before you do, because I stand in Parri's stead, the death watch would fall to you. You can reclaim the knife and use it as your own, and then it will be burned with your possessions. Either way, you'll both be released together. I can do no more than that. The choice is yours. No one else but Ashamad knows what you did, but we will settle the matter between us, since Parri is willing. And, Ashamad will keep your secret if I speak for you."

"You would do this for me?"

"Yes." Hamli nodded solemnly.

Soela looked down at herself with a rueful laugh. "I

doubt anyone else would want me now, anyway." She paused, chewing on her lip for a moment. "Look, I know you never liked me, Hamli, but I'll try to be better. Maybe, we could be friends after all. I think Parri would like that."

"We will be sisters," Hamli said, putting on a good face, "just as we would have been if Parri had lived. But, you need clothing and we have a long journey ahead of us."

"Not so long," Soela said, giving Hamli a puzzled look. "We are only a little way from the village, in the hills near the edge of the plain."

"But you struck off into the deep forest when you left the village," was Hamli's embarrassed protest.

"That is true, but I got frightened and doubled back the next day and came here. It was the secret place Parri discovered when he ran away when he was a boy. He never showed it to anyone but me."

"Then there is no reason we should not return," Hamli said, pushing back a pang of envy. "If we start now we may be home in time for supper."

"That would be good," Soela said, smiling as she rose to follow Hamli from the cave, but she paused at the entrance to catch the other girl's hand shyly in hers.

"Thank you, Hamli," she murmured, giving her a quick hug before she turned to lead the way down the slope.

NECESSITY AND
THE MOTHER

by Lee Martindale

Lee Martindale made her first professional sale in 1992—to Marion Zimmer Bradley's *Snows of Darkover* anthology. Since then, her work has appeared in *Sword & Sorceress XIV* and *XVII*, the tenth anniversary issue of *Marion Zimmer Bradley's Fantasy Magazine,* Sharon Lee and Steve Miller's *Low Port,* Selina Rosen's *Four Bubbas of the Apocalypse,* three collections of her stories from Yard Dog Press, and Esther Friesner's *Turn the Other Chick.* Lee also edited Meisha Merlin's first original anthology, *Such a Pretty Face,* which she dedicated to Mrs. Bradley.

When not slinging fiction, Lee slings sharp pointy steel as a member of the SFWA Musketeers. She's a Lifetime Active Member of SFWA, a member of the SCA, a filksmith, and a Named Bard. She and her husband George live in Plano, Texas.

Donta had been a hiresword, come from a long line of same, and one thing she'd learned was there was no use crying over spilled mead or lost limbs. If one survived, one picked up and moved on without remorse.

So when a fireball from the opposition's battlemage took her shield and the arm to which it was strapped, she healed, drew her injury pay, and made her way back to Hemfrock. Her grandmother, who'd "retired" from mercenary service in much the same fashion, had built a tavern there. Her father, after a profitable career as a contract caravan guard, expanded the place into an inn with the help of Donta's mother, an archer he'd met when her bandit clan had tried—and failed—to raid one of his commissions. By the time *The Mercenary's Mother* passed into Donta's hand, it was a thriving concern.

Well regarded by the townsfolk for its reputation of being so respectable that an unescorted woman, young or old, could enter and leave in safety, it was also the first place they came to when trouble threatened. *The Mother's* clientele was the cream of the hiresword trade, and Donta actively encouraged that cream to rise to the occasion when there was need. The resulting goodwill had its advantages; those seeking local opinion for the best place to find good mercenaries were invariably directed to Donta and her patrons.

The end of both peaceful reputation and mutually beneficial goodwill came one spring afternoon, announced by the sound of Donta bellowing, "Goddess' nightgown!"

Donta's voice had risen above the considerable din of battle to rally squads and shout orders, and the loss of an arm had affected it not at all. It cleared the rooms above, brought people scurrying from neighboring businesses and, in very short order, assembled a large crowd in *The Mother's* common room. A large crowd that saw Donta standing in front of the bar trembling in barely contained rage, hand clenched as if on the hilt of a sword, as she read from a scroll being held in front of her by one of the patrons.

"You wanted proof the Ruling Council has been infested with spellslingers? That proof lies here on the page. Quote: 'Resolved this thirteenth day of the Colt Moon, that the defense of our fair community can no longer be left to the weapons and charity of whatever mercenary troops happen to be within the walls at any particular time.' As if there's ever been a time when a call for help was refused."

"Donta here included," a man growled from near the hearth, "I doubt there's more than half a handful of trained fighters in residence who *don't* hire out regular. What do they mean to leave it to, feather pillows in the hands of willing chambermaids?"

"Magick," Donta snorted. "The fools intend to defend

the town with magick alone." She moved her eyes to the scroll. "And that's not the half of it. Quote: 'Henceforth, in recognition of the debilitating effects of iron and steel on the flow of arcane power and the wielders of spell-craft, all weapons not made of wood and all armor not made of leather are banned from within the walls of Hemfrock and a distance of two hours' march in all directions.' End bloody quote."

The *Mother*'s reputation as a quiet hostelry dissolved altogether in the sustained and incensed howling that followed. Periodically, something intelligible rose above the din, more often than not having to do with the personal predilections and unnatural familial habits of those who had crafted the resolution under discussion. Finally, the furor began to die down, and general consensus was reached, as voiced by one of the regulars. "The Ruling Council might as well throw open the gates and invite every bandit clan within a hundred days' ride to come for dinner."

Donta concluded reading the scroll and signaled for quiet. "According to this, they're going to start confiscating weapons at noon day after tomorrow. Put 'em all in storage, with wards to keep the spellslingers all shielded and comfy from all that nasty steel. We'll get receipts for what we have to give up, of course." A newly sharpened labrys could not have cut through the sarcasm with which that last was delivered.

"Then we might as well just close up shop and take to begging in the square," opined the blacksmith whose shop and livery stood next to *The Mother*. "Our businesses were built on the hireswords' trade, and that trade won't come where their weapons aren't welcome."

Blue eyes twinkled as one strong hand wadded the parchment into a ball. "We'll close up shop, for true. But I have something better in mind than begging."

*

When, at noon on the fifteenth day of the Colt Moon, mages and their leather-armored, quarterstaff-armed escorts went to enforce the new law and collect weapons, they found them already gone. As were their owners and the proprietors, patrons, and contents of several notable establishments. At the blacksmith's place of business, the mage reported no more than iron filings and scraps; forge, bellows, anvil, billets, and tools were gone. The same greeted them at two nearby armorers. At *The Mercenary's Mother,* they found the rooms, upstairs and down, bare of furniture, the kitchen stripped of provisions and cookpots, the wine casks, ale barrels, mead bottles, and jugs of spirits likewise absent. Posted at each place was a plaque of wood on which had been painted a simple map and a symbol none of them recognized.

Upon receiving these reports, the Ruling Council congratulated itself on having avoided what could have been a nasty situation and turned its collective attention to more important matters.

The symbol was, of course, mercenary code that directed those who could read it to a farm in the hills some three hours' ride to the southwest. Like the inn, it had passed into Donta's hand from her family, and from the time of her grandmother, it had supplied much of what *The Mother* served. A great deal of hard work and cooperation, all under Donta's keen eye and sharp direction, turned it into a self-contained haven for those made unwelcome by Hemfrock's new order.

One of the barns she gave over to the blacksmith for a livery, and it was there that he and both armorers set up a cooperative forge and work area. The main house's kitchen and great hall were soon functioning as the relocated tavern, while several of the outbuildings were converted into comfortable barracks. Latrines were dug in areas safely away from water sources, while the water sources themselves were enlarged. And one luxury that the Hemfrock inn had not enjoyed, a natural mineral hot spring of precisely the right temperature for soothing aching muscles and healing hurts, quickly became a popular and profitable addition to the amenities.

By the time the Colt Moon gave way to the Calf Moon, the new incarnation of *The Mercenary's Mother* was a going concern. Tired hireswords, confronted by the weapons policy at the gates of Hemfrock and seeing the plaques nailed to their old haunts, gratefully accepted their first tankard free as a thank you for having made the journey to Donta's. One of the two physicians in Hemfrock moved his practice into one of the parlors. Several guilds, among them the goldworkers', minstrels' and brothelers', gladly paid Donta a fee—much smaller than what they had been paying in taxes—to bring their wares from Hemfrock on a regular basis. Before long, word passed among those who hired mercenaries where the best of them could be found. And it wasn't within the walls of Hemfrock.

*

There's nothing like a crisis to prompt the rethinking of a decision and, for the Ruling Council, it arrived in the form of a ransom note. The importance of the individual to whom the accompanying big toe had once belonged sent its members scurrying to the city coffers, where a slight oversight in stewardship was brought to light.

So immersed had the Council been in reveling in the departure of iron and steel that it failed to note the departure of other metals, specifically gold and silver. Taxes from the sale of good and services, taxes from the sale of food and drink, taxes levied on the occupation of beds, taxes collected as a percentage of hiring and finders' fees, all but a trickle had been banished along with the hireswords.

Which reminded the Council of the second part of the ransom demand and brought the realization that, while the decision had been based on sound theory, it might not hold up all that well in practice. Hemfrock was going to need help and lots of it. A representative was immediately dispatched. His return was just as immediate, the response short, historical, and concise: "Throw spells at 'em."

A second representative was dispatched. When he returned, it was with the reply that, if the Ruling Council wanted to negotiate for services, they could "bloody well send someone besides a barely past-adolescent apprentice to do the talking."

*   *   *

The Ruling Council's third representative glided into the relocated *Mother* a vision of blue-black hair, sea-green eyes, porcelain skin, a heart-shaped face, and dainty figure clad in dark, rich velvet. Those sitting at various tables took immediate interest. Donta, leaning on the bar, regarded the young woman as if she were something a stableman had forgotten to scrape off the sole of his boot. "A glamour," the one-armed woman said by way of greeting, "is a shabby opening gambit to negotiations. And your true appearance, Katrin, is no more than of a princess of Faerie than is mine."

The new arrival answered with a gesture that was half arcane, half rude, and colors began to spin in nauseating fashion around her. When they dissolved, it was to reveal a loose-jointed, lanky body a good six inches taller, thinning gray hair braided close to a pointed skull, and a long face covered with parchmentlike skin. A tabard of Council-crimson over sickly green mage robes had taken the place of the velvet dress. "We need help."

"So I gathered," Donta replied. She pointed toward a table, asked what the mage would have, and gave instructions to the server who slipped behind the bar before joining the other woman in the quiet corner. "Well now," she said after the tankards had been delivered. "Let's see if I understand the situation. One of your spellslingers has gone missing."

A sour looked crossed Katrin's face before she replied. "One of the Three Great Mages. He was coming to Hemfrock to preside over a special convocation, a very great honor for us. And he's not 'gone missing' . . . he's been kidnapped."

"Ah, yes. By bandits."

"Yes."

Donta was almost successful in hiding her smile. "Who haven't killed him outright, but are holding him for ransom."

Katrin nodded.

"And the nature of this ransom?"

The mage raised an eyebrow and pursed her lips. "Why would you need to know that?"

Donta chuckled. "Because I'm trying to decide what the help of mercenaries is worth to you."

Katrin was taken aback. "We've never had to pay for help before."

"You've never made that help unwelcome before. Now, once again, what has been demanded for the supposed safe return of this Great Mage of yours?"

Katrin paused, then answered with some reluctance, "The weight of their captive in gold and unchallenged entry into Hemfrock."

"Interesting. A man of wide girth, is he?"

"He is, as befits his station, impressive in size and stature."

Donta chuckled. "Unfortunate from the standpoint of Hemfrock's treasury, though. And this 'unchallenged entry' by a pack of uncouth bandits with big nasty steel swords and lots of nasty metal armor . . . doesn't bode too well for the citizenry. Quarterstaff, leather armor, and magick not being up to the task and all."

Katrin bristled. "That has not been stipulated."

Donta barked a laugh. "It was stipulated the moment you dispatched the first messenger, spellcaster. The only questions remaining for you to answer is how many hireswords you need and how much you're willing to pay for them. And the only question remaining for me to answer is whether or not I can talk any of them into dealing with you."

*

"Let 'em rot!" seemed to be the near unanimous, and not unexpected, opinion when Donta first laid out the situation that evening to the hundred or so hireswords gathered in the courtyard. There *were* mercenaries who sold their loyalties and ethics along with their blades, but few of that breed ever came to Donta's, and fewer still stayed. The men and women listening to the Council's offer that evening had either been present during the disarming of Hemfrock or had learned of it from those who were. And all considered it a personal affront to themselves and to one who had been one of them.

"They wanted a city free of steel, and they got it,"

argued one old veteran. "They said they could defend themselves using magick alone, and now they've got the opportunity to try. I say we sit back comfortable and snug right here while the bandits show them the error of their ways. Poetically just, it would be. We let the bandits clean out the mages, then we go in and clean out the bandits."

"We could do that," Donta agreed when the furor had died down a bit, "and be perfectly justified in doing so. Mithras knows what Katrin can afford for our services is paltry enough to warrant turning it down. On the other hand, it wouldn't just be mages that the bandits cleaned out. There are people within those walls that have no more love for magick than I do, not to mention the women and children. Do we leave them defenseless as well?"

"Why not?" another man called out. "They let the Ruling Council be taken over, and then, without so much as a protest, handed over their weapons. If they think so little of defending themselves, why should we take the risk of defending them? They let the bed they're lying in be made. Good riddance to them all!"

Donta noted that few gave voice in support of letting innocents be slaughtered. "I've been thinking, though, that there's a certain appeal to having the very folk the Council thought so little of be the very folk who haul their sorry carcasses out of harm's way. And to have one of their supposedly most powerful magickers rescued in the process. . . . The tales of that alone will keep us in work for the next two years."

* * *

When dusk fell a few hours later, a small party of scouts slipped away from the farm to locate the bandits. They were back before moonrise with the camp's layout carefully mapped, including the location of the captive.

Just after sunrise, Donta and three helpers—actually the blacksmith and both armorers—headed for Hemfrock with three wagons ostensibly loaded with produce for sale. In actuality, they were loaded with as many fighters, along with their arms and armor, as could be

hidden under the wagons' covers. By midmorning, the
wagon sat in the livery in Hemfrock, the mercenaries,
unseen by townsfolk and any bandit spies who happened
to be lurking about, had a command post set up in the
deserted *Mother,* and Donta's three "helpers" were busy
checking, cleaning, and distributing weapons from the
Council's confiscated stores. Donta, after meeting with
the Council and making sure the plans were well under-
way, climbed into one of the wagons with one helper—
actually the young mage who'd served as the second
representative—for the trip back to the farm.

Several hours after sunset, two forces moved out from
the farm. The smaller of the two headed for the bandit
camp, while the much larger moved, as quietly as possible, to join their compatriots in Hemfrock. Donta, a few
remaining mercenaries, the physician, and the young man
who'd come back with her, made preparations to receive
a wounded Great Mage.

Bandits rarely impress mercenaries, but those who had
waylaid the mage had done so by the remarkable nature
and consistency of their stupidity. So lacking in organiza-
tion were they that, despite their captive's value, they'd
not even bothered to put guards on him. The only difficulty the rescuers encountered was with the slightly
maimed-but-otherwise-unharmed mage himself; the
man was in pain and anxious to wax petulant that no
one seemed to care. Careful reasoning—in the form of
a gag and the whispered promise that he could either
be quiet or have his throat slit and the whisperer didn't
really care which—convinced him to move as quickly
and quietly as possible toward the horses and his freedom. He was back at Donta's, being pampered to his
apparent satisfaction by the physician and the young
mage, before dawn.

At about the same time the former captive was down-
ing his third tankard of drugged wine, the bandits were
just discovering his absence. Angry at having lost such a
rich prize, they decided to take it out on Hemfrock and,
just incidentally, do a little looting and pillaging while

they were at it. So off they rode, confident that the un-
armed town would fall to them quickly and profitably.

The sight of the walls of Hemfrock bristling steel and
nocked arrows like some mythological beast bristling poisoned quills changed the bandits' minds. Without benefit
of arrow taking flight or sword being swung, the would-
be pillagers decided that elsewhere was a desirable place
to be and rode off to find it with right good speed.

*

The sounds of celebration, muted by thick walls and
heavy tapestries, could still be heard by those within the
Ruling Council's meeting chamber. Katrin, the blacksmith, Donta, and the mercenaries' representative sat
around one end of the long table. Several sacks sat heavy
with coin on the table between them.

"My comrades will be glad of this, madam," the mercenary commented. "Thank you."

"And as to the remainder of the agreement, Katrin?"
Donta said with a slight smile.

The mage's lips compressed into a thin, angry line before she said, "As agreed, all members of the Ruling
Council, mage and no, have stepped down, but not before rescinding the ban on iron and steel. And, as also
agreed, we have admitted that the ban came out of blind
adherence to our particular discipline."

"It *was* stupid to act from the thinking that all brands
of magick were like your own."

Katrin shrugged. "As may be. But for now . . ." She
lifted a large key ring from the table and started to hand
it to Donta.

"Goddess forfend!" the former mercenary laughed as
she indicated that it was to the blacksmith they should
be given. "Borik, here, will take over as head of a Ruling
Council. I'm going to have my hand full running two
businesses."

"Two?"

"*The Mercenary's Mother* is being reopened as we
speak. And it seems a shame to let all that work done
out at the farm go to waste. Truth be told, I hadn't done

much in the way of improvements since my father died, and might not have if this whole business hadn't forced me into it. In a way, you can think of it as necessity spawning another *Mother*."

SUN THIEF

by K.A. Laity

Marion always liked stories that take a familiar motif and turn it on its head. In this tale, based on the folklore of her Finnish heritage, K.A. Laity takes the story of the sacrificed maiden back to its roots and beyond. She also gives the lie to the adage that "those who can't, teach." She is a medievalist with a tenure-track position, and drew on that knowledge for her first novel, *Pelzmantel: A Medieval Tale,* from Spilled Candy Books, published in 2003. She believes that the heart of all myth is a search for the stories that live on and on. Luckily when her feet fly too far off the ground, her husband Gene is there to pull her back, to give her hope and great feedback.

She is a volunteer for the Mythic Journeys conference (www.mythicjourneys.org), a center with an ongoing interest in the use of the mythic in storytelling and life, inspired by the work of Joseph Campbell. In this tale, reality becomes mythic indeed.

She was a sacrifice. Not because she was pure—though she was—but because she was their best. Much fame to her family, for she would be their second offering. Many long winters before, her sister Sari had gone. "Sari is with the Winter Giant," Mama had often said to the little ones, smiling while her eyes sorrowed. And now Arja must go, too, and add to the sadness in her mother's heart.

The village honored them all. The hunters insisted that Arja choose from the best of each kill. Old Pekka grumbled by with a skin of his berry liqueur, mumbling a grudging word of thanks to Papa before stomping off into the snow. Linne crafted a fine necklace of jangling bones and reindeer horn and shiny bright blue stones that lit up the twin gems of Arja's eyes. The elders had walked all together one night to present her with a fine bearskin cloak. Her papa crowed over its thick pelt, holding it aloft so Arja and her mama could trace the fine stitches embroidered on the inside. Three scenes told the story of Aino, the salmon maiden—her spurning of old Väinämöinin, and her watery death and final transformation. This cloak was her people's treasure. Arja thanked them humbly, blushing with terror and enjoyment, even as she wondered to herself how much good it would do her in the Winter Giant's realm. But she took it gratefully— such a prize! Papa swelled with pride. "Even Sari did not receive such a magnificent gift," he said, pulling playfully at her long braids. Arja glowed as if the fire reflected in her cheeks had caught and burned. She loved to clap the bear paws together under her chin and hear the claws clack.

That sound was less enjoyable as she waited on the frozen tundra, the many gifts surrounding her under the three-sided tent. The open side faced north. He would come from there, Arja knew. After rising long before their men would stir, her mother and the other women had led Arja to the sauna for a careful cleansing. They had beat her skin with the birch twigs until she felt the pleasant glow of well-being, as the steam belched up with each ladle of cold water poured upon the hot rocks. Arja could almost forget why she was being so pampered. Mama had woven red and white ribbons in her hair, braiding the colors into her waist-length plaits. The women had helped her slip into the beautiful red dress they had all had a hand in making—Mari's fine stitching, Linne's beads, Hanni's weaving—and pulled on the warm fur boots that had belonged to the eldest of the elders. Fine silver bells ringed the ermine tops and jangled when she walked.

These bells rang out across the plains as Arja stamped her feet to keep warm, and her little chimes were answered with further ringing from the north. She squinted into the darkness, trying to find movement within the white. If the sun were rising, Arja thought, I would be able to see him. But this day, again, the sun did not rise. Hiisi had taken it away, further and further, until darkness fell upon their land without respite—as he did every winter. *And I have been chosen to appease him.* Arja clacked the bear claws together under her chin and felt her heart beat faster.

Now she could see a shape against the drifts. The steady chime of the bells melted into Arja's thoughts until she could no longer hear it. The occasional crack of the whip, to urge the beast on, ran through her head and snapped through her body. Closer now. The animal drawing the sled seemed to be an elk of immense proportions, but there was something odd to it, too. As it plunged through the wind-sculpted banks layering the plain and covered the distance with surprising speed, Arja puzzled at the beast's strange silhouette. When it was yards away, she could make out the yellow eyes that twinkled like lilies on the pond's surface, the head like a stump rotted by winter's cruelty and crowned with a broken branch. The legs that ran so fast, leaping through the snow, looked like saplings or maybe fence posts. The fur of this creature, now pulling up before her, appeared to be as rough as the bark of a fir, winter hardened and wind teased. Could such a thing live? This sorcery made her shudder.

But Arja's wide eyes had not even taken in the one who had conjured such an alarming creature into being. He was taking her in, though. As he threw down his whip and shook off several layers of white bear skins, his eyes—dark as a night-flying raven—hungrily swallowed her body. Arja felt faint. He was so tall! And his shoulders hunched with power, like twin eels ready to spring. White hair rippled out the sides of his cap, but it brought her no comfort—this was no grandfather. The Winter Giant stepped down from his sleigh accompanied by a ringing as the massive elk shook his traces, pawing at the snow. Arja's body was a river of trembles that shook music from her boots and tears from her eyes.

A foot away now, he looked down upon Arja, then shifted his gaze to the goods behind her. At last, a smile.

The Giant moved with surprising speed—and grace. He crowed like a small boy, delighted with the fresh-baked breads, the exquisitely smoked meat—Matti used special herbs along with the birch twigs to flavor the reindeer flesh—and of course, Pekka's berry drink. He lifted the skin above his head and squeezed the fermented juice into his gaping jaws. Such sharp teeth! And so many—Arja gulped, but her mouth remained dry.

It took him scant minutes to load the sleigh. It had taken half the village to bring all the gifts out here in the darkness, then go one by one—Mama holding on as if she might not leave, until she too had turned away and walked off into the night. The Winter Giant carried armfuls to the sleigh, piling them quickly, but with care, so nothing would get squashed in the ride back. He did not ask her help, so Arja stood silently by. The loading done, he rubbed his hands—paws? They were so rough, the nails so long and sharp—together with satisfaction and turned to Arja.

"Well, my bride, it is time we go."

Arja took his offered hand, her toes curling under as her small fingers were grasped by his frigid ones. Their cold was a new shock, even after the hours alone in the tent on the plains. A cold that came from within, from his cold heart, no doubt, Arja thought. *How can I bear this?* But she was already seated beside him and he was drawing the white bearskins over their laps. He paused to run his fingers over her own bearskin cloak. "Not bad for a little creature." Again he laughed, smiling down at Arja. The smile was terribly frightening. Arja could only think of how those teeth would feel in the morning.

"What are you thinking, my bride?"

Arja opened her mouth but no sound came out at first. She swallowed. "I was wondering what it will feel like to be in Tuonela."

Again the giant roared with laughter. "You will not go to the Land of the Dead, child. When I eat you, I eat your spirit. Why do you think I am so strong? How can I pull the sun so far from your land? I eat spirits of human folk! Tasty they are!" His teeth scraped together as he spoke, like knives on bone.

Though warm under all the bearskins, Arja felt chilled to her heart. She had resigned herself to death. Someone had to die after all, for the good of the tribe—and there was honor in it. But to be consigned to oblivion! Trapped forever in the brutish hulk of this ogre—no, no, that she had not prepared for. Sitting next to the great giant as he urged on the huge elk with growls and whipcracks, Arja strained to hear the lost souls trapped within him. To be so cut off from the world of the living—she could not fathom it. There had been some comfort in the thought that Mama would be able to call forth Arja's spirit from the grave already laid for her, the grave without a body. Only a lock of her hair, braided then cut off—only that was buried in the hollow with the other folk of their tribe. A scree of carefully chosen stones marked the place where her body would not lie. A shiver had run through her then, too, but it was balanced with the thought that her spirit might commune with family again at that spot. We go on, Papa always said. But Sari was always "with the Winter Giant." Had they known? Then why make her grave?

"You are silent," the giant said gruffly, pausing to wipe his streaming nose.

"I am unhappy," Arja said.

The big teeth gaped wide once more as he threw his head back laughing. When he stopped, the big gray eyes regarded Arja perplexedly. "Well, at least you are quiet." And without another word they rode for hours with only the elk's jingling traces to break the silence of the wind-swept plains.

The Winter Giant's home was a cleft in a cliff that opened into an immense cavern. One could never find it in the landscape's vast blankness without knowing just where to look. Arja watched as the giant released the elk, who shook his head and ran for the edge of the forest to make his dinner of what he could paw from the drifts. Just as easily as before, the great ogre carried all the precious gifts deep into the cave, motioning with a jerk of his head that Arja should follow within. A merry fire burned there, as if determined to cheer the poor girl, but still she shivered.

Here I will die, Arja thought glumly. She was too tired even to work up any anger or to fight. What could she possibly do against such a foe? Her eyes followed him. He was pawing through all the gifts with a childlike eagerness that somehow made his powerful frame that much more menacing. He could hurl her against the wall as easily as a boy might throw a snowball. And then eat her. It was too much.

"Here." The Winter Giant had opened all the packages and finally settled on the liqueur, some of the braided breads, as well as the pickled herring in the earthenware jar. He held out a piece of bread to her, ripped from a loaf. His claws held it fast. She hesitated. He laughed. "Yes, have some!" Gingerly, Arja reached for the bread, sure the claws would dart out and stab her hand, but he released the piece of bread and it dropped into her tiny palm. "Well, how do you like your wedding night."

"Will there be no ceremony even?"

"What does it matter? You are only food, in the end."

"It matters to me. I am offered by my people as your bride—that I must perish after is not my concern. But the ritual is very important to me."

"Well, you may leap over the fire if you wish. I believe your people do such a thing." The giant chuckled as if this were very funny. "Then are we married?"

Arja stood up and felt the prickly skin of her legs as the blood began to flow sluggishly. "It will do."

It should have been such a joyful moment. Her family should have been around her, her village. Some young man should have been standing on the other side of the fire—not this great hairy beast of a creature, gnawing his way through her people's precious goods as the water sweated down the ice of the cavern. The fire should have been a symbol of blessing and fertility, filling her with the potential fruitfulness that their harsh life demanded.

But here she was in the cave of the Winter Giant, his wife, his food. Let there be some blessing in this, Arja thought, eyes closed. Mother Sun, may your presence return to my people and this fire warm my heart and spirit. After a moment's reflection, she gathered her skirts and leapt over the crackling flames. The orange and yellow fingers reached up as if to caress her sturdy legs, and buoyed Arja with a warm pillow of heat. She landed on the other side, her mind buzzing with half-formed thoughts. So I am married, so our souls entwine, until death claims one. Must it be me? Arja regarded her husband without emotion. "It is done. Now you will return the sun to my people?"

"It is already done," the giant mumbled with a mouth full of herring. "The sun is returning, a little more each day." Again his raucous laughter echoed through the cave. "You can know my secret now. I do not control the sun. She moves on her own. Her yearly path takes her far from this land, but she always returns. Your foolish people! One very very bad, harsh winter, they believed the bragging words of this one," he thumped his chest proudly, "so now they pay me, and I eat when the sun is farthest and the nights are coldest and game scarce. I eat well—tender young flesh."

Arja burned, her eyes grew flames and her heart sizzled.

"None of the others asked, you know. Terrified they were. No wedding, no fire jumping. Just tears. Is it better knowing? No," he cackled, "I can see it is not."

Arja's blood raged through her flesh, her anger gathering momentum. But she could not strike out—what good would it do? Make him roar with laughter all the more? No, she could not attack him. In Arja's heart, the hot rage turned to cold tin. The questions inspired by her leap over the fire continued to whip through her thoughts. She did not even realize there was a smile on her face— grim as it was—as she turned to the giant once more. "Husband, may I ask a boon of you?"

"You know, you may call me Hiisi, as you are my wife—for now." He smiled over the skin of berry liqueur, his lips stained red. Arja felt a deeper chill, realizing how he would look with her blood splashed across his greedy mouth. "You may ask a boon of me—provided you do not ask to be spared death."

"I shall not ask that. But as I am never to rest in the land of the dead, may I at least be allowed to see Tuonela once before I die? Surely that is not so much to ask."

"Hmmph," Hiisi grunted. He was quite comfortable sitting cross-legged upon his bearskins, the many gifts gathered around him. Clearly he had no desire to make such a journey. "There is little to interest anyone there. And you could only stand on the shore. I could not take you into the land itself. My power is not such."

Arja controlled her smile. It must not look happy, only ingratiating. "This is all I ask. It is not so much. After tonight I shall see nothing. Let me have one glimpse of the land from which my ancestors speak to us."

Hiisi considered her request as he chomped on the salty fish, stopping occasionally to slurp at his claws. "I suppose there is no harm in it. But there is little of interest in it, either. You will be disappointed." He looked at Arja, her chin jutted out implacably, and sighed. "But I cannot refuse a final request from my delicious wife."

He sighed and put down his treats, with a careful pat, as if to bid them await his return. Arja bundled her cloak around her shoulders once more, her eyes brightly eager. Hiisi stretched, wiped his jaws with a huge paw, and belched noisily. This made him laugh even more loudly. His young wife smiled agreeably, but her thoughts already ranged ahead: Tuonela! Never would she have thought that so much hope could dwell in the Land of the Dead.

If her journey to the ice cliffs had been swift, then she had no suitable word for the speed of her second ride. Arja struggled to stay upright as the sled whistled over the icy banks. The white skins shifted with every bounce, and her teeth chattered with the cold and terror. But she must be brave. It had been her choice to come, to face once more the pallid expanses and the rattling winds, to risk what little life she had left. Tears flowed freely down Arja's cheeks. Even she could not tell whether they sprang from the whips of frigid air or from her fears. She was going to die, Arja knew it truly now. But the question still hung before her—how?

Just at the horizon, white turned to black, a darkness that was yet not so dark as that overhead. With alarm Arja saw that the first presages of dawn—not that they would see the sun that day—had whispered across the sky. The heavens were still black, but no longer the dark of a raven's wing. Hurry, hurry, she silently urged the bark elk, who—as if he had heard her plea—seemed to have saved a final burst of energy to reach this far-off goal. Through her tears Arja could see the dark lake, its sooty surface broken only by the gliding swan's wake and the whirlpool's hungry swirl. Tuonela, the Land of the Dead: beyond the mist she could not see, but she knew in the center an island lay. No one knew how big or small, even those who dwelled there. Some things could not be known.

"Well, my wife," Hiisi roared too loud for the silent shoren, as he pulled hard at the elk's reins. "Here is your land of dead. We must hurry back now, it is time to eat!" But Arja was already clambering down from her seat, squirming out from under the bearskins. Hiisi stared, his mouth hanging open. Arja looked into his eyes. For the first time all fear fled from her heart, and she saw her own truth. He cannot guess. "Aino, share your gift," she muttered, then turned and ran toward the clouded banks. Hiisi gave a yelp of surprise, threw aside his whip, and hopped down from the sled. But he was not so fast this time. He would not catch her. She did not even try to shake off her heavy clothes, her beautiful boots, the clanking necklace that chivvied her throat. She only ran. Her feet felt light and swift. Arja spread her arms as she approached the water's edge, and the swan— as if in sympathy with her flight—spread its wings, too, and hissed a threat to any who might stop her, raising up from the water and arching its neck.

From the bank, Arja jumped. Her body arced, palms

together now; she hit the water like a leaping pike and plunged into the black spiral whirling down from the surface. Cold, so cold—and she had thought the mid-winter air frozen! It was nothing to the glacial grasp of the midnight waters, fingers of ice that wormed through her garments and probed into her soul. I am dying, Arja realized. Her dive seemed to gain momentum, as if the whirlpool were greedily drawing her to its heart. Down and down she spun, losing all sense of direction, feeling her life slip away. Arja's eyes remained open, but she saw only her memories against the inky depths. It was all disappearing, washing away, trailing behind her, perhaps bursting at the surface. She did not even notice when the last bubbles of air left her nostrils, for the force of the water drew her on imperiously, until she saw nothing but blackness and felt no cold on her skin. Like a stone, Arja hit the bottom with a soft thump. Unlike a stone, she flipped and nosed her way toward the surface, her strong tail propelling her up once more. Long before she breached the water's skin, Arja could see vague clouds stretching across the sky. It was the first midwinter dawn.

Arja leapt from the water, droplets dappling her new scales. It was a shock to slam down on the surface, gasping for air, then remembering, dive once more to pull the rich liquid through her gills. It was cold and pure and invigorating. But she had to go up one final time. She twisted around, trying to get her bearings. There, over there! Arja paddled her fins vigorously to keep her head above the waves, and looked back at her husband. Hiisi had fallen to his knees at the very place where she had leaped. It was not anger she heard in his voice now, only a terrible sadness. He would have eaten me, Arja reminded herself as she plunged back into her new watery world. Yet his aching cry followed her down.

"But you will tell them! And then I will be alone!" Hiisi wailed. "Alone!"

LOSTLAND
by Rosemary Edghill

Rosemary Edghill is a lady of wit and wide interests whose novels I had been enjoying for several years before I actually met her. Her first professional sales were to the black and white comics of the late 1970s, so she can truthfully state that she once killed vampires for pay. She is the author of over thirty novels and several short stories, and has collaborated with both Marion and with Andre Norton, worked as an SF editor for a New York publisher, and as a freelance book designer and professional reviewer in addition to being a full-time writer. Her hobbies include sleep, research for forthcoming projects, and her Cavalier King Charles Spaniels.

You can find her on the Web at: www.sff.net/people/eluki. Her personal favorite Web site is a tarot and divination site (it's free!) http://www.facade.com.

This story is the second about Ruana Rulane, a sequel to "The Ever-After," published in *Dragon* #149, June 1989.

They say that in Lostland you can find anything you've ever renounced—whether you want it again when you have it is another matter. They say that no one knows the way to Lostland; they say that Lostland finds the people meant to find it. They say the one thing you can't find in Lostland is the way out.

Once again the truth is a thought different.

*

Her name was Ruana Rulane, and she was a hero. Practically speaking, in terms of semantics and sex, she should have been a heroine, but heroines are rather more associated with the staunch maintenance of husbands, children, and the gentler arts of domestic order. Ruana

Rulane was a hero—which is to say, vastly inconvenient except in times of war.

This was not to say she wasn't a well-tried and acceptable hero, as self-willed anarchic moralists go. In her time upon the Glory Road she had slain giants, faced down bandits, meddled where she wasn't wanted for the sheer joy of it, gotten brief glory and a little legend and even—much against her will—found herself the custodian of a magic sword.

For there *were* magic swords.

Once, a very long time ago, before, in fact, the universe was made, there was war. It was a war of gods, and gods' weapons, and the human cat's-paws fated to wield them for their masters, and in that time there was a weapon.

This weapon was a living thing: self-willed and self-aware, and conscienceless—and powerful. Those who made it wrought cruel as the grave and more cunning than Death. It was created for one task, and fitted to it supremely well, and once it had done its work the gods slept, and all the world was gone.

But the weapon remained, seeking to perform its function again. Its makers thought they had been careful. The weapon was powerless without a companion to use it. And so, since before Time began again, it had awaited a companion to make it invincible. A hero, to carry it into a battle that would grow to claim the stars.

And since heroes require swords, it was a sword. And since the swords of heroes require names. . . .

Call it Shadowkiss.

Destroyer of universes.

The glass-green god-sword, companion and weapon of heroes—which (in this age), if it was not the Starharp Itself, could surely lead her to it, so that Ruana could play the song that would wake the Sleeping God, the Crownking, and bring an end to all the world.

If she would only let it.

It was only mad luck that had led her to claim the sword—a thing she had never meant to do—and when she had, Shadowkiss had tried to bend her will to its own. The sword had promised her everything that it had promised a thousand heroes before her, thinking those things would be enough.

And perhaps they would have been enough, if Ruana Rulane had been an ordinary hero.

The Gray Duke, ruler of Corchado, greatest of the cities of the North, had sought Shadowkiss, seeking to bury the god-sword forever beneath the stones of Corchado before it could take a companion. He had brought Ruana Rulane before him, to beg her to set down the sword which she could not—or to offer her the chance to face him in battle—which she would not.

She spoke to him of a third course: of turning Shadowkiss to the simple work of heroes.

And against all odds, the Duke had trusted her.

Trusted a hero.

And so a partnership was forged, which would endure beyond the End of Days.

*

"Crownking and Starharp!" The oath rang flat against air that—it seemed—had never before been made to carry human voice.

She had ridden out three days ago—at dawn, with ten good men—to find out what was keeping all traffic on the Eastern Spur Road from reaching Corchado. It was suitable work for a hero.

And Ruana Rulane was a hero.

Or so men said, she reminded herself bitterly, as she cast about—alone—for some sign of the road. So the Gray Duke had said, when he gave her soldiers and horses and supplies. He was dismantling the battle-engine he had prepared against her coming, but that was not the action of scant days, and the absence of traffic and messages from the East could be the forerunner of war from rival cities made anxious by Corchado's past preparations. The Duke needed a hero to determine why the trading caravans had stopped, he said, and so Ruana went.

The men she had taken with her had been soldiers of the garrison of Corchado. Steady, experienced veterans, unfazed by riding as companions of hero and hellsword, and not one of them a fool. And in ones and twos they had vanished, stolen away by night and day and river-mist and a sobbing from somewhere just out of sight, until at last Ruana Rulane was left to ride alone.

She'd made up her mind to turn back at the end of the second day, when she'd still had half her men. Shadowkiss had not wanted to retreat. The sword had pulled at her, luring and coaxing, demanding she seek out the destroyer and give battle. But the Gray Duke needed even this much information more than Ruana needed glory, and so she had fought down the sword and put the sun at her back and turned the remains of her men back toward the gates of Corchado.

It hadn't made any difference. She'd lost three more before another night fell, and this morning she awoke to find herself alone, still a day's ride from the city walls. Knowing it was useless, she had ridden out to look for some sign of them, and managed to lose the road entirely, a thing that should not have been possible.

Before the sun was an hour higher she knew she would not find the road again, no matter how hard she looked, and the sword's thrill of triumph told her how badly she was lost.

But it was battlejoy, not malice, that echoed through the sword. Shadowkiss loved her in its fashion and would not betray her, nor was it in its power to carry its wielder out of the world. Shadowkiss destroyed worlds, but its whole purpose was to kill.

Ruana Rulane would change that, if she could.

If she lived.

She gazed around herself, taking stock of her surroundings. All around the landscape was the same: trackless, featureless, and flat. Dun-gray below and iron-gray above, and like nothing within two weeks' ride of Corchado.

Sighing, she started the horse off briskly, since the direction did not matter. Any direction would serve to bring her to the attention of whatever had stolen her men away in the night and trapped her within this eldritch not-land, and she had words to say to that when she met it. More sorcery. She should have known. Ruana despised sorcery: it was the path of fools and cowards, and no work for honest folk.

And you, she said, fingers skimming lightly over the translucent scarlet pommel stone of her sword. *You're no help at all.*

Shadowkiss did not answer.

*

The bone rings braided into her hair clicked faintly with the horse's gait, and her saddlecloth, a gift from the Duke, did not bear the golden tower of Corchado upon it. Ruana Rulane bore no one's colors but her own: her saddlecloth was black with a fiery sword worked in green and gold and silver. Ruana Rulane carried Shadowkiss, and it was much safer for the world if the world knew that at once.

Not that there seemed to be anyone in the immediate area to take note of who she was and what she carried, Ruana noted with disgust. No one, and no road to follow. Perhaps all roads were the same here.

Wherever "here" was.

*

As she rode, the land began to subtly change. It rose up around her like folds in a cloth; hills on each side of a narrow valley. The folds of the hills were filled with mist, and the sky darkened to twilight, though it had been dawn only a scant few hours before.

More sorcery. The unnaturalness of it chilled the Twice-born's pragmatic bones to the marrow. What use were her wits and her skill and her experience of the world if, in the world through which she now rode, all laws were changed? How could she predict if and when this realm would release her, and how and whether she could stay alive?

What was there to fight?

"Well, if there's no more field nor fare than this, the nag and I'll both starve to death—and then where will you be, my hinny?" she said to her sword.

Again, there was no response from what she carried.

Then her horse slowed, and threw back its head and neighed. Ruana swore, and dragged its head down, but she could already hear the hoofbeats of another horseman approaching in the twilight. She eased Shadowkiss halfway from its sheath at her back and waited uneasily for the rider to appear.

He rode a white horse, and his armor was the color of winter's ice; a deep clear blue that darkened even as she stared at it, until it was the color of the air all around and its wearer a seeming illusion. His hair was finer and fairer than that of any man or woman she had ever seen, and on his brow he bore a black iron crescent-crown holding one star-clear gem.

She knew him. How not? The god of soldier and slayer, whose symbol decorated every soldier's tavern she had ever seen. Chayol, the Rising Star. Chayol Warhammer.

"Stop." She drew Shadowkiss as she spoke, and the broad gem-starred green glass blade of the hellsword seemed to hang supported by the air itself.

Chayol Warhammer reined in his glistening stallion and touched the hammer that lay sheathed against his thigh.

"Consider well, swordbride, before ordering Chayol of Lostland," he answered.

Lostland. It ought to be a name to frighten drunks, fools, and children, or perhaps to fascinate poets, but here and now it held a terrible credibility, a sense of being nothing dramatic or fabulous: not meant to shock or amaze, but only the simple truth.

"Consider well, Chayol-of-Lostland, before riding on. I'll fight if I must, but I'd rather not," Ruana said evenly. "I'd have answers."

But answers, it seemed, were a thing she was not to have.

"What sort of a hero won't fight?" Chayol said mockingly. "A poor one, probably."

"A live one, certainly. I'm not minded to spend my life just to amuse the gods. Tell me where I am, and how I may find my men and leave."

"And have I not?" said Chayol Warhammer once more. "Lostland is my kingdom."

"A pretty name to frighten children," said Ruana evenly, even though she believed him.

"If you like. You'll find that heroes and children are not so unalike, if you stay here. Here is the country of lost things, and all that are lost are within its borders. Consider carefully whether you truly wish to find that which you have lost. But come, hero, I'll bargain with you. Give me the sword you carry and you can go. As for your men. . . ." He shrugged, and said nothing more.

Shadowkiss described a small flourish on the midnight air.

"I've had that offer before. Answer is always the same. No." She could not give up the sword, nor let it be destroyed while she lived. And the sword was invincible in battle, nor would the sword's companion wither and age as did ordinary folk. . . .

"Then I will kill you and take it," Chayol said, as if he had expected no other response. "But before you die, swordbride, consider who you face. I am Chayol Warhammer. A thousand generations have cursed my name, and there is no kindness in me. Hear me: once, before your world was made, I was a king of men, and in those days I was kind. I had enough wit to be a coward, and sufficient imagination to foresee the things that happen to a man who has no allies. So I held my tongue and my temper; I thought I was wise and tried to be just, and I assured myself that I would never be so outcast that no one in the whole tribe of Man would speak for me when evil days came. But I was wrong. Turn against me they did, and there was no refuge for me anywhere, despite soft words and softer deeds in the days of my fame. All my forbearance had won me nothing, and I died knowing it was so.

"When I was reborn I had learned to dispense with inessentials."

"Then you'll kill me here, or try?" Ruana's question was interested, nothing more.

"That is my nature," answered the king who had become a god. His mouth twisted, as at some black personal joke, and he closed his hand over the weapon at his side, lifting it from its holster.

Ruana raised Shadowkiss to meet the challenge, and for the first time in her wielding the sword seemed reluctant to offer battle. For a dreadful moment she wondered if Shadowkiss meant to betray her here in this unreal place, and then Chayol Warhammer too had raised his weapon and spurred his warhorse forward.

Ruana wore no more armor than a light chain mail shirt, and the weapon Chayol carried did not need to pierce it to hurt her. One strike from his hammer would break her bones; two would kill her. But in the last instant Shadowkiss dragged her arm forward, and the warhammer echoed off the flat of her unyielding blade. The shock rang achingly up her arm, numbing it, and for a dreadful instant Ruana could not tell whether she still held Shadowkiss. Chayol had already reversed his weapon, and once again the sword was barely there in time to meet it.

Hammer clashed on sword with a sound like a starsmith forging a new creation, until there was no time for the echo of one blow to die away before the next was struck. Ruana felt the drag in muscles that were merely mortal; Chayol did not give her the extra moment she needed to turn a counter into an attack, and a magic sword, however powerful, was only as good as the hero who wielded it.

But Chayol seemed to weary after the first exchange of blows—or perhaps he looked to an ally who did not come. He drew back.

"Do you not know me?" he said, and when Ruana drew breath to answer she saw his eyes were not on her. She followed his gaze to the hellbright flare of rubies in a green glass blade. Chayol looked to her sword.

Shadowkiss.

A god-sword, many had called it, and Chayol Warhammer was a god. Was he the god who had once carried it into war and now sought to summon it to his hand once more?

The fury that she felt in that moment penetrated every defense she had. Ruana dug her spurs savagely into her horse's sides and flung her unstoppable traitor sword up to shear through the chest and neck and skull of her enemy.

Only Chayol wasn't there. He had vanished, reclaimed by the mist that had given birth to him.

Despite his absence, battle-rage and jealousy made her goad her mount forward, hunting through the mist for her foe. She brandished Shadowkiss, testing the air of the path before her, but still there was nothing there. Chayol Warhammer was gone.

And then at last the absurdity of it struck her, and she laughed.

"Jealous. . . . Aye, like some maudlin mooncalf; fighting a dream to get what I already have," she said aloud.

Shadowkiss had chosen her—for now, and for the duration of this world. She had, and could have, no rival. She sheathed Shadowkiss again, shaking her head.

The rings in her hair made cool impacts upon her cheeks. She forced herself to think of all she had just heard and seen: how much was truth, and how much was illusion bred from the dust of this unchancy place? Had Chayol Warhammer truly been a human man before he became a god . . . the man who had last borne the sword she now carried—if in a different shape—and summoned the end of an age?

If he had been, it had been a very long time ago. The sword was hers now.

While she lived.

Yet she could die. Others had possessed the Dreaming Sword, and died, failing to accomplish the task Shadowkiss had set for them. A hundred times—a thousand— the sword had been found and lost and found again since the world had been reborn, and still the Crownking slept.

But in her heart, she knew Chayol had spoken truth, if of a twisted kind.

"Once I was kind. . . ."

She forced her mind to turn from things that didn't matter to things that did. Chayol had said her men were

here—or if he hadn't, he'd said that lost things were, and
for a certainty, her men were lost, not dead. Urging her
horse forward more gently now, Ruana went to find the
men she had lost, here in the country of lost things.

*

The village lay on the shore of the lake; a half-circle
of skin-covered lodges, primitive by every standard she
had come to know in her wanderings. The fishing nets
lay drying down at the lake edge, and beyond lay the
sweep of ice-covered lake. Somewhere near the middle
of the ice was a star of dark water, as if the ice had been
lately broken.

She had not expected anything like this when she rode
over the last ridge, and so it took a moment for Ruana
to realize where she was. And then the drums began.

"No," Ruana whispered. The jagged rhythm of the
sound caught at her, dizzying her with memory. This was
the place where she had been born—and where her girl-
self had been lost forever.

Once she had not been Ruana Rulane the Twiceborn.
Once she had been any ordinary young woman, with a
husband and a father.

Once.

But then, there had been an eclipse, and in its shadow
that young woman was brought to bed of her firstborn
in the same hour its father died. She lost husband and
daughter in that hour, and then her name, because to
baffle the vengeance of the ghosts of child and husband
it was decreed by the elders of that small village that
Ruana must become a man. The bone ornaments for her
hair were quickly brought, and the drums and herbs for
the ritual, and when the dance was over there was no
grief spent on husband and dead girlchild, for Rulane
Twiceborn had neither.

And when Rulane Twiceborn had been schooled to an
honorable man's estate, a warrior skilled with sword and
bow and sling, the woman reborn as a man left the village of birth and rebirth, never to return again.

And for a dozen years afterward Ruana Rulane the
Twiceborn, went where she pleased, and did as she

chose, until the day that she meddled in the affairs of priests once too often.

And claimed Shadowkiss.

She had sworn never to return to the village of her birth and rebirth. And she never had.

Until now. Because in Lostland all that you had lost was waiting for you.

The beat thundered on, peopling the empty village with her ghosts. In her imaginings the men drummed, the women danced, the ritual to make the suffering bleeding girl into a man of the Sassenach against the spirits' vengeance sped onward to the end that would thrust Ruana Rulane outward to walk the Glory Road.

Could she save the girl that she had been from the hero she had become? She tensed, half-ready to ride down into the village, to disrupt the ceremony. . . .

To take back what she had lost.

But if she could, if she did, who would take up Shadowkiss when that time came in turn?

In her imagination, the future unfolded.

The captain closed the door behind the priest and his acolyte. The room held one man. He stood at the tall desk by the window, turning the pages of a book with jeweled covers.

"Do you have what I sent you for?" he asked the priest.

His eyes were a little darker than amber, his hair already streaked with gray. Without waiting for an answer, he came forward and drew back the caul of silk shrouding the sword. In the dim room it gathered all the light and gave back color brighter than the tapestries.

:Name me: the sword whispered, for the Duke's ears alone. :I have waited for you since the universe was made; together we are complete. With me you take up a mad god's curse and a glorious destiny; to play the Starharp and bring order to all the worlds. Beloved. . . .:

"Shadowkiss," the Duke said huskily, clasping the black bone hilt and raising the sword high.

He had prepared an army to guard and hide the sword. In that moment all that prudence was forgotten. Shadowkiss had claimed him, and the Gray Duke's heart turned

*to thoughts of vengeance and power, love, glory, and re-
nown, and a name that would endure beyond the end of
the world.*

"Summon my generals," he said to the waiting priest.

No.

The Gray Duke was a good man, a kind man, but he
was not strong enough to stand against Shadowkiss.

She must be there to take the sword.

Consciously Ruana forced herself to relax, taking her
hand from the hilt of the sword and sitting back in her
saddle to wait, and after a time—a very long time—the
drums stopped.

*

She knew that she had to find a way out of Lostland,
for herself and for her men. Perhaps they were somewhere before her in this mockery of her past—but when
Ruana Rulane finally dared to ride down into the Sassenach village, dismount, and enter the priest-chief's lodge,
it was empty except for the girl.

The child was blond like the people of the tribes north
of Ruana's own, and stood naked among the sleeping
furs of the lodge like a silver bolt of moonlight shining
to earth. She was the age that Ruana's daughter would
have been, if she had lived.

"What are you? Spirit?" Despite the god-sword in her
hand, Ruana's voice was hoarse with superstitious fear.

"I am cold," said the girl with dignity, and held out
her arms in supplication.

There were furs to wrap her in, and all the things that
Ruana's memories told her belonged in such a lodge as
this: bark-tea and fish and porridge. She lit the torches
and coaxed the fire in the fire pit to life, and felt the
wrongness of the heeled boots of the south striking the
skin-covered floor of the lodge as she walked about gathering her needs from what was there. The child regarded
her with wide grave eyes while Ruana prepared the meal
for both of them.

"How are ye come here, hinny?" Ruana asked, when
the food was ready. The tea was more bitter than she
remembered it; thick and flat and musky. She took a

deep swallow and watched the child over the rim of the wooden cup.

"I . . . am here," the child said, as if that were an answer. The day had waxed to brightness again while Ruana had worked, and the light from the smoke-hole in the roof above whitened the child's hair and made her face the brightest thing in the lodge.

"And my men?" The question came almost in spite of herself.

The child regarded her with a wide-eyed unspeaking gaze, in which Ruana might read what she would.

What now? She could not remain here, in this shadow of her past, for she would not find her men here. Yet to leave its shelter was to risk some new confrontation.

There was no choice, really.

She found clothing for the girl-creature, wondering all the while if she brought her peril with her in bringing the child along. She suspected Shadowkiss could tell her, if it would, but stubborn pride kept her from consulting the sword. In the end, it hardly mattered: human child or otherwise, Ruana would leave no living thing to fend for itself in this desert of shadows.

Leading the girl by the hand, she left the priest's lodge. Her horse, she noted with faint relief, was where she had left it. She mounted, lifting the child to sit before her on the saddle.

"Where do you take me?" the child asked.

"In search of what I have lost," Ruana said simply.

"That was here," the child said.

The statement startled a laugh from Rulane Twiceborn. "Think you, my hinny, that I've lost only the one thing? Happens I'd choose which lost things I want back."

At that the child settled into place, and said nothing more.

They rode from the village, and Ruana did not look back.

*

Once more the landscape evened into a featureless gray plain, and the light dimmed again toward an unending twilight. The longer nothing happened, the tighter Ruana's nerves stretched. Waiting.

And suddenly it came.

In the distance, through the mist, a sparkle of light, as if—somehow—sunlight danced on water.

But there was no sun, and no water.

Then came a sound like the distant roll of thunder, and if she were afoot, Ruana knew she would feel the ground shake beneath her feet.

Cavalry at the charge.

She reined in and stopped, waiting. It would be a fool's trick to attempt to outrun the horsemen. She could not yet tell how long the line was, but a lone rider who was quick and clever—and Ruana was both—might gallop between the soldiers and win to safety, if she could not pass around the end of the line.

She reached back and drew her sword, looping the reins around her free wrist. It might yet come to fighting.

She spared a moment's regret for the child seated before her. She dared not set the girl down to be trampled, and to protect her would make her own defense harder.

Then at last she could see the other horses clearly.

Not cavalry, for they did not run in a line, or in any order that Ruana could see. They ran as wild horses run, in a great herd, their bodies straining to the utmost—monstrous silk-skinned horses with tails like flaunting bannerets of maiden's hair, hooves of steel and eyes of fire; lunging, foaming, running forward, the spearhead of some unimaginable charge.

And upon each one's back, a rider.

Warriors and queens, kings and princes; their armor as fantastic as sculpture; their headdresses plumed and jeweled, the light sparkling off swords and crowns.

Her mount was a steady and reliable creature, but it began to fret as the Wild Hunt drew closer. Ruana tightened the reins and resolved to stand her ground. By her estimate, the riders would pass her merely. If they kept to their present course, they would offer no true threat.

But as they came closer, and the thunder of their coming woke a thunder in her blood, the quickening of her heartbeat warned her that their presence was a danger in itself. Her mount began to fight in earnest, desperate to go with them. Too late Ruana remembered fireside tales from a hundred roadside taverns, of hungry lonely ghosts condemned to search endlessly for others to join them, and wondered if, perhaps, not all who now rode with the Hunt had joined it of their own free will.

And she knew that the gaze of sorcery could bend the mind and destroy the will. . . .

"Don't look!" Ruana cried to the child, as the riders began to pass the place they stood.

But she looked herself, and in that instant she was caught, dazzled and yearning.

Somehow she understood everything about the Hunt and all who rode within it. Her men were there, too, lost and enchanted, caught by the desire for glory that lived within every man's soul . . . the desire that she felt as well, the desire that was Shadowkiss' greatest weapon against her.

She would not surrender to it, no matter how much she yearned to, and in that moment, seeing the Hunt, Ruana mourned her own refusal, knowing that in that refusal to submit to the Dreaming Sword's will she destroyed something fine, something glorious, something that deserved to live.

But all was not lost. There was still a chance. The ground still echoed to the drumbeat of hooves, the air was still scintillating with the flash of jeweled armor. Her mount danced madly beneath her; if she loosed the reins for an instant, she could join them. . . .

:These do not change: said Shadowkiss, roused to speak at last. Against all expectation, she felt the god-sword join its power to hers, protecting her from the enchantment that fought to claim her—

Then the child in her arms struck the sword from her grasp and jerked the reins from her hand with more than human strength. Ruana's horse lunged forward. She clutched at emptiness where the child had been a moment before, and her ears were filled with the sound of Chayol of Lostland's mocking laughter.

A trap!

There was time for one last thought, caught halfway

between anger and despair, as her maddened mount lunged forward to join the spectral *rade*. . . .

And Ruana Rulane was lost.

*

Here was glory and legend, a hero's deeds and the heroes who had done them, their fame outlasting the world they had known. Here she was among her own, in a way she could never be elsewhere. Here was the home she had searched for in all the years she had walked the Glory Road, an end to all uncertainty and pain.

She was sick-dazzled by the glory of it until she nearly missed its grief. But slowly Ruana became aware that beneath the wanton ecstasy was a joyless, choiceless desperation. Here indeed was all the joy of battle, of war, and of slaughter—of every art that the Twiceborn had first learned, then forsworn to take up Shadowkiss.

And nothing more. Only the need to go on and on in the only way they knew, without hope of release.

Trapped.

As she was trapped.

These do not change, Shadowkiss had said. Was she, too, condemned to ride forever, a helpless prisoner of Lostland?

In that moment Ruana Rulane realized what she would have known from the first, without the *rade*'s strong spells to trick and dazzle her.

Shadowkiss was gone.

Pure panic struck her. To be without the dreaming sword was a bereavement unspeakable, a loss too profound for words.

Yet it must, in some fashion, be an illusion. She clung to that knowledge as to a weapon in battle. She could not surrender the sword, nor could it be taken from her while she lived. And no one living could touch the sword and live while she was its companion.

But they could be kept apart. And she would be responsible for all it killed in that time.

And she could die.

And Shadowkiss would be free to mate again.

Suddenly she saw a flash of green fire on the horizon.

Shadowkiss.

The sight of it gave her strength beyond her own. She forced her mount to the edge of the Hunt, but not all her will could break free of them.

There was no need. The glint of green fire upon the horizon was the destination of every one of the riders. The emerald flame of the blade drew them onward like an earthbound sun, like the first hint of spring after winter, and she could feel through the link that bound her to the *rade* the yearning of every member in it for her sword key to the chains that bound them prisoner, for the god-sword was Death Itself.

She must reach it first. No living thing could claim her sword, but she did not know what might happen if these members of the spectral *rade* should try.

She raked her spurs along her horse's ribs, working her way forward along the edge of the Hunt. Now she could see it clearly. Shadowkiss stood thrust into a cairn of skulls that stood heaped as tall as the shoulder of a horse.

For one brief instant as the Hunt reached the cairn, its members ceased to think as one. They turned upon one another, each fighting to prevent his fellow from reaching the cairn first. And in that instant, the sorcery that had bound Ruana Rulane to the eldritch Hunt failed—for just an instant—and she was free.

She jerked her horse's head aside, putting distance between herself and a tall woman with furnace eyes who swung at her with a hooked sword. In the last instants that the Hunt swirled, indecisive, behind her, Ruana drove her flagging mount toward the cairn. Behind her, the Hunt reformed itself, at last seeing her as an enemy. Again, the riders swarmed around her, but this time Ruana would not look. She kept her eyes fixed upon her sword.

And she reached it first.

Her hand slipped over the naked blade and was flayed to the bone, but she forced her bleeding fingers to close upon the hilt. The Hunt was all around her now, circling her, never stopping. She flung the sword up and brandished it defiantly.

But still she did not look.

Shadowkiss flashed in her hands, as if it drew illumination from some place outside this world. The tempo of the circling riders increased, and the thunder of their horses' hooves, and from every throat issued a wail of such despair as made Ruana wish somehow to stop her ears so that she could not hear it.

But the sword was hers again.

Then all at once the Hunt was gone, and she was alone.

Or nearly.

"I have tried to save you."

He had returned, the pale king on his pale horse. With an effort, Ruana forced herself to meet his eyes.

"Do you know what you have done, and what you will yet do?" Chayol of Lostland asked.

He was as she had first seen him, in his armor the color of the night sky, a hammer at his hip. The black iron crown was dark upon his brow, and perhaps its pale gem now shone less bright.

"No one knows what they *will* do," Ruana answered evenly, slowly lowering her sword. Her blood dripped down its blade, dimming the light of the flaring jewels.

"Yet you have chosen the future," Chayol Warhammer answered. "For yourself and for many, knowing or otherwise. And so, in the end, just as it was for me, there will be no refuge for you anywhere."

She tightened her aching hand upon the sword hilt, feeling it slippery with blood. She wondered if she must fight again for Shadowkiss and wondered if this time she would win. But Chayol's face was becoming hard to see, growing small and distant at the same time, like something seen through the lens of a dream, and even her pain was a far-off thing.

*

She roused, as if from momentary inattention, and heard the rattle of cart wheels on the road not far ahead.

Her hands were empty, her sword a reassuring weight upon her back. The morning sun was bright.

Her hands were whole and unscathed.

She took a deep breath of air—true honest living air,

ripe with the smells of horse and decay. She heard the creak of leather and the sound of horses behind her, and turning in her saddle, she saw her men behind her, all present.

She touched her heels gently to her horse's sides, and rode forward, and a few minutes later, saw a caravan's outriders moving toward them along the road. She greeted them in the name of the Gray Duke, and rode to the wagonmaster to get his news.

The road was open to the east. A tree had fallen, a rockslide had blocked the road for many days. . . .

And she knew somehow that what the wagonmaster told her was both true and not-true; a truth that had only become true because of what she had done in Lostland, and what she had brought out of there.

—If she had surrendered to Chayol, or fallen to him in battle—

—If she had lost herself to the Hunt, or if someone else within it had claimed the god-sword Shadowkiss—

—If she had simply never come out of Lostland at all—

Then all these things might be different, and the Eastern Spur Road still bare and silent, haunted and empty, choked with ghosts, herself and her men vanished forever.

But Ruana Rulane was a hero, and she had prevailed. And having prevailed, so it was that the silence on the road turned out to have had such a homely ordinary cause as no man might wonder at.

She looked back at her men, and from their faces she knew that none of them remembered the cries in the night, nor wakening in the morning to find their numbers dwindling day by day. She had ransomed them from a dream, and as dreams do, it had faded upon wakening. They remembered merely that they had ridden out upon the road and met the caravan upon the way. Nothing more.

But she remembered more. She had brought not only herself and her men out of Lostland, but memory as well.

But if she had taken something out of Lostland, then she had left something behind as well.

Certainty.

When she had first taken up Shadowkiss and set her will against that of the god-sword, she had thought only of the deaths she would avert by keeping the sword from wakening the Crownking and setting men's feet on the road to the Final War.

She had not thought, when she made that vow, that there might be something worse than such a war. Before she had journeyed into Lostland, she had thought the Dreaming Sword was Death alone, forgetting that every sword has two edges.

But she had ridden with the Hunt, and now she knew differently. The other edge of the blade she carried was Change. And perhaps all that she had pledged her future to save might die a worse and different kind of death without the Change that she held in her hands and would not release into the world.

If all things died in their season, then surely worlds died as well?

She would not break her vow. She dared not, for the sake of all the innocents she had sworn to save. But on this day, and every day to come, the sky would be less blue, the air less sweet, than they had been before she had ridden out along the Eastern Spur Road. She would remember for ever more the Hunt, the desperate unchanging eternity of it, the special hopeless terror of creatures condemned to go on forever, without any capacity to be other than what they were.

To learn. To grow. And perhaps, in the end, to die as they were meant to.

:These do not change: Shadowkiss had said, and in the sword's words had been something like grief.

She was what she was. She knew she was set upon her course and would not turn aside from it. The world before hers had made the sword, and while Rulane Twiceborn held it there would be no world after. That was the vow she had made, and she would keep it.

But was she right?

PLOWSHARES

by Rebecca Maines

Medieval fantasies has to work hard to transcend the stereotype, and I think this one does the job nicely. Author Rebecca Maines has published short fiction in *The Magazine of Fantasy & Science Fiction* and *Amazing Stories* (writing as Pamela Hodgson), and assorted anthologies. Her short story collection, *Ex Cathedra,* will appear as part of the *Twilight Tales Presents* series in 2004. When not writing, she spends her time working as a medical editor, living and dying with the Chicago Cubs, proving to the guys in her Krav Maga (martial art) class that a woman her age should be taken very seriously, and being worshipped by a husband and five cats.

Elisabeth's feet ached with each footfall against the still winter-hardened dirt of the road, but the exhilaration from the pilgrimage helped her rise above it; she had just to remember the magnificence of the soaring cathedral, its sculpted face gleaming heavenly white against the overcast sky as if the stone itself were lit from within by divine power. Now, tramping between the wheel ruts, three days' walk from Canterbury and three days yet to her home village, she wanted rest but permitted the memory of the divine vision to sustain her. And drive out of her mind the fear of what might await.

"We'll stop for the night at the next town, only an hour's walk on," said William, the pallid, gray-haired priest who had become by mutual assent the leader of their group of a dozen travelers. Despite a complexion the color of an ice-covered pond, he was muscular, a sturdy bulk that exuded such a sense of security that Elisabeth couldn't help but trust him and feel safe in his presence.

And safety was important in these times. Especially after what they had seen at the previous night's stopping place.

The sun, already starting low, peeked for a moment from behind a cloud, brightened the spring green of the fields on either side of the path, and a breeze carried their sweet grass scent. Elisabeth had chosen to undertake this journey early in the year because she would be less missed now than later in the season, when she would work with the men at harvest time. She was young and strong, a widow in a village whose men had been taken in greater numbers than women by illness in the past winter. Her new husband had been one of those. And so, because she had a strong back and no children, she would work as a man when she was needed. But first, she had needed to make this pilgrimage. In a year that had made her doubt the existence of God, she had needed to see something to inspire her back to faith. And she had needed time away to think, to grieve, to learn to live without the young man she had so recently learned to live with, who had so easily become a part of her.

The memories made her sad, and once again she retreated to thoughts of the glorious cathedral, recollections of running her warm fingers over the icy marble pillars, watching the colored light cast through the windows' edge across the floor with the passing of the hour, kneeling on the hard stone floor at the memorials to martyrs. And yes, praying. She had prayed there, too. But that was not what had restored her faith; it was the building itself, the fact of something so immense and magnificent. It could only exist if God Himself had inspired the men who had built such soaring towers, cut the intricate figures in the stone. In that knowledge of inspiration, she found her renewal of faith. In that recollection, she would find strength to determine what work it was that God wanted of her. She still had no idea, but she was certain God would reveal it to her in time.

At nightfall they reached the town Father William had mentioned. This was a larger town than last night's village, with thatched houses crowded near one another, and even a priest in residence. She sighed and pushed her unruly hair back up under her cap. Bandits like the dreadful Dark Men would not terrorize a town of this size. She hoped.

Father William talked with the town's priest, and soon they found themselves welcomed. The inn was full for the night, but they supped there, and then Father William and the other priest, Father John, found them accommodation with families in town.

Elisabeth spent the night sharing a straw bed with the three young daughters of the town's blacksmith and his wife. The oldest girl, Hannah, was ten years old. She had spent the evening begging Elisabeth for tales of her journey, stories of faraway places like Canterbury that she dreamed of seeing. Now, as they settled themselves in the loft of the house, the burnt-wood aroma of the dying fire below wafting up to them, Hannah was not sated. She leaned close and whispered in Elisabeth's ear. "Did you hear of any bandits?" she asked conspiratorially.

Should she tell the truth, and risk frightening the child? Or herself—she wasn't sure she was ready to talk of such things. The previous night, she had seen the result of what bandits might do.

But she was saved the decision as the child rattled on. "I've heard men who come see my father from other villages say that the Dark Men are about. Do you know about the Dark Men? They're the most evil bandits . . . they take what they want and go on their way, with a promise that they'll return—and you better have something else to give them when they come back, or they might kill all the men and take all the women with them.

"That's what I heard said, anyway. But I don't believe it. You couldn't travel around being bandits with all the women from whole towns in tow," the child concluded smugly.

They might kill them instead, Elisabeth thought but didn't say. After they've defiled them.

"I wonder what they're like, the Dark Men," the girl

mused. "If they came here, I would hide by the forge and peep out and watch them and see what they were like, and then when they were gone I would come out again.

"Unless they tried to hurt my sisters," she said in a reassuring tone to the two smaller girls, both of whom were almost but not quite asleep. "Then I'd leap out with a knife and cut them wide open just like butchering a stag! Their innards would spill out—"

"Hannah, do I hear you talking?" the blacksmith's wife's voice filtered up from below. "Be quiet and let your sisters—and our guest—sleep."

Hannah let out a long-suffering sigh and closed her eyes. Elisabeth stroked the girl's thick, charcoal-colored hair and hoped that her innocent fantasies wouldn't be intruded upon by the reality of the Dark Men and their works any time soon.

It was too late for such a hope for herself. She thought of the previous night's stop—the sign of a trio of crossed sticks in the road, upright and meeting in a point, the mark the Dark Men left. The woodsmoke smell, which at first she'd taken to be cookfires, took on a new meaning with that sign, and sure enough, soon they'd come upon a village where three of the houses closest to the road were still smoldering.

The Dark Men were known to be the worst of the bandits in these parts. Their sign made it known to other bandits that this town was theirs now. Just as Hannah had said, it was their custom to take what they chose from a village or town, including some of the young women, but leave enough goods behind for the villagers to rebuild. Then, having laid claim to this village, the Dark Men would return and harvest its goods and women again.

And their sign reminded passersby that no village was safe from them.

She had heard of the works of the Dark Men, but they had never been close enough to her own village for her to have seen what they had done before. When she'd seen their sign in the center of the road as they approached the village the previous night, she'd felt her knees weaken and smelled fear on herself and her companions.

William had called for quiet so he could be heard. His voice was as strong as his body, and so in a moment, they all quieted. When he'd addressed them, his voice had carried and echoed around them as if they were in a cavern rather than a wood. "At least we know the bandits are gone," he'd said, gesturing at the marker. "Better than coming on them at their work, and risking ourselves." Several people nodded. "And perhaps we can be of Christian service to the people here."

Not all the travelers had left Canterbury as inspired as Elisabeth had, she knew from talking with them, but they all knew better than to contradict the priest. Whether they felt inclined to be of service or not, they would do as he said, because it was politic—and because if there were bandits in the area, they would rather be under the protection of the burly priest than not.

As they had approached the village, an old man had burst from the doorway of a house that was damaged but still standing. "Who are you? We have nothing! You've seen the sign!" he'd shouted, waving a shaking finger toward the road. There were deep, angry lines in his face.

Father William had raised his hands as if in benediction. "We are pilgrims. We had hoped for your hospitality, before we saw the sign. But now, seeing that, we've come to see if there is anything *we* can offer *you*."

Reluctantly, the man had led them into the center of the village, shouting out as they went. "They're pilgrims, not bandits. They have a priest."

Father William's services were wanted, to say a blessing at the burial of two men the bandits had killed. The other men in their group went along to help dig the graves.

The rest of the travelers set their hands to preparing a meal of soup with the women of the village, and gathering straw to make beds in corners and stables, wherever there was space for them to sleep. The able-bodied

agreed that the next morning they would help the villagers with a few tasks of repair before the group went on
its way.

Elisabeth found herself sitting on the dirt floor of the
largest house in the village, where the women of village
and pilgrimage had assembled, chopping vegetables next
to a woman whose chestnut hair was newly streaked with
gray. Where the men she'd seen so far in this village
were bent, almost cowering, this woman stood strong and
tall, with a fiery glint in her hazel eyes. She'd said her
name was Merylla. Hesitantly, Elisabeth asked her about
the bandits.

"They took my daughter," Merylla said matter-of-
factly.

Elisabeth gasped.

The older woman nodded. She glanced toward the
open doorway and the sounds of two small children
squealing and running outside. "The strongest of the
older girls here, three of them, are gone now. I don't
know . . ."—she turned away—"when we'll see our Maggie again."

Elisabeth wanted to ask what they'd done to the girls
and women of the village, whether they'd been violated,
but she couldn't think of a proper way to ask it. She
looked across at another of the village women, a young
one with a bitter line to her mouth and dark circles under
her eyes, and drew her conclusion from that. Her stomach fluttered with fear knowing that she was walking the
same ground these villains had trod. She drove thoughts
of her own village out of her mind, as if thinking of it
might draw the evil to it.

"The two men . . ." Elisabeth tilted her head toward
the direction Father William had gone with some of the
village men. "Did they fight the Dark Men . . . ?"

The hard-worn younger woman snorted, and Merylla
shot her an angry look, and another look over her shoulder to where the men had gone. The younger woman's
chin tilted upward and she looked past Merylla to Elisabeth. Her knife thunked sharply through a root. "Not
much of a loss, those two, if you ask me."

"Shush! Don't talk that way!" the other women in their circle chorused.

"Please pay no mind to her," Merylla said softly to Elisabeth. Elisabeth waved her apology away. She understood that terrible events might lead a person to say things she never would otherwise. She knew it from the days after her own loss. She put her attention into the paring of carrots, and the rest of the women worked quietly as well.

In the morning, she rolled her sleeves and lent her strength to the repair of the burned houses. As she'd walked around the village, she'd noted that the damaged buildings were the ones closest to the road; those farther away were mostly left in no more than disarray, as if the bandits had wanted to make a sign of the damage, like their sign in the crossroad.

After they'd helped with the work and taken a breakfast of porridge, the pilgrims set off. The men of the village warned them to beware the bandits. Merylla had patted Elisabeth on the shoulder, gave her strong arm a squeeze. "You'll be fine," she said. "If anywhere in your travels you hear of a golden-haired girl of fifteen named Maggie . . ."

Elisabeth squeezed the woman's arm in return, lifted her small pack onto her back, and followed after her companions.

At a crossroads they'd seen again the sign of the Dark Men, down a cross that wasn't in their path. Father William didn't suggest that they turn and see if those villagers needed aid; instead he'd hurried onward on their own path toward the town where she now laid her head next to the three young girls, finally sleeping, piled across one another like puppies. She curled herself against them and drifted off to her own sleep.

When she woke it was still deep dark. Hannah was shaking her, hard. "Lisbeth! Lisbeth!" the child hissed. "They're here!"

"W-what?" Elisabeth muttered, still half asleep.

"The Dark Men. I think it's the Dark Men!"

Elisabeth sat upright. "What?" And as she came fully

awake, she heard clatter and shouts outside. She pulled her cloak tight around her, but it couldn't stop her shivering.

Below them, the door to the blacksmith's house was thrown open with a sharp crack, and three hooded figures burst through it, brandishing torches. "Out! Everyone outside!" a young man's voice shouted. One of his compatriots prodded the blacksmith and his wife where they slept, urging them toward the door.

Elisabeth was torn—should she and the children stay in the loft and hope they were overlooked? Or would these Dark Men burn the house, and them in it? She drew Hannah and the slowly waking younger girls close to her.

She was spared the decision. As the blacksmith's wife was herded toward the doorway she shot a frightened look over her shoulder toward the loft ladder. It didn't go unnoticed. One of the bandits turned and bounded toward the ladder.

It should have been the other way around, but Elisabeth took her strength from Hannah. The ten-year-old peered over the rim of the loft. Elisabeth prayed the bandits would at least spare the children. For herself, she didn't dare pray.

The bandit was lithe as he climbed the ladder. Beneath his hood, his face was swathed in dark cloth. Only bright blue eyes were visible. The eyes didn't look angry; they weren't cold. Elisabeth let that give her hope that this one would be merciful.

"Come down, girls," the bandit said. "How many of you are there?" He reached over and drew Mary, the youngest girl at four, toward the ladder. Mary rubbed her eyes and with a look of question to Hannah, she followed the bandit down. The others followed in order of age, with Elisabeth last.

They stood in a line at the foot of the ladder, waiting to see what would happen next. The bandit looked them up and down. Elisabeth shrunk back a step. The bandit laughed. "You look a sturdy young woman," he said. He reached out and felt the muscles of her arm. "You help in the smithy?"

It took her a moment to find her voice. "No," she whispered. It was all she could manage.

"She's a visitor," Hannah piped up. "A pilgrim. She's been to Canterbury." Torchlight glimmered and reflected in the little girl's dark eyes.

"Ah. And you, you're the smith's daughter then."

"Uh-huh." She sounded proud. Elisabeth admired her courage, hoped it would not cost the child.

A shout echoed from outside—a gravelly voiced shout, and another, and a third that rose into a scream of pain. Elisabeth grabbed Hannah's shoulder and drew her back, away from the bandit. Her fingers dug into the girl's shift and the skin below it.

"It's all right," the bandit said.

It's all right? What a stupid thing to say! Elisabeth thought. What fools did he think they were? She found her voice all of a sudden, and a strong voice it was. *"Get out of here!"* she bellowed, her voice deep with anger, full. "Leave these girls alone!"

To her amazement, the bandit backed toward the doorway. He leaned half out and called to someone outside. "I've got a likely one here! Bring the others."

Had she sealed their doom? It didn't matter what happened to her, Elisabeth thought, but she should have found a way to get the children to safety. Perhaps she could still bargain; perhaps she could consent to the vile deeds they would demand of her—she shuddered at the thought—in return for the children's release. She felt herself trembling, and wrapped her arms around herself to give herself strength. There was clamor and shouting rising from every direction now outside the house, and she could smell smoke.

She prayed for herself now. She prayed that when they were done with her, they would at least kill her.

Other women were shoved into the blacksmith's house. Most were young—not as young as the three children, but some only a little older; others were Elisabeth's age or more, but none were much more than a score. The bandits who herded them in prodded the women to form a line. They closed the door.

Elisabeth urged the two younger girls back toward the wall behind the loft ladder. She and Hannah stood their ground along with two dozen others.

The bandits—there were again three, though by their builds, Elisabeth didn't think it was the same three who had first entered this house—walked up and down, reviewing the women, looking at them the way one might examine cattle.

One of the bandits stopped, fingered a bruise on a fair-haired woman's face. "How came you by this?"

The woman didn't speak, turned her eyes down. The bandit took her chin between fingers and raised it to look more closely.

Hannah leaned in close to Elisabeth and whispered. "There are only three of them in here, there's a lot more of us. Why don't we just fight them?" the child asked.

Elisabeth tilted her head toward the nearest bandit, nodded toward the gleam of metal at his belt, matched by the other bandits. "They are armed."

Hannah snorted. "So what. How many of us can they stab at once?"

It was a child's logic. Elisabeth took the girl's hand to keep her from trying something that might cost her life. "Shush," she whispered.

The woman with the bruise had still not answered as to its cause. Finally, another young woman answered the question. "Her husband did it. That and more, I'll warrant," she said. "He's a worse villain than any bandit."

"Is that true?" the bandit asked the fair-haired woman. The woman nodded. "His name is?"

"Ewan Baker," the woman answered softly. She began to tremble.

The bandit nodded and went to the door. He stuck his head out and said a few words to someone outside and returned.

"See, there are guards," Elisabeth whispered to Hannah, to further cure the girl of dangerous ideas.

"We could still do it," the child whispered back petulantly.

"Still do what?" a bandit asked, turning toward them. Elisabeth's breath caught and held. She drew Hannah back, tried to put the girl behind her. But the bandit reached out, grabbed the child's arm and drew her forward, away from the others, and spun her around, so the bandit's back was to Elisabeth as he faced the child. He stooped to the girl's eye level, leaned close to her face, and pulled at something near his face—took down his mask? The child let out a gasp.

And then the little girl laughed.

The bandit turned back toward the line of women, the scarf that had been a mask now dangling. Elisabeth saw under the hood the face of a young, golden-haired girl. "Maggie?" she asked.

The woman laughed. "No. Maggie's elsewhere." She nodded in the general direction of the door. Things had grown somewhat quieter outside, although the sounds of movement, people passing back and forth, were still evident. And she could smell something burning.

"All of you—" she addressed all the women "—have a secret to keep now. We'll trust you with it, but not your menfolk." The other two bandits drew their masks down, and revealed themselves to be a swarthy woman of Elisabeth's age and an older woman—the age Elisabeth's mother would be were she still alive—with a strong mouth and sparkling eyes, and a deep scar across her cheek.

The older woman fingered the scar on her face, looking toward the young woman with the bruise. "My husband did this," she said. "He'll not hurt a woman again." She looked along the line, then back at the blonde woman. "And your husband won't hurt you again." The young woman's eyes widened.

"You may call me Eve," the older woman continued. "This is how it works. If you are asked what we did to you, each of you will claim to your fathers and husbands and brothers that some of the other women were ravished here, but that you were spared. Other than that, you'll not talk of it.

"Then you will bring us all of your valuables, and show

us where you keep your supplies. We will take what we need, and a souvenir or two to prove we've been here. You will hide the rest, and tell your men it was all stolen. Gradually, as need arises, you may each 'find' an item here and there that we must have forgotten or dropped." She grinned.

"Then we'll erect our symbol in the road, and that should frighten off any others who might rape and rob you in truth.

"Do you understand?"

The women had all been silent, but now they erupted in mutters and whispers. This couldn't be, it just couldn't—they'd heard so much of the work of the Dark Men—

"But where are the Dark *Men?*" Hannah's high voice pierced the noise and silenced it.

The woman called Eve laughed. "You're looking at three of them.

"And if any of you would care to join us, you would be welcome."

"You're all *women?*" Hannah was incredulous.

Eve nodded.

"Do you fight?" The child pointed at the knife on Eve's belt.

"When we have to. And we'll teach any of you who join us."

Another woman, the one who'd named the blonde woman's husband for what he'd done, put her hands on hips. "You want us to think you're on our side, but your friends are out there burning our town, and for all we know killing the rest of our families and neighbors."

Eve nodded, in understanding rather than agreement. "We've burned two houses, one at each end of the town nearest the road. The women there were allowed to remove their most necessary possessions first. If we don't leave damage, we can hardly persuade the other groups of bandits of our reality. Otherwise they will think you've simply erected our sign in your road. We need there to be proof."

"But you killed two men in the last village I visited!"

Elisabeth said, her anger rising. "That was no ruse—I saw their bodies. You're murderers!"

Eve drew a knife, and Elisabeth shrank back. She pushed Hannah away from her, and the woman to her other side drew away as well. She was a stranger here; no one would help her. Elisabeth closed her eyes and waited for the strike, waited to meet her husband in heaven.

Eve's breath was on her face as she spoke. "Girl, did you ask who those dead men were?" Her voice rippled with anger.

There was a long silence, and finally Elisabeth filled it with a whispered "no." Her voice echoed in the silence. She could smell the mix of road dirt and sweat on Eve's tunic. She could taste her own fear like blood on her tongue.

"They did to their people what we are accused of. One of them raped his daughter when she was no older than this one." Elisabeth opened her eyes and saw the woman gesture with her knife toward Hannah's next-younger sister. "The other's wife was dead—of a beating he had given her. And was ready to do the same with his new wife."

Elisabeth remembered the woman who'd said the men were no loss. She remembered how Merylla and the others had shushed her. Yes, it made sense. She saw from the corner of her eye that the other women were looking at her, awaiting her judgment. She nodded. With a long exhale, Eve stepped back from her. It felt as if the entire room had exhaled as one.

"Your mothers and grandmothers—all of the older women—are in another house," Eve said. "They too are learning who we really are. But we are not offering them the chance to join us. This is younger women's work." She smiled toward her two younger compatriots, and Elisabeth could see the weariness in the corners of her eyes.

"If you want to join us," Eve went on, "to travel, to make your own choices and your own way, to do good for yourselves and others like you—to *be* protection rather than to need it—we will say that we've abducted you." She raised the knife. "We will cut your hair, and once we're away, we'll clothe you as a man and teach you what you need to know.

"If you want a different life than the ones you can have here, speak."

Hannah leaped forward. "Me!" she squealed. "I want to go!"

"You're too young yet, little girl," Eve said. "Too small yet to disguise yourself as a man. But when you are a little older, we will be back. Then, if you still want, you are welcome."

The dark woman looked past Hannah to Elisabeth. "But you, traveler—you have spirit. And strength. What waits for you in your home village?"

She thought of the empty bed, the lonely days and nights. The tide of sadness at her core spilled out through every part of her, overwhelmed her. She felt hot all over, on fire.

She stepped forward and in a single move snatched the knife from Eve's hand. Eve didn't resist, simply eyed her, waiting, tensed ready to move, but yet motionless. Elisabeth raised the knife and used it to slash through a hank of her own long hair. She let the tresses scatter on the floor at her feet.

*

"This is the place," Elisabeth said, waving an arm toward the tiny village at the foot of the ridge they had just crested. She smelled the familiar pine that ringed the village, and the dirt rich from the previous night's rain. She recognized the tiny house she and her husband had shared, next to a field that had been her father-in-law's. The previous year's furrows were still visible as mounded lines in the dirt. And in the distance, she saw the too-long line of graves where all who'd fallen to illness had been buried. Her eyes filled.

"We'll camp in the woods until dark," Eve said. "And then, when we go, Elisabeth, you can lead us."

Elisabeth nodded. She felt strong. It was good to be home from her pilgrimage.

STEP BY STEP

by Catherine Soto

Every editor has received submissions that are really novel outlines masquerading as stories, but when an author comes up with a story that has the potential to develop *into* a novel, the reader is left wanting more. That's the case with "Step By Step." I hope we'll be seeing these characters again.

Catherine Soto works in Homeland Security, and that's all she's allowed to say about her job if she wants to remain on the outside of the Federal prison system. She admits to an occasional longing for the old days, when working security required weapons skills instead of a dozen technical certifications. (If this stuff weren't classified, you could get a great Trivial Pursuit game out of it.)

Her favorite hobby is research: her Internet home page has links to a bunch of reference sites—plus the Google toolbar, of course. One of her favorite sites is one that gives relative prices for things in the Middle Ages, but the one she goes to every day is www.thehungersite.com, where you can give food to people who need it with a click of your mouse.

The wind whipped a spatter of rain into Lin Mei's face as she looked up at the dark mass looming ahead of them. The temple was much larger than it had appeared from the road, as well as being very old and abandoned.

The caravan came to a stop in front of it, twenty-two pack horses, four grooms, and ten guards, all soaked from the rain and glad of a place to shelter from the storm.

"There's a barn or something off to the side!" Shin Hu, the caravan master, yelled over the wind. "Get the horses in it and the packs off and under a dry roof!"

Lin Mei dismounted, slipping in the muddy puddles.

She and the other grooms held reins and leads in cold wet hands barely able to grip them and led the horses toward the dark outbuilding beside the temple.

Biao Mei, her brother, paused for a moment as he passed her. "Keep moving," he told her quietly. "You shiver when you stop." He looked at her worriedly. Although he had only fifteen years to her seventeen, he was stocky and muscular while she was slender and willowy, although far tougher and stronger than she looked.

She nodded and walked as quickly as she could to the outbuilding and the welcome shelter under the roof. It was just as cold inside as out, but at least the walls cut most of the wind and the leaky roof kept out almost all of the rain, and unsaddling and grooming the horses would warm her quickly enough.

It was hard work, Lin Mei thought, but it was better than their last job had been—and much better than the death her uncle had planned for her and her brother. They had survived, and now they worked toward the restoration of their house and their honor.

"Grain for the horses!" Togrul Magh said, coming up with a heavy bag on his shoulder. A long bow protruded from over the squat and stocky nomad's other shoulder. Lin Mei gave him a quick smile. He had been kind to them, getting her brother a job as a guard and her as a groom with this caravan.

"Good if we get some for ourselves too!" another guard said. "These horses eat better than we do!"

"Rice is cooking in the temple building," Togrul said. "We eat as soon as the horses are seen to!" He balanced the sack on his shoulder and slit it open with a slash of his dagger, then poured a golden spout of grain into one of the troughs alongside the wall.

"Now we can eat!" Togrul said. There was some low laughter and he led them all through a door to the main hall of the temple, each of them stopping for a moment at the door to make obeisance to the front of the hall. There was no longer an image or idol of whatever deity the temple had been raised to, but no luck was gained by disrespect to the gods and spirits that ruled these mountains.

A fire burned in the center of the empty hall where a hearth had been laid. A frame of iron rods supported a trio of kettles over the flames.

"The rice and tea are ready," Shin Hu said. "Everyone, get your bowls out." Rice bowls and teacups came out from their packs. Biao Mei took a spot near the fire with the other guards, and Lin Mei squeezed into a small space next to him.

Togrul heaped a mound of steaming rice into her bowl with a wide grin then poured her some tea. She nodded her thanks and held the bowl close to her, enjoying the warmth for a moment before digging into it and wolfing down mouthfuls of the steaming rice.

She smiled wryly to herself. To such simple pleasures had her life shrunk to. The past was gone, she lived in the present, and the present was good, if sometimes uncomfortable. It was also a step toward the future. Lin Mei was determined, but not impatient. She and Biao Mei would reach their goal, but there was much to be learned before they could return to their distant home and take on their uncle.

"We'll sleep in one of the back rooms," her brother said. He indicated a door by the wall near the back of the hall. He stuck his sword back in his sash, and then gathered up his pack and a glowing torch from the fire. She took up her pack and followed.

The door opened onto a short hallway with two doors at the end. He went to the left hand one and opened it to reveal a room that had apparently been a storage space at some time. Straw baskets were stacked against the corner and a pair of cracked pots lay in the other corner. He grabbed one and stuck the torch in it, making a crude lamp. They unrolled their sleeping mats, and they lay down, covering themselves with their wool cloaks for warmth.

But as soon as she lay down, Lin Mei noticed an odor she was all too familiar with.

"Biao Mei," she whispered urgently. "I smell something dead!"

His hand reached out to his sword, pulling the long blade to his side as he sat up on his bedroll. "Pine needles, mold, damp grass," he cataloged, sniffing the air. "Horses, people, but nothing dead."

"I smell it!" she insisted. He looked at her. "Maybe it's on this side," she said.

Sighing, he got up and came over to her side of the room, sitting down beside her and inhaling the air.

"You're right!" he said. "It's here!" He stood, his sword scabbard clenched in his left hand, right hand on the hilt ready to draw.

"It's not too big," she said. "I suspect it may be some small animal. But it's recently dead. It's under us," she said, standing up and pulling her dagger from her sash. Grumbling, Biao Mei took the torch out of the cracked bowl and swung it around, causing the embers to blaze again. Lin Mei was already prying up the floorboards with the point of the dagger.

Biao Mei stepped forward to shine the light of the torch down into the darkness under the floor as she pulled the last of three floorboards up. The stench of death rose.

Biao Mei leaned over, the flame dangerously close to his face as he peered into the opening. He made a face.

"It's two creatures," he said. "Joined together in death." Lin Mei looked down and gasped.

In truth there were two animals dead under the floorboards. Two dead animals, so tightly wound around each other's bodies were they that an immediate identification was almost impossible, but Lin Mei had seen this exact sight before—in a dream six years earlier.

That had been the dream she dreamed the night that their home was attacked, the night their family had been wiped out. The dream had wakened her and enabled her to hide herself and her younger brother among the servants who survived the attack. She learned the smell of death well on that night.

"The cat and the weasel!" she exclaimed in a low

voice. The weasel's jaws were locked in death on the cat's throat as tightly as the cat's jaws were locked on the weasel's spine. Her brother made a sound of disgust as he looked into the opening.

"Weasel," he muttered. "That explains the smell!" They both examined the tangled bodies below them. The fur on both was matted with blood and torn, but color and markings were still visible. The cream color and dark face markings of the cat were a sharp contrast to the dark reddish brown of the weasel.

"They died together in combat," Biao Mei noted.

"It was a mother!" Lin Mei said. "See her belly?" Biao Mei looked, nodding unconsciously. The skin on the cat's underbody was distorted; she had obviously been a nursing mother.

"She was protecting her cubs!" Lin Mei said. "The weasel came hunting and she fought him!"

"Dead men tell no tales," Biao Mei said, "and neither do dead cats. Do not be so sure you know what happened here."

"What else?" she asked in reply. "Be quiet!" Her eyes grow cloudy as she listened to the sounds around her. The details of her long-ago dream resurfaced in her mind, as clear as if she were just now awakening from it.

"Over there!" she said, indicating a direction closer to the door. She stepped quickly to the door and began prying up more loose floorboards until she heard a low mewling sound.

"There!" she exclaimed, reaching down into the void. Carefully she pulled up a mass of dried grass, obviously bedding for the two tiny furred bodies resting on it.

"They're near death," her brother said brusquely. "We were too late to save them. With their mother dead, they are doomed."

"No," she said. "They are not. We were not, and they will not be!" She cradled the two kittens in a fold of her sleeve. They were barely breathing, their eyes still shut.

"But they will die!" Biao Mei said in exasperation.

"No!" she said. "There is a mare with milk in the caravan. She can spare a few drops for such a pair of small mouths as these." She stood and went to her pack taking out her teacup, then went back to the door and opened it, stepping quietly out into the hallway. Biac Mei followed in silence.

Lin Mei padded quietly back into the main hall of the temple, which was filled with the snores of sleeping men. One, Togrul, was missing, doubtlessly outside on the first watch. The others were sound asleep. She passed through the door into the stables, not waiting for her brother to catch up. The mare was at the far end, her colt curled up on the straw next to her. Lin Mei cut a strip of cloth from the sack Togrul had used to bring in grain for the horses and twisted it into a wick. With soothing words and hands she gentled the mare, then milked a small amount of the milk from her udder into her teacup. When it was half full she sat cross-legged on the floor and settled the kittens onto her lap, then dipped one end of the twisted strip of cloth into the warm milk and held it to the mouth of one of the kittens.

Slowly, almost painfully, the kitten was trying to open its mouth. Lin Mei held the strip of cloth against the tiny snout, letting a drop of warm milk form on the muzzle.

It was enough. The moisture on the drop of milk was sufficient to moisten the caked tissues and allow the mouth to open just enough for her to squeeze a drop of warm mare's milk into the tiny open mouth. She dipped the cloth back into the teacup and held it against the other kitten's muzzle. She alternated between them for a while, feeding them drops of milk as they grew in strength and began to suck from the scrap of twisted cloth as if they had been nursing at their own mother's side. Finally the milk was gone and the two tiny bodies were satiated.

"They're asleep," she said.

"As we should be," her brother commented. She made a face and wrapped the two kittens into another scrap of cloth cut from the grain bag.

"We won't be likely to leave early," she told him. "Shin Hu won't want to start in this storm until we've had some food to keep us warm on the journey. We might even be able to sleep late!''

"I wish,'' her brother muttered. "But let's not tempt fate by staying out here. Those cats set a good example. Let's get some sleep ourselves!'' He led her out of the barn and back into the main hall where the snores of the sleeping men told them no one had been disturbed by their nighttime antics.

"The rain is fierce tonight,'' Lin Mei said in a low voice, pointing to the roof where the sound of drumming raindrops made a low staccato on the tiles. "Maybe we should take some tea out to Togrul, since we're already up anyway.''

"First the cats, now Togrul,'' he sighed. He followed her as she picked her way to the fire and lifted the tea kettle off the hook over the embers.

"It's still warm, and there's almost a cupful,'' she said, hefting it. "Enough to help Togrul stay awake.'' Biao Mei looked at the door, listening to the rain hitting the roof above them.

"I'll take it out to him,'' he said. "No sense you getting cold and wet, especially since you're carrying those two kittens.'' He took the kettle from her and began to pick his way through the dark around the snoring men on the floor. Lin Mei smiled in the darkness, holding the bundled kittens against her body with one hand.

She looked around her at the dim interior of the temple. The cream colored cats with dark faces were often used as temple guardians, she recalled. Most likely these two were descended from the temple's cats left behind when the temple was abandoned. Suddenly a flash of lighting flared in the night outside, illuminating the hall through cracks in the door.

"Intruders!'' she screamed, seeing a shadowy form perched on a beam above her. She jumped to the side, pulling her dagger loose with her free hand, while she tucked the kittens into her sash with the other.

Biao Mei spun on his heel, dropping the tea kettle and grasping a lance from where it lay on the floor. With a sudden snap he threw it upward into the dark at the movement he had spied up there, a dark shadow against darker background.

A grunt showed he had struck home. All around them bodies stirred to wakefulness, alerted by Lin Mei's scream. Shin Hu was on his feet first, his sword flashing loose from its scabbard, a flash of steel in the light from the fire's embers.

"Alert!" he yelled. "On your feet, you sluggards!"

Suddenly they were in a fight. Black-clothed men dropped down from the rafters, hooded and masked, swords and knives glinting in the firelight. One swung a weighted chain attached to a sickle. The guardsmen came to their feet with the quickness of veteran swordsmen. Biao Mei was fighting in a corner near the door, backed into it by two opponents, his sword out and held two handed. He stepped forward, parried a slash from a shorter straight blade, and dropped to one knee, cutting off the leg of one of his opponents. He left the screaming man to die on the floor and turned his attention to his second opponent. The masked assailant came forward, sword held before him.

Lin Mei took the opportunity to step forward and slash her dagger against the back of his head. In the theater plays of the large cities the heroes on stage disdained such behavior, deeming it ignoble and beneath them. She knew better. Heroes like that just got killed.

The man yelled in pain and turned his head slightly to see who had attacked him from behind. Biao Mei shot forward from the wall and slashed with his blade. The hooded assailant went down with a shouted curse that ended when Lin Mei stepped forward with her dagger in both hands and slashed downward with all her strength, cutting into his rib cage and ending his life.

Biao Mei nodded to her with a grin and jumped past her to join the fray in the room. Lin Mei went up to the first man he had left behind and cut his throat with a quick movement. More than one mortally wounded man had taken several foes with him to whatever hell awaited foolish warriors, and she knew better than to take chances.

That taken care of, she grabbed the man's sword and turned to face the room. She was alone in her corner of the room for the moment. Near her Biao Mei was fighting a heavyset man almost a head taller than he was, his blade clanging as he parried and blocked the man's sword blows. Biao Mei was a good swordsman, but even so he was being forced back by the man's savage strokes.

Lin Mei took her short dagger, flipped it to grip the tip, and threw. In the darkness she misjudged the distance and the dagger struck hilt-first, bouncing off the man's cheek. He turned his face to see where it had come from, his eyes fixing on Lin Mei's willowy form and scowling.

He fell in a jumble, Biao Mei's sword embedded in his skull. Biao Mei jerked his long dagger out and turned to face the next man coming at him, a quick and wiry form with the chain and sickle. But before they could come to blows the hooded man fell, a dagger between his shoulder blades.

The fight was over. All around them there was the sound of heavy breathing as men recovered from the sudden burst of combat.

"Start the fire again!" Shin Hu ordered. "We need light!" Someone stepped up to the hearth and stirred the embers. In moments they flamed and a handful of wood was added. The fire rose, making light where there had been darkness, and they took stock.

Shin Hu was eyeing the rafters above, looking for more enemies. After a few moments, assured they had all been dealt with, he sheathed his sword and eyed the scene about them.

"Biao Mei. See what happened to Togrul!" Biao Mei nodded and went outside to check on the nomad. In moments he was back inside, his face doleful. He looked at Shin Hu and shook his head.

"Poison dart," he said. Shin Hu pursed his lips and nodded, before looking around.

"Who gave the alarm?" he asked.

"Lin Mei did," her brother said. Shin Hu looked at her for a long moment before nodding his head. It seemed almost a salute. He looked around. In a far corner the other grooms cowered, eyes wide and staring at the carnage. Shin Hu looked back at Lin Mei and at the sword in her hand.

"We lost two men," he said. "But it could have been much worse had not you given the alarm. My thanks."

Lin Mei bowed her head in thanks for the praise. Coming from a warrior such as Shin Hu it counted greatly.

"Now," he went on, stepping forward to pull his dagger free from the chain and sickle man, "how is it that you two were up and about?"

"I found some cats," Lin Mei answered, "and we went to the stable to get some mare's milk for them. That is how we happened to be up."

"Cats?" Shin Hu asked. Lin Mei took the bundle from her sash and opened it to display the two tiny forms inside.

"Cats," she said, holding out the bundle for inspection. "Two kittens." Shin Hu looked down at them and grunted with what might have been amusement.

"Cats," he repeated. "Well, it's lucky for us that you were up, or we would have been caught in our sleep by these vermin." He kicked a nearby body with his boot toe. He looked around.

"You three," Shin Hu went on, looking over at the grooms, "go and check on the horses. And be careful." They nodded and left.

Shin Hu looked back at Lin Mei. "Not a bad night's work," he said quietly, "and you fought well, for a groom. With a bit more training," he continued, "you could be a guard, instead of a groom. It's hard work, but the pay is higher. Would that please you?"

I'll need all the training I can get, to win back what is ours, Lin Mei thought, as she bowed assent. "Yes," she said aloud, "it would please me greatly."

FAVOR OF THE GODDESS

by Lynn Morgan Rosser

Lynn Morgan Rosser is a musician who currently directs a choir and teaches private voice lessons for a living. She performs occasionally as a singer-songwriter and has recorded back-up vocals for several contemporary folk artists. Lynn lives in the mountains of western North Carolina with her musician husband, Chris, and her amazing two-year-old son, Aram. Writing is a passion that Lynn has not pursued on a professional level, except through *Sword & Sorceress* (her first sale was in *Sword & Sorceress* XV). She is still working on a few novels and has many unsubmitted short stories lurking in her computer.

Having written my own first stories while working full-time and raising small children, I understand the challenge. I can remember one particularly frustrating day when I had to pour juice for one child or another between every sentence, culminating in a visit from the Fuller Brush man just as I reached the climax of the scene—but I do hope that Lynn will send more stories out and even finish one of those novels one day!

The whirling tumult of West Market, jam-packed and brightly decorated for the month of Holy Moon, blared and flashed just beyond the skulking shadows of the alley where she crouched, nursing a bruised hand. Her fingers were painfully swollen. Her nails, which had started out so finely shaped just three moons ago, had become broken and crusted with grime. A constant cacophony of hawkers, conflicting melodies from street musicians, and the haggling of merchants and pilgrims assaulted her aching head and blurred into her thoughts. Festive rainbow-colored flags painted with the Life Spiral and the Imperial Dragon stirred listlessly in the light ocean breeze.

She had modestly strung up a pair of them in the shadows behind her for privacy, hiding the area she used as a privy. Another flag she had torn into rags for more personal usage. She did not think the City Planners who supplied the pennants would appreciate her creative use of the Sacred Symbols, but then none of them had to live as she did, either. They all resided in the opulent security of the Governor's Quarter with running water and marble sewage systems. She imagined one of the city lords having to camp in a slum alley for a few nights and cracked a wicked grin; it would be far too cruel, really, given they couldn't do the simplest bodily tasks without an army of servants in attendance.

Idly, she bled a small wound on her left pointer finger, worrying it until she thought it cleansed enough to prevent infection. She had fought fervently two nights ago to make this rude corner her own, as if it were holy ground wrested from the grasp of Draonite infidels, and she a Jessonian priest. The pack of six men who had attacked her, thinking her a prostitute and easy prey, would not soon forget the lesson. She'd let them live only for practicality's sake; murdered men tended to attract too much attention.

She smiled grimly underneath her veil, which covered her nose and mouth not out of piety, but to filter the stench of the refuse dump behind her. She knew she stank as well. Her flesh crawled with scents best left to the midden heap and she felt the itch of a constant layer of dust and filth that lay over her once fair skin. Flies felt at home lighting on her body and face; she had given up swiping them away. She sighed. Her limbs felt sore and disjointed. Hunger was a dull weight of stones in her belly that pulled down her shoulders and curved her into herself, and she would not last much longer without food, pure water, and decent shelter. She could see a day coming when she would no longer be able to teach humility to those who would molest her, or to so nimbly escape the Empress Jessiopia's Guard.

She had run for her life from the Guard's persistent efforts to catch her and lost herself in the nameless masses that crowded into the northwest corner of the city. The West Market bumped up against a layer of nicer tenement houses, behind which the slums began. Caravan traffic occasionally flowed in with livestock and wares from the desert tribes bringing trade from the fair-haired peoples in the far northern reaches of the Empire. West Market also bordered Crescent Harbor, which was where the cheaper goods came into the city from the poor Hadasi and Verkoli nations. In addition to those goods, West Market held the stalls of the lesser craftspersons and fabricators that lived on the edges of the slums.

She had run here from East Market near the grand shipyards of Empress Harbor, keeping to shadows and alleys. She had managed to exist there, hiding on the fringes, for a whole week before her robes and body became stained with hard living and the Guard noticed her. She remembered East Market quite fondly. It was a bedazzlement of fine wares, of jewelsmiths, silk merchants, and all manner of amazements and entertainments from far off Maconia, Albatha, and Sennis, the wealthy nations under the rule of the Empress. But East Market was also crawling with Guards who had a knack for arresting lost souls such as herself. The sea-gate walls were bedecked with crows and cages where such unfortunate persons could find themselves if they hadn't the coin to pay corrupt judges for their freedom.

She looked out into the section of the West Market that her alley emptied into, assessing her chances of finding a meal. Across the main avenue, tanners and leather crafters with brown dyed hands showed their wares while to her left, a gap-toothed metalsmith sold cheap brass Goddess icons, singing bowls, meditation gongs, and Crescent Horns along with practical implements for homemaking. On her side of the avenue there was a thin, shifty-eyed rug merchant who sold third rate weavings for second rate prices, and a pretty, olive-skinned wood crafter showing her first efforts in the next stall, with furniture that could grace a middle-class home. Lastly, and most importantly, the food stalls began with semi-fresh vegetables, fruits, and the briny stench of salt-preserved fish and fresh seafood.

Smoke from grilling goat meat along with the wafting fragrances of garlic, onion, cumin, and fresh-baked bread billowed towards her like a fat merchant's breath from the multicolored tent stalls. She licked dry lips. A man who sold figs, dates, almonds, yogurt, and cheeses from a wheeled cart walked by with sharp eyes of warning to her ragged presence, the Jessonian dagger glinting wickedly at his waist. In the City of Jewels, charity was the highly limited province of the Empress' temple and the individual believer was not to be troubled.

She sighed again and slunk back into the depths of the alley to sit with her back against the rough, cool stucco of the wall. Her choices were simple and hard. If she went to beg, the Merchants would call the Guard. If she were caught stealing, they would also call the Guard. If she went to the Temple for bread, the Guard would be at the gates, screening the needy and looking for criminals. If she tried to find honest work, she would have to get the Seal of the Empress and official papers, which would once again alert the Guard. If she fell into the hands of the Guard, she was worse than dead. If she did nothing, she would die of thirst and hunger anyway.

She dropped her head down to stare at the dust at her feet. It was still there, the great black void in her head that kept her a mystery to herself. It was as if she had been born on the street that day when she awakened to find herself with no name, no rank, nothing but servant's robes on her back and no one looking to bring her to an unremembered home. She didn't even understand why the Guard pursued her. Her fighting skills were masterful and honed, which provided some clue. Perhaps she was a renegade Guard, or an assassin, or any number of options that involved skill at killing. She wished she knew—it would make dying for her crimes a little easier to bear if she didn't feel like such an innocent.

A crooked silhouette filled the alley entrance. "Myst?" a high, harsh voice whispered. "You in here?"

She unfolded herself from the shadows and came forward to meet her visitor. "Well met, Magpie. Where have you been? I found us a place to stay." She gestured grandly to the narrow, refuse-filled alley. The hodge-podge tenements on either side created a partial arch and a semblance of shelter from the elements.

"Oh! A room at the palace, I see. Very fancy!" Magpie danced into the alley on her uneven legs. Her black- and silver-streaked hair was a nest of snarls and her clothes a collection of rags and beads. "I knew you'd be a friend to have, Mystery, my girl. That's why I saved you." The woman turned to someone who existed only in her broken mind. "Yes, and the Empress will come to tea with us today? Very fine, very fancy indeed!" A shrill, crazed laugh bit the air. Magpie whirled back to face Myst. "Did you hear? Calopia said we'd take tea with the Empress."

"Yes, yes," Myst soothed, then a smile lit her eyes. "You saved me?" An eyebrow arched over veiled features. "Those two very rude men and I might remember it a little differently."

Magpie grinned, her blackened teeth showing behind thin chapped lips. "Of course I saved you. Who showed you the streets? Who showed you the secret places to hide and the way to beg and the way to borrow?"

She smiled at her friend's questions. "Borrowing," in Magpie's view, was a perfectly fine thing to do, regardless of whether the owner wished to lend and, as her memory for what she had taken from whom was far from stable, most "borrowed" items became permanent possessions.

"Yes, you did do that. But only because I followed you back without your knowing."

Magpie looked crestfallen. "What? No thanks?" She shook her head sadly then crossed her arms and pouted. "Then I shan't tell you what makes today the most special of days." She cocked her head then, as if listening, then stamped her foot. "No, Calopia! She's too ungrateful. I shan't tell her even if you say please!"

"That's fine, Magpie. I don't need to know what makes today special."

"What! But of course you need to know!" Magpie

hobbled over and brought her face close enough so that the tiny red veins that covered her cheeks could be clearly seen on her wizened face. "Today's the Full Moon Procession of the Empress! She hands out all kinds of good things, like coins and sweets and bread and we're going to get some!" Magpie pulled on her as if she were a misbehaving child.

"Magpie, you know I can't go. The Guard will be out in double force during the procession. You go without me."

"I won't!" Magpie stamped her foot again.

"Who will make sure we keep our room at the palace? What if someone takes it?" She gestured again to her hard-won shelter.

"What, this stinking alley?" The old woman chuckled and punched Myst's shoulder. "Coins could buy us a room, dearie, and I'm very good at collecting them." Magpie punctuated her argument with a predatory grin and a poke to Myst's chest.

"Fine. If the Guard catch me and torture me until I scream to die, it will be all your fault." With that Magpie cackled a laugh and twirled her way out into the throng. Mystery followed like a shadow.

*

The Golden Gate of the Imperial Palace opened to the chanting masses and the Empress Jessiopia's ornate divan made its way out slowly amid the protection of a full regiment of her personal Guard, all clad in their deep purple tunics, shining black leather belts, pants, and boots. Sabers with gold tassels swung at their sides, the scabbards glinting gold and silver. The divan was carried by twelve powerful male servants, six to a side, who were naked to the waist with billowing silk pantaloons all the colors of the rainbow and shining silver arm bands. They had turbans swathing their heads that trailed thick cloth down onto the shoulder that carried the heavy wooden beams, padding them from the weight they hefted. As a sign of her Imperial favor, they were tattooed with the Mark of the Empress on their chests; a dragon curved into a Spiral of Life.

The purple velvet and gold thread curtains of the

divan, which also sported the Imperial Dragon, were drawn closed. The cumbersome couch was smothered in gold leaf, with sparkling gems catching the morning light. It was shaped into a stylized dragon whose ferocious head sprouted from the front and whose tail curved and twisted into the Life Spiral behind its body where sat the Empress herself.

"Would you look at that!" Magpie chimed, "One chip off the Empress' chair and we'd be buying a house in the Merchant's quarter." She whistled appreciatively and shook her head in disbelief.

"It could be empty, for all we know. How do we know she's really in there?" Myst said, her eyes narrowed. "I wouldn't be surprised if she's really in the palace taking a bath." Myst stood on tiptoes to see over the throng of chanting pilgrims. "No, wait. I see her hand!"

The curtains parted briefly and a white hand bearing the Dragon Ring gestured at the crowd. The wealthy pilgrims energetically cheered their Empress in her role as the holy representative of the Goddess on earth, while singing her praises as the Bringer of the Harvest, the Light of the Night Sky.

"They should add to her titles, if you ask me," said Myst. "How about 'Protector of Noble Fortunes' or 'The Abandoner of the Poor'?"

Magpie squealed in pleasure. "Calopia says we should call her 'The Many Plowed Field' instead of the 'Bringer of Harvest.'"

Myst laughed at the coarse joke. The servants that bore the Imperial Seal were commonly known as "The Pleasure Guard." The Empress was notorious for her excesses in both men and luxury.

"Let's get closer. Follow me." Magpie darted into the crowd, creating an empty path out of her madness and filth as surely as a noblewoman might with armed servants. Myst followed at her heels, ducking the occasional outraged fist or elbow from a high-ranking servant. They wound closer to the spectacle, ladies and gentlemen stepping away in horror lest their silks be stained or their purses be cut.

"Hsst. Magpie. You're going to attract the Guard!" Myst nearly ran over the old woman, who abruptly stopped in front of her.

It was too late. Master Guardsman Hebron of the Empress' personal fighting unit had broken form in the parade with several masked soldiers, his massive plumed helmet towering above the crowd as he bellowed at people to get out of his way. Myst stood frozen for an instant, as if a memory were trying to rip itself out of the blackness of her mind. He was a lion of a man and for an instant she thought she knew the face that lay hidden behind the frontpiece of his helmet.

"Oh, Goddess! We're dead. Run!" Myst grabbed a cursing Magpie and tore through the throng in the opposite direction from Master Hebron. The masked warriors were the Dragon's Claws, a special force whose only mission was the protection of the Empress. A net had been laid and Myst could feel it closing in. The warriors who had broken off from the parade were being joined by others in the crowd who materialized as if sprung from the ground.

Myst dragged Magpie along, attempting to get out of the net before it closed. She headed straight for one of the masked Claws who stood at the entrance to a side street that would take her back to the West Market. The crowd parted easily, seeing the danger in her eyes as she dodged through, pushing and elbowing her way forward. A second Claw reached the first warrior she had aimed for and they both stood still, waiting to fight her as a team. Hebron and his team gained from behind. Curses and shouts of alarm filled the square as the singing stopped and the people realized what was happening. Her lungs hurt, her ankle twinged, and she lost time hopping several steps until she could run again. Her vision narrowed towards her goal.

The world seemed to slow and go silent around her as her training took over from someplace deep within sinew and bone. Magpie was left to fend for herself. Myst's joints loosened, her breathing steadied, and she leveraged herself off the shoulders of two onlookers, leaping forward with a fierce yell, legs brought up high for a double kick, her dagger dropping into her hand. A small part of her registered surprise as the masked Claws seemed to shrink back a few paces. Then Hebron's bellow broke into her hearing and the world returned to normal speed. The Claws leapt forward to counter her move and she twisted in time to save herself a blow to the head. Then all was too fast for thought as Hebron's net closed and her chance of escape fled with a shock from behind that brought stars to her eyes, then the black void swallowed her whole.

*

They'd placed a sack over her throbbing head and had dragged her down the street into a dead end where the corners of the temple wall began and commerce ended. Gently, the hood was pulled off, though she was bound at the wrists and ankles, unable to do more than sit upright on her knees, an act which took most of her concentration. Looking up, she saw the Grand Dome of the Empress Temple arching to the sky where it was topped with a golden crescent. She glanced to her left and saw Magpie bound next to her. Hebron himself loomed over them both, his face hidden in shadow.

"She's awake, Commander." A voice said to her right, but Myst kept her eyes turned up to where she thought Hebron's stared down at her. Hebron knelt, and the Guard followed suit.

"You are safe now. Though our lives be sacrificed for this treatment of you, we do so willingly, as it was the only way."

She looked disbelievingly into his softened features as he removed his helmet in respect.

"Release us, then, and perhaps I'll spare your life." Myst, being no fool, decided to play along.

"Not until you tell me who you are," came Hebron's reply.

Myst looked at the ground. The seconds stretched out in the waiting silence, but she had no answer. Magpie moaned and her hood was removed.

A bright flash of blue light, smelling of copper, erupted

from where Magpie was bound. Time slowed. Through the glare Myst saw Magpie's human shape fold into a small ball and a bird emerged, streaking from the center, its black and white wings tearing into the sky, to land on a rooftop above them. Cries of alarm burst from Hebron's men, but there was nothing they could do, having only swords and daggers among them. The ropes that held Magpie had fallen useless to the ground.

A wave of heat and magic swept through Myst as the bird gave a raucous cry, seeming the echo of her friend's laughter. She tumbled back into the void in her mind, then through it to what lay buried underneath.

She glanced at the representative of the Northwest slums. He was a second-rate Merchant with presumptions of leadership. From the height of her jeweled throne in the public audience chamber of the Moon Palace, he looked like a brown lump kneeling in the elegant Circle of Compassion, a low marble platform inlaid with silver moons in all the Phases of the Goddess. The air felt stifling and close in her heavy velvet robes. She thought she could smell the unwashed stench of the supplicants in the hall and she pressed a scented kerchief to her nose to breathe in the sweetness of lavender and rose.

The man before her claimed something about conditions of danger and disease, of roaming bands of criminals, of poor living conditions and squalor. Everyone knew the Goddess provided the worthy with her favor and the unworthy got what they deserved. Or something like that. She had never been good with theology. Light caught the diamonds and sapphires, rubies and emeralds of her three rings and bracelet, which attached to each other in intricate bands of silver.

The jewels were Dragon Ring, also the Seal of Might. She remembered the day it had been placed on her hand at the same time the Moon Crown had been placed on her head; she had been nine years old. Twelve years later, the memory was just as sweet. She played with the rings, letting the prism lights bounce off the man's head, the vast columns of white marble with their ornate silver filigree, and the heavy black velvet curtains dotted with diamonds.

She let the colored spots dance across the immense statue of the Goddess, over her pale marble skin and bounce off the sightless eyes.

The man droned on. How did he get in to see her? Shouldn't someone else have dealt with this and kept him from her sight? She shifted slightly, her body stiff from this morning's cursed warrior-exercises; she was seriously considering putting Hebron in a cage on the city walls for a week as payment for the bruise on her back. But like the weekly torture of listening to supplicants, the training was traditional, the Lords would protest if she stepped a hairsbreadth from their precious traditions.

She barely stifled a yawn and began to twirl her luxurious dark locks as a signal to the Guard. The Guard moved quickly and silently. She did not look to see the man removed from her presence, nor did she hear his quickly stifled protest. The line of petitioners froze, no one wanting to approach. Boredom threatened to consume her and she stirred restlessly. Glancing at her favorite servant she came up with a delicious alternative to hearing the bleating of her malcontented sheep.

Standing, she flicked a finger in his direction and her retinue leaped into action, anticipating the direction of her thoughts. He gave her a warm smile, his dark eyes promising far more interesting things to her than the sheep left to wait for another Day of Mercy. She took his hand and he brought his lips to her wrist. She was a mystery no longer. She wept with shame.

Hebron recovered quickly and knelt at her side, working her bonds.

"Help me up, Hebron, we both know who I am." He leapt to his feet and drew her up, releasing her immediately and bowing to the ground. "Who is it that rides in my divan in my place?"

"Your cousin, Dreama," Hebron said, apologetically. "The Council thought the people needed their Empress during Holy Moon. They thought it best not to let them know you were missing."

"Hmm. I hope little Dreama has not gotten too comfortable on my couch, though the Goddess knows that gaudy thing is as comfortable as riding a three-humped camel."

Hebron and two of the Claws worked frantically to get her bonds cut and to help her to her feet.

Empress Jessiopia rubbed her sore joints and glared at her Guard, who were pitching stones at Magpie. The bird merely mocked them.

"Don't bother with her, Hebron," she said, gesturing at the comical attempt to attack the bird. "She has done us all a great service." She pushed away well-meaning hands and brushed herself off. "No. On second thought, I need a decent advisor."

"Your Majesty?" Hebron's face registered shock.

"I had forgotten who I was long before she took my memory and placed me in the midst of my own negligence to my people. I deserved to know the truth, Hebron. It is time the Empress grew up. Perhaps next year even the poor will have something to celebrate."

The bird transformed on the rooftop, but instead of the ragged form of Magpie was a striking woman with ebon hair and pale skin. "You choose wisely, Empress." The voice was rich and sweet.

Jessiopia's mouth hung open for a moment, her eyes round with surprise and wonder. The woman's gown was stitched with the phases of the moon and on her head was a simple crescent diadem; around her neck hung a silver horn. Jessiopia gasped, came to her senses, and dropped to the earth, her forehead pressing into the dust. Hebron and his warriors stared at their Empress in amazement.

"Great Goddess!" Jessiopia whispered.

The Goddess stood and stepped down from the rooftop, floating as easily as a bird. She landed in front of Jessiopia and cupped the trembling woman's chin in her pale hand. Jessiopia wept silently. Then the Goddess was gone, as if she had never been.

"Empress?" Hebron spoke tentatively.

"Did you see Her?" Jessiopia turned her head towards Hebron, eyes streaming.

"See whom, Your Majesty?"

"Never mind." Jessiopia stood again and faced her loyal subjects. "We should return to the palace, through the servants' passage, I would think. I could use a bath." She smiled to think of the ambitious Dreama enclosed in the stifling Dragon divan while she luxuriated in a hot bath. "And then we'll see about hauling the City Planners and the Council out of their comfortable homes for a tour of the slums."

"Yes, Your Majesty." Hebron gestured to her Guard and they gathered close around her. They walked a moment in silence. "Your training served you well, your Majesty." Hebron offered, a trace of pride in his voice. "You eluded us most effectively."

"Yes, I did, didn't I?" She smiled wryly. "Hebron, I'll never curse your name again for all the battle readiness you've given me."

Hebron puffed his chest and gave her a stern look. "Then I'll see you as soon as possible for further training. You need more sparring against multiple opponents."

"After the bath, Hebron. After the bath."

ROSE IN WINTER

by Marie M. Loughin

Marie Loughin began her writing career and motherhood in the same year, while continuing her job as a consulting statistician. As if this weren't enough, Marie accepted a position as editor for *E-Scape: The Digital Journal of Speculative Fiction*. She held this post for three years, until the demands of two small children toppled the slush pile. She lives in Kansas with her husband, Tom, and two daughters, Hannah and Juliana. She is now working madly on her own writing.

This is Marie's first professional publication. As an editor, Marion always loved discovering new talent, and I'm delighted to have a chance to do so as well. I didn't know this was a first sale until the biographies for those I accepted came in. Congratulations, and I hope this will be the first of many more!

Snow fell on Aerovale. Lacy feathers whirled in the flickering torchlight to vanish into the dark of the longest night of the year. One flake stalled before the window, dancing to the music rising from the festival below. Rosabel Damask leaned over the cold stone ledge to capture it and brought back a single tear shed by the winter sky.

So fragile, and yet her lifelong dreams had melted away just as easily on the floor of the great hall. She touched her tongue to the drop and felt tears answer in her own eyes.

The gentle drum of her father's voice rumbled through her. "You invite illness, standing before the window like that." His arm, warm and strong, encircled her shoulders. He drew her away to the gallery rail overlooking the great hall. "It would not bode well to begin the new year with a chill. Come, rejoin the festivities, little lady."

Rosabel smiled. Throughout childhood he had teased her with that nickname, "little lady," a meaningless title in her father's poor barony. But on this night, her first at Castle Nemaurel, she truly was a lady. And perhaps, she thought, it *is* time to rejoin the swirl.

Then a wave of laughter swelled from below, drowning the piping and strumming of the court musicians. A cluster of courtiers had gathered around Princess Camilla like a bouquet of gaudy flowers. Rosabel's smile faltered. A flush rose in her when she thought of facing those pretty strangers again, of what they might say and how she could possibly answer.

"I think, if you don't mind," she said, hesitating, "that I'd like to rest here a moment more. I found it a bit . . . hot in that crowd."

"Ah, I see!" He pulled her closer. Hairs from his full red beard tickled her cheek when he spoke. "I'll stay with you, then, and make sure you don't freeze. It wouldn't do to present the eminent Lord Damask's daughter to King Eldrid for the first time with an icicle hanging from her nose." His smile teased, his words mocked, but his eyes remained gentle with sympathy.

She laid her head on his shoulder. Together, they watched a skinny, eager lord tie a silk blindfold over Princess Camilla's eyes for a round of hoodman's bluff. *They play it just the same, here,* Rosabel thought, remembering the tattered rag tied to her own eyes, the coarse feel of a peasant's tunic escaping her fingers, the smell of the dried sheep dung burned for warmth in her father's keep. She felt a pang of longing for her friends, children of farmers and craftsmen running barefoot over the uneven yard.

But she was here to make a place for herself in finer society, no matter how awkward she felt.

She looked to her father for reassurance, but his eyes strained toward the king's table. There, the older men told outrageous stories and toasted the worst with a clash of tankards. Shame flooded her. She was sixteen, and her father was no nursemaid. She slipped from his hold and forced a smile, pushing him toward the stairs. "Go on down, Father. You must be thirsty after the long climb up to the gallery. I'll follow in a little while."

He shook his head, frowning in mock embarrassment. "You see through me as always, little lady." But he paused before leaving and brushed a callused hand across her cheek. "You do look beautiful—like your mother reborn."

Then he was gone, and Rosabel fought a panicked urge to call him back.

A ten-day before, she had felt as beautiful as her father claimed. Her new gown, ordered for her debut at court, had arrived. She draped herself in the emerald velvet and danced around her room. In that tiny chamber, in the small barony that was her home, her dreams came alive. She laughed with unseen courtiers, flirted with imagined gentlemen, whispered secrets into Camilla's ear, and, blushing, accepted the wreath crowning her Snow Queen, awarded each year to the loveliest maiden of the Festival of Renewal.

But here, within the solid walls of Castle Nemaurel, the fantasy could not survive. The lords and ladies, many no older than her own sixteen years, flitted like jeweled butterflies behind shields of cut crystal. She could not approach them, could think of nothing to say to them that did not involve crops or sheep or ways to preserve fruit, and she could not follow their tittering court gossip.

She did not feel the glances of men admiring her slender curves, the shine of red-gold hair, and eyes as green and soft as the velvet she wore. She only felt out of place. At last she had fled to the gallery.

Excited shouts drew Rosabel's gaze from the courtiers' game. An odd voice sailed over a crowd gathering near the entrance. It had a rasping quality that should have been irritating, but somehow compelled her to listen. The crowd, too, fell silent. Even the musicians faltered and stilled their instruments. Left to itself in the echoing hall, the voice settled into sprightly song.

> *I walked along one windy day,*
> *The air so still, I heard it say,*

"Whither away? Whither away?
Where are you going, this windy day?"

"Whithersoever the sky is green,
The hills run deep, like a clay tureen,
On grass of blue is where I'll be seen."

"Why do you walk, sans gelding or mare?"
Queried a voracious carnivorous old hare
As he supped on wine and a round red pear.
"When I do walk, I ride on my mare."

"My frolicsome donkey has rolled in morass.
All oily with sludge, oh woe and alas!
Now afoot I go, lest I fall on my ass."

Groans and laughter rippled through the onlookers. The crowd swelled from the door until a tall figure in brightly mismatched clothing burst through. A caricature drawn by the gods, he capered through the great hall on legs like stilts. The three prongs of his hat flopped, bells tinkling, with each jaunty step. Beneath the hat jutted yellow hair, straight and stiff as straw.

He wove through the revelers, conjuring paper flowers and presenting them to each lady with an off-balanced bow. Upon reaching King Eldrid, he knelt and doffed his hat. He held it forth like an empty sack and sang another verse.

Highpockets, grasshopper, scarecrow, twig,
Hoppity hoppity, jiggity jig,
Teller of tales, player of pranks,
The name, my lord, is Spindleshanks.

Impassive, the king stroked his beard and studied Spindleshanks for a moment. Then his mouth twisted in a grin and he nodded. With that, Spindleshanks tossed the hat to the floor, baited it with silver, and somersaulted to his feet. He pulled another hat from his sleeve, twin to the first, and stuffed his head into it.

The revelers had stopped their games to watch the shenanigans. Princess Camilla and her retinue, of an age that placed them above such silliness, snickered at Spindleshanks' lanky build and awkward gait. The children flocked to him, squealing and tugging at his clothes. Their elders smiled indulgently.

Spindleshanks folded his legs until his knees poked above his shoulders and his head hung level with the smallest child. He waddled among them, one hand pulling treats from ears while the other dropped little toys into pockets, to be found later.

Suddenly he leapt from their midst and landed at the center of the banquet table. He cartwheeled its length amid shouts and gasps. With a flip, he vaulted from the far end, a chicken leg clenched in his teeth. He stripped its meat in one bite and dropped the bone into the tankard of a lord who had turned away to joke with his comrades.

Sticky-fingered tots trailed Spindleshanks into the area cleared for dancing. There, Lord and Lady Antilion remained paired as though frozen mid-step. Lord Antilion, a portly man with limp brown hair, gaped indignantly at Spindleshanks' approach. His Lady, taller by an inch, wrinkled her nose and hissed in her husband's ear. Rosabel's own ear grew hot just watching.

Spindleshanks bowed before the affronted couple and indicated a desire to cut in. Outraged, Lord Antilion raised an arm to stop him. Spindleshanks shrugged and grabbed the proffered hand. Dancing to thunderous laughter, he swung Antilion about the floor.

Antilion's face darkened. With a furious tug, he pulled free. He opened his mouth to speak, but Spindleshanks had already pranced away.

Rosabel watched the boisterous tide sweep Spindleshanks to the platform below her perch. She strained over the rail to see what the fool would do next. The platform held a high-backed chair, bedecked with evergreen leaves and berries. The throne of the Snow Queen. Banners of red and green silk hung from the gallery, framing the throne. A wreath of snow-white feathers lay upon the seat, awaiting the selection of this year's mistress.

Spindleshanks mounted the platform. He removed his hat and knelt, head bowed, at the foot of the throne. With a slow, deliberate motion, he raised the wreath and settled it onto his own head. Then, to jeers and catcalls, he rose and flung his arms wide, throwing his head back as if to absorb the adulations of his admirers.

For the first time, Rosabel could see his face. She had expected ugliness, but instead found features of exaggerated beauty, like those of a theater mask. The nose, though overlarge, arched in the strong lines of a hawk's beak. High, sharp cheekbones and a long pointed chin lent an outlandish beauty at odds with his foolish tricks. But his eyes . . .

His eyes spoke of alien lands, of green skies and grass of blue . . . of magic. And when they met her own, a shock exploded from her core, as though her heart were plunged into fire. Though her hands never left the rail, she felt herself fall toward the gold-speckled brown of those eyes.

Spindleshanks faced her squarely. Gone was the jovial clown, the prancing fool. His features grew strained, as though he suffered a deep, ancient pain. And from those eyes of gold-speckled brown a tremulous heat rose up to ensnare Rosabel in the grip of their desperate longing. She recoiled, afraid of the intensity of that gaze.

Spindleshanks stepped past the throne to the back of the platform. The courtiers, sensing a departure from the show, muttered in confusion. Then he reached for the hanging banners and began to climb. Rosabel gasped, certain the delicate fabric would never hold. But so fluid was the movement of Spindleshanks that he seemed to weigh less than a feather, less than a snowflake. The fabric held, and his eyes never once let go of hers.

Trapped by the crowd, Lord Antilion watched in growing rage. "Ho there!" he bellowed. "Stop that miscreant—he's ruining the festival!"

The courtiers, unsatiated in their desire for amusement, did nothing. The lord huffed and threw his weight against the bystanders. Those in his path were knocked aside in his rush to reach the platform. As he hoisted himself up, a seam in the seat of his breeches burst with a resounding tear. Amid whistles and laughter, Antilion swiped one-handed at Spindleshanks' dangling legs while clutching his own gaping bottom.

Above, Rosabel did not see the antics of Lord Antilion. Her vision had narrowed to the sway of straining fabric, the curl of Spindleshanks' fingers in red silk, and the deep well of his eyes. The higher he climbed, the more fearful she grew that he might fall, still more fearful that he would reach the top.

She thought to offer help, but fear stopped her. She was alone in the gallery, and he was, after all, a stranger. A fool. A self-proclaimed trickster. And the power of his passion was more than her young heart could bear.

With a final effort, Spindleshanks swung into the gallery. There he waited, one long-fingered hand resting on the stone as though he were ready to vault down onto the crowd at her request. So still was he, so tense was his posture, that the audience quieted. Even Antilion quit his bellowing and sagged, gasping and panting.

Spindleshanks took one step toward Rosabel. Whispers hissed through the courtiers like grease spattering hot embers. Lord Damask stiffened at the king's table and set his tankard down.

Another step. Emotion so raw shone on Spindleshanks' face that Rosabel felt her lips part. She longed to immerse herself in that passion, ached to wrap herself in its unquestioning acceptance. And she wanted to flee.

A final step and Spindleshanks towered above her. He smelled of clover in the rain and cinnamon. He took the feathered crown from his head and placed it over her red-gold braids. Lord Damask leapt to his feet, upsetting his chair. "Your Majesty, my daughter is unattended—"

King Eldrid frowned and signaled the guards.

Spindleshanks knelt before Rosabel. He took her hand, and fire ignited her blood where his skin touched hers. It burned through her veins until she was nearly overcome by its smoldering heat. For a moment, she was transported to a different place, where flowers bloomed in winter and the sky matched the emerald shade of her dress. Then, in a rasping whisper that somehow resounded the length of the great hall, Spindleshanks said, "I would crown you my bride, if you will it."

His soul reached through his eyes, asking, begging. That same look had lived in her father's eyes when he gazed at her mother, eyes that had gone empty with her mother's death. Rosabel had dreamed of seeing that look in her own lover's eyes, had hoped to find such a lover in this court, and yet . . .

Emerald skies gave way to gray walls and bright banners. Clover and cinnamon melted before the acrid odor of charred pork. Over the railing, the faces of richly dressed courtiers stared in disbelief, amusement, and contempt. Princess Camilla and her friends sneered and turned away. Anger twisted King Eldrid's face. His men boiled around him. Her father fought through the crowd toward the gallery stairs.

Rosabel looked again at Spindleshanks, not meeting his eyes. To marry this—this wandering trickster! What sort of life could she hope for?

Spindleshanks must have seen "no" in her face, for he pulled away even before her father reached the gallery. She felt a terrible rending as his hand left hers. A chasm opened within the man before her, and, for a moment, she glimpsed the vast loneliness that filled it.

Then, with a hop and a sweeping bow, he presented her with a single white bud on a long thorny stem.

> *Three I have to give to you,*
> *Though not without a cost.*
> *Here is one, and that leaves two,*
> *My heart to me is lost.*

His voice was light, his manner silly, but the look in his eyes was not. With a trembling hand, she accepted the gift as her father charged into the gallery. The guards followed hard behind him. Spindleshanks laughed aloud. As they reached for him, he grabbed a handful of air and dashed it to the floor. Thunder clapped, smoke billowed, and when it cleared, Spindleshanks was gone.

Rosabel looked at the flower in her hand. A rose, blooming in winter. For no reason she could name, she turned and cried into her father's shoulder.

The icy fingers of winter gripped Aerovale clear through equinox that year. When at last spring chiseled the land free, crops stretched upward, only to shrivel in rainless summer heat. Hungry winter followed lean fall, until once again banners of green and red draped the great hall of Castle Nemaurel on the shortest day of the year.

The roast pig may have been smaller, the ale more bitter, and the table lighter, but for Rosabel, no Festival of Renewal had ever been finer. Her gown of midnight blue was well in fashion. Her hair coiled about her head in a more sophisticated manner than last year's braids. She danced, she laughed, she even whispered with Camilla, for Rosabel's distress at the previous Festival had softened the crystalline heart of the princess. At festival's end, she had invited Rosabel to remain at the castle as a lady-in-waiting. Rosabel had accepted, and watched her father ride off without her.

Lute, flute, tambourine, and drum sounded a merry rotundellu. Rosabel swung and twirled through the newly learned steps of the circle dance. Faster and faster went the music, until she abandoned the steps in her struggle to stay in formation. The dance reached a frenzied peak. Her feet scarcely touched the floor.

Then she swung left where she should have skipped right, and collided into the broad chest of a young lord. She fell hard on her back. A rope of hair broke free and spilled down her dress like molten copper. She lay struggling for breath—a task made more difficult by the laughter blocking her throat.

The other dancers gathered around, also laughing. The young lord fingered his chest and winced as though bruised. "There are easier ways to break a man's heart, m'lady."

With that, Rosabel laughed all the harder, until her stomach ached and she thought she might faint for lack of air. But the lord's words touched deep within her a memory of infinite loneliness glimpsed through eyes of gold-speckled brown.

"Now that Lord Kenneth and Lady Rosabel are properly introduced," Princess Camilla cried, "perhaps they would be willing to start a game of hoodman's bluff!"

Lord Kenneth! The name swept memory away. She had collided with the first cousin to the princess, returned from fostering in another kingdom. He was the lord most desired by the ladies, and Rosabel could see why. Every part of him signaled strength. Square jaw, broad forehead, wide of shoulder and narrow of waist, the only softness about him was a well-groomed beard. Even his clothes were bold: a black brocade tunic and a scarlet cloak fastened at the throat by an emerald-studded brooch.

"As you wish, Camilla," he said. He bowed to Rosabel and extended a hand. "Though as I am the injured party, 'tis only fair that Lady Rosabel wear the hood."

Rosabel laid her hand in his. He hesitated, letting his gaze linger on her face. Then he lifted her with gentle ease. The hard feel of palm callused by sword and rein sent a thrill through her. He held her hand a moment too long before offering his arm.

At the circle's center, Kenneth accepted a hood of black silk from another player. Rosabel looked to Camilla, letting her nervousness show in her face. " 'Tis not exactly fair, Your Highness," she said. "I've just met some of these people today. It could be a very long round."

The princess arched an eyebrow. A corner of her mouth lifted in a sly smile. "Don't worry, my dear. I'm certain you'll make a good catch."

Kenneth lowered the hood over her head. In the sudden darkness, she caught the scent of cedar. Lord Kenneth? She sniffed again. Definitely cedar, probably Lord Kenneth. She could do worse than to aim for that smell. Much worse.

He spun her around. Hands out, she shuffled forward. Her fingers grazed satin. A gasp and a giggle, then nothing. She felt the rush of air as players dodged. Beneath the hood, her face turned grim. Why worry about identifying a person if she could not even catch one?

Smells of wood smoke, hay, and ale drifted by. She veered from the sour odor of stale sweat. The fire crackled, the king's robust laugh rumbled forth, music jangled. She shuffled toward what she hoped was center circle, sweeping her hands before her. And was rewarded by a cedar-scented draft from her left. She whipped her arm to the side. Her fingers tangled in brocade, and she was pleased to feel a hard-muscled arm beneath.

"Ah ha!" she cried, "You are my prisoner." She reached for her captive's face, hoping for a trim beard and a stone-studded brooch at the collar. Excitement warmed her when her hand brushed soft whiskers. Now if only . . .

Her fingers curled over a round, stone-encrusted brooch. Ecstatic, she shouted victory. "I name you . . ." The players quieted, awaiting her answer.

Cedar? . . . or was it clover? She hesitated, confused. What she had thought to be brocade now felt coarse—wool. The arm beneath it—long and lean muscled, not brawny. "I-I name you . . ."

Clover and cinnamon. A burning chill blazed through her. A year of denial collapsed before a memory of golden flecks in brown. Trembling, she whispered into the silence, "I name you . . . Spindleshanks!"

Cries of disbelief rang from the players. Deaf to their demands for a replay, she lifted the hood. The man, a stranger, had shaggy brown hair and a mustache. He wore a cloak of gray wool, ringed by a beaverskin collar—the beard she had felt. At his throat sparkled Kenneth's brooch. Then he smiled, and a summer breeze stroked her cheek and flowed through her hair. Every part of her tingled as though thawing from a year's frozen slumber. When she met his eyes, her joy nearly outmatched her dismay.

The other players grew restless, ready to continue the

game. They had not recognized the trickster. In their midst, Kenneth fumbled at his throat for the missing brooch. A torchlit glitter at center circle drew his gaze to Spindleshanks' collar. Kenneth took a step forward, then shrugged and relaxed, though his eyes remained watchful.

"Here now, Rosabel," a roguish voice called, "throw that fish back and cast again!"

Shouts of agreement rang out. Rosabel heard, and a part of her warned that court favor was easier to lose than it was to gain. But her hands stayed, one on Spindleshanks' arm, the other resting on his chest. In his eyes, she saw a place where favor was granted unconditionally. There lay a love that bit deeply and held fast, though it threatened to tear him asunder.

She shivered, knowing that she too could be torn.

Her eyes traced his long, angular face. His lips were strangely soft among such sharp features. She imagined them brushing hers and leaned closer, trembling. Joy sparked in his eyes, a joy birthed of pain and loneliness. For a moment, it seemed they were alone in the hall. For a moment, Rosabel thought he would kiss her.

"Rosabel, just what are you doing?" The voice, cold, imperious, returned winter's chill to her blood. Camilla stood not two paces from her, arms crossed. The other players gathered closer. Their questions and demands battered Rosabel. She felt herself spiraling away from Spindleshanks, though neither had moved.

It was, at last, Spindleshanks who pulled away, before the demands grew angry. To the astonishment of all but Rosabel, he pulled off his wig and threw it in the air. A trickster once more, he waited, tapping his foot with exaggerated impatience, until a three-pronged hat fell into his hand. Grinning, he perched it on his straw-colored hair.

Chattering confusion ensued. Rosabel felt grateful relief as the weight of their attention lifted.

The noise caught the interest of other revelers. The crowd around Spindleshanks grew. Calmly, as though no one were watching, he removed the brooch and tossed it over his shoulder. It arched over the onlookers, almost floating, and dropped at Kenneth's feet. Before anyone could react, Spindleshanks removed the cloak from his shoulders and began to swing it over his head. As it whirled, the gray flaked away in a shower of sparkling crystal, leaving multicolored patches behind. Faster the cloak whirled, and larger became the patches, until the cloak transformed into a kaleidoscope of undulating color.

Overtaken by wonder, Rosabel lifted her hands to the falling crystal. Laughing, she pirouetted, sparkles catching in her hair, flashing in her eyes. The courtiers around her stood awestricken, as though faeryland had open its doors. Through it all, Spindleshanks spun on his heels, bells bouncing and jingling on his hat. When the last of the gray was gone, he stopped.

Rosabel—" he said, her name a fair, soft thing cradled by his voice. He reached a hand to her and she took it, again feeling the flame of his touch. The young courtiers cavorted about them, scooping crystals out of the shimmering air. The older lords and ladies at the king's table laughed among themselves. No one noticed the still, intent couple at center circle.

Spindleshanks lifted the twist of red-gold hair from Rosabel's shoulder and touched it with a kiss. When he spoke, his voice was low and rough. "I ask you again—please, will you come away with me? Will you be my bride?"

Yes, Rosabel thought. *Yes, oh yes!* But she could not say the words, though his love lay like an open door in his eyes.

"Spindleshanks!" a hard voice broke in. Rosabel gasped and jerked away. Camilla confronted them once more. "Again, you have disrupted the Festival of Renewal. Look!"

She turned and glared at her friends gamboling in the sparkling air. "I simply will not stand for this—this distraction! Rosabel, come." With that, she marched toward the banquet table, where the king drank with his lords. Rosabel stared after her, afraid. Camilla had given substance to the dreams of court life Rosabel had cherished as a girl. Dreams she had lived this past year. All that she had most desired now walked away with the princess.

Though Rosabel's heart cried within her, she backed away from Spindleshanks and would not look in his eyes.

Alerted by his daughter, King Eldrid rose from the table. His face reddened at the sight of the trickster. "Seize the fool!" he bellowed. No one reacted. Startled, the courtiers let the last crystals fall and looked toward their king. Still sputtering his rage, he signaled for the guards.

Spindleshanks, the merry prankster, doffed his hat and bowed to the king with a flourish. As the guards approached, the jingling hat swept through the air, releasing a rainbow avalanche of marbles to the stone floor. With shouts of happy surprise, the courtiers bent to gather this new treasure. A short, wart-nosed lordling clutching a hatful of crystals squatted in the guards' path. Unable to stop, they skidded and flailed, crashing into the little man in a dazzling explosion of glitter.

While the guards fought through the cloud, stumbling over marbles and the courtiers who collected them, Spindleshanks turned once more to Rosabel. From that surprising hat, he drew a red rose in full bloom.

> *My heart is gone,*
> *The wound so deep.*
> *My mind now, too,*
> *Is in your keep.*

He sang in a jester's voice, full of laughter. But when Rosabel dared search his eyes, she found only pain. Their gazes still locked, he flung his cloak around himself. Folds of colored wool swirled, then fell to the floor, empty, at the feet of the fumbling guards.

Loss ran Rosabel through like a sword. She crumpled to her knees, the rose clutched to her breast. Pain lanced her palm. *How fitting,* she thought, *for a winter rose to have thorns that drive so deep.*

*   *   *

Rosabel touched the feathered wreath that crowned her elaborate fall of curls. How different life had become since her arrival at Castle Nemaurel, now two years past. She smiled at the memory of watching from the gallery, fearful that she would never be accepted, that her hopes for position and romance within these walls were but childish fantasy. Now she sat on the throne of the Snow Queen, betrothed to Lord Kenneth, who stood at her side. He smiled down at her and took her hand.

How different, indeed.

This was the pinnacle moment of the Festival of Renewal, and Rosabel Damask was at its center. The courtiers crowded the platform like supplicants. Rosabel's ears still rang with the roar of approval at her crowning. She looked down upon faces red with long hours of frolic and drink. Tankards of ale made their way through the crowd to be raised in toasts to her beauty, and then passed along. Lord Antilion reached for the nearest only to be cuffed by his wife. He winced, his ear glowing under her spitting vituperations. Rosabel stifled a giggle and looked for her father, who stood with the king. He beamed at her with drunken pride.

The king, to whom all tankards eventually traveled, held one in each hand and plowed a course for the platform. More than a little tippled, he heaved himself up, wobbled, and then faced his subjects. "A pronouncement!" he bawled. "Lord Kenneth, where are you? Come forth!"

Kenneth, not three feet behind him, stepped forward. Startled, the king floundered a bit "Hum—ah yes, there you are, lad!" He laid a fatherly hand on Kenneth's shoulder and left it there for support.

"As you all know, Princess Camilla is now betrothed to King Darius of Gigliam." Cheers echoed through the hall. Tankards crashed together. Ladies flocked to Camilla, offering words of congratulations. Camilla blushed and gripped the arm of the tall, long-bearded man at her side more tightly. The revelers, thinking the king finished, returned to their festivities.

"Hold!" King Eldrid bellowed. Surprised, the courtiers

quieted. The king hiccupped and smoothed his stained robe. "Now, unless you all wish to become subjects of Giglium upon my death—" he paused until the onslaught of good-natured boos died out, "—I must choose a male heir."

He drew himself straight, pulled his belly remarkably flat, and said with great dignity, hardly slurring a word, "Being of sound mind and devoid of male progeny, I declare Lord Kenneth, brother's son, heir to the Kingdom of Aerovale. May he rule in popserity—propserty—ah, wealth and peace."

It was a popular choice. Kenneth stood capable and strong before the clamor of the crowd.

The king waited for silence. "And now, I would like to offer a toast." He raised one tankard, then the other. Finding both empty, he pitched them aside and snatched another from the lips of a duke standing too close to the platform. Sloshing it high, he said, "To Lord Kenneth and Lady Rosabel! Let the first day of the new year be the first of many in their happy future together. Tomorrow they wed—shall we cheer them on their way?"

Cheers shook the buttresses. A musician piped an impromptu jig. Ladies lifted their skirts and danced with their lords. Lord Damask ambled about like a laughing bear, hugging all who got in his way until someone dumped a pitcher of ale over his head. He made great show of ringing out his red braid and launched into a rowdy song.

Amazed happiness washed over Rosabel. Marriage to one so impressive as Kenneth was overwhelming enough. To become Snow Queen was sheer fantasy. But to become Queen of Aerovale. . . !

It was too much for Rosabel. She felt detached, as though viewing the celebrations through a distant window. Beside her, Kenneth waved and grinned at the crowd, absorbing their adulations. She watched him, bemused.

He is like a character from a dream, she thought. She knew how lucky she was. Anyone would tell her so.

It's all like a dream. The throng swirled about her in

a collage of sound and color. She fought for a fixture, a detail she could focus on. Slowly she became aware of a low hum weaving through the fabric of the noise. A thread that grew into a wordless tune. Memory burst over her, and with it came joy—and pain.

The dancers and musicians heard it, too. The jig faltered and stopped. Shouts and laughter fell to a puzzled murmur. Heads swiveled in search of the source of the mysterious voice. Many faces turned to the door—the courtiers also remembered the prankster who made his entrance there two years before, singing a similar tune.

No one thought to look up until a rope dropped from the truss overhead. From it dangled Spindleshanks. Lowering himself, he stepped lightly to the platform. He wore the same mismatched clothing in which Rosabel had first seen him, now tattered and not so bright. The bells were gone from his hat. Beneath it, his hair hung limp and colored of ashes. The crowd saw none of this, however. They only saw the same comic fool who had dazzled them with tricks and antics before.

Spindleshanks skipped to the platform's center and bowed to the astonished king. Then he turned to Rosabel. She trembled, wanting to turn away, to deny the torture of a love she could not accept. But the desire within her was greater than her fear, and she met his gaze. His own desire answered through his eyes. Opening his mouth once more, he sang,

> *The wind I ride*
> *Like a feral horse,*
> *She carries me where she will.*
>
> *She swept through me*
> *and plucked my heart,*
> *From me she holds it still.*
>
> *We soared too deep*
> *Where none dare go,*
> *And there my mind was lost.*

*The wind, she tears
What's left of me,
My soul will be the cost.*

The courtiers shuffled their feet and muttered to one another. "What sort of riddle or rhyme was that?" someone called out.

"Yes, Spindleshanks," came another voice, "Give us a trick, or a randy tale!"

Spindleshanks did not move. His eyes never left Rosabel. In his words lay a question, in his face, a truth. His skin stretched over his bones as if he were empty of substance. He moved in the taut manner of one forced to wait beyond endurance, holding life to a skeletal body, void of heart, void of all thoughts but one—that he must win her or lose his soul.

Her own soul responded—not in pity, but in longing. To Kenneth, she was a symbol, chosen for her beauty, perhaps even chosen out of fondness. But he would not die for want of her. She rose from her throne and lifted her hands to Spindleshanks.

The scrape and ring of a drawn sword shattered the transcendent moment. Kenneth stepped before Rosabel and leveled a sword at Spindleshanks' chest. His eyes glinted. The muscles in his sword arm bunched and stretched as though he fought to hold it back.

"Twice now you have come to claim what is not yours," his voice boomed. "Begone, lest I forget this is the eve of new beginnings and end your life!"

A grim smile stretched Spindleshanks' face. He studied the blade, then raised cold eyes to Kenneth. The young lord was fierce and strong in his anger. Spindleshanks was terrifying. An aura of power radiated from him, dimming the light of the torches. The courtiers gasped and drew back from this fool who had once seemed so harmless. The word "sorcerer" was muttered by more than one. Even King Eldrid stepped back, signaling frantically to his reluctant guards.

Only Rosabel remained unafraid—and Lord Kenneth, who held fast and readied his blade with the bravery

inherent in such men. The golden flecks in Spindleshanks' eyes began to glow. His hair crackled and stood
out. Kenneth raised his sword.

"No!" cried Rosabel. She rushed forward to insert herself between the men, but it was too late. Already Kenneth's sword arched toward Spindleshankss chest in a
killing blow.

Spindleshanks smiled, and, for a moment, Rosabel saw
the playful trickster in his eyes. Before the sword could
connect, Spindleshanks puffed out his cheeks and blew.
Kenneth flickered and vanished like a candle flame in
the wind. His sword clattered to the platform.

The crowd erupted in hysteria. Ladies screamed, some
fainting. The courtiers closest to the front fought to push
away, while those at the back struggled forward for a
better look. King Eldrid shouted for the guards, who
were trapped in the press. Rosabel drew a breath and
waited. She could not believe Spindleshanks would hurt
anyone, even Kenneth.

"He's a sorcerer!" Lady Antilion shrieked. "Take his
head and throw it in the sea—and burn the rest of him,
or he'll destroy us all as he did Lord Kenneth!"

Even as she spoke, a woman's scream rang out above.
The crowd followed the sound to the gallery, where three
figures scrambled in panic. One was Lord Kenneth looking about in confused anger. Beside him stood a lady, her
hair in disarray, breasts hanging bare from an unfastened
bodice. The third figure was Lord Antilion, yanking his
hose into place.

Lady Antilion shrieked again—this time in outrage.
The rest of the crowd roared in relieved laughter. Still,
none approached the platform, for Spindleshanks had
displayed a power far outweighing that of an itinerant
trickster.

While all eyes were focused overhead, Spindleshanks
again turned to Rosabel and took her hand. "I would
not have hurt him," he said.

"I know." She also knew what he would ask, and that
she had only the moment bought by his trick to decide.

"Rosabel," he said, and the pain came flooding back,

"I ask you one last time, and will bother you no more. Will you come away with me?"

Rosabel looked at his face and saw past his words. She clasped his hand to her breast and again immersed herself in the passion, the utter acceptance in his eyes. She felt the wonder of dancing free under skies of green, of the warm breeze of endless summer. And she felt joy— the joy of twining her soul with another.

And then she saw her father, red-faced and laughing, as Lady Antilion threw a roasted squash at the gallery. She saw the happy camaraderie of the courtiers— ordinary people, really—decorated in velvet and lace just as she. She saw Camilla and her handsome king. And she saw Kenneth, a future king. Her future husband. The manifestation of the deepest fantasy of her childhood.

To leave would be to deny everything she ever wanted, everything she was. Who, then, would she be?

Love spilled like tears from her eyes as she looked again at Spindleshanks. And she let his hand fall.

The light went out of Spindleshanks' face. He laid his head back and a dreadful keening poured from his throat. The sound tore into Rosabel's heart like the jaws of a wolf, but she would not relent. As she watched, Spindleshanks faded into nothingness.

The mournful wail spiraled after him through the echoing hall, piercing every heart it touched. It drew each member of the court, each servant, entertainer, and guard, to their own memories of pain and sadness.

The wail rose in pitch and volume, until a voice cried out, "A storm! A great wind has arisen outside."

As if a spell had been broken, the courtiers heard it too—the howl of wind blowing over the battlement, ripping through barren winter trees. Dazed and a little frightened, they returned to their festivities, forcing merriment to cover unexpected pain. But Rosabel heard more than the wind. She heard the cry of Spindleshanks, now outside the great hall.

"Rosabel!" Kenneth's deep voice called to her from the gallery stairs. She tried to smile in reassurance when she saw his concern. He started toward her, but was swarmed by admirers. Lords slapped his back and commended his bravery. Ladies hung on each arm, simpering at every word. Concern for Rosabel slipped from his face as he laughed with them.

Watching, an understanding came to Rosabel. As wife to Kenneth, heir to the throne of Aerovale, she would live a life at court that she had only thought possible in her dreams. The clothes, the elegance, the dazzling trappings of power would all be hers, never to be taken away by the turn of court favor.

But she would never know passion, or the bliss of joining her soul with another.

Looking about the great hall, everything she had once thought to be beautiful and perfect now looked drab and coarse. Color drained from the banners. The music soured, the instruments out of tune and played by awkward fingers. Every blemish glared from the ladies' faces, each lord seemed puffed up with air and arrogance.

In that moment, she knew where her true choice lay. With shaking hands, she removed the wreath and placed it on the throne. She climbed from the platform and pushed through the crowd. No one noticed her passage from the hall, and she did not look back.

Freezing wind buffeted her, but she did not feel it. Snow swirled into her face, stinging her eyes. She stumbled into a half-buried postern. Foot-high drifts dragged at her skirts. She squinted into the darkness, screaming "Spindleshanks" over and over.

At last she came upon a still form huddled in the snow. A three-pronged felt hat lay beside it. She threw herself down and wiped the snow from Spindleshanks' face. "Please, please come back to me," she sobbed, and kissed his lips.

She held his head and rocked back and forth, the wind howling and tearing at her, until she felt cold fingers on her arm.

"Ah, Rosabel." Spindleshanks smiled at her with cracked lips.

She placed a shaking finger over his mouth. "You are

going to be all right," she told him, pleading. "You have to be all right."

"I'm afraid it's too late for that," he said. *"The wind, she tears what's left of me . . . ."* He stretched a shaking long-fingered hand to trace her cheek. "Oh, what price has love." The hand dropped lifeless to the snow.

As his last breath stilled, so too did the wind. The clouds parted and a moon shone down on Aerovale. Blue light fell on Spindleshanks' lifeless face. His body began to shimmer, glowing brighter and brighter until she could no longer bear to look. Then the light was gone. And so was Spindleshanks. In his place lay a perfect rose, unhurt by the snow. Its petals were black.

It was the last he had to give.

Rosabel came to her feet and let the moonlight bathe her tear-streaked face. In the snow-muffled stillness of the night, she found a sense of calm, even peace, within herself. Music drifted from the great hall. A jig, for dancing, but tinged with sorrow. Somehow she knew that, for her, music would always be so, and the brightest colors would appear in shades of gray.

She crossed the castle grounds where she would one day be queen and knew, too, that there would be contentment. Laughter. Even love, of a sort. But for her . . .

She brought the rose to her face, breathing its bittersweet scent. For her, there could never be joy.

KAZHE'S BLADE

by Terry McGarry

Terry McGarry is the author of the fantasy novels *Illumination*, *The Binder's Road*, and *Triad*, as well as over forty short stories. This is her second appearance in the *Sword & Sorceress* series. She's a copyeditor by trade, and plays Irish traditional music on the side in gigs and pub sessions around the New York area. She has earned a Longsword 1.0 Certificate from the Association for Renaissance Martial Arts (www.thearma.org), and holds an orange belt in the Israeli self-defense system Krav Maga. In her spare time, she volunteers at a local animal shelter and is studying Japanese with the aim of watching Akira Kurosawa films without English subtitles.

Since the first volume of *Sword & Sorceress*, a whole generation of women has grown up that knows what it means to train as a fighter and use a blade. They also know that it's not all glamour and glory, as this story shows.

Her cheekbone cracked against the table. No pain in the back of her head—a shove from behind, not a blow. She was on her feet in the time it took an eye to open, with an instant field awareness of the posture and position of every form in the room. No threat from front or sides. The stool her rising knocked backward scraped and tottered but did not hit flesh. Whoever had smashed her head down was not directly behind her. He was likely right-handed. There was no blade in her. He was either reaching his bare hand for a weapon or drawing his fist back.

She spun left, blade hand sweeping a knife from her belt. Her off elbow whipped through air. She jerked her blade arm back hard to halt the rotation even as the carry knife came fluidly into a thrusting grip.

No one there. No one diving through door or window. Just a side wall of chinked gray stone, hung with horseshoes, mule shoes, ill-matched halves of steer shoes.

Though she had pulled up, the low, smoky room continued to rotate. The floor tilted. She came full around and braced herself on the table. The flamewood's grain ran in queasy waves.

"All right there?" A man set a tankard of dark beer down on a cluster of rings in the old waxseed polish. Publican? Innkeeper? Taverner—place was too small for an inn, and in a public house she would have smelled stew.

"Your furniture's making me seasick."

"That'd be the stout," the man said cheerfully. "Chuck bucket's in the corner there."

Kazhe fingered her cheekbone and found it numb but not bloody. Low rafters, smoke-filled air, tables stained and scarred. The drink spill smelled rich and bitter, the pipe smoke piquant. The Fist, then. She was still in the Fist, where they drank stout and crumbled dry crampbark into their briar pipes. Hobblebush, they called it. She wasn't anywhere near numb enough if she could remember a thing like that.

A set of ninestones strewed the table. A winning configuration, possibly arranged by the impact of her face. Beside her was a modest pile of old clenched nails. Beside a larger pile, across from her, sat another tankard, empty. Who'd finish his drink but leave his stones?

The boot knife plunged point-first into the table beside the stones gave partial answer. She worked it out and slid it home. "Sorry about that," she said to the taverner.

"The cut'll wax in, like all the others," he said. "And nice work, by the way. I was in the cellar, but my boy saw it. Will the fellow come back for his stones, do you think?"

Kazhe gauged the time of day from the shuttered windows and oily lampglow and said, "Not tonight. Why don't you keep them safe for him?" She scooped the nails into their box but left the stones for the taverner, not trusting herself to cope with the drawbag.

"It's more than nails I'm rolling for," he'd said, with a tense, expectant glance as he rattled the stones in his cupped hands, and she'd snorted and told him to yank a younger pair of breeches.

She remembered now—the offer of a friendly game, the way he demanded the strongest stout. Called himself Arron, a Heartlands name but in a Highlands accent. She'd let him stand her the drinks, although the taverner gave her all she asked. For keeping the peace. She remembered now. The Blue Dunnock had thrown her out for starting more brawls than she stopped. She'd packed the blasted Fist in, set off for home. But now she was here.

She remembered. It was a partner Arron wanted, but the bladed kind. *"A rousing workout once a nineday, when the caravans come through,"* he'd said, *"and you'll never have to wipe up another tavern."*

She hadn't heard of roadside attacks in the Fist, though merchants traveled in caravans for fear of just that, with hired blades to protect them. The folk they hired wouldn't know a point from a buttcap—she'd said as much when they tried to hire her—but this lout didn't know that, or didn't want to find out the hard way that he was wrong.

At least they fear me enough to want me, she'd thought. The merchants, and the lout.

She'd turned him down. He'd turned nasty. Said she was selling herself cheap, working protection for crossroads fleatraps.

"Aren't you tired of being a washed-up legend? Kazhe n'Zhevra, bodyguard to the Lightbreaker. Can't make choices for yourself, without some darkmage pulling your strings?"

"His name was Torrin," she'd growled.

"His name was traitor," Arron had said, his burred accent thickening, and that was when her knife went into the wood and he stumbled up and away. He'd mistaken her for someone else, she said, and if she saw him again she wouldn't be aiming for the table.

"I only made one mistake," he'd said as he backed to

the door. *"I didn't wait for you to get through the next barrel of stout."*

Bleeding spirits, she hated Highlanders.

She retrieved her stool and gripped the seat to guide herself onto it. She picked up her tankard with two hands. It seemed like years since the last draught, as if in the moment of keeling face-first into the table she had journeyed to a far time and place. The shakes eased as the bitter, creamy liquid went down. A meal in a mug, that's what this stuff was. Forget your ales and shandies. You could live on this. Forget careering brigandage you could have prevented with a maiming blow. Forget the insults you shouldn't have let pass.

Forget the past. That was the point. Somewhere was the memory of drinking with shielders—the looks of disgust, even pity, as they went on their way. Today? The day before? It didn't matter. Lift the tankard, take a swallow, there went the memory. Somewhere below that, the memory of driving her lover off; lift, swallow, drown that memory a little deeper. Worse hurts lay wrecked in the depths. The draughts of stout blended into draughts of ale and beer and wine, a stream running backward through the years and disappearing into a swallowhole, down and down into the darks of the earth.

Yet somehow the bottom of even the dullest tankards showed the same clear moment. Only when they were filled would the vision of Torrin Wordsmith's fall ripple and grow dark.

"I see you're still keeping your back to the wall."

The familiar voice made her blink, though she was too well greased to startle. She'd taken no interest in the woman who came through the door. Folk came, folk went; it was a tavern. Now she absorbed the watchful demeanor, the grip of a longblade peeping over the shoulder, the extra belt sheaths. She should have noticed this one. Shielder or brigand, someone that bladed deserved her attention. How many tankards had she downed since kissing the table?

She took in the long black hair, the olive skin, the green eyes, and knew: Not enough. Not nearly enough.

"Verlein."

"Hello, Kazhe. Long time."

"Not long enough."

"Longer than you know." Shieldmaster Verlein n'Tekla swung a leg around the lout's stool and sat. "A lot's happened while you wallowed in the bottom of a cask."

Kazhe's lips drew back in a snarl that would have passed for a grin in other company. "Straight to the point. I taught you to dance better than that."

"I've made some modifications in your teachings."

"I saw," Kazhe said on a belch. "Your shielders waddle by now and then. You've done ill by those blades, lengthening them. *Tapering* them."

"To a finer point," Verlein said. "They thrust through the holes in mail."

"The hole's in the opponent's guard. If it's down to his mail he's dead anyway."

"I'm not here to argue bladecraft. We do things my way now."

Kazhe barked out a laugh and wiped spittle from her mouth with the back of her hand. "And may the spirits save you all."

"How long since you've eaten, Kazhe?"

Kazhe lifted her tankard. "This is the only food they serve here. And you won't buy me with this or any other meal, whatever it is you want." She drained it off, and the serving boy was right there to take it for a refill.

"You've trained him well," Verlein said after passing him a tallystone to fetch her a brandy.

"Better than I did you."

"I took what I could use and left the rest."

Kazhe made a sloppy gesture toward a particular sheath at Verlein's belt. "Yet you still wear that."

Verlein touched the yellowed grip of the dagger in that sheath and said, "A memento. A relic of friendship. A reminder that there's a world out there and I can fight it when it comes."

The dagger was a cheit, the smallest of a kenai blademaster's three magecrafted weapons. Two of those weapons—the cheit and the tain, or lesser blade—went to prentices when they showed mastery. The third, the greater blade, the kenai longblade sheathed on Kazhe's back, no blademaster bequeathed until death—and then only to her finest student. Verlein had been meant to receive that blade. Kazhe had trained Verlein in blade-craft, bestowing the cheit upon her as the first acknowl-edgment of skill. Kazhe had trained Verlein in bladecraft that Verlein might overthrow an Ennead of malicious mages. But the rogue mage Torrin, Kazhe's charge, had destroyed them in the magewar—and himself in the process—and the magelight that had shielded Eiden Myr from the outer realms. Verlein was left to form a human shield in magecraft's place, defending their land's coasts with what had been her rebel horde. As the years ground past and no attacks came, Verlein built that human shield into something else, something more, something new: an armed force that could turn all too easily on the land it shielded.

Kazhe had chosen ill in choosing her.

The boy brought her freshened tankard. She washed the tightness from her throat with a long pull, then kept pulling, and handed it back to him empty. Her father's shade was long gone to the spirits. If they were kind, he'd never know the fate of the dagger that had been his, and his master's before him.

"Aren't you going to tell me the outer realms are a tellers' tale?" Verlein said.

Tellers. Holes. Didn't they have tellers in this hole? She felt the maudlins coming on. A wistful tale to bring a tear to the eye, now, that would suit her. To have her heart lifted and crushed by events that hadn't touched her, to exult and ache and grieve for things that never were. She wanted a teller, a fantasy, not some haunt of the past made flesh.

"You should have come at another time," she said. Her words were blurred, distant. "Earlier. Or another day."

Now was a time to be mawkish, to laugh and cry at wisps and vapors, to find the illusory camaraderie of vine and grain among shadowy strangers in a wayside place whose name she didn't even know. To feel, for a space of breaths, something that felt like sentiment. To paint an illumination of life over the hard numb plank of herself—and then go black, know nothing, and wake under a table or in a ditch with simple, burning needs that could be met. A drink of water. A mug of elderbark tea. A thirst that could be quenched, an ache that could be soothed. She'd plunge her head into a stream, then spend the time from waking till noon with her longblade driven hilt-down into the ground. Watching its shadow contract against it. Waiting to see whether midday came before she accepted the blade's justice. When midday won, she could unearth the blade, and sheath it, and walk through some alehouse door and feel the first cool blessed flow of relief in her gullet.

She would be happy then. She would be entertaining and entertained, she would welcome reminiscences of youth and fervent beliefs. That would have been the time for this. Not now.

"All the days are the same, for you," Verlein said, and in that faraway voice, on that faraway face hazed by smoke and long years, Kazhe thought there was a quiet pity.

"Why do you *plague* me?" she snarled, expanding from her seat, blooming from the small tight kernel of herself. Her voice came out of that distant, muted place and swelled into a roar: "*Why do you plague me?*"

"I need you, Kazhe. Sit down."

No tales. No laughter. No sweet tears. She sank back onto the stool, dead weary. "Go away, Verlein. You're a ghost. Haunt someone else."

"I'm real, Blademaster, and I have need of you."

Kazhe drank, and when the mouthful struggled back up as bile, she drank again to wash it down. She waved a hand in resignation: *Say what you will.* She laughed, belatedly noting the honorific, and then sighed. *Blademaster.* Her father's name. She'd never been meant to take it up so soon. But when she killed the turncloaks who'd killed him, she'd done it with his blade. It had become her blade, bequeathed by him in death, and she could never be free of it thereafter. She couldn't lose it, she couldn't cast it off. It always came back to her. It contrived to hide itself, keep itself safe, and then return to her keeping, whatever she did.

"We fought the Ennead," Verlein was saying. "Together or apart, it was the same fight. But it's not over. There's one left of the Ennead. There's one left of you to kill her."

Ennead. How long since she had heard that word? How much longer since she had cared? *"We both only ever tried to keep what we loved alive,"* someone had said to her once. *"For me it was a way of life. For you it was a man."*

But Torrin fell, and Torrin died, while she was bashing herself against the magecrafted warding that kept her from his side in the magewar, her throat screamed raw, her blade useless, and Torrin fell, and Torrin died, and all the long stream of ale had done nothing to soothe the burning screams.

"There's no one left to fight, Verlein," she said, so clearly that for a moment she thought someone spoke for her. "I lost the only fight that ever counted."

"No, there's one fight left," Verlein replied. "And you're losing that one."

Kazhe came back to herself at the table, saw the undulating grain in the flamewood, the gouge her boot knife had made, the layers of polish, the pewter tankard in her hand. She tilted it, peering close, but the gray metal gave back no reflection.

As dull as the metal, she said, "Tell me who you want me to kill."

"No. Not while you're like this." Verlein sipped her brandy—the first sip she'd taken—then rose from her seat. "I'm staying in the inn in Tilgard, down the road. Your blade was sworn to protect, Kazhe. The man you protected is gone. I'll give you all Eiden Myr to protect in his stead—if you come to me tomorrow at sunset, clean and with no drink in you."

Kazhe huffed in disbelief. "I won't join your fool shield."

"I wouldn't have you. You don't follow orders."

"*What*, then?"

"Meet my terms and I'll tell you."

"Fine," Kazhe said, throwing her hands up. Then, with a twist to her mouth that was meant to be wry but turned out crafty, she said, "You going to drink that?"

Verlein stared at the brandy cup and said, "I remember the night we met." *No*, Kazhe thought, *don't*, but Verlein didn't hear. "You were two nineyears old, all white-blond fluff of hair and blazing eyes. Full of rage and courage. Don't drown that wild, bright flame. I loved you Kazhe. So did Torrin, in his way. But my heart is still beating. *My* heart can still be broken."

Then she was gone, on a swell of pain, leaving Kazhe alone in the midst of strangers, with a tankard of dark grief and failure at one hand, a cup of pungent Koeve brandy in the other.

"Till tomorrow," she said, lifted the cup in a toast to the closing door, and downed the brandy in three searing gulps.

*

She was wet. Not the river. From the stink, not a ditch.

"Wake up," someone crooned, not for the first time. Then, harder, "Wake up, runt. I have to see you take the lesson."

A fist in her shirt, pulling up, shoving back. The ooze and squish of an open midden under her back. She smelled a barn or stable. Another voice, lower. More than one of them. Life came back into her limbs on a surge of exhilarating fear, but she left them limp. She kept her eyes closed, and listened.

Only two. One was Arron. She knew the voice. He'd been alone. Or so she'd thought. The rest blurred. It didn't matter. He had a friend now.

"Pick her up."

"I'm not touching that. You pick her up."

An oath. Muffled thuds of boots on dirt. A bucket swung by its handle, slapping into a stream. Maybe nine feet away. She cracked open a crusty eye. One had turned to watch the other fill the bucket.

Novices.

She took the near one out with an elbow across the jaw as he turned at the sound of her sucking rise, then a knee to the crotch, all before her body's state caught up with her. She shoved him into the dungheap; she wobbled but didn't go down. Arron was visible in the light of stars and a hangnail moon. Running from the stream, awkward with the bucket. She stepped back into the shadow of the barn. The bucket was too heavy to swing around in time. He flung the water at where she'd been, a pale arc. She came at him from the side, less an attack than a headlong stumble. He was just off balance enough for the impact to knock him down. Even impaired, she got his arms locked while he was still trying to flip over.

He swore at her, and she jerked hard, feeling ligaments strain—not all his. "Wasting your time," she managed through a swollen, grit-thick mouth. "Taverner has your stones. Taverner has twice your bloody stones."

He answered with a choking sound. The smell was unbearable. She grinned, feeling it soak into his clothes.

A yellow light came around the side of the stable barn. The taverner and his boy. The boy held the lantern. The taverner held her scabbarded longblade.

She pushed away from Arron and stumbled up. Not graceful, and she dropped the weapon when the over-eager taverner tossed it to her, but once she had the grip in her hand the blade centered her. She stepped away as the louts got their feet. The friend had the worse of it, and was swearing at Arron, something about how this was supposed to be an easy one-off, just a scare. Kazhe frowned.

The taverner said, "They kicked through the bolt on the door. Good thing you were sleeping there, Blademaster. From the looks of it nothing was taken. But I told you you should have hung on to your weapon."

The bloody taverner had heard the crash and cowered in his room while the two men dragged her out and around the side of the stable. Kazhe wanted to close her eyes and hold her head, but her line of sight along the blade was the only reason she hadn't fallen. She supposed she should credit him for coming down to bring her the blade. She didn't remember entrusting it to him, but at least that kept it out of the dungheap. Any of her eight smaller blades would have done if it came to that. Some instinct must have told her that Arron might return while she was passed out and take her blade as a consolation prize.

She wondered why she hadn't left it for him.

"I'll only need the flat of this," she said. "Neither of you will do much robbing with broken arms, I'd say, and if you're careful, the gangrene shouldn't get you."

"Bloody spirits!" cried the friend. "We're not robbers!"

"You could have just asked for the stones back," Kazhe went on. "And if you take such insult from a knife stuck in a tabletop, you have no business drinking in taverns."

"We were sent," said the friend, ignoring Arron waving him to silence.

"*Sent?*" Her own raised voice sent a spike through her head, but didn't kill the ironsmith using her skull for an anvil. She bit down on a groan. A fractured, painful glare haloed the lantern, and all movement took on a throbbing translucence in the approach of dawn.

"Her shielders saw you drinking here, couple of days ago, and she sent us on ahead to see how far you could be pushed, then knock some sense into you," Arron said at last, bitterly. "She told us the day you lost a fight because of drink, you'd never look at an alehouse again. She said if we could shame you enough . . . But there'll be no deal now that I've told you."

"The deal broke when I didn't lose the fight." A little stable muck never hurt anyone, though it was going to be a cold job washing it off in the stream.

"They came here to mess you about?" the taverner said. "If not for you and them, I'd still have a bolt on my door?"

Kazhe nearly burst out laughing, but it would have hurt too much. Poor, naive taverner. It was so nice when he was legendstruck. She'd be sleeping rough the rest of this night.

Unless she put it to better use.

She sent Arron and his friend off on foot with hard words and a slap of her blade. Let them walk back to Verlein, or the Highlands, or wherever they belonged. She told the taverner's boy to fetch her horse; he glanced at his father or master for permission, got only a bewildered shrug, and went into the barn. *I still have a horse,* she thought with mild surprise. She remembered gambling it away somewhere, but perhaps she'd won it back. Or perhaps it was a different horse—but it was Comfrey led sleepy and rankled from the barn, and her saddle on his back.

"Which way is Tilgard?" she asked, taking the reins.

The taverner pointed downland. In the bluing light, she saw that the road followed the stream. That suited her. She'd have her wash, and clean and oil her blades, and the morning sun would dry her. She started off, leading the horse although he nipped her shoulder hard.

"Who were they talking about?" the taverner called after.

"Who sent them, you mean? That bladed Souther."

" 'Her shielders,' that man said. Was she . . . ?"

Kazhe kept moving. "Verlein n'Tekla," she called without turning. "You had the first of Eiden's shield in your tavern."

She left them to whisper excitedly about their new brush with legend, and contemplated the joys of stuffing legend's beating heart down its throat.

*

At midmorning, Kazhe burst into the Tilgard inn and strode toward the big oak table where Verlein and two seconds, a man and a woman, were only just breakfasting.

"An ale!" she called to the innkeeper, whose wide eyes peered from the cookroom. "Make it two. And none of that black stuff. One for now, and one for after I break the first shield over my knee."

She dropped the man with an elbow to the stomach pit while he was reaching back for his longblade, and spun the woman away with a kick to the hip so that her blade, coming into play, had only air to cleave. Her gloved hand closed on the blade of Verlein's battle knife, forcing it wide, while her forearm across Verlein's throat bore its wielder back against the wall. Fingers hooked around the knife's guard twisted it from Verlein's grasp, and she laid the blade on her own forearm, pressing the tip up into the soft flesh under Verlein's chin before the taller woman could land a blow or draw a different blade.

"Weapons turn on you if you misuse them," she growled.

"The ale was a mistake," Verlein managed through a constricted airway. "You have only till sundown to meet my terms."

"I chewed up your terms," Kazhe said. "They went in the midden."

"And you, from the smell of it."

"I took your message boys with me." Without looking, she said, "I'll drive this through her brain in the death spasm," and the seconds withdrew as noisily as they'd tried to sneak up.

"Stand down," Verlein rasped at them. "She won't hurt me."

"I wouldn't say that," Kazhe crooned.

"Don't you want to know what the mission is?"

"Not on your terms."

"State yours, then."

Kazhe shoved back and flipped Verlein her knife. "Outside."

The shielders obliged her on a nod from Verlein. Kazhe crooked a finger at the innkeeper, who stood frozen with two mugs in her hand, then swore and walked over to take one from her. She picked up an elderflower fritter on the way by, and washed it down with the tepid ale. "Ahhh," she said, wiping her mouth with the back of her hand. "Better already. My thanks."

The seconds had positioned themselves to either side of the door, which opened inward. Kazhe ducked out and back and let them tangle with each other in trying to grab her, then cocked her head at Verlein and waited.

"Good training for them," Verlein said with a shrug, and gestured them back to her side.

Kazhe stepped into the grassy yard. Comfrey was tied to a hedge around the side of the building. Tilgard was a pleasant village, all whitewashed stone, thatched roofs, dark-leaved trees. "You and me," she said, flipping knives into a neat column in a mulberry's trunk. "Long-blades. You best me, I do whatever it is."

"And if you best me?"

"Then I win."

Verlein removed her own shortblades from belt and thigh and boots, laying them down with care, and the cheit with them. "You needed a cause to fight for, once."

"I fight for the bloody thrill of it. But since you asked . . . I'll have that cheit back, too."

Verlein looked up sharply. "I don't think so."

Kazhe grinned. "Does my little dagger make fools take you for a kenai blademaster?" She shrugged out of her crosswise harness and slid the oiled, ancient scabbard off the magecrafted kenai, the weapon that had been her father's, the weapon no blademaster bequeathed until death. "Or are you just sentimental?"

Verlein drew her long tapered blade and thrust forward in answer. Kazhe, flinging the scabbard aside and adding her left hand to the kenai's grip, countered with a bark of glee.

Verlein's opening thrust was arrow-straight and aimed at the belly, meant to prove the merit of her blade's design. She gripped it one-handed and turned her body, presenting a narrowed target—as though they stood on a practice strip, as though they fought along a single line. Had she abandoned the eight directions of movement? In her obsession with meeting straight-on invasion, had she conceived battle as only advance and retreat?

Kazhe passed forward and to the left and bore Verlein's blade down easily. The same motion served as a cut to the legs. Verlein sprang back to save her thigh and stop Kazhe bearing in on her from the side. Kazhe followed onto her right foot with a rising false-edge cut. Verlein halfbladed to block it, left hand on the weak of the blade. Kazhe did the same, and grinned at the shriek of iron on iron as they vied to slip past each other's point of resistance, to yield to the strong and draw the other off balance, to dart over or under and hook blade with guard or lever arm with hilt. Verlein made a bid to grapple. Kazhe sprang free and spat at the ground. This would not descend to wrestling. This was a contest of blades.

They resumed their guards at middle distance.

Verlein's flat stance was strange. Kazhe danced around it, testing her footwork, making her pivot, trying to force her back into a square-on stance. Verlein persisted in turning her body, shoulders angled to legs when she passed forward. Power derived from the alignment of hips and shoulders. It was a dramatic change in style, a weakening of all Kazhe had taught her. Kazhe moved fluidly through guards, seeking a way in. Verlein, voiding and winding and disengaging, never met her full in the bind, never jeopardized her weaker weapon. Instead she exploited her longer reach, her slimmer, swifter blade.

A tapered blade. A thrusting blade.

Verlein counted on her fluid wrist to be more deft than the two hands with which Kazhe levered and spun her grip. She turned her body to protect it as she maneuvered herself to dart in for the thrust or the harassing slice, again and again.

Verlein was a shielder. She was meant to be holding a shield in that off hand.

Or a dagger. A cheit.

Understanding at last, Kazhe attacked with full intent.

Burning, exhilarated, she turned Verlein in circles, backed her against trees, broke her stance again and again, made her leap and hop, sway and duck. Then she slashed under a high assault for a clean cut across Verlein's midriff, taking a slice to the shoulder for it, gasping with the ecstasy of pain—laughing to see Verlein's eyes fly wide.

To Verlein, this was a demonstration. A first-blood

bout to prove supremacy of style. She had let Kazhe attack the blade while she waited for her to tire. The first cut should have ended it; the two cuts should end it in a draw.

Verlein had not forgotten the eight directions—six forward and back on the straight and diagonal, one to each side. But she had forgotten the ninth direction.

The ninth direction was down. To death.

Kazhe drove in through a reddening haze, heedless of the damage the longer blade would inflict should she blink or falter. Under her own sharp, powerful exhalations she heard Verlein order her to stand down, as if she were one of her toy fighters. Under the next "Hup!" and clang of iron, it sounded like an offer to yield. But there was no yielding here. There would never, ever be any yielding.

Only a ruse of feigned yielding. The teacher's oldest trick: the invitation to underestimate. Would Verlein remember the hard lessons in the fields? Or had the sight of the drunken wreck wiped the memory clean? Still appearing to give her all, Kazhe hunched her shoulders and let her point drop below eye level in middle guard. Just a tad, a nearly imperceptible change of angle. She set Verlein's next thrust aside and failed to press through. She dropped her elbow in hanging guard, let her cut fall just shy, flopped her arms into low guard and let her blade point brush the ground. Just enough to signal that, ravaged from drink, out of practice, short on sleep, off her stride, she was beginning to flag. She drew Verlein in with each strike made too close to her own body. She invited her in, with elbows too bent, cuts too short. She passed back, but not quite out of range. When Verlein, still wary but irresistibly tempted, committed to one flung-out cut at the legs—meant to pay Kazhe back for the belly slash, delivered with only the pommel retained in her grip—Kazhe stepped in, whacked Verlein's forearm with the cross of her hilt, and lifted her blade above her shoulder to deliver the strike of wrath.

"Die, Verlein," she said, and brought her blade down with all the power of her body.

Verlein dove headlong past her. She groped for her fallen blade, failed to snag it as Kazhe pivoted, and rolled aside just a hair before Kazhe's reversed blade would have brained her with a hammer blow. Disarmed, she scrabbled to regain her feet and put a tree between herself and the vicious madness that was Kazhe, shouting for her seconds.

Kazhe let them grapple her, let them drag her away from Verlein, but would not release her blade even when one of them cracked a pommel on her knuckles. The blade was part of her. She was the blade. There was no word for blademaster. The word for blade and wielder was the same. She was kenai. She was the blade.

"There are no bouts, Verlein," she said through blood after the gauntleted second whacked her in return for a peremptory shin kick. "There are no terms. There's only dying, and not dying. You've forgotten that."

"The drink has cracked you. You were never like this."

"I was always like this. That's why you loved me. Come on, Verlein. Pick up your iron hazel switch. We're not finished."

"We're finished, Kazhe. I am going to tell you what to do, and for once in your bloody benighted life you are going to do it."

"Or what? You'll hand me the pieces of your *broken heart?*"

"I'll hand you the pieces of this broken land. The Khinish are going to march. I'm going to stop them if they do. The Ennead's ghost is whispering in their ear, inciting them to conquer. Assassinate the ghost, and chances are they'll pull their thrust and go back where they belong. Terrorize that poor innkeeper into pouring drink down your throat, and my shield will battle the Khinish and this peaceful land will soak in blood."

"You had to best me. Those were the terms. I owe you nothing."

"You refused the terms. The shield bested you." Verlein gestured at the seconds who held Kazhe's arms.

As though just noticing them, Kazhe buckled one with a heel behind the knee, freed that arm by cocking its elbow under the woman's jaw as she fell, dispensed the other with a groin strike, then asserted her space with a lazy sweep of blade. "Relying on shields is only one of the flaws in your new technique."

With a hiss, Verlein opened her arms and her empty hands and moved inside the blade, close enough for Kazhe to smell the scallions on her breath, the sweat on her body. "You listen to me. It's going to be them or us. If the Khinish carve out supremacy, they'll have us in irons. You will do whatever I tell you to do in order to keep them off us."

"The Khinish are olive growers. They have no reason to carve anything."

"The Khinish were formidable conquerors once. Warriors who invaded and took control of other lands."

Control.

Kazhe blinked. "You want to *rule*."

"No, I command. I already have that. I want to save us."

Kazhe shoved away and turned to sheath the kenai. "You seek to wield me like a blade."

"You are a blade," Verlein said. "You are kenai. The only one left." She strode halfway to where Kazhe was picking her knives one by one from the flesh of the tree. "Be good for something. *Do* something."

Kazhe sheathed the last knife in her belt as she sheathed Verlein's words in her mind. Newfangled shielders and ancient warriors: Two forces vying to conquer *their own land*. Spurred by some surviving member of a corrupt mage cadre, or merely inventing justifications for war—it didn't matter which. All that mattered was that one of them would win.

Kazhe turned with a roundhouse punch that sent Verlein sprawling on the grass. She watched unseeing as blood gushed from the shieldmaster's nose.

No one had ever ruled this land. Not even the Ennead, manipulating their web of mages from their dark fastness. No one.

Her blade was sworn to protect. For as long as there had been people of light, there had been kenaila—their shadows, their blades, pledged to kill in their defense, to take the stain of death on their souls in order to keep the mages safe. Pledged to die for them.

Most of them had. Kazhe should have, too. She should have died with her father in the silken grasslands of home, when the Ennead's turncloak kenaila came to kill him. She should have died with Torrin in the magewar. But she had not.

Now she knew why. There was one thing left to defend, protect, preserve. One thing still to die for.

Freedom.

The blade had come back to her. As it always did.

"You will not rule," Kazhe told Verlein. "You will not rule the world that mages made. And you will not rule *me*."

She mounted her horse, ignoring his irritable nip at her foot when she reined him from the tasty hedge, and rode straight through the shielders, scattering them.

That was her answer. That was her vow. *I will ride through your forces with the forces I will raise, and I will scatter you, and your enemies, and there will be no ruling then*. Whether Verlein would understand it, she didn't know. Verlein had been a slow study, though relentless. She let words sway her when she should have looked only to actions.

Kazhe had no use for words. Only deeds would save Eiden Myr.

Only a victor who refused to rule.

Or be ruled.

That night, in another public house, Kazhe regarded the tankard in her hand, her knuckles blanching on its handle, the dull nothing it reflected and the ale it no longer held. "*You* will not rule me," she said, very softly. She rose, and left that place, and got back on her horse. He bit her arm, but he bore her true.

The next morning, on a ferry bound across the water that lay between her and the myriad grasses of home—between her and the proud, loyal folk she would forge into a blade, a bladebreaking blade, the greatest blade, a breaker of armies—she sent the tankard spinning end over end into the sea.

THE SKIN TRADE

by Heather Rose Jones

In all of Heather's *Sword & Sorceress* bios so far, some mention has been made of her grad school career in linguistics. Two days before she received the acceptance notice for this story, she delivered the final (we hope!) draft of her Ph.D. dissertation, "Cognitive Aspects of the Grammaticalization of Medieval Welsh Prepositions," to her committee.

Now she plans to turn her writing energies back toward fiction and her many research projects. As we assemble this anthology, she is working as a technical editor for Bayer, but it's a temporary contract so there's no guarantee what she'll be doing when this story sees print.

A good prediction is that it will involve doing things to language. When Ann Sharp sent out contracts, she asked writers to recommend a Web site that readers would find interesting or useful. Heather says she decided to be slightly self-serving (since she has a few articles on the site) and recommend the Medieval Names Archive at http://www.panix.com/~mittle/names/. Fiction writers—whether of sf or any other flavor—usually share the need to name their characters, and when those characters have a historic setting, or one inspired by history, brainstorming for the "right" names can be a stumbling block. The Medieval Names Archive, while not aimed specifically at writers, is an extensive collection of articles intended to help people create historically accurate names for particular times and places. It certainly sounds useful to us.

Looking back, the moment I walked through the gates of Wilentelu, I set my feet on the trail that led me home again. But I would have laughed at the thought then, because we stayed in Wilentelu far longer than we ever intended.

We came there to deliver horses. Eysla's brother Toral
had made a contract with the Marchalt of Wilentelu and
because Eysla and I had never traveled in that direction
before, we were more than willing to take the offered
chance. Toral and I had come a fair distance since our
first meeting. Then, I was the witch who had bespelled
his sister. Well, and by his eyes it was true—I made the
skin-song for Eysla's dead mare that let her wear it and
run four-footed across the hills. We Kaltaoven don't
think of that as witchery any more than you would think
it of fire or of language itself. But in the face of his
sister's determination, he retreated by small steps: first,
not to kill me; then, to allow us within his clan's lands
but only in human shape. Then, one day last winter,
when the need was great, he had begged us to put on
our skin-cloaks, when only those bodies could prevail. I
counted it a victory when, at last, his only remaining
grudge was that I was his sister's lover.

Now there were horses to deliver at a long distance,
and Toral had no more doubts about asking us to take
them than if he had done it himself. And for once Eysla
and I approached a new town riding side by side, instead
of Eysla wearing her skin to carry both me and our belongings on her back. I'd had no experience with horses
until I met Eysla—I had to learn to ride all over again
on this trip.

My teacher, Laaki, had told stories of the stone-built
cities in the north, but I'd never truly believed that many
people could all live in the same place. When we first
saw Wilentelu at a distance, it was just a collection of
walls and roofs on a rocky rise that stood out from the
broad green river valley. But then we rode all morning
and it grew only slowly nearer. The "little river" turned
into a wide but sluggish flood and the horses balked at
the crossing until Eysla lost patience and sang her cloak
about her to lead them across. She had finally learned
the trick of taking our baggage in under her skin as well,
so we made the crossing dry. A rest on the far bank gave
us the chance to repack our gear, stow our skin-cloaks
away, and to brush the horses into a more impressive

show. No harm in making sure the Marchalt knew he was getting full value. Three riders from the city met us halfway from the riverbank—wiry, compact men on horses that made me understand why they had searched so far to find better. They shouted orders at us and at each other in a thick version of Eysla's native tongue, and together we gathered the herd into a rough pen set against the city wall. When the gate was closed at last, the first of them nodded briefly in our direction then turned back to watch the horses mill and circle in the pen. It was clear he thought he had dismissed us. I moved back into his path. "Forgive my discourtesy, but we were told to deliver them to the Marchalt himself."

He looked me up and down as if only noticing me for the first time. "You have." And then as an afterthought, "Come to the Shalen later for your delivery fee." Then it was clear he had no more attention to give us, even to hear that we hadn't expected a fee, so we gathered up our bags and set off around the curve of the walls toward the main gate. They were built in a warm yellow sandstone that was only just beginning to soften around the edges. It had glowed like gold from a distance. But the walls were thick and high—meant for some hard purpose—and the guards who stopped us at the gate questioned us closely, even though our purpose must have been obvious. If we wanted to sell goods, we must pay a fee at the guildhall; when we found lodging we must register at the Shalen; before we left, we must have permission from the Marchalt. We entered with our heads whirling, and if not for the promised fee and the itch to see what lay within, we might have turned back instead.

*

The wonder was worth it. Even more than my own memories, I remember watching Eysla take it all in. Walking through the streets of Wilentelu was like galloping in horse-skin across rough ground: exciting; with new sights rushing past wherever you looked, every moment thinking you can't continue at that pace, but never wanting to stop.

"Ashóli," she whispered to me. "Where do they all live? How do they feed them all?"

And then we came out from a canyon made by two buildings into an open, stone-floored field and there was the answer: people selling every kind of food, and more.

"We may leave with everything we brought," I grumbled. We were more used to small villages hungry for anything from outside. Even more, we were used to being obvious strangers and stared at, but here no one seemed to notice us, and we did all the staring. Perhaps everyone was a stranger to them—we saw people from every place we'd traveled through, and more that we hadn't.

We tired of walking, or rather, of carrying all our goods, before we tired of looking, and asked the way to the guildhall as we'd been told. And once we'd paid our fees and been told the rules of when and where we could sell, we were directed to a house with rooms available, by chance belonging to a cousin of the guildhall clerk.

"I want to do nothing but sleep!" Eysla said, testing out the first real bed we'd seen in a month.

I sorted out the bundle of our spare clothes from the goods we carried to sell. "We need to find this Shalen first. At the gate they said we need to tell where we're staying, and I want to collect that fee while the Marchalt still remembers he offered it."

Eysla groaned and sat up. "Both of us?"

I focused very carefully on smoothing out our clean garments. "I'd rather we stayed together."

She heard in my voice what I tried to conceal. "It's all so strange, but do you think there's any danger?"

I shrugged. "I don't know. I just . . . I'd rather not be separated for now."

She took my hand and stood up. "But at least let me fetch some water to wash."

And because there seemed no reason not to among such exotic sights, and because it made for a finer display, we took our skin-cloaks with us, as well as wearing our best clothes. Sometimes we were more cautious. Laaki had tried to teach me to be wary of all strangers and assume there were enemies everywhere, and I could understand why she felt that way, given what she had seen. But I had Eysla as an argument on the other side, and all the people on our travels who had not cared—or not known—what the cloaks meant. It seemed to me that if you did not put on or cast off a skin-shape in front of people, they were mostly content to let you be. And we had survived the few exceptions well enough.

Shalen, as we understood, meant "king's house," but the Marchalt was not the king—he only led the king's soldiers in Wilentelu and collected the fees and kept watch for raids. It seemed an awkward way to live, to have a clan so wide that you might only see your ruler once in the year. Strange as well to have people whose only work was to carry weapons. But in every town, they said, there was a Shalen, not simply for the king to live in when he passed through, but so those who were his eyes and hands would stand under his roof and so in his authority. It stood near the center of the city, or so I guessed, and the sandstone had been covered by a smoother, harder face, with veins of color. The first room we entered was like a stone forest, with the roof held high above our heads by tall columns. At the far end, raised up, stood an empty chair, and then a smaller chair before it to one side, but it, too, was empty. People came and went along the aisles to either side, and just as in the market square they took no notice of us until we asked the way.

I think I had expected to see the Marchalt himself, but it was a quiet, piercing-eyed clerk who gave use the money and had us mark his book and then took the information on our lodgings. But as we left, the head man was sitting in the side chair in the main hall, talking to a group of people. He looked up and saw us passing and sent a guard to bring us close while he dismissed the others.

"You're Keltowin," he said abruptly, pointing to my cloak.

It took me a moment to untangle his pronunciation. "Yes," I said hesitantly. "I am Kaltaoven, a skin-wearer.

We—" I shot a glance at Eysla. It was too complicated to explain the full story. "We are."

"You should have told me. I like to know these things."

He didn't seem angry; he only said it as a fact, but my heart was racing and every sense was alert to what lay between us and the door. "We didn't know," I stammered. "Forgive. . . ."

He made a dismissive gesture. "What shapes do you wear? No, let me guess." He reached out to finger my cloak and I tried not to flinch back. "A forest cat and," he glanced at Eysla, "a horse. A pity—I might have had work for you if it were something more useful. There's a bird-man lives off by the east gate who carries messages to Mergenel for me, but a cat's not much practical use and real horses serve as well as magic ones."

I think I was struck dumb for several moments. I had known people who feared us or envied us, and even one or two who thought we were gods, but I'd never heard us taken so much for granted. "Bird-man" indeed. Eysla filled the gap.

"We regret there is no service we can do for you."

He waved off the apology once more. "A pity," he repeated. "I sometimes think what I could do with an entire troop of your people. To combine the best skills of men and beasts. . . ." He shook his head. "But Keale says there are few of you in these lands, and too far scattered."

When we had first set out on our travels together, Eysla might have blurted out the truth—that I could sing skins for anyone, as I had for her, and not only for my own people. And then I would have had to make excuses and we would have quarreled. She had learned the value of secrets since then. And I had come to the truth of Laaki's accusations: that I had sung a skin for Eysla to show off my own power, to impress her, and to prove that I could. There was more to being Kaltaoven than wearing a cloak, and few who weren't born to it managed well.

And so we were dismissed and had nothing to worry us but sleeping in comfort until well into the next morning.

*

But when we rose finally and had eaten, rather than searching out a place in the market to begin selling, I suggested that we explore the city some more . . . beginning with the east gate.

"To find Keale?" Eysla asked.

I nodded.

"Perhaps you would rather go alone."

"What's this nonsense?" I demanded. "Do you think I plan to abandon you for the first Kaltaoven I meet since I left home?"

She shrugged but didn't meet my eyes.

"Don't be silly. You're my skin-daughter, my road-sister, and my heart. Birth couldn't make you any closer than you are already. Do I worry every time we visit your family that you'll shed your skin and leave me?"

She tilted her head and smiled sideways at me. "Yes."

I laughed. "Be fair! Not since that first time, and confess that you gave me reason!"

Then she stood and threw her cloak around her and kissed me. "The east gate, then, and a man we've never met who may or may not be wearing a feathered cloak."

*

But as it turned out, the search was short. The east gate market was for goods from far foreign lands: cloth and spices, fine jewelry and rough gems, songbirds and strange books. And just when I was ready to begin asking where the man named Keale lived, I looked down between two hampers of small furs—ermine, sable, and miniver—and sitting in a wicker tray was a small, intricately carved wooden bowl of a design my cousins made. Then I looked up into the pleasantly plain face of a woman, framed by a collar of soft gray fox fur, who was staring with equal intensity at my own cloak.

I scrambled for the words for a moment. Eysla and I spoke the Kaltaoven tongue between us all the time, but the last time I had addressed someone in the formal mode was when Laaki was newly come to our village.

She, I think, had the same difficulty, and stammered out a response at last as Eysla wandered over from the next stall to join us. The small child at the woman's side had no such difficulty and cheerfully cried out a family greeting, only to be shushed and corrected.

"I think you must know Keale," I said, as Eysla murmured her own formal greeting. "The Marchalt mentioned his name yesterday when we arrived," I added quickly when her face tightened in suspicion.

"My husband is at home working," she answered. And then after a slight pause, "Perhaps you will join us for a meal at midday?"

"If it's no burden to you," I responded.

Eysla took the carved bowl from me and turned it over in her hands. The woman switched into market-patter. "It's a fine bowl—well-made and beautiful. Brought at great expense all the way from Karskar. Perhaps it reminds you of home?"

I had to laugh. "More than you know! But it hasn't come anywhere near as far as from Karskar—there's my cousin Goalnen's mark on the bottom."

A bright eagerness came into her face. "Your cousin? Then you—" She broke off. "It isn't the appropriate time for questions. But you will come? We live down the fountain lane." She gestured towards a narrow street by the public well at one side of the square. "Near the end, with the red door. We . . . oh, never mind, if you'll help me carry these things we can go now."

And so, in the end, we gathered her wares back into their hampers and followed her bemusedly to the house with the red door.

*

When he had been fetched out of the back workshop, Keale greeted us with the same bright eagerness. "We don't get many Kaltaoven passing through, and most are far-wanderers like we were. We haven't heard of any settled clans since we each left our own."

And as we were settled onto cushions in the main

room, and plied with food and drink, their story emerged. Keale and Haalan had each left their families, intending it only for a wander-season, but they had lost touch. Keale's family had migrated on, and if they had left signs for him to follow, those had been lost by the time he returned. Haalan's had fled before attackers and she dared not try to follow in case she betrayed them. But the years had cast them both up in Wilentelu and they had found each other.

"It's been a good home," Haalan said. "The Marchalt is a hard man, but he values the service Keale can do for him, and we have been under his protection." There was an edge in her voice that I couldn't sort out yet. "But lately we've been hoping to return to our people, or find a clan to join. Vék is old enough to start wearing a skin, and we have another to come." She laid her hand briefly on her belly. "And they won't find skins here in Wilentelu."

I shot a warning glance over at Eysla and she nodded in understanding. Almost certainly I would offer to sing skins for their children, but I wanted to hear the whole story first. "But you trade with my people," I said. "It's a far distance, but not too far if you have the reason to travel it."

Keale shook his head. "We get those things from travelers. People will pay more for Kaltaoven goods if you wear a skin-cloak even if you bought the goods from another, which benefits us both. But the traders won't tell us anything of where they travel—they're afraid we'd cut them out of the bargain. And even if we knew . . ."

"He wouldn't let you go," Eysla broke in.

I looked at her in surprise. "Who?" The other two clearly knew what she meant.

"The Marchalt," Eysla said. "He does more than value your service, I'd guess—he depends on it. And he doesn't seem the sort to give up something he depends on."

Haalan nodded. "Oh, it's always couched in soft terms. 'It's not convenient at this season, we'll talk about it later,' and 'There's no sense leaving until you have some place to go—let me see what I can discover about these traders for you.' And somehow the seasons turn again. He has us watched."

"I think you're wrong there," Keale said, but she hushed him with an angry glance.

"We might be able to leave the city if we were careful, but we can't travel quickly or quietly with Vék. If he wanted to fetch us back, he has all the way to the border to do it." Her voice grew bitter.

"And what do you want from us?" Eysla asked. I grabbed her arm to warn her but she shook me off. "No, Ashóli. I know it's horribly bad manners to ask such things directly, but we need to know. Why do you trust us with all this when you barely know our names? What do you think we can do to help, and what danger will it bring?"

"I should think we could trust other skin-wearers," Haalan began, then she turned away and started crying. Keale threw up his hands helplessly as the child began bawling in response and I calculated that our welcome was wearing thin.

"You've given us a great deal to think about," I said. "Perhaps tomorrow we could offer you an evening meal and we can talk further? We're staying at the House of the Lilies near the guildhall. May we expect you then?"

Keale nodded with a wry but grateful smile. "We will come."

*

We talked about it, Eysla and I, that evening when we'd had our fill of exploring the city. I'd expected her to argue more for their side, but for once she was the more cautious.

"There's more to this than helping them escape a trap. There's power here and a long reach. If we trick the Marchalt to help them flee, then we can't stay either, and I want more time to taste this place. And what if he takes his revenge on my brother's bargain? There's still the second half to be paid, and the promise of more dealings in the future. This isn't life and death where we need to snatch any way out that offers. There's room for bargaining here."

"Bargaining . . ." I echoed, thinking about the possibilities. "I wish Laaki were here. No one else I know can craft a bargain like she can." She'd taught me how far bargaining could stretch when she bought my death and sold my life back to me.

Eysla smiled—she'd heard the story often enough, although there were parts I'd rather forget. "What sort of bargain would she make?"

"Oh, something complex and interwoven that leaves everyone thinking they've gotten the best of everyone else. I don't have that skill. Even you're better at it than I am." But that gave me ideas, and we talked for a long time about what Keale and Haalan might want, and what the Marchalt might want, and what we might gain between them.

*

We tried our hand as merchants the next day. The crowded market was a hard place to sell. People wanted to be coaxed, cajoled, seduced into considering the possibility that they might have a use for our goods. But the prices they were willing to pay, and in coin, not trade, were startling. By the afternoon opening, we were both enjoying ourselves and there was a promise of high gains, although hard won.

We packed our goods early to have time to pull a meal together before the food market closed as well, but when we returned to the House of Lilies a group of the Marchalt's men were waiting for us and would say nothing to our questions but that we were wanted in the Shalen. So we followed, hoping that the empty room and abandoned food would tell the necessary tale.

We needn't have worried—Keale and Haalan were there before us, standing rigid in the hall before the Marchalt's chair. Vék was in a corner being entertained with a game of sticks by one of the guards.

Haalan looked like she might spit when she saw us. She advanced as far as the guards would allow her and said, "You betrayed us!" Her husband laid a hand on her shoulder and whispered something in her ear, but she shook him off. "You betrayed all our secrets, but I know secrets of yours to tell."

"Which secrets would those be?" I asked. I wasn't going to guess and give away more than they might have already.

The Marchalt had been watching us from his chair with an expression that was impossible to read. But when he raised his hand and pointed at me everyone else fell back and was silent. "Perhaps," he said, "it would be better if you told us what secrets you have to be known. I told you before: I like to know these things."

Eysla's hand slipped into mine and tightened. We'd discussed this the night before. One thing we might bargain for with him was knowledge, but not if he thought he was bargaining. This was a man comfortable with his own power and accustomed to being obeyed. He might reward something freely given, but he wouldn't pay for something he thought he was owed. I took half a step forward and bowed.

"I am a *byal-dónen,* a skin-singer. I can take the skins of beasts and make a song for them so one of our people can wear the skin. It's not a skill we all have." I gestured towards Keale and Haalan. "They needed a skin-cloak for their son to wear and for the child to come. This evening I was going to bargain with them for the cloaks."

I could tell from the surprised look on Keale's face and the expectant look of the Marchalt that this wasn't the secret they had expected to hear. That left only one. I looked back at Eysla, since it was hers to tell.

She stepped forward to stand beside me and said, "I'm not Kaltaoven—it's no secret." She gazed coolly at Haalan. "My tongue and my face make it plain enough to anyone who is."

The Marchalt rose from his chair. "And yet you wear one of these skin-cloaks. For show or for use?"

I could see that it crossed her mind to show him, but she only said, "For use."

His eyes widened as if he hadn't believed that would be the answer. He looked over at me, "Your work?" I nodded. "How is it possible? I was told . . . did you lie to me?" he asked Keale.

"It isn't done," I said quickly. "It's forbidden—I broke the rules."

"Then you can break them again," he said confidently. He gestured to the soldiers who stood by Keale's family. "They can go, but not outside the city walls Not until this is finished." And they left, without looking back at us. Keale, I think, because he was ashamed, and Haalan because she was afraid.

*

Haalan was right: he couched everything in soft words. There was never a time when he said, "Do this, or that will happen," or commanded anything directly. But we soon came to understand that life would be very convenient and pleasant if certain things came to pass that he desired. And then he let us go. It was masterful—he would have been a match even for Laaki, and I had only a fraction of her skills in that field.

When we were alone again in our room we spoke only briefly of leaving. I could take the skin of a night-bird and sing it around the both of us and all our goods for long enough to escape beyond his reach. But all the same arguments remained. We were thoroughly tangled in this tapestry now: by Toral and the horses, by Keale's son and his hope for a skin-cloak, even by that mythical loyalty that I was supposed to share with all Kaltaoven. Like Eysla, I wanted more of a taste of this place—I didn't want to lose the choice of returning. And, strangely enough, I *liked* the Marchalt. What he wanted was impossible, but I could understand why he wanted it. He'd had a taste of how useful we Kaltaoven could be: messages delivered at the speed of birdflight; sentries with eyes and ears beyond what any enemy could manage. To him, we squandered our skills. To us, wearing a skin wasn't a tool; it was what we are.

We didn't sleep well that night, but we slept.

*

In the morning, we didn't wait for soldiers to fetch us—we went to the Shalen as soon as people were stirring in the streets and waited, while whispers ran around us, until the Marchalt appeared.

I told him about the three-fold bargain. "It's a practice we Kaltaoven have, to make ties between families. Three exchanges proposed and accepted. Not marketplace exchanges, but something of deeper value."

He looked amused. "And you would propose one of these triple bargains with me?"

I shook my head. "It's not something I could make with an outsider, but with your permission I would like to propose one with Keale and Haalan."

He was still amused—I counted on that. So he sent for the others to be brought to join us. And when they came, hesitant and nervous, I spread my skin-cloak there on the stone floor of the hall and sat on it to chant the opening call for the three-fold bargain.

They looked at each other, then at the Marchalt, then Keale shrugged and spread his own cloak to sit. He had nothing to lose. He could refuse the bargain, if he chose, with no shame attached.

It was an awkward bargaining—the formal phrases didn't come as easily in a language the Marchalt could understand, but he was my target, even if he'd been willing for us to bargain in the Kaltaoven tongue in his presence. "Here is my first offer," I said, "that I will make a skin-song, as you choose, for your son, and in exchange you will give me your contract with the traders from the north."

Keale considered silently for a moment. "It is a fair bargain," he said at last. "More than fair, but I cannot answer yet. Without those trading contracts we would need to find a new way to live."

I nodded and continued. "Here is my second offer. I will make a skin-song for the child to come, and in exchange you will give me your rights to your house and workshop."

I think he saw, then, the hope of a way out, but he protested the exchange. "The child is yet unborn and anything may befall." He made a sign to avert bad luck. "The house and workshop have solid value. But trading contracts, like an unborn child, are a promise only. Reverse the exchanges and I will consider it fair."

I nodded again and felt my heart begin to race in anticipation. "Here is my third offer. I have rights in a clan for which I have no need." (It was the simple truth—a skin-singer would be welcome back, clan-right or no.) "You have the trust and dependence of a man of power and importance. Will you exchange that for my clan-right?"

I could hear the Marchalt stirring behind me but I dared not look. Keale stared past me, searching for some sign of what to answer. At last he said, "It seems an unfair exchange. That trust and dependence have become a burden to me, but you offer me something of great value for it. For my part, I would accept, but you ask for something that is not mine to give."

I heard the Marchalt's voice behind me. "I have never kept you here against your will. I never refused you permission to leave." But I guessed that he had found ways to discourage the question.

Keale swallowed visibly. "If the Marchalt is willing to give you his trust and rely on your skills, then I gladly surrender them. Is the bargain well-made?"

"*Gyel-dón a-don,*" I said. "It is well-made."

He rose and took up his skin-cloak again, then waited to see what would come next. I rose too and turned at last to face the Marchalt. As always, his face was hard to read. I had committed myself to serve this man for some time to come and I wanted badly to know more of what went on behind that face.

"What bargain will you make with me?" he asked at last.

"The bargain is yours to offer," I countered. I wanted to hear from his own mouth what he thought he could ask for.

"You will carry my messages as a bird—you can take that form?"

I nodded. "I'm a skin-singer—I can take any form I choose. But you needn't bargain for that, it's yours already."

"And you can make a charm for any one—anyone at all—to become a beast as you do?"

"I can sing the skin," I answered, "but it isn't so easy to wear it." I nodded in Eysla's direction where she had been waiting, the more tense for not having a part to play. "When her skin was new, she sometimes lost herself in the beast. If you give a man a skin and he forgets himself, he may never come back. Which of your men is willing to risk that?"

He looked around the room, weighing them. "My men would do much for me." But I saw no volunteers and neither did he. It was one thing to watch witchery unfold in front of you; it was another to have it worked on you.

I knew then where to place my shot. "Would you order a man to do what you would not do yourself?"

For the first time that morning, I saw him smile broadly. "You drive a hard bargain indeed. But my own life isn't mine to risk, it's pledged to my king. Is the danger so great?"

I shrugged. "If I put the skin on you, I can take it off. A taste, if you like. It's safe enough unless you go mad in the first moment."

He shifted in his chair. I had pushed too far. He could not afford to back away now. Abruptly, he headed past me toward the door and snapped his fingers for all of us to follow. In the center of the courtyard he turned to me. "What shape will you give me?"

"Now?" I looked around. "I can only use the skins that are here." But before he could make a choice, Keale came forward and offered his cloak. It wasn't the one I would have picked. A natural falcon is a crazy bird. Beautiful and noble, but completely insane. If I left enough of the bird in the skin to carry him, would it be more than he could handle? Wasn't that what I wanted? To frighten him? But if he took flight there was no easy way to bring him back.

To my relief, he shook his head. "The horse, I think, if your friend will lend it."

Eysla wasn't happy about it, but I could see that she agreed with the choice. If he went mad, it was the one skin that would be easy to retrieve. So she slung it off from around her shoulders and placed it around his. I could see him steeling himself, and before he could lose his nerve I whispered, *"Wear thy skin!"*

His body blurred and stretched as he fell to all fours. There was a clatter of hooves as he danced backward. His horse-body gave away what his human face would not. His ears were back and the whites of his eyes showed. He wheeled away, half-rearing as if trying for a human posture again, and then circled the courtyard growing visibly more comfortable in his skin. Then, snorting and dancing, he came back to me and bent his head in a nod. I whispered the words that took the skin off him once more and we all pretended not to watch while he composed himself. When he handed the cloak back to Eysla he looked at her in new respect. I could see there were questions he wanted to ask later.

But at last he shook his head. "No, that would not be such a good idea, I think. Such power . . . a man who gets a taste for that would no longer make a good soldier. And a man with no taste for the change would be no use at all as a beast."

I couldn't tell how much of that was honest and how much was to save face, but it didn't matter. We had come to a truce without my refusal or his retreat. The bargain was well-unmade.

*

He caused no further trouble for Keale and his family. They left a few days later, not from fear that he would change his mind, but because the child would not delay its coming for their comfort. With the map and instructions we gave them, they would arrive in good time, and I sent letters and a token for Laaki to tell her of the bargain and let her know I was well. The next year, when the traders came over the mountains in the spring, bringing the furs and carvings my cousins had collected through the winter, they brought Laaki's letters in return. That was when I knew I would go home someday, after all. Not to stay, but, like Eysla, to weave new and different ties with them. But for now I had bound myself to stay in Wilentelu until we forged a different bargain, and for now we were content. Eysla was busy training her brother's horses and arranging to sell others. There was time and more for everything we might plan.

MULTIPLE CHOICE

by *Leslie Fish*

Leslie Fish is probably best known for her music; she plays any kind of guitar, recorder, and pennywhistle (not terribly well), auto-harp, hand-drum, and can fake it on electric bass. When she got her first guitar at sixteen she was already into folk music, singing it anyway. Her mother had tried for years to teach her piano (and classical lyric-soprano singing—even though her voice was obviously alto) because she wanted her to become a proper classic-music pianist/singer and maybe wind up at the Met—and none of it took. (MZB tried the same thing with her daughter, without much more success.) Instead, Leslie was busy "wasting time with that awful cowboy music."

These days, her CDs of gutsy, inspired lyrics are renowned throughout fandom. She's making a living at "That Wretched Stuff," and she has gone from writing songs to writing fiction. We had the privilege of hearing her in person when she lived in the Bay Area. Now she has moved to Arizona and we miss her a lot. Stories in the present tense are hard to bring off, but this one has Leslie's authentic mix of irony and unexpectedness.

> *"So now I stand amid the circles I have drawn*
> *upon the floor.*
> *I have no further answer if this spirit's friend or foe.*
> *No god-sign has been granted me, though I have*
> *prayed full often,*
> *Nor can I this moment answer if I will say 'come'*
> *or 'go.' "*
>
> —Mercedes Lackey, "Lammas Night"

Enough waffling; finish the spell. I know perfectly well what I'm going to do. I must have known it in my heart, weeks ago, when I called on Oaksley for help.

See him there, sitting in the corner: long hound ears

and sad brown hound eyes, paws placed neatly together, so polite and patient that anyone seeing him would automatically think "good dog"—and think no more about him. My good old hound, yes: and waiting for my word.

No, no thought to spare for him now. Draw the power together and focus on the pattern. Now say the word.

"Come."

The multicolored mists swirl, thicken, condense: tighter, brighter, faster—I can hardly bear to look. The glowing core darkens, solidifies . . . ah, so heavy, drawing on me. . . .

No, hold on. Stand up. Complete the chant, the ritual. Seeing success, close down the circle. Mumble the proper words of dismissal and unbinding, so long practiced that I could do them in my sleep. Say them all, leave nothing unfinished. Magic is an exacting business.

By the end, I'm barely standing: exhausted, drained, woolly witted, not rowing with all oars in the water, I know. Maintain the last thin circle by the force of my own Talent and Will; the gods have departed and left the consequences of the spell to me. I'm not grateful for that.

In the middle of my wizard's circle, which now barely glows on the scrubbed wooden floor of the cabin, stands a handsome young man. Of course: he's the former wizard of this little village, who died of unknown causes six months ago—thus giving me this job opportunity. This is the spirit that's been troubling the house, and me, since I moved in. Now, reincarnated by my spell, he's . . . distracting. He's easily six feet tall, with curly black hair running down to crisp sideburns, smooth-shaven square chin, enormous green eyes framed by velvety eyelashes, slender body sheathed in pale fawn-tone skin, generous mouth curving already into a warm sweet smile, long-fingered hands spreading out in a gesture of welcome, the more interesting parts. . . . Yes, he reincarnated stark naked. Quick, throw him the robe and sandals.

Be honest, woman; he's a romantic wet dream—everything you've ever imagined while rubbing the button and thinking censorable thoughts. Yet my magic didn't shape him like this; he did it all himself. This is either his self-ideal or his true original form. He's gorgeous.

"I'm alive," he whispers, awed, delighted, wondering. "I'm alive again!"

"Yes," is about all I can say. "Alive. Speak."

"Uh, what should I say?" he asks, charmingly awkward as an innocent boy. "My family name's Kayar. I'm Loren, and I was born in the village of Heartmore. That's in Wengella, sheep country." He pauses to wriggle into the clothes. "I couldn't stomach wool-twisting forever, I was bored to tears by sheep-herding, and I loved books— so I became a scholar. My folks sent me to the nearest city to learn letters and numbers and religion and all that. They found that I had Mage-Talent, so I was sent to the Highscarp school. You know of it?"

"Yes," I whisper, tired, tired. Indeed I know the school, having gone there myself. It's a good, broad, general school that pipelines Talented young things into the specific studies that can make the best use of their particular Talents. One can indeed learn much there, and not all of it in class.

"Well, then I was apprenticed to Master Jundrup to learn, ah, finesse."

"Ah." Yes. Jundrup has a good record of finding specific and esoteric Talents, training their strength and depth, training with impeccable protocols and no bias whatever. He says little about psychology or ethics, unless given pressing reason. The gods bless independence and tolerance, but there are times when Jundrup could give people a little more warning about the characters of his graduate students. . . .

"So, after a year's apprenticeship, Jundrup told me to stop wasting his time, get out from under his roof and get a full-time job."

I can't help grinning, remembering when I last heard that same piece of advice. That was after we glued the horse to Master Alwing's ceiling.

Loren shrugs, coltish, beautiful. "So I went out looking

for work. Ye gods, do you know how hard it is to find decent work these days?"

"Oh yes!" I laugh out loud. Yes, gods save all dewy-eyed innocent young things, fresh out of college or graduate studies, from the horrors of the real, middle-or-older-aged, work-for-a-living market. How well I know! "So you made your offers all around campus-town, right?" I can't help chuckling. "And then you went to the Big Mean City itself, right? And after . . . what, half a year?—of starving in the Big City, you decided that maybe the hicktowns would give you less competition, better job opportunities?" Gods, how well I know that story. Of all the Holy Words our old college masters taught us, the holiest by far is "job."

Ah, ye gods, see the play of expressions across his face! Yes, he thought he'd be welcomed in the workaday world as the new Intellectual Savior, given his proper due—and proper pay and rank—first crack out of the barrel. And, oh, the shock—the dismay, the sense of betrayal—when a whole dozen or more potential patrons turned him down, one after the other. Oh no, my academic brother-in-wit; the big, mean economic world doesn't really like good minds, let alone select for them. Patrons select for "efficiency" and "experience" and for—ah, let us be blunt—kiss-butt. So, how well can you lie? Fake? Fawn? Politic? How willing are you to accept the rules of a very old, very dirty, and very well-entrenched game?

. . . Yes, much easier to drift out into the hinterlands where a complete education is something marvelous and rare, where the locals stand in awe of anyone who can even name—let alone practice—any two sciences. Oh yes, you took the same path I did: out to the boondocks to impress the yokels. Let's be honest, since I'm too weary for anything else; no matter how cheaply the country towns pay, it's enough to live on. It's better than starving in the city among critics who know too well what you're really worth in the game.

Loren smiles, spreads his hands, so merrily self-deprecating. "Hey, what were my choices?"

My smile is false. I know what his choices were—much better than mine were. I would have killed for an apprenticeship to no less than Jundrup. Instead, I worked crap-and-scrap jobs in the city, developed my skills, moved to the boondocks-circuit the same as young Mage Loren Kayar did, but with far fewer illusions about my place in the world. I made my reputation slowly, the hard way, at every town where I stopped. I swapped spells, fortune-telling, music, gossip, whatever I had—in exchange for a meal, a drink, a bed for the night. . . .

Come on, my winsome, whinesome brother: I've played this game the same as you. Don't expect my pity; you had it much easier than I did.

"At last. . . . " He smiles, so warmly that it could make any unprepared heart melt. "I found a town that needed a full-time wizard. Ideal, right?"

I smile again, knowing damned well what this village meant for me: security—at the price of obscurity, loneliness, occasional boredom. I worked at improving my situation. Yes, I'd call this place ideal for me, but did it satisfy Loren?

"So I settled in, did weather-spells, healings, love-charms. . . ." His smile takes on the faintest suggestion of a knowing leer. "You name it. Little things. A quiet, comfortable life, right?"

I nod, still smiling. Yes, after a year as a wandering mage, that much seemed very good to me, too. But what then? Do go on, Loren.

He does. "But after a while. . . ." His expression grows sweetly thoughtful, hopeful. "After dealing with so many simple, mundane problems, always the same . . . well, I wanted to explore my craft further. Gods know, I had plenty of time on my hands. . . ."

Did you indeed? Given the same chance, I would have turned my attention to study, experimentation, writing for the scholarly journals (or for something more mundane, low-class, and profitable) until I managed to spread my reputation around the countryside. I would have gone that route—if it hadn't been for this odd young mage who managed to get himself killed so strangely. All those ghostly distractions of his: the eerie dreams, the fresh rose on my plate, the invisible caressing hands, the long and subtle and elaborate seduction. . . . Who in hell could concentrate on serious work with all that going on?

"So I began experimenting." He tests the boundary of my circle with a sandal-shot toe. It doesn't yield. "I got so many requests from the locals to contact their long-dead relatives. . . . Well, you know." Again, that heart-melting wistful smile. "So I took up necromancy. Oracles of the dead, and all that." He shrugs, half-embarrassed, half-artful. "That's what people wanted of me. How could I refuse them? I made a serious study of the phenomena. . . ."

Oh gods, I see where this is going! Too many of us try that study, and learn—too late—that the dead can tell lies just as easily as the living do. They can also be malicious, and greedy for one's life-force. Always remember that.

"Well. . . ." He shrugs again, and paces around the circumference of my circle. "I got in too deep. Some really cunning, greedy old ghosts . . . I was grabbed and sucked down before I realized what was happening, let alone had time to put up adequate defenses. Life-force and soul yanked right out of my body, left me stuck here. . . ." He gives a deep, sorrowful sigh.

Just a sigh? Not an involuntary shudder at the memory of what must have been a truly ugly experience? . . .No, this is calculated, artful, planned. "So what did you do then?" I ask, as if I didn't know.

"What could I do?" He spreads his arms wide, graceful and charming and apparently artless. "Even disembodied, I could visit the places where I'd spent most of my previous life, you know?"

Yes, I know. So why didn't he go back to the college, or to Master Jundrup's laboratorium, and appeal to his old professors for help? Disgrace is nothing to a disembodied spirit, and after a good scolding Jundrup would have helped. With the power of necromancy, Loren certainly would have had the power to travel that far. I determined before I started my spell that no geas held the spirit to this spot, and certainly he knew his old college halls as well as this tiny country house. Could it be that he tried, and was refused? Did his old teachers know something about him that discouraged them from hauling Loren's chestnuts out of the fire?

"At first I could do nothing," he goes on, wringing his hands in gestures of classic tragedy. "Then . . . you came." He flashes a super-intense smile at me. Gods, if I were just five years younger and less experienced, I'd fall on my face for that.

"I sensed your presence," he goes on, voice sliding subtly into the classic declamatory mode. I'll wager anything that he spent a year studying theater. "I knew that you had a pure soul, a kindly heart, and the magical power to help me, so I tried to contact you. You were my best hope." He gives me a soulful look that by rights should melt a stone.

Gods, I'm so tempted to drop all pretenses and believe!

With an arm as heavy as lead, I lift up the oak branch. With lips as stiff as wood, I recite the ancient, simple, limited, and irresistible words: "I abjure thee to tell me thy purpose in this world."

He steps back, looking hurt. "Was that necessary?" he asks. "Of course I'll tell you my purpose! My purpose is simply to get back to the life I had before I, uh, made that fatal, uhm . . . mistake."

Yes, by the blue light edging the branch, he's telling the truth. He goofed, he died, he wants back into the world. If there's more that he hasn't said, I can't compel it out of him.

I have no choice but to proceed.

With fatigue-heavy fingers I trace the sigils. With weariness-clumsy hands I lower the branch, draw the line, break the circle. With exhaustion-thickened tongue I say, "Come ye forth."

He does. Long strides step boldly across the broken boundary of the circle. "Darling!" he cries, sweeping me up in his arms. "Thank you! Oh, thank you forever! I'm back in my body—and free!"

"Yes," I whisper, drained to the core. "Let's . . . go lie down. So tired. Tomorrow . . . we can decide what to do."

He gives me a knowing look—then a hot and mind-blazing kiss.

"Yes," he promises, coming up for air, "we'll speak of it tomorrow . . . but I have something important to do tonight."

I can feel his Talent searching out mine, all down the ends of my tired-to-death but experienced nerves, seeing what I have, probing my strength. He pulls back, satisfied that right now at least I can't possibly stop him.

"Sweetheart. . . ." His eyes are already shifting away, to some other distance. "I've got to, uh, deal with those who trapped me. Close the gate. Stop the evil. Uh, you understand? Yes, dearest. Let me finish that, and I'll come right back to you."

It's a lie. There is no gate, save the one I made—and just closed—myself. He wants something else, and has no compunctions about lying or seducing to get it. Any man will lie, cheat, even kill, if his case is desperate enough—but where's the desperation here?

I press my head against his shoulder and use the contact to probe, as little as I can now, for his uppermost feelings.

I find no gratitude, only impatience. He wants to be done with me, and on his way somewhere else.

Gods, I've seen this happen too many times. Maybe I spent too long in college, replaying in graduate studies all the games I'd played earlier to make certain they were all done the same way. I know too damned much about affairs of the heart, the Love Game, and all the common patterns of cheating therein. Is there nothing else here?

"Help me," I whisper, reaching tired arms upward to wrap around his neck. "I brought you back from death . . . gave you body . . . drained myself. I'm so tired. Stay and help me."

Just for an instant, the true thought shows on his face: *Gods, another clingy female wanting something. . . .*

Then the sweet phony smile spreads back across his

face, product of years in practice at lying to women. "Of course I will," he promises, as if to the stars and the earth below. "I'll help you, sweetest."

He drags me over to the nearest horizontal surface, which happens to be the couch, murmuring his simple litany, "Lie down, darling. Lie still. Go to sleep. I love you. Of course I love you. I'll take care of you. I'll always care for you. Go to sleep. . . ."

His expression, caught in the corner of my eye, is bored to death. It's the face of a pimp sweet-talking a reluctant whore into work, for the dozenth time. He dumps me on the couch and turns away, unwilling to put out the effort to even kiss me before he leaves. He's already looking toward the door, planning the next move in his campaign. He's unshielded enough that I can see it.

—damned Jundrup never got me the tenure or connections he promised, wouldn't help me out of limbo, just sneered about old Raymond's stupid daughter, and said a few years as a ghost might cool me off . . . get him first. . . .

As his plan unfolds I can hear all the unguarded thoughts, all the resentment, all the spite. Yes, he expected to walk out of school and straight into the palace of some king, or baron at least. When that didn't happen, his resentment grew to encompass the whole hard world that demanded he work for a living like the rest of us Lower Orders: illiterates, women, animals. . . .

And what was that thought about Master Raymond's daughter? Look further, as he pulls a cloak off the peg and tosses it around his shoulders. Being mine, it's too short for him. He resents that, too.

*—next town back down the road, biggest landowner, wouldn't pay me anywhere near decent price for his daughter's abortion, and after all the work I did disguising myself as her stupid lover, getting the sow pregnant in the first place. . . . Get him first. Town before that, bitchy old chief weaver dared complain that my dye-fast wasn't as good as her sister's. Give her bone-rot. Then back to the city, get Jundrup. Then that jumped-up little

city baronet—bet he never had any real plaguey nightmares, let alone watched them come true. Bet the wizard
he said he already had can't help. And old Raymond's
whiney daughter, make her brat look really ugly. Things
I've learned while waiting around on the darkside. . . .*

I can see it all. He thinks all humanity is no more than
meat for his eating, or a dog for his whipping. And he
thinks he can run free in the world.

He starts to lift the bar on the door.

"Oaksley!" I call.

SNAPtwanggggg.

At the door, Mage Loren Kayar of Highscarp school
jerks, steps back, looks down in astonishment at the sudden oddity: the head of a crossbow-bolt protruding from
his chest.

"Whuh. . . ?" he grunts, falling backward.

A solid thump on the floor, then silence.

Oaksley stands up carefully, the doggy illusion dissipat-
ing, his joints crackling from suddenly relieved stiffness.
"D-did I do right, Lady Wizardess?"

"Absolutely," I pant, firmly as I can, while trying to
pull myself up to a sitting position at least. "A good,
solid heart-shot. Nobody could have done it better."

As I look, I see Loren's body changing. The changes
are subtle, nothing really spectacular, but they reveal
how he really looked rather than the way he saw himself:
still handsome, yes, but with the childishness apparent
now in the sulky pout, the slightly soft belly, the distinctly
soft hands. Yes, I recognize him now. That nasty little
scandal my first year at school, old Master Raymond's
daughter, the forcibly expelled graduate student. . . .
Well, so that was Loren Kayar. He got no worse than
expulsion, and resented even that.

The little woodsman tiptoes carefully to the door, in-
spects the wide-eyed body on the floor, and automatically
reloads his crossbow. "Uh, Lady Wizardess, just when
did you know that the pestering spirit was . . . evil?"

"Just an instant before I signaled you, Oaksley." The
smile I give him is perfectly genuine. "I wasn't sure until
then. That was the whole problem with calling him back;

I didn't know how he died, or what he truly wanted, or what his character was—not until I brought him back to life and questioned him."

The village woodman turns wide round eyes at me. "But . . . ma'am, you were so tired. . . ."

"Yes." I twitch a faint grin at him. "After the restoration spell, I knew, I'd have no strength to stop him or restrain him. All I could do was question him, learn as much as I could. I knew that someone else would have to stop him if he turned out to be . . . the wrong kind."

"Me?" Oaksley gulps, shivering. "B-but I know nothing o' magic."

"Precisely." I drop back onto the couch. "You had no feel of magic about you. Just a simple illusion from me—making you look like a faithful dog in the corner—that was all you had. He didn't look twice. He was so arrogant, so sure he could charm or magic his way around people he thought less clever than himself—he didn't look any deeper at me, let alone you."

Oaksley gulps again, and prods the corpse with a shy foot. "He was a real, true wizard . . . and I killed him . . . with a common crossbow bolt."

"Yes." My voice is down to a whisper. "Common, nonmagical, physical crossbow bolt. Last thing he expected. Physical attack, and from a Lower Form of Life. Stupid, arrogant bastard. . . ."

"Aw, Lady, you're tired." Oaksley tiptoes up to the couch, opens the folded blanket at its foot and tenderly spreads it over me. "Y'oughtta rest. Ye've had a hard bit o' work, this Lammas Night."

"I have," I grin at him. "So much effort . . . to bring him back."

"But why'd you do it, Lady?" he asks, wringing his hands in serious intellectual distress. "If ye thought he might be evil, needed to call on the likes o' me with my poor crossbow for protection. . . . Oh Lady, why'd ye bring him back at all? Why not be safe, send him on to his proper rest?"

"Because I couldn't know." Fatigue is dragging me down, but I have to answer the man's honest concern.

"If I sent him on, I'd never know the truth. If I brought him back and he proved to be evil, well, I could always send him on again. It was the choice that gave me . . . more choices. Thank you, Oaksley."

"Aye, and thank you too, missus." Oaksley smiles back, understanding.

I close my eyes and hear his soft footsteps patter across the floor, then the door quietly unbarred and opened, borrowed clothes and crossbow bolt being pulled away from the corpse. Gods, yes, I've lived long enough to know an honest man when I see one—looks and manners and charm be damned.

I slide into sleep, hearing Oaksley drag the wizard's body out the door.

OULU

by Aimee Kratts

Deadly passions can flourish as well in small towns as on battlefields or in palaces, as this story by Aimee Kratts shows. Marion bought Aimee's first short story for the *Leroni of Darkover* anthology. From that jumping off point, Aimee has published several other short stories in magazines and anthologies, including *Sword & Sorceress XIX*. She writes, "Marion will always have an important place in my life because she believed in my fiction and a gift like that is not forgotten."

Currently, Aimee resides in Virginia where she makes her living as a technical writer. "Oulu" was inspired by two months she spent in Norway where, she says, "The weather isn't appreciably different from the dark cold winters in Saranac Lake, a small town in the Adirondacks of upstate New York where I grew up. I think living where the weather was really harsh influenced my habit of including the weather as an important aspect in many of my stories."

She recommends http://www.arkeodok.com, a Web site about Viking history.

Aimee says, "This story is for my friend Bonnie Chauncey."

Hilda Lajutar studied the cards on the table before her. She felt Lisbet's eyes upon her, expectant. Hilda paused to listen to the cows lowing in the pasture. It was time for milking. She'd rather be doing that.

When Hilda finally spoke, it was with great weariness. "Lisbet, if you continue seeing Olaf, the cards are warning you to be careful. It would be good if you didn't see Olaf at all." Even as she said it, she knew the girl would ignore her advice. As always. Olaf, her boyfriend, would beat her again while her cuckolded husband Edvard, who loved her dearly, would pretend not to know.

The autumn wind howled outside, tearing leaves from the branches and throwing them against the door. Lisbet chewed her lip for a moment. She leaned forward, peering at the cards. "Is there anything else? What do those cards mean?" She looked up, worried.

Hilda tapped the Harvest and the Judge cards and frowned. The cards weren't clear or maybe it was just that she was tired. She should have insisted that Irena try harder to read cards. Or at least she should have started to send people to Charlotta more often. "A test of your strength will come soon. You should resist wrongdoing."

"And this?" asked Lisbet touching a third set of crossed cards apprehensively.

"Yes. A storm tomorrow. Have Edvard pull his fishing boat from the harbor soon. The ice is coming early." She needed no cards to tell her that. The cold was in her bones.

Lisbet breathed out slowly. Hilda gathered up the deck and stacked them on the table. Pulling her wool wrap around her, Lisbet fumbled in her apron for a coin, found one, and pushed it across the table to the old woman. "Thank you, Hilda. Next week on this day, yes?"

Hilda sneezed and blew her nose. "There is something else." She dreaded the telling. Lisbet was as unpredictable as a snowstorm. "I'm leaving Oulu, the day after tomorrow."

Hilda watched bewilderment in Lisbet's eyes. Then the girl recovered herself and smiled. "Of course! You're visiting someone. Who is it? When do you return?"

"I'm not returning."

Lisbet frowned. "But who will read the cards for me? I need your help with Edvard and Olaf. You can't leave! How will I manage?"

Hilda coughed. "Lisbet, I'm getting old. My fingers ache and winter hasn't even come yet. I'm leaving for the south lands where it's warmer. I'm leaving on the *White Seal*. Charlotta can do your readings from now on."

Someone tapped on the door. "That'll be Irena Bernsdotter," said Hilda.

"But—"

"I'm sorry Lisbet. I know it's unwelcome news, but you'll be fine." Hilda patted her arm.

The young woman stalled. "Please—"

The door opened and Irena peered inside. "Are you finished, Hilda?"

"Yes, yes, come in. Good-bye, Lisbet."

Stricken, the young woman ran out.

Irena smiled at Hilda as she closed the door behind Lisbet. "How did she take it?"

Hilda shrugged. "As I thought. As you thought."

The younger woman nodded. "Well, it's over now. I've come to tell you that I'll bring you some dinner tonight so we can eat together."

"That's kind of you. Isn't Valentin home yet?"

"He'll return from Raahe later this evening." Irena paused. "Did any of the others take it as hard?"

Hilda shrugged. "Some. You should have started doing readings long ago."

Irena gave a good-natured smile at the familiar jab. "What about Anneliese Ryky?"

Hilda nodded. "Yes, she will be angry." This town makes extreme people, Hilda thought. Saints and beasts. It was the harsh weather. As time went on, the lucky ones had hearts that became warmer like the fires in their hearths. The unlucky ones had souls that became as cold as the sea and as fractured as broken ice. Then they'd hurt themselves or others with little or no provocation. Those were the ones she felt she needed to help and it had taken all her strength to do so. She had nothing left to give anymore. It was time to leave.

"Anneliese 'will be angry'? you haven't told her?"

"I see her tonight after I milk the cows and feed the pets. She's the last. She's the only one from whom I fear a tantrum."

Irena chuckled. "You shouldn't have given her such

good business advice. You made Anneliese and her husband very wealthy."

"They made themselves wealthy. I just read the cards."

Irena snorted. Hilda did more than read cards for people. She was a wise old woman who gave good counsel and had managed to improve many lives with her advice. The townspeople would miss her.

Hilda stood and leaned on the table for a moment. "Do you want some beer and warm bread?"

Irena nodded. "Have you made a decision about your cows? And what about your 'pets'?" She smiled. Hilda's one eccentricity was keeping a few livestock as pets, which any farmer knows is a bad idea. It was expensive for her and made for extra work. But Hilda seemed to get attached to an animal every so often and would not be talked out of it.

"I sold the cows to Torvald at a good price since he promised to take on the pets and not slaughter them for meat as soon as I left Oulu."

"They'll love Torvald as much as they loved you," said Irena.

"Yes, I know. Whoever feeds them last is their best friend."

Hilda smiled but to Irena, the old woman's face was strained. As silly as it seemed, Irena knew that leaving behind those old pigs and goats and chickens that were her pets was hard for the old woman.

"Here," said Hilda, putting a deck of cards before Irena on the table. "Let's try to improve your card-reading skills before I go out to milk the cows. You have the knack for it. I'm determined you'll focus it before I leave Oulu."

*

After leaving Hilda's, Lisbet ran the short distance back to town, tears drying cold on her face, her mind working frantically. Hilda reads cards for everyone! She's been in Oulu my whole life! How can she just leave me? Who can I talk to about this? Olaf won't understand. Edvard would scold me for wasting money on a card reader. Who will help me then? Who?

The answer settled on her as she crossed the deserted harbor marketplace. Anneliese Ryky, the tar merchant's wife. She is no friend but she is smart and she depends on Hilda, too. She will know what to do.

Lisbet ran to the side entrance of the tar merchant's shop. The shop was closed for the evening, but the side entrance led to the family quarters. Lisbet pounded on the door.

The oldest daughter of the family threw open the top half of the door one-handed while holding one of the new twins in the crook of her free arm. "Yes, what is it? The shop is closed." Seven children milled around the room behind her with their mother, Anneliese, in their center holding the other twin. When Anneliese saw Lisbet's tear-streaked face, she scolded her daughter.

"Never leave a guest in the cold! In! In! Lisbet, what's wrong? Are you hurt?"

"No," moaned Lisbet, ducking inside and closing the door. "She's leaving!" Lisbet slumped in a chair and put her hands up to cover her face.

Anneliese patted the baby who began to cry because of Lisbet's noise. Irritated with the young woman's histrionics, Anneliese snapped, "Who's leaving?"

"Hilda," said Lisbet.

"What! Hilda? She can't leave! When did you hear this?"

"Just now," said Lisbet miserably. "She finished my reading and gathered up the cards and looked at me and said, 'I'm leaving Oulu. I'm old and I'm going to the south.'" Lisbet wiped her nose with the cuff of her blouse.

Anneliese handed the fussing baby to another daughter and nervously fingered her expensive necklace. "She can't leave," Anneliese said matter-of-factly, which pleased Lisbet. Anneliese understood.

"Who will read the cards? I can't guide my children's futures or my husband's business without Hilda. She can't go. No. She can't. I need her."

"We need her," said Lisbet.

Anneliese said, "All we have to do is explain how much we need her and she'll stay."

"She doesn't care," said Lisbet.

"Huh. Well, then, we must persuade her."

*

By the time Hilda had finished milking the cows, feeding the pets, and putting them all in the barn for the night, darkness was upon her. She went inside to consider her belongings. There wasn't much to pack. An extra skirt and blouse. A few pieces of silver coin jewelry for festival days. Two blankets. Her cards.

It was autumn and the starlings had already left for the season. In two days, she had passage on the *White Seal*, the last fur ship traveling south before the harbor froze. The winds raged down from the hills. She spread her hands before the fire in the hearth. Her fingers were numb again with cold. She held them closer to the flames, flexing and rubbing the life back into them.

She took a deep breath of warm air from the fire. Even in the cold, the burning oak couldn't mask the scents of manure from the barn or the old, wet leaves on her shoes. But it wasn't the smells she despised. It was the bone-biting cold and the oppressive darkness of winter. The scarce, fickle sun never bothered her before. Now the blackest winter days had the knock of death. The dark months crushed her like an ice floe crushes a ship's hull.

"No more," she said to the empty room.

Someone knocked at the door.

Finally, she thought. Anneliese Ryky is here for her last reading. She moved to the table and picked up her deck. "Welcome!" she called out. Anneliese entered the house with Lisbet behind her. They licked their lips nervously and refused to meet her gaze. Hilda shuffled her cards and slapped the deck on the table aggressively. Here it is, she thought as she looked at the women. The madness has come into my home.

"Lisbet. Why are you visiting so late? I would ask you to stay and for a bowl of soup but I have a reading to give Anneliese." She smiled pleasantly at the women, trying to forestall them. Maybe Irena would return with dinner a little earlier than planned.

"We are h-here—" Lisbet's voice shook.

"We are here," said Anneliese, standing as tall as her plump little body would allow, "to take you to a safe place."

"I am in a safe place," said Hilda.

"To a safer place, then," said Anneliese.

Hilda felt a sick twist in the pit of her stomach. With all her powers of sight, she had never foreseen this. These women meant her harm. Lisbet and Anneliese were desperate, that was obvious. Led or dragged, she was going.

Hilda moved slowly, wrapping her wool cape around herself, pulling up her hood and tying her scarf around her neck. Pocketing her cards, she left her mittens behind, hoping to further stall by having to go back and get them. Both women knew she suffered terribly from the cold. They'd let her get her mittens.

In the moonlight, they walked past the footpath going into town. Hilda made a show of flexing her fingers and blowing on them. "Oh, dear. I've left my mittens behind. I need to go back and get them."

"No," snapped Lisbet.

Hilda felt a sharp metal point against her back.

"I don't understand," said Hilda, suddenly understanding full well what was going on. They meant to keep her from the *White Seal* until it left Oulu. What she couldn't figure out was how they meant to do it without killing her. She was a friend to nearly everyone in the town. Where would they hide her? "Lisbet, what is troubling you so that you should treat me like this?"

"Your leaving troubles us," said Anneliese, in a hard voice. "You read the cards. We need you. You can't go to the south lands."

"Nonsense," said Hilda. "Charlotta can read for you. She is a fine reader. Or even Irena. She told me she would begin readings soon." It was a lie but a plausible one.

"Charlotta can't read a raindrop," said Anneliese. "I went to her once and she upset me with such tales about my husband that I lost the child I was carrying."

"Anneliese, that is not true. You lost that baby because you insisted on traveling to that spring festival instead of staying in bed." Hilda raised her voice hoping that it would carry in the cold air. "Shame on you to blame such a thing on Charlotta!"

"Shush!" Anneliese ordered, poking the knife into the old woman's back harder. "Come quietly."

Lisbet was beginning to feel brave and shoved Hilda just a little, not even as much as Olaf shoved her sometimes. She smiled to herself when the old woman stumbled.

"Down the road," Anneliese hissed in Hilda's ear.

Frightened, Hilda did as she was told, speaking no more, trying to see her way out of the danger she was in. If she was not such a worn-out old woman, she could have saved herself. But she wasn't young anymore.

The women walked the north road outside town along the frozen shallow bay. Goran Martensson's abandoned trade ship, *The Beauty,* was locked in the ice, slowly being crushed. Soon it would lie with the rest of the scuttled ships at the bottom of the inlet.

"Down there," ordered Anneliese, pointing toward the ice below.

Lisbet gave Hilda another shove, tumbling Hilda down the embankment, making her skid on dead birch leaves until she hit the shore ice, twisting her knee. The old woman moaned. Running was now impossible. Hilda sat up with a grunt. Her hands were numb to her wrists.

When Lisbet and Anneliese reached her, they each grabbed an arm and slid her backward twenty paces to *The Beauty.* Some small calm part of Hilda's mind wanted to point out that even if their plan worked and she was trapped in Oulu for yet another winter, she would never read for them again, but she held her tongue. Either one of them was capable of killing her at the moment and she knew it.

They hauled her into the ship's hold. Once settled in the darkness against a broken barrel, they bound her hands and feet and gagged her.

"We're sorry," said Anneliese, "but you must understand this is for everyone's good. Once the *White Seal* has left harbor, we'll come get you."

Hilda closed her eyes in defeat but raised her bound hands up to Anneliese and wriggled her fingers. Anneliese nodded and removed her scarf. Warmed by Anneliese's neck, the scarf eased some of the ache in Hilda's hands. Following Anneliese's example, Lisbet removed her scarf and wrapped it around Hilda's nose and mouth.

Without warning, the sea ice groaned, snapping a plank in the hull. All three women jumped at the noise, then Lisbet laughed nervously. Hilda opened her eyes, meeting Anneliese's gaze, and pleaded silently with the woman.

Anneliese set her jaw and shook her head. "You'll be fine," she said.

You stupid women, thought Hilda. You stupid selfish women. You're leaving me to die.

Lisbet and Anneliese climbed the stairs out of the hold without looking behind them.

*

At dinner hour, Irena knocked on Hilda's door and pushed her way inside without waiting for an answer. She put the fish soup and bread on the table and looked around for Hilda. She thought that her friend might be out in the barn with the animals but she couldn't see any lantern light spilling out of the cracks in the barn door. The kitchen fire was low. Hilda's mittens were on the bench but her wool cloak was not on its peg. Irena walked over to Hilda's bed and pulled back the curtains. The old woman was not there.

Irena frowned. Hilda would never leave her mittens behind for any reason. Something is wrong. Her last reading was with Anneliese Ryky. Maybe she has gone to Anneliese's home.

Irena ran back to town and toward the tar merchant's shop. Before she rounded the last corner, she heard familiar laughter. Coming slowly around the side of the bakery on the corner, she saw Lisbet and Anneliese walking into Anneliese's husband's shop. Through the windows, Irena could see that the two women were happy about something—that was obvious by the way they were patting each other on the shoulders and hugging. And it didn't look as if Hilda was with them.

If Hilda's not at Anneliese's, not at home, and not on the way in between, where is she? Irena chewed on her thumb and thought about knocking on Anneliese's door but decided against it. Lisbet was not a friend of Anneliese. The fact that these two women, who would barely exchange greetings at a summer fair, were acting like giggling sisters meant that something was happening. But Irena couldn't puzzle out what it was. Maybe Valentin is home by now, she thought. He might know what to do.

Her husband was eating his soup and drinking beer when she opened the door. "Were you out visiting Hilda? How is the old woman?" he asked between slurps. "Is she sad to be leaving?"

Irena kissed her husband on the forehead. "She was expecting me for dinner but she's not home."

Valentin shrugged. "Perhaps she's out visiting and lost track of time. She's an old woman with lots of good-byes." He took a sip of beer.

"Yes, I know. But her mittens were on the bench in her kitchen."

"Old women forget things."

"Hilda doesn't forget her mittens, not with her cold hands. Besides, she told me she said good-bye to everyone already." Irena took her own set of cards down from the kitchen shelf and shuffled them, laying them out on the table. Hilda had tried to teach her how to read them, but Irena never felt she learned. The cards were still obscure to her, only useful as objects of nervous habit. Where is Hilda, she thought to herself. Where is my old friend? She laid the cards on the table looking for an answer to her question. She pondered the figures. The Flower, The Midnight Summer Sun, The Maiden Playing at the Waterfall. All the beautiful cards. They told her nothing. She gathered them up and put the deck back on the shelf.

Watching his wife pace about the room, Valentin offered, "Maybe she is out walking in the moonlight like those other two women on the road."

Irena rounded on her husband. "What women?"

"That Anneliese Ryky and that other one, the one who cuckolds her husband and lets her boyfriend beat her. They were walking into town along the road when I came back from Raahe. I offered them a ride in the wagon but they said no."

"Anneliese Ryky and Lisbet Tallus?"

"Yes. Them."

Irena drummed her fingers on the table. "Lisbet doesn't want Hilda to leave. But why was she with Anneliese? They're not friendly. The only thing they have in common is . . ." Irena chewed the side of her thumb and thought hard. "They've taken Hilda somewhere."

"What? Why?" Valentin bit off a mouthful of bread.

"To keep her here in Oulu." Irena gazed into the fire. "I'm going to Hilda's to check again but I know she's not there. Fill the iron bucket with hot coals and put it in the wagon. And take enough fur rugs for two. Take the road to where it turns past the hill just beyond Hilda's farm so no one will see you. I'll meet you there."

Valentin shook his head. "Nothing good happens when a man gets involved in women's battles. It makes you old before your time."

Irena slammed her hands on the table. "Hilda's in danger! You can either drive the wagon and meet me on the road or you can spend the winter sleeping in the wagon."

"Irena!"

"She's been good to us for so many years . . . and now she's in danger." Irena added more softly, "I know it."

Valentin wiped his mustache with the back of his hand. "I'll get the wagon."

Irena was frantic by the time she met him on the road. "Hilda is not home," she said breathless from her hurrying. "No one has seen her. Drive the wagon slowly. I'll walk ahead." She took a lantern from the wagon and carried it with her.

"Hilda?" Irena called. "Hilda, are you out here?"

All she could hear in reply were the wagon wheels behind her and the sound of the ocean waves in the distance as she and Valentin traveled farther along the inlet.

Valentin began calling out, too. "Hilda Lajutar, can you hear my voice?"

The moon was high overhead, making it easy for Irena to look along the roadside. She found nothing but dark stones and undergrowth. "Hilda, please! Tell us where you are!"

Small animals scurried among the weeds along the roadside. The wind began to pick up again.

Two hours into their search, they found no sign of the old woman. Cold and distraught, Irena climbed into the wagon next to Valentin who turned them toward home. "She's probably at home in bed," said Valentin as he put his arm around his wife. Thin snow began to fall.

Almost back to town, along the edge of the bay, they heard the sea ice moan. A crack that sounded like musket fire made Irena jump. Valentin, very tired, still managed to chuckle at his wife. "It's just Goran's ship being scuttled by the ice."

"Goran's ship?"

"The Beauty."

"The Beauty?" Irena thought back to the cards on the table. The Flower, The Midnight Summer Sun, The Maiden Playing at the Waterfall. All the beautiful cards! The Beauty! Irena gripped her husband's arm. "Valentin! She's in *The Beauty!*"

Valentin reined in the horse. He and Irena leapt out of the wagon and skidded down the embankment. "Hilda! Hilda! Are you there?" called Irena.

Valentin skidded across the ice and boarded the ship first. With a quick glance, he saw that Hilda was not on the deck. He hurried below, Irena at his heels. They found the old woman unconscious. Valentin untied the ropes while Irena removed the gag and patted her friend's face. "Hilda, wake up. You have to wake up. We're here. Come on now. You're safe."

Hilda opened her eyes groggily. "Irena?"

Irena noticed the two extra scarves. One was familiar to her. "Did Anneliese and Lisbet do this to you?"

Hilda nodded.

Valentin carried Hilda to the wagon, Irena following,

already planning, weighing the advantages of quick over slow punishment. Those wicked women will suffer for this. They will suffer for the rest of their lives.

"Take her home," Irena said to her husband, "To *our* home. Warm her up. Feed her if you can. I'll be home soon." She took the ax that Valentin kept in the wagon in case a tree fell across the road while he was traveling.

"What are you doing?" asked Valentin.

"Helping the ice," said Irena. She searched Hilda's apron until she found her cards and took them. "I'll be home soon. Take her now and whatever you do, don't call her Hilda when you're in town. No one must know we saved her. As soon as she is warm and full of food you must take her to Raahe and get her passage to the south lands. Think of some reason you must go for business. Make up a good lie. A business lie."

Valentin nodded.

In the belly of *The Beauty,* Irena set aside Anneliese's and Lisbet's scarves before she raised the ax and hacked through the hull where Hilda had been sitting. She cut a hole large enough for a woman to fall through. Water sloshed in the opening. The scarves she caught on the rough edges of two planks were well above the water so they would be found. The cards were last. She took the pack and threw some of the cards into the icy hole, scattering the rest in the puddles forming in the bottom of the ship. Many of them would still be floating there in the morning. At the last moment, she hid two coins in different places behind the ribs of the ship. There, she thought grimly. A recipe for justice.

Returning home, she found Hilda bundled in furs and sitting before the fire. She let Valentin take her wet mittens and cloak before she sat herself near the fire as well. After giving Hilda an enormous hug, Valentin went to bed grumbling about the entanglements of women's lives.

Irena found herself getting sleepy and dozed off, only to be awoken by a sharp question from Hilda.

"What have you done?" Hilda asked.

Shivering and reaching forward to stoke the fire, Irena

eplied, "I made it look like you drowned. Tomorrow
'm going to hint to Mari, the baker's greedy wife, that
Goran Martensson might have left a couple coins on *The
Beauty* by mistake. She'll go out there and find the
scarves and your cards and the hole. She'll tell the whole
own that you were killed." Irena couldn't help but
sound righteous. "They will pay."

"But I wasn't killed," said Hilda softly. "You can't
punish someone for something they didn't do."

"They tried."

"Oh, Irena, you're so young. Don't be so quick to
condemn."

"But they must be punished!"

"Shh. You'll wake Valentin." Hilda sighed and rubbed
her hands before the flames. "You have to think of how
t will affect their families. If an angry crowd kills those
women, what will their families do? All of Anneliese's
children would be motherless. And Lisbet's husband
would be a widower. No, what I think they need is some
counsel about the wrongness of their intentions. But I'll
need your help."

"You've never explained to me how you give counsel."

"Yes, well, I didn't want to. It's not always easy."

Irena nodded. "What should I do?"

*

In the morning, Valentin, Irena, and Hilda walked
back to Hilda's farm. Valentin milked the cows, fed the
animals, and set about chopping wood. At Hilda's request, Irena fetched a hen from the hen house and
brought it inside.

"Now when you bring Anneliese up here, you're to sit
beside me on the bench and concentrate on the card that
I hold up before the both of us. Put all the power of
your heart into it. It will be as if we are putting Anneliese
inside the card to make her experience the power of the
symbol before we put her back into herself again. We
are going to change Anneliese for the better. Now go."

Irena hurried into town and found Anneliese at her
husband's shop.

"Yes, what is it?" Anneliese asked Irena.

"Hilda Lajutar is at home in her kitchen and she wishes to see you for a reading."

The color of Anneliese's cheeks went as pale as frost. "I don't have time for this."

Irena leaned forward over the counter and said, "My husband and I know all that happened and if you don' come with me now, I'll be forced to tell everyone in town. Now get your coat."

Anneliese narrowed her eyes at Irena but retrieved her coat and put it on. "Watch the children," she said to her oldest girl as she left the shop.

*

At the farmhouse, Valentin was chopping wood. He waved to Anneliese and Irena as they approached the house. Anneliese turned her stony gaze away from him and walked into the kitchen.

Hilda said, "Good morning, Anneliese. Please take off your coat and sit."

Anneliese remained standing.

Irena removed her own coat and sat on the bench next to Hilda.

"Why don't you let me read some cards for you, Anneliese, since we didn't seem to have time to do it last night."

Anneliese stared at Hilda, her fists clenched at her sides.

Shuffling the deck, Hilda laid out the cards before her on the table. The Great Mother card figured prominently. Hilda picked it up and held it before her. "This," she said to Irena and Anneliese, "means that your skills as a mother are going to increase greatly in the near future." She tapped Irena on the knee with her free hand.

Irena stared at the card. She thought of pulling Anneliese's soul from her heart and putting into the Great Mother card, the card that symbolized love and succor, abiding faith in children and their importance in the world. Her head spun with the effort and she grabbed the edge of the table to steady herself.

Beside her, she felt Hilda's own efforts as a physical pulling and pushing, a twisting around of things in the air. A part of her heard Hilda breathing with effort, as though she was moving a large table across the room. To her amazement, Irena actually felt something of Anneliese slip into the Great Mother card but then it slid back out in another direction.

At that instant, she felt herself go limp, as if she were a marionette and the puppeteer had dropped her strings. She leaned against the table listening to herself breathe roughly.

She looked around when she heard the caged chicken in the corner of the kitchen start to squawk and scream. She turned toward the animal but could see nothing bad happening to it. Then she heard Hilda ask, "How do you feel, Anneliese?"

Irena turned her head to look at Anneliese who was smiling so broadly, she didn't look like herself. "This is wonderful," said Anneliese. She held her hands up before her eyes, turning them this way and that, then running her fingers lightly over her face. "Thank you," she said to Hilda. "Now I must get back to my children. Um . . . I seem to have forgotten . . . where are they?"

"In town," said Hilda. "The tar merchant's shop. Go on and give your husband greetings for me."

Anneliese waved at Irena and left.

When the door closed behind Anneliese, the chicken in the cage went wild. Tired, the old woman turned to Irena. "Do you understand?"

Confused, Irena looked at Hilda. "No."

"Did you feel the movement of Anneliese's self into the Great Mother card?"

"Yes."

"Did you feel her slip out of it again?"

"Yes."

"Did it feel as if she went back toward her own body?"

"Yes. No, wait. No. Now that you say it aloud, it didn't feel like she went into her own body." Irena's eyes widened. "You put her somewhere else."

The chicken squawked again, beating its wings against

the cage. Irena pushed back from the table and got up to look at the animal closely. "You put Anneliese into this chicken?"

The chicken began throwing itself against the cage.

"Yes."

"Then what walked out the door? Is Anneliese now a golem?"

"No. The chicken is now in Anneliese's body."

Irene thought of Hilda's special pets. How she cared for them and worried about them and yet never seemed to enjoy them. "The animals . . . !"

"Yes."

"Then you haven't been changing the lives of the really bad people by giving them good counsel. You've been replacing them with animals."

"Yes."

Irena sat down hard. "I don't think I could do that to someone."

"You created the appearance of my death in order to fool an angry crowd into killing Anneliese and Lisbet."

Irena looked up at the old woman. She imagined she felt a cold lump where her heart used to be. "Yes. I did," she admitted.

"I'm not strong enough to change people anymore," said Hilda. "I needed your help to change Anneliese. Now, before I leave on the *White Seal* tomorrow, all that remains is giving counsel to Lisbet. Her husband has a dog that he loves as much as Lisbet herself. It's up to you what kind of counsel she gets. I can't do this alone."

"What about Charlotta?" Irena asked. Her shoulders felt leaden.

"She's a good card reader but she has no real power. You have the power."

Irena gazed at Valentin through the window. When the silence had stretched itself out long enough, Hilda said, "She was ready to kill for what she wanted, Irena. We don't know that she hasn't already done so. Did Olaf's last girlfriend, the one before Lisbet, really drown off the docks by herself?"

Irena had forgotten about the death of that young

woman. She felt that everything she knew about everyone was shifting, as if the sun had changed color.

"And what would have happened if you hadn't found
me? What happens if you aren't around to save the
next—"

Irena held up her hand. "Stop. I'll get the dog and
bring Lisbet here."

As she walked past the barn, she noticed that Hilda's
pets had stopped whatever they were doing and crowded
up to the fence to stare at her. The human emotion
trapped in the eyes of the filthy pigs and tethered goats
was too much to bear. Irena turned her head away. She
walked slowly to town, her eyes staring down at the frigid
dirt road dusted with snow.

*

During high tide the next morning, Irena and Valentin
waved to Hilda as she stood on the deck of the *White
Seal*. As the ship pulled away from the dock, Valentin
hugged his wife. He could tell something was wrong by
the stiffness of her embrace. "What is it?"

"Her pets," said Irena. "They'll be a burden on Torvald. You should advise him to put them down as soon
as possible."

Valentin nodded. "Of course."

As soon as he agreed to her suggestion, Valentin felt
his wife relax into him and lean her head against his
chest. She is tired, he thought. He hoped she wouldn't
take the old woman's leaving too hard. Hugging her
tightly to him, he rubbed her back and thought about
what she said.

Even though Irena had been adamant yesterday about
protecting the pets, Valentin decided he wasn't about to
disagree with her about wanting to put them down today.
It was never wise to become involved in women's business. It makes you old before your time.

A KIND OF REDEMPTION
by John P. Buentello

Of all the genres John has dabbled in, fantasy continues to be what he enjoys the most. There just seem to be so many more possibilities there to explore. Fantasy holds a unique kind of wonder and excitement. He has recently finished his longest work in the field in collaboration with his brother, Larry. A sequel is in the works. He is also currently at work on a fantasy for younger children. His stories have appeared in *Marion Zimmer Bradley's Fantasy Magazine, Sword & Sorceress, Adventures of Sword & Sorcery,* and other publications.

He says "I owe Ms. Bradley all the thanks in the world for the encouragement and the opportunity she offered. My writing career would be entirely different, and not nearly as satisfyings, if not for her."

That would certainly make her happy. When she talked about how she wished to be remembered after her death, she used to quote Christopher Wren's epitaph: "si monumentum requiris circumspice" (if you seek his monument, look around you). He was buried in a cathedral he designed, so in his case it was literally true. In Marion's case, you may need to go only as far as the nearest bookstore or library.

Tavis spied the waxy glow of firelight as she made her way up the road from the deep, winding woods behind her. She made out the framework of a tall structure, an inn of some kind, set slightly off from the road. In another moment she heard the soft neigh of horses, the sounds of revelry leaking through the broad, oaken walls of the inn. She stopped, fingering the heavy hilt of her broadsword, wondering at the image before her. For so long she had been traveling this road, it seemed to her, without another sight beside the borders of sad, mis-shapen trees and the flat, muddy road for company. What was an inn doing in such a place? A better question came to her: what was *she* doing in such a place? Tavis realized she had no memory of how she had come to be here.

As she approached the inn, she searched her mind for some clue of why she was here. Had she been traveling? Yes, traveling for a long time now. She recalled the image of marching boots, legions of them, soldiers massed and armored and armed for battle.

Faces appeared before her, blending into mists and shadows before she could recognize them. The memory of wielding her sword against an enemy came to her, the bite of her blade as it cut through metal and bone. The roar of her war cry filled her mind. Then the darkness swept over her memories. She could draw no other pictures to fill the spaces that wound through her senses.

She put her left hand on the door of the inn and swung it forward. The smell of freshly spitted meat and roasting vegetables met her nose, and her stomach churned. She walked stiffly toward a long wall where the innkeeper had a row of tables and benches. Across from her a great fire blazed. Tavis regarded the tired and hungry travelers who sat beside it. They looked docile enough. Still, her hand stayed close to her weapon. She took a table with a single chair and felt her body collapse into it.

"You look like a woman who needs a drink," a voice said as a tankard of ale was placed on the table. "How bout some soup to go with that? There's nice chunks of meat in it."

Tavis took the tankard in her hand and raised the rim to her lips. She savored the sweet taste of the ale, the heavy feeling that coated her throat and stomach. She nodded and looked up. A woman, in her later years and fleshy about the face and midsection, regarded her. There was a strange expression in her eyes that troubled the warrior, but Tavis said nothing as the woman signaled to another for a bowl of soup to be brought and slid a chair next to the table. The older woman sat and said nothing.

When the soup was brought she allowed Tavis to eat i
peace. When she had finished Tavis became aware tha
the other woman was still staring at her.

"I am called Salandri," the woman said. She signale
for the empty bowl to be removed. "I am the owner o
this place."

Tavis' eyes widened. "A woman owning an inn in
place such as this?" She looked around the room, notin
that every eye was on her. "Surely that invites trouble."

Salandri shrugged. "Trouble comes when it wishes. I
doesn't need my invitation." She glanced at the swor
hilt Tavis was resting the fingers of her right hand upon
"Take you, for instance. Why have you come?"

Tavis wished she had an answer. She would hav
gladly declared "I'm on my way home," or "I'm travelin
to meet my friends." But nothing appeared in her min
as the reason for her being here. She was here for som
reason, and each time she tried to recall what it was tha
had brought her to this place, the only image she sav
was a dark blanket of cold and ice.

"I'm a traveler," she answered.

"Are you a mercenary?" Salandri asked. Her face be
came hard. "Because they aren't welcome here."

Tavis shook her head. "I'm no mercenary." She looke
at the armor she wore, traced the crimson design of th
dragon that had been painted there. The cold metal stun
her fingers. Another image came, the sting of metal, th
cry of her fellow guardsmen. Her hand shook as sh
reached for another tankard of ale.

"I think I am a soldier."

Salandri's expression changed. She studied the war
rior's eyes more closely. "You're not sure?"

Tavis shook her head. "I know I've been traveling fo
a while. I don't remember where I was going, or from
where I came. I remember my name, Tavis, and that'
about it. I'm dressed as a warrior, I feel like a warrior
but I'm not sure who or what I am."

Salandri sat back. She rubbed her reddened hands to
gether. "You must have been a soldier. You wear th
armor of the Red Guard."

An image rolled over in Tavis' mind, unfolding like carpet. The battlefield was moving with soldiers, her Red Guard caught at its flanks, her strongest warriors fighting to keep control of their front ranks. She was running through the crowd, shouting and crying, her hands lifted high above her head. She looked up, expecting to see the bloody sword in her grip, but both hands were empty. The image crumbled at the edges, then broke apart completely.

"I am the commander of a legion," she said quietly, while the other woman watched. "There was a terrible battle. I cannot remember more." She turned to Salandri and reached out to take her hand. "You know of the guard. You must tell me how to rejoin them."

Salandri withdrew her hand. She stared at the warrior, her eyes hard and suspicious. Then she shook her head and said, "There is no way, for there is no more guard. The entire legion was wiped out in the battle that took place years ago in the Wildwood. They are all dead."

Tavis felt her head explode, light blinding her eyes and harsh, blaring sounds rocking her senses. She saw torches bobbing and swinging, the outline of a full, bloody moon dancing through the trees. She saw a man to her side bend down to get a better look through the tree line. A lance hurtled forward to bury itself deep in his head. A pain gripped her deep inside her stomach, but she ignored it. She screamed, pulling her great weapon free, feeling the surge of blood in her ears. Other cries joined hers, first in triumph, then in awful, bloody wails that threatened to deafen her. Then the pain returned, the terrible, gnawing pain that she had lain contorted with the day before. She saw herself drop her sword and raise her hands in supplication as the enemy came relentlessly on.

The screams rose from her lips then, awful to hear. She felt the hilt of her weapon and almost withdrew it from the scabbard, but the gnawing was like a rodent in her belly. She pounded the table and screamed until she felt two strong hands shake her by the shoulders. She opened her eyes to see Salandri holding her, the woman's

eyes fixed in bewilderment. Tavis unclenched her fists as
the pain began to subside.

The tavern part of the inn had been pretty well abandoned by the time Tavis came fully back to herself. She
still shook from the effect of the vision, but she could sit
by herself, and her breathing had steadied. She watched
as Salandri directed her staff, acting as if strange warriors
came to her inn and went berserk before her on a nightly
basis. The innkeeper finally returned to the table when
things seemed settled for the night.

"You had us scared, warrior. Are you well now?"

"I may never be well again," Tavis replied. "I am no
warrior. I am a coward. I remember pieces of it now.
We had been ordered to engage the mass of insurgents
that had taken refuge in the woods. They were cutthroats
and mercenaries who had been pillaging the king's villages and killing his subjects. The Red Guard, my warriors and I, were sent in."

"And fought to a man," Salandri said quietly. "We
heard the battle rage for days. In the end, the Red
Guard fell."

Tavis shook her head. "Save for one. One coward who
chose to run when the odds seemed too great." Tavis
put her head in her hands. "I left them to die."

Salandri said nothing for a time. She reached out at
one point and grasped Tavis' hand firmly, then released
it. Finally she said, "You were crying and screaming in
pain, not fear. Something about your stomach?"

Tavis waved the question away. "I had a belly ache
the night before."

"That returned in the middle of battle." Salandri
pursed her hands. She closed her eyes and began to
breathe deeply. "That was strong enough to cause a warrior to drop her sword, leaving her open to attack."

"So I ate the wrong thing," Tavis said. "I abandoned
my warriors."

Salandri opened her eyes. They were fixed on some
point far away. "You were poisoned," she said loudly.
"One of your enemy poisoned the meal the night before.

They wanted to remove you from battle. Many others died on the battlefield of the same poison."

"But I ran and got help and survived." Tavis brought her fist down on the table. "*I was their commander!*" She watched as Salandri jumped, her eyes clearing. "They were my friends," Tavis whispered.

"There was a terrible battle, and you were a flesh and blood warrior who was badly poisoned. That poison affected your mind and body both."

"Certainly my memory." Tavis stood, flexing her hands, looking through a near window toward the woods beyond. "I must go."

"Since the battle," Salandri said, "no one goes into the section of forest known as the Wildwood. Not even the insurgents who still hide within the forest. Each night there are noises, clashes, shouts, screams, that are carried upon the wind. Some say the ghosts of those who fell in battle fight that small war each night over and over again. I imagine their pain is great, great enough to keep them chained to the earth."

"The bloody souls who cannot rest," Tavis said. "Delivered to their hell by me."

"There is more," Salandri said as she rose to embrace the warrior. "Much more than you know. You have been wandering a long time, warrior. Perhaps it is time to meet your ghosts face to face."

Tavis nodded, staring through the window. Mist had begun to wind its way through the trees. Distant sounds began to be heard. "I'll see what they have to say to the living," she told her new friend.

Salandri smiled. "All creatures have the need to speak their piece," she told her.

Tavis left the inn and walked slowly up the road, following the tree line until she came to a place where the trees grew dense, and reached high into the night sky. She followed a path that was unseen, allowing it to take her off the road and deep into the woods. Above her a full moon began its slow creep into the sky. Tavis tested the draw of her sword and continued forward.

Soon she came to a great expanse where the trees thinned, and the undergrowth receded. She strained to see past dark trunks and dripping boughs. At times she thought she saw movement in the growing mist. Finally she stopped, because a pain had become born in her stomach, a raw gnawing and tearing that threatened to drive her to her knees. She bent double in pain, and felt the contents of her stomach begin to move.

Then a hand was at her shoulder, and she felt herself being drawn up. She stood, still holding her stomach, and saw a similarly clad warrior standing next to her. She saw the gray eyes and dark beard and grasped his arm. "Shandar! You're alive! How can that be? I saw you die that night . . ."

"And dead I remain," the booming voice she had heard so many times in battle replied. "Waiting for you to return to us." He waved a hand about the forest, and the trees came alive with movement. Members of the Red Guard, walking, talking, smiling at her, moved forward. "Remember your friends?" Shandar asked.

Tears came to Tavis' face. "Of course I do. Your faces have never left me." The pain in her stomach returned twofold. This time she did lose her stomach. "I am sorry!" she cried, staggering to draw herself erect. "I did not mean to leave you."

"You are here," Shandar said. "And that is all that matters." A chorus of voices started around them. "You will lead us to victory, as always," Shandar said quietly.

Tavis heard the other sounds then. Mass movement through the trees. Shadows moving beyond them in a great circle. The glint of many weapons in the light of the bloody moon. The pain gnawed at her, great waves of it moving through her. Her legs grew weak. Her hands trembled. Her mind began to unwind.

"They have come," Shandar told her. "As they come to us every night. But this night will be different. You have returned."

"I should have stayed away," Tavis said through clenched teeth.

Shandar's voice lowered so only she could hear. "You

had no choice but to return," he said. "To end your pain."

Tavis felt the shock of his words rush through her. Their pain was greater than any she had ever experienced. She remembered the battle in full detail now, all the bloody spectacle of it. She ran through the woods, ripping at her belly, trying to get the pain to stop. She'd heard Shandar's voice calling for her, but she ran on. She had almost made it to the road, to safety, when the pain bloomed within her to a hot fire that enveloped her completely. Her legs had buckled, she had seen her warriors fighting on as she fell, fighting hopelessly on.

"I imagine their pain is great, great enough to keep them chained to the earth."

Tavis remembered Salandri's words. She looked at her hands, her body, touched her face. Her flesh was as translucent as the mist. She stood then, regardless of the pain that had become a hot brand in her sides.

"Shore up our flanks," she shouted to her squad leaders. "Shandar, spread our people out. We have a deluge to deal with."

Shandar smiled and boomed out her orders to the men. Tavis watched as they drew weapons, assessed the enemy's great strength, and turned back to gauge their leader's courage. Tavis grinned, baring her teeth, spitting at both the enemy and the white hot pain that kept her chained to this existence.

"Now!" she screamed, drawing her sword, rushing forward to spit her enemy upon it. The others followed, moving into the mass like a great scythe. Tavis watched her ghostly troops decimate the greater force, which shifted and faded from sight. She raised her sword high, laughing through the pain, conquering everything that stood before her.

"Fight with me!" she shouted with more life than she had ever felt before. "Tonight, we shall have our victory, and our freedom!"

JOURNEY'S END

by Dorothy J. Heydt

Dorothy J. Heydt is getting past middle age into Late Antiquity by now and lives placidly at home with her husband, four cats, and entirely too many computers. She reports that her first novel *The Interior Life* (under the pseudonym Katherine Blake) has become a cult classic with about forty-two cultists following it (I would disagree with that—at least she should count me in as number forty-three). Her second novel, *A Point of Honor* (DAW, 1998, did a little better but not well enough, and its sequel, *Pastures New*, failed to fly and is currently being taken apart and rethought. But the stories about Cynthia, physician and reluctant witch, that have appeared in *Sword & Sorceress* over the years will metamorphose into a collection, with a current working title of *The Witch of Syracuse,* some time after *S&S* XXI comes out. Meanwhile, she hangs out with the SCA and plays too much *Asheron's Call*.

We always look for strong stories to bring the anthology to a close, and this seemed an appropriate place for Cynthia to end her journey.

It was to be expected that Gaius Duilius Nepos, having determined to do a thing, would do it properly: whether fighting a battle, adopting a son, or sacrificing to the spirits of the dead. Cynthia had told him how Odysseus had sailed northward into the stream of Okeanos, to Persephone's grove, where he had dug a pit and poured food and drink into it, and lastly the blood of a black ewe and ram, before the spirits of the dead would rise to taste the offerings and speak to him.

Duilius in turn had told her how Aeneas, guided by the Sybil, had made his way down into the caverns of Awornos. Some of the songs he knew were so old that they were not written in hexameters, and the antique Latin was hard for Cynthia to follow. One of them said Aeneas had sacrificed seven bullocks and seven ewes; another listed four bullocks, a black lamb, and a heifer. No Sibyl dwelt in the birdless groves any longer, to advise them what offering to make.

"Let me have a little while alone," Cynthia told Duilius. "Perhaps the gods will tell me."

She went into her own room, shooed the maid Rhodopë out, and shut the door. "Aretë," she said. "If you hear me, help me."

"Oh, of course," the goddess said, and Cynthia whirled around. The young goddess was standing there, bright as spring sunshine, crowned with the immortal flowers of asphodel, so welcome a sight that Cynthia forgot herself and embraced her. Her body was light, but far from frail; it seemed her bones were of adamant.

She held Cynthia at arms' length and looked her up and down. "You have been busy, haven't you?" she said, smiling. "Listen, about your sacrifice: you know and I know that what the high gods truly want is not sacrifice, not blood spilled and the thighbones wrapped in fat to burn on the altar, but a loving and merciful heart, such as Komi's was. But you might have trouble explaining that to the good Duilius; he is a formalist. So tell him—" she paused to think for a moment—"tell him, one black bullock, one white heifer, both unblemished, in honor of Night and Day. Bring them to the cavern's mouth, and kill them, and follow the path downward. And we shall be with you, though you may not see us." She smiled again, and vanished in a scatter of sunlight.

So now Duilius, who always did things properly, walked at the head of the procession with a fold of his toga pulled over his head. Behind him walked his young daughter Camilla, and the other freeborn youths and maidens, carrying the implements of the sacrifice, and men of Duilius' household leading the unblemished bullock and the spotless heifer, their horns gilded and their heads wreathed with flowers.

Demetrios was with them, walking gingerly in his new

dignity as Duilius adopted son. He had told Cynthia, "I shall not venture to speak to the shade of your husband; not unless he wants to speak to me—to sound me out, maybe, on how well I would serve as his replacement? But I will come; this concerns me."

Duilius led the procession around the shore of the dead lake, through the fumes of brimstone and the whistle of the wind in the grass. An ancient city cut into the hills above, now the home only of ghosts, looked down on them from windows like dead eye sockets. Ahead, the trees grew thicker, till they could no longer see the westering sun.

The cavern's mouth opened suddenly ahead of them, tall and wide, with branching tunnels opening up inside it, easy to get lost in. Duilius spoke prayers in antique Latin, raised the knife and cut the animals' throats, while the youths and maidens sang something Cynthia could not follow at all. The blood made a pool in a hollow in the ground, and overflowed and ran in a little trickle into the mouth of the cave. No ghost appeared to drink it, as Elpenor and Teiresias had done, the blood loosening their tongues that they might speak to Odysseus. It simply ran in a little stream, gurgling over the stones. Cynthia followed.

The little rivulet of blood ran into one of the tunnels, twisting and turning busily among the pebbles on the floor, seeming to know where it was going. It was soon too dark for her to see, but there were no more branches to confuse her and she continued steadily downward.

Aeneas had seen monsters, Duilius had told her, beast-headed men and man-headed beasts, harpies and gorgons and Discordia with her snaky hair bound with bloody ribbons. Cynthia saw nothing, only vague shapes the darkness made within her own eyes, and she heard the song of the little bloodstream and the whisper of her own hand along the wall of the tunnel.

And footsteps. She stopped, and the other feet stopped at once, not dying away like echoes. Her friends the young goddesses, whose names were those of abstract qualities, went neither before her nor behind her, but within her. She straightened her shoulders and went on.

When at last a faint light appeared far below and far ahead, she had to rub her eyes with her free hand before she could believe in it.

The light widened as she approached the tunnel mouth, and she found herself on the brink of a sheer drop into a huge cavern awash with red light, pale like blood trailing away into water. The little bloodstream at her feet trickled over the edge and fell, drop by glistening drop, into a wide underground river that ran from darkness on Cynthia's left into darkness on her right.

Before she could nerve herself to think of jumping, she saw that there was in fact another way down: a little path that wound like a vine tendril through the air, spiraling downward from right to left. It turned against the path of the sun, as fitted a road through the realms of the dead, and it brought to her mind all the old sayings about walking on the knife's edge, but in fact the path was an ell wide, maybe more, and if she could only make her will rule her feet, she could walk it.

Between Komi and myself lies this path. Komi, her husband of a few short months, the only man she had ever loved. Komi, who had risked his life to save his sister and her baby, and lost his life under Tanit's curse. He lived nowhere now except in her heart. In the years since his death, she had kept the breath in her body, kept one foot moving in front of the other, only by considering, *Who will remember Komi if I die?*

She closed her eyes and tried to bring to mind the image of Komi's face, the wide brow and narrow chin, the dark brown eyes alight with intelligence and love. When all was quite clear in her mind she opened her eyes and set foot to the path. Thin as a shaving of wood, delicate as a child's forelock, it held firm beneath her and she followed it around and down.

Then the images began to take shape. At first she thought they were only drifts of steam rising from the garnet-red river below, which seemed to be very warm.

They roiled and writhed and took on hands and faces, and she was able to discern what they were doing before she could recognize any of them. Those on the left threatened, those on the right beckoned. Those swirling mist shapes, tinged with the red light from below: those were the flames of the old goddess of Phaneraia, the silken veils of Tanit, faceless between her outstretched fingers. There were Roman soldiers in tall-crested helmets, brandishing their swords of bitter bronze, and thugs and ruffians from the alleys of a dozen cities, clutching at her arm, clawing at her face: but they were phantoms and could not touch her. Stormclouds dripping rain, and the Siren in their midst; Isis in her linen wrappings, holding up something, a mirror maybe, and she averted her head. And the Punic shapechanger in his ratskin, and all the little boys who had tried to harry her on the docks at home: everything that had ever threatened her was on the attack, but they were illusions and could not touch her.

The shapes on her right hand were harder to pass by. The first that showed her a face was, of all people, old Demodoros, who had been kind to her in those few months when she had been a frightened maiden and then a sullen wife. He smiled at her, and tried to beckon her in, but seemed to lose heart and waved her away again. He began to fade, and other shapes moved forward: women great with child, women with infants in their arms, sick and injured people, all beckoning to her to come and put them right.

Cynthia, though awed by the vast blood-colored airy vault of the place, and nervous about where to set her feet, was not so dim as to miss what this was all about. On her left, threats and tumults, from which she was supposed to recoil, and so fall off the path. On her right, images of love and need, toward which she was supposed to be drawn, and so fall off the path. It was all meant to deceive.

So the next shape, with its great outstretched arms like sheltering wings, and the soft folds of its bosom like the breast of a brooding dove, and the void where its face should have been, blank as the pitiless head of Tanit, must be the mother of whom she had no memory. Well, that wasn't going to work. She felt no desire to fly into its embrace, or to bend down and pick up the faceless small form at its feet.

But some of the others had faces: old Xenokleia, her shining hair wound round her cow's-horn headdress and smiling like an afternoon of sunlight, and Enzaro, her baby at her breast, looking at her with Komi's eyes. Her heart turned over, but she made her feet keep steady. To the best of her knowledge both women were still alive. These were phantoms, meant to frighten and deceive.

The only image that might have tempted her was Komi's, and the deceiver had not presented him yet; perhaps it was saving him for a final deception, or perhaps it could not wield him at all.

Assuming this place was a test, this gauntlet between hates and loves . . . what was being tested?

She was now three parts of the way down to the floor of the cavern, where the dark stream sparkled. There was something moving underneath, something that went on two feet like a man, but its head was strange.

She took the last step from the spiraling path to solid ground, and the thing turned to face her.

Cynthia had seen her like this before in a vision, devouring her children, but the Goddess had aged. Her breasts drooped like half-empty waterskins, the skin of her belly lay in folds upon her thighs. Tanit's veil hid her face, but all her flesh hung upon her like a translucent mist, revealing all her bones but the skull. Within the cage of her ribs something moved. Half-hidden, half-revealed by a dark heart that beat slowly as a wave of the sea, Komi's face loomed: Komi, undying and unborn. Cynthia raised hands like claws and leaped to tear the cage apart.

They rolled over the warm sandy ground, one over another like two sluts on the Alexandrian docks fighting over an obol, like two cats fighting over a dead fish. Sharp talons raked Cynthia's back, and her own fingers groped through smoky jelly flesh to pry the ribs apart.

The creature heaved up suddenly onto its knees, breaking Cynthia's grip. She clutched again and got it by the throat within the veil, squeezed and twisted till something snapped. The head toppled from the neck; Cynthia let it fall and groped again for the rib cage. Komi's face floated inside, white as a lily on a lake, its eyes closed. She gave a great twist and wrenched the ribs apart, but overbalanced herself in doing it and fell heavily to the ground.

She came back to herself in silence, lying on the sandy floor that was cooling under her cheek. Painfully she got to hands and knees and looked over the strewn bones, but she could see nothing of Komi. The scattered ribs lay empty. Perhaps the last of him had died with the last of the Goddess; perhaps he had never been there at all.

She tucked one leg under her and sat down again, hard. She had fought, and won, and lost, and there was nothing more to be done, and she could not see or hear or feel her friends the Qualities anywhere.

The veiled head lay in a heap to one side, and after a while she reached out and tugged at the trailing end of the veil till the head rolled toward her, unwrapping itself as it came.

The face was her own, of course. That was only to be expected. Cynthia/Aretë/Elpis/Sophia had killed Tanit/Isis/Demeter/Cynthia, and now she was dead, and that was why her heart lay unmoving like a stone in her body. A pair of cold tears crept down her cheeks, like dew on a gray morning. She sat there for a long time.

The red light had faded, and the air was cooling: there was a feeling of space and emptiness around her that had not been before. She could not see the roof of the vault anymore, nor the ramp she had descended to reach the sandy floor. It was as if all had opened out, and an empty sky hung overhead. There was a thin breeze blowing from her right, with a cool fragrance of leaves in it, and after a while she got to her feet and went that way.

The sandy path was the color of silver, but the stream that ran alongside it was dark, like ice under the stars; it did not seem to be of blood anymore, and perhaps it

never had been. There were trees around her, their trunks
reaching high overhead, and as she walked among them
birds began to sing in the branches, tentatively, tuning
their throats in little runs and trills, as if the dawn
were near.

She was coming into a great open space now, and four
large stars hung like jewels in the vault overhead, but
over the distant treetops the sky was growing pale. There
was a soft sound, like wind through grass, and from behind her a white hare came leaping, its long ears tinged
with rose. With a single bound it crossed the stream and
vanished into the woods.

Cynthia followed as far as the water's edge, and
stopped. The stream seemed neither very wide nor very
deep, but it looked icy cold, and she did not know
whether she could cross it.

"No, you can't. Not yet."

Cynthia raised her eyes. Komi was standing on the
other side of the stream, smiling, and for a moment all
the stars were drowned out in his light.

"Why can't I?" she asked, when she could speak again.
"Am I not dead?"

"No. Well, yes, you are, and no, you're not." He
shrugged, and spread his hands. "A fig for all the poets
who said the dead could speak to the enlightenment of
the living; they lied. I have so many things I want to tell
you, and the words have not yet been made."

"A pity," she said. "I was hoping you would tell me
what to do."

"What you'll do? That's simple. You'll go back to the
world above, cure the sick, marry Demetrios, and have
children. And your son Marcus will marry Enzaro's daughter Enzollahar, and our lines, joined at last, will take part
in the history of Rome and all that will follow upon it."
And seeing that she was weeping, "You've already done
the hardest part of it, you know. You've torn me from your
breast, and set me free, and you've slain the Goddess."

"Have I? Who is the Goddess?"

"You know her," Komi said. "She's part of you; she's
part of every woman. And if she's allowed to have her

will, she becomes the monster that eats her own children. She must be killed, so that she can be reborn, and then she can become a Goddess indeed.

"In the same way there's a god in every man—I said that once, didn't I? I didn't know what I was talking about. He's the tyrant who wants to see the power of his own arm, the seed of his own begetting spreading out over the land, blotting out all others. He's the bull Mithras slew at midnight in the dark cellar. He's a cruel bloody bastard, and he too must be killed and be reborn, before he can be a god.

"When the false gods go, the true gods can come: your friends the Virtues, and the love that moves the sun and the stars. Cynthia, all our lives we have lived in shadow, but now the dawn is at hand. Look: the sun is about to rise."

And the dawn light was indeed brightening, and the birdsong rose in a deafening chorus, and Cynthia raised her hands to shield her face from the sun's blaze. When she lowered them again she was kneeling at the cavern's mouth, with the chill breeze of morning blowing upon her. Gaius Duilius and his companions were singing in their antique Latin, of which she could catch only the word *Sol*, the sun; and Demetrios came to raise her up, his hands strong under her forearms, and led her out of the cave to where she could see the sun rising, splendid over Rome.

LOVE POTION #8½

by Marilyn A. Racette

The other kind of story that Marion liked to put at the end of a volume was one with humor, which you can probably guess from the title, so I'm not giving anything away. This is Marilyn A. Racette's second sale to *Sword & Sorceress*. Since the last one, her son has married and moved into his own home. She now lives with her father, a ninety-year-old wiseguy with a ponytail, and her cat, Midnight, a three-year-old cuddlebunny who likes to sit on anything she's trying to read. She has recently become a grandmother and thinks her granddaughter is the best thing since sliced bread.

She works in a small bookstore in Winchester, Massachusetts, which is just about the perfect job for a doting grandma in love with books and storytelling. She would like to dedicate this story to the memory of her mother.

"Your prices are ridiculous . . ." Sofran rose from his chair, "absolutely ridiculous."

I raised an eyebrow. I was not about to lower my prices, not for Sofran, filling my best chair with his well-fed frame, expensive lace spilling from the sleeves of his tailored jacket and fine gold chains tangling in the dark mat of sweaty chest hair revealed by the cut of his tunic. He could well afford double the price I had quoted. I looked at his face, still red from the effort it had taken to climb the stairs to my little apothecary above the glassblower's shop. I thought Sofran was bluffing, but I really could not afford to lose the sale. My landlady, kind and understanding as she was, liked to be paid.

"Perhaps . . ." Sofran settled back into his chair. I hoped it would not break. "Perhaps I might engage the services of your apprentice for a slightly lower fee?"

"Celi?" I could barely hide my disbelief, but I should
not have been surprised by this suggestion, not coming
from Sofran. "It's true that she is my apprentice, Sofran
and therefore well-trained, but this is a very delicate matter you propose, and just this side of ethical. The propen-
sity for mischance is enormous."

My aristocratic clients seem to like it when I use bigger
words. It makes them think they are smarter than the
love-struck farmer who comes to me for a charm.

"But she could do it?" Sofran leaned forward eagerly
one of my delicate teacups barely visible in his great
red hand.

"Yes," I sighed. "She could." And that would take
care of the rent issue, I thought to myself, and maybe a
bit more too.

"You'll have to sign a contract, of course, indicating
your recognition of the risks involved . . . no guarantees
you understand, for Celi's work in this instance. If the
charm doesn't work, you'll be out the money. Are you
certain that you wouldn't rather pay a professional price
for professional results?"

Sofran shifted uneasily in the chair. But his greed
won out.

"I understand," he said. "I'm sure you've trained Celi
well." He pulled an ornate snuffbox from a pocket and
concentrated on extracting exactly the right amount of
snuff, then sneezed noisily into his sleeve. *Well,* I thought
*so that's the way of it. If things go awry, he'll blame my
training. We'll see about that.*

I rang the bell that connects me to Aban's shop on
the floor below, and he came upstairs to witness Sofran's
signature to our contract. Celi went out to gather the
necessary ingredients, and some hours later the scent of
rose and lavender filled the workroom and the office. I
listened as Celi recited the spell, watched her long, delicate fingers trace the proper signs in the air above the
vial holding the distillation. I had no doubt the potion
would work. That's not what usually goes wrong with
love charms. And really, they're not love charms. It
wouldn't be ethical to make someone love you, even if

you could. But drawing their attention, well that's a bit different. Exciting the senses—that falls within the realm of fair play. But I digress. What usually goes wrong is a matter of degree. How much attention do you want?

There was a fine spring rain falling when I heard the stairs groaning once again under Sofran's heavy tread. It had been a week since his last visit.

"Roshan!" he bellowed, once he'd caught his breath. "Call her off!"

"Sofran, it is so good of you to stop by. Please, sit down. What can I do for you?" I took his damp cloak, and he let himself be settled into a chair that I prayed would hold together. I'd already repaired the last one he'd sat in.

"Some of your mint tea, Roshan. And no additives." He waggled a beefy finger at me.

"Celi," I put my head in the workroom, "we need a pot of mint tea for Sofran."

Her hands flew to her mouth, and a blush began to spread across her fair complexion.

"Oh, Roshan, is there a problem?"

I winked at her. "Nothing that can't be fixed, my dear . . . for a small fee. And no fault of yours, not when a man of Sofran's age thinks he wants a young girl to find him attractive. Just bring the tea when it's ready. All will be well for us, and for Sofran too. You'll see. Have a cup yourself, it will calm you."

I returned to the fretful Sofran. "Just what seems to be the trouble, Sofran. Did Celi's charm fail?"

"Alas," he said, mopping sweat from his face, "it works too well. The girl follows me everywhere! It's an embarrassment! I cannot turn around but she is there, giving me an idiotic grin, a sly wink. And she giggles! I am a laughingstock! It must stop."

"Well, Sofran, I warned you. . . ."

"You warned me against using an apprentice. . . ."

"And if you had hired me, I would have taken the time to talk you out of an ill-considered notion. If you are lonely, Sofran, and wish to attract a mate, there are more suitable women available."

Sofran snorted. "Are you a matchmaker now?"

"I might know of someone with similar tastes, who might be aided to see your attractions."

He narrowed his eyes—hard to do, for Sofran, and still have eyes. "My money, you mean. I'm no fool."

"And I do not take you for one. Do you wish to wed, and end your lonely sojourn? I can provide a charm to help you attract a suitable mate. You will do the rest. I am confident enough to wait until you have proposed— which I expect to happen by the next new moon. And, of course, we'll have to see to the other matter. For that I would like payment now, and the matter will be resolved by morning."

Sofran drew a very ample purse from his pocket. I felt sorry for the girl. She would feel a fool when she came to her senses, but perhaps it would teach her a measure of discretion.

"I'm sorry, mistress," Celi said later, once Sofran had left.

"Whatever for, girl? What have you done?"

"The spell for Sofran."

"Oh, you did nothing wrong. If Sofran had been seventeen instead of a man of forty and five, he would have been thrilled with the attention. Believe me, Celi, the fault was not yours."

Two moons later Sofran wed the widow Marsden, a woman closer to his own age, with a comfortable income, a minor title, and estates of her own. If she was past the first flush of youth, she still had womanly charms, slightly enhanced by certain incantations and herbal preparations. Sofran received a bit of help as well. Celi and I were invited to the nuptial celebration; several days later a thank-you gift arrived, as well as the remaining balance of Sofran's payment. I believe it might be safe to say that the couple lived happily ever after—with a bit of help, of course.

Marion Zimmer Bradley & Deborah Ross

A Flame in Hali
A Novel of Darkover

On Darkover, it is the era of the Hundred Kingdoms—a time of nearly continuous war and bloody disputes, a time when Towers are conscripted to produce terrifying laran weapons—weapons which kill from afar, poisoning the very land itself for decades to come. In this terrifying time of greed and imperialism, two powerful men have devoted their lives to changing their world and eliminating these terrible weapons. For years King Carolin of Hastur and his close friend, Keeper Varzil Ridenow, have dreamed of a world without war. But another man, Eduin Deslucido, hides in the alleys of Thendara, tormented by a spell so powerful it haunts Eduin's every waking moment—a spell of destruction against Carolin Hastur... and all of his clan.

To Order Call: 1-800-788-6262
www.dawbooks.com

DARKOVER

Marion Zimmer Bradley's Classic Series

Now Collected in New Omnibus Editions!

Heritage and Exile
0-7564-0065-1
The Heritage of Hastur & Sharra's Exile

The Ages of Chaos
0-7564-0072-4
Stormqueen! & Hawkmistress!

The Saga of the Renunciates
0-7564-0092-9
The Shattered Chain, Thendara House
& City of Sorcery

The Forbidden Circle
0-7564-0094-5
The Spell Sword & The Forbidden Tower

A World Divided
0-7564-0167-4
The Bloody Sun, The Winds of Darkover
& Star of Danger

To Order Call: 1-800-788-6262

www.dawbooks.com

Kristen Britain

GREEN RIDER

As Karigan G'ladheon, on the run from school, makes her way through the deep forest, a galloping horse plunges out of the brush, its rider impaled by two black arrows. With his dying breath, he tells her he is a Green Rider, one of the king's special messengers. Giving her his green coat with its symbolic brooch of office, he makes Karigan swear to deliver the message he was carrying. Pursued by unknown assassins, following a path only the horse seems to know, Karigan finds herself thrust into in a world of danger and complex magic....   0-88677-858-1

FIRST RIDER'S CALL

With evil forces once again at large in the kingdom and with the messenger service depleted and weakened, can Karigan reach through the walls of time to get help from the First Rider, a woman dead for a millennium?   0-7564-0209-3

To Order Call: 1-800-788-6262

DAW 7

John Marco

The Eyes of God

"THE EYES OF GOD isn't just about warfare, magic, and monsters, although it's got all of those: it's about the terrible burden of making choices, and the way the seeds of victory are in every failure, and tragedy's beginnings are in every triumph."
—Tad Williams

Akeela, the king of Liiria, determined to bring peace to his kingdom, and Lukien, the Bronze Knight of Liiria, peerless with a sword, and who had earned his reputation the hard way, loved each other as brothers, but no two souls could be more different. And both were in love with the beautiful Queen Cassandra. But unknown to anyone, Cassandra hid a terrible secret: a disease that threatened her life and caused unimaginable strife for all who loved her. For Akeela and Lukien, the quest for Cassandra's salvation would overwhelm every bond of loyalty, every point of honor, because only the magical amulets known as the Eyes of God could halt the progress of Cassandra's illness. But the Eyes could also open the way to a magical stronghold that will tear their world apart and redefine the very nature of their reality.

0-7564-0096-1

To Order Call: 1-800-788-6262